ABOUT THE AUTHOR

When *USA Today* bestselling author Alissa Callen isn't writing, she plays traffic controller to four children, three dogs, two horses and one renegade cow who believes the grass is greener on the other side of the fence. After a childhood spent chasing sheep on the family farm, Alissa has always been drawn to remote areas and small towns, even when residing overseas. She is partial to autumn colour, snowy peaks and historic homesteads and will drive hours to see an open garden. Once a teacher and a counsellor, she remains interested in the life journeys that people take. She draws inspiration from the countryside around her, whether it be the brown snake at her back door or the resilience of bush communities in times of drought or flood. Her books are characteristically heartwarming, authentic and character driven. Alissa lives on a small slice of rural Australia in central western NSW.

THE
RED DIRT
ROAD

THE
RED DIRT
ROAD

ALISSA CALLEN

mira

First Published 2018
Second Australian Paperback Edition 2019
ISBN 9781489263568

Published by
Mira
An imprint of Harlequin Enterprises (Australia) Pty Limited (ABN 47 001 180 918),
a subsidiary of HarperCollins Publishers Australia Pty Limited (ABN 36 009 913 517)
Level 13, 201 Elizabeth St
SYDNEY NSW 2000
AUSTRALIA

Cataloguing-in-Publication details are available from the National Library of
Australia www.librariesaustralia.nla.gov.au

Printed and bound in Australia by McPherson's Printing Group

MIX
Paper from
responsible sources
FSC
www.fsc.org   FSC® C001695

To Luke

CHAPTER
1

Life can change in a heartbeat. For Dr Felicity Knight, life changed in the space between a newborn's cry and the last, shallow breath of a young mother.

Fliss walked along the dusty hallway of the farmhouse that had become her new home. Her thick socks left smudged footprints on the timeworn floorboards. No matter how much she swept, fine outback dust seeped in through the loose window frames. She repressed a shudder. She wasn't going to think about what else might take advantage of the cracks and crevices in the old homestead.

Her practical sister, Cressy, had already warned her about covering the gap beneath the back door. A mouse or a shingleback lizard could squeeze through the opening. Fliss also wasn't in a hurry to meet any of the brown snakes calling her overgrown garden home. She hadn't seen any yet but the snakeskin by the gate let her know the tiny blue-and-black wrens weren't the only wildlife enjoying the spring sunshine.

At the front door, Fliss bent to put on her work boots. She had to tug hard to pull them over her bulky socks. When Cressy gifted her the navy, wool-blend socks last Christmas, Fliss could never see herself wearing them in Sydney. But after the first day of blisters in her new life, she'd unpacked them. Now the socks had become her go-to fashion item. Last trip to Woodlea she'd bought six new pairs.

She pushed open the screen door and stepped into a world she'd never thought she'd again inhabit. No shrill sirens echoed throughout a concrete landscape. No scent of fumes hung heavy in the air. Instead the warmth of a fresh breeze washed over her, carrying the sweet scent of wisteria and the silence of the bush. The only sound in the past ten minutes had been the cheerful calls of two cockatiels whose wings had dipped low over the bluestone stables.

Fliss stopped on the top veranda step and scanned the granite-grey sky. More rain was coming. It had been a wet winter and now a wet spring. The roadside verges were lush with grass, paddocks saturated and creeks swollen with rain run-off. It was as though Mother Nature cried the tears Fliss couldn't yet let fall.

A rush of grief and anxiety engulfed her. Knees weak, she lowered herself to sit on the veranda step. No matter how hard she pushed her emotions into the depths of her subconscious, they continued to shoot to the surface like a cork in water. She took a slow, deep breath and allowed the serenity around her to soak into her soul.

She couldn't waste another second wallowing in her failure or second-guessing every decision she'd made that cold, dark night. She owed it to the family whose future had forever been altered by a drunk driver to not let their tragedy taint another life. Karl regularly sent photos of baby Jemma to show how well she was doing and to remind Fliss that his wife slipping away wasn't her fault. She'd done everything she could.

Fliss swallowed past another swell of emotion. But it was her fault. She should have done more. She hadn't been able to save a patient's life.

The throaty chug of a diesel ute engine cut through the intense quiet and the torment pressing upon her shoulders. It was the sound Fliss had been waiting for. She came to her feet. City habits were hard to break and she brushed off the seat of her jeans. She might have swept the veranda, but dust was still embedded deep in the wooden grains.

She shaded her eyes against a brief shaft of sunlight and stared at the narrow road into Bundara. The previous night's rain had turned the powdery red dirt into a dark, thick sludge. She'd made the mistake of believing she could walk to the milk can at her front gate to collect the mail. She'd only taken four steps before her left boot had slipped and she'd almost face-planted.

The engine noise intensified as a once white Land Cruiser ute negotiated the dip in the road filled with running water. The windscreen wipers worked hard to clear the spray that funnelled over the vehicle. Fliss admired the skill and ease with which her younger sister navigated the wet conditions. If she'd been behind the wheel she'd have slid into the table drain or a tree. She had no desire to end up like the car crash victims she'd once worked on.

Cressy continued at a steady pace, her momentum only slowing as the tyres fought to gain traction on the soft patch where the driveway curved alongside the garden gate. Fliss left the veranda and kept to the firm gravel path that led through her untidy lawn. She needed to win her power struggle with the temperamental ride-on lawnmower. If it could start for Cressy's fiancé, Denham, then it could start for her.

Cressy climbed out of the ute. Fliss's heart warmed. She may have missed the country-girl genes but their differences had never divided them. Her sister was far more than a sibling, she was her best friend whose love and support remained unconditional.

The gathering wind caught at Cressy's black Woodlea rodeo cap and she settled it more firmly on her head. Today she wore her usual boots, purple work shirt and faded jeans. Unlike other visits, her aged kelpie, Tippy, and young dog, Juno, weren't by her side.

'Hey, you.' Fliss stepped through the small garden gate to hug her sister. Cressy always smelt of orange blossoms. 'No dogs today?'

'No. I left Juno rolling in the mud. She definitely doesn't take after her show poodle mother. Sorry, I'm late.'

'That's okay. I wasn't sure you'd make it. After the rain last night, there must be water across all the roads.'

Cressy's hazel eyes, so like her own, shone. 'It was … and it can be our little secret Denham's ute did some fishtailing to get here.'

'My lips are sealed. I know how precious his ute is.' She watched as Cressy opened the passenger side door to reveal an assortment of bags filled with grocery items. 'As much as he loves his ute, he loves you more.'

Cressy flashed a sweet, contented smile over her shoulder. Fliss banished a tug of loneliness. Her tunnel-vision, and single-minded pursuit of a city medical career, hadn't been the sole reason why none of her relationships had lasted. No one had ever looked at her like Denham looked at Cressy. And, if she were honest, she didn't deserve to be loved so deeply. She'd always held a part of herself back. She'd never found a man who made her breath falter or made her want to risk everything to be with him.

Cressy handed her a large container filled with jam drop biscuits. 'Meredith sends her love.'

'Thanks.' Denham's aunt's jam drop biscuits were her favourite and she could never stop at one. 'I needed a sugar fix.'

Cressy tilted her head to assess the heavy blanket of cloud cover that sunlight could no longer break through. 'We'd better get everything inside.'

After the third load, Fliss stared at the large bag of pasta she'd sat on the kitchen bench. 'I know I might get flooded in, but there's enough food here to feed all of Woodlea.'

Cressy put her own bags on the table. Seriousness tempered the light in her eyes. 'You know the talk we had about how I was worried about you being out here alone?'

'I do. And like I said before, I'm fine, really. I can take care of myself. I'm not the risk taker, remember?'

A brief smile shaped Cressy's lips as she reached into the bag closest to her. 'I know. Usually you're the one worrying about me.'

Cressy took out a tin of coffee. Fliss frowned. She didn't drink coffee.

'When exactly is Denham's old rodeo friend staying? It's next week, isn't it?'

Cressy carefully sat the coffee on the table before she spoke. 'There's been a change of plans. He's coming ... today.' She reached out to touch Fliss's hand. 'I didn't call and give you the heads-up because you'd find any excuse not to be around.'

Fliss sighed. Cressy knew her too well. These past months, talking and engaging with people hadn't been high on her priority list. Anxiety had a way of stealing her words and her confidence when she least expected it. 'I was hoping you'd forgotten about asking Hewitt to stay.'

'No such luck. You need someone to help out around here. This house hasn't been lived in for years and your garden's snake heaven.'

Fliss stayed silent. Everything Cressy said was true. The first thing Fliss had seen when she'd walked into the dilapidated farmhouse she'd bought last autumn was a dead snake tangled in the living room's lace curtains.

Cressy placed a large box of tea beside the coffee tin. 'It's not enough to get your garden under control, there's the very real risk of you being flooded in … alone.'

'I happen to like being alone. I need to be by myself.'

Cressy's expression softened at the pain Fliss couldn't completely strip from her words.

'Don't worry, you'll still have space. Hewitt won't be any trouble and as he'll be over in the stables, you'll hardly know he's here.'

'Can't we go for Plan B? I'll have Reggie stay. I'll feed him carrots and he'll keep me company.'

'Your veranda floorboards are not up to the weight of a Brahman-cross bull who'd wait at your front door every morning for his breakfast.' Cressy's tone sobered. 'Hewitt coming here is as much for his benefit as yours.'

Fliss slowly nodded. Cressy had already explained that Hewitt was also in need of space. Fliss hadn't pressed for details as to why the cowboy needed to spend time on an isolated farm. Personal demons were best kept hidden.

She hadn't revealed to anyone in Sydney how the death of Caitlyn, the young mother, had rocked her, not even her trusted university mentor, Lewis. There wasn't a hospital stairwell or hallway she hadn't sought refuge in, until she didn't have the strength to fight anymore. Adrift and uncertain, she'd left the frenetic pace of the emergency department to head west to where the sun tipped gum leaves in silver and the slow blush of a sunrise brought with it a sense of peace.

Cressy's chin angled. 'Hewitt will get that mower of yours working. He'll keep the garden under control, fix the fences to stop my cattle straying and keep an eye on them when they calve. He'll be here should anything go … wrong.'

Fliss sighed. She had as much of a chance of convincing Cressy that Hewitt didn't need to stay as she did of driving her impractical two-wheel-drive car along the muddy back roads. 'Nothing will go wrong, but okay, I'll be on my best behaviour.'

'Thank you. I just hope our definitions of best behaviour are the same. Need I remind you that you hold the record for the shortest date ever?'

'It would have been one minute, not five, if my so-called date had stopped to draw breath while listing the ways I reminded him of his ex-girlfriend. But for all of those five minutes I really did behave.'

Cressy's lips twitched as she placed the remaining grocery items from the bag beside her onto the table. 'I'm sure you did for two seconds.' She headed for the door. 'All we've left to unload are the plants Sue's potted up for you. The pink geraniums are the ones Mum gave her cuttings of years ago. Then we'd better put the kettle on. The boys shouldn't be far away.'

Mouth dry, Fliss followed. Her sanctuary was about to be breached and her fragile peace compromised. The deep croak of frogs erupted from the corrugated-iron water tank around the side of the homestead. More rain was coming. The rumble of an engine cut through the happy frog chorus, causing her stomach to lurch. She eased out a tight breath. Whoever this Hewitt was, at least if he was prepared to stay this far out of town, he wouldn't be wanting her company.

An unfamiliar black ute negotiated the dip in the road, a quad bike strapped on the back. Denham sat in the passenger seat and he lifted a hand in greeting as Fliss and Cressy walked through the garden gate. Fliss returned his gesture, her attention focusing on the man beside him. Through the windscreen she glimpsed masculine features guaranteed to make any single woman take a second look.

The ute navigated the soft corner with ease before rolling to a stop next to the white Land Cruiser. Denham left his seat while Hewitt strode around the front of the ute. Her first impression hadn't been wrong. Tall, broad-shouldered and lean-hipped, by anyone's definition her guest would be considered gorgeous. Dressed in a blue shirt, jeans and boots, and with his dark head bare, he'd send the Woodlea grapevine into a frenzy.

She studied the tanned angles and planes of his set features. Despite the ease with which he approached, he seemed guarded. Relief slid through her, reducing the tremors in her nerves to a tremble. He'd want as little to do with her as she would with him. Nothing would change just because she had a cowboy living across the garden.

Then Hewitt smiled. Even though his focus was on Cressy, Fliss felt the effect of his slow grin as though he was looking right at her. The rigid landscape of his face relaxed and softened, revealing the humanity beneath. Unable to look away, she fought a frown. Since when did the warmth of a man's smile flow through her like a sugar rush after night duty? Normally she was a slow-burn girl. The only sparks she believed in were the ones she could see.

Another city habit she couldn't let go of was reading people. Once a patient had been triaged by the emergency department nurse, Fliss would remain alert for signs of what the patient mightn't have revealed. Was their pain real? Were they coping? What would their pain threshold be? And just like then, when Hewitt's grey eyes met hers, she really looked at the man before her.

He might stand still and straight, his arms loose by his side, but in the bleak darkness of his gaze she recognised untold emotional suffering. The slight hunch of his left shoulder and the grooves beside his mouth confirmed he was also in physical pain, and not just a small amount. A lesser man would have his shoulders bowed.

Something within Fliss tightened. Cressy had reassured her Hewitt wouldn't be trouble and she'd hardly know he was there. Nothing could be further from the truth. He already was trouble and she already knew she wouldn't forget he was around.

For this strong and stoic cowboy, whose eyes crinkled at the corners when he smiled, was unlike any man she'd ever met.

Hewitt Sinclair stared at the woman who was to be his new neighbour and realised he'd made a grave mistake.

He should never have accepted Denham and Cressy's offer to stay at Bundara.

Cressy's sister was beautiful. When Denham had described her as a taller version of Cressy, Hewitt had been prepared to find Fliss pretty with long, dark hair and hazel eyes. But what he wasn't prepared for was the jolt of intense awareness when he met her thick-lashed gaze.

He suppressed the urge to roll his shoulders. The action would reveal his tension and ratchet up the pain-meter on his fractured shoulder. Fliss continued to look at him, the sharp intelligence in her stare leaving him in no doubt she'd analysed him with the accuracy of a polygraph. Cressy had warned him she didn't tolerate fools easily. Over the years, he'd heard many stories about her astute and strong-willed older sister.

A raindrop splashed his cheek, reminding him to speak. But as a faint frown creased Fliss's forehead he remained silent. He couldn't blame her for her wariness. He looked as though he'd just come off a wheat harvest. His hair needed a cut and his jawline a shave. Even without Cressy's brief explanation that Fliss was going through a tough time, the shadows beneath her eyes confirmed her vulnerability. He couldn't cause her any more concern.

'Hi, Felicity, I'm Hewitt.' He held out his hand. 'Thanks for having me.'

He didn't imagine her slight hesitation before she slid her hand in his. 'You're welcome. Please … call me Fliss.'

He could feel her tension in the fine bones of her fingers. He gentled his touch to let her know he wasn't there to cause trouble. For a moment, her hand relaxed and the amber flecks in her irises intensified before her lips pressed together and she slid her fingers free.

Movement flickered in his peripheral vision as Denham moved to kiss Fliss on her cheek. 'Glad to see you haven't been washed away.'

'Me too. I can't remember there ever being this much rain.' She paused to tap the pocket of Denham's emerald green shirt. 'So, Mr Bull Rider, is there something you need to tell me?'

Denham groaned and glanced at Cressy.

She held up her hands. 'Don't look at me, Denham Rigby. I never said a word.'

Laughter tugged at Fliss's mouth but when she spoke her words were firm. 'I thought your bull-riding days were over? You said your bones creak as if you were a hundred.'

Hewitt had known Denham for over a decade and it was a strong woman who'd take him to task about the toll his rodeo career had taken on his body. He'd once tried to stop Denham from riding with a broken hand and had failed.

Pain, which had nothing to do with his broken shoulder blade, lanced through him. Not only was the woman before him breathtaking, she had a strength of character that would ensure she'd stand beside a man, never behind him. But he had no right to find any woman compelling or beautiful, just like he had no right to allow his loneliness or his longings to steer him off course. The day his brother Brody died was the day he committed his life to looking out for his family.

Denham shifted on his feet as he stared at Fliss. 'They do but … it was just one ride.'

She arched a fine brow. 'One ride on a bull no one had ridden this season.'

'I wore a helmet and protective vest. If I'm to buy this bull's offspring I need to know what he's capable of. Cressy was there.'

Fliss exchanged a look with her sister. 'Which is why I'm not reading you the riot act.'

Denham's expression turned sheepish. 'So how did you know?'

'The internet's a wonderful thing, even if my dial-up connection is slower than the turtle who lives in my garden.'

Denham flicked Hewitt a wry look. 'Just as well I stayed on and didn't make a fool of myself. I'm getting rusty in my old age.'

Cressy went to Fliss's side and slipped her arm through her sister's. 'You know I would have called if anything happened. You're the only doctor Denham listens to.'

Pain flashed across Fliss's face.

A large raindrop hit Hewitt's forearm where it was left bare by his rolled-up shirtsleeve. Another raindrop targeted the toe of his left boot. No words were needed as they all turned towards the ute. While Denham collected the tool box stashed beside the quad bike, Hewitt reached for the esky. As his right hand wrapped around the handle the twinge in his upper arm reminded him he wasn't capable of lifting something so heavy.

He swapped hands and, bracing himself, hauled the full esky over the side of the ute. He sat it on the ground before reaching for the navy duffle bag. When he turned, he realised Fliss stood behind him, her attention on his bad shoulder. He bit back a sigh. Somehow Fliss had homed in on his physical weakness. Even Denham didn't know the true extent of his motorbike injuries.

Her eyes briefly held his before she took the duffle bag from out of his hand. 'I'll put this in the stables, if you want to head into the kitchen with the esky?'

He nodded, not trusting his words to emerge as anything but a hoarse rasp. His shoulder hurt like hell plus Fliss was too close. Far too close. He could see the smooth softness of her lips and caught the faint scent of gardenias. His tension must have shown on his face, as her mouth firmed before she turned away.

He ground his teeth. Whatever first impression Fliss had formed, it couldn't be good. Not only did he look rough around the edges, the tightness of his jaw reminded him that his default expression this past year had become more grim than reassuring.

Uncaring of the raindrops that now splattered the top of the esky, he continued his unhurried pace towards the main house. After the dry years on his family farm further out west, he still appreciated the earthy scent of rain and the novelty of getting wet. Water trickled past the collar of his shirt, cooling the heat of his skin.

To his left, Denham and Cressy carried the tool box and a garden rake over to the tin shed tucked beside an old cedar tree. Hewitt studied the yard through the thin curtain of rain. Everywhere he looked there was work to be done.

The lawn needed mowing, the beds needed weeding, the fence posts needed straightening and the wire needed straining. He scanned the front of the Federation-style bluestone homestead that loomed before him. And that was only the garden to-do list. The house required some urgent TLC. Windows needed new glass panes, wood needed painting and gutters needed replacing. Water coursed through a hole in the rusted front gutter, spilling into the bucket below like a high-country waterfall.

A cow mooed and he looked beyond the house to the green slopes dotted with Cressy's Black Angus cattle. Denham had mentioned that Bundara backed onto Glenmore, allowing Cressy easy access to the rye and native grass pastures for her breeding herd. At the moment Fliss wasn't interested in the land of her new home, just the house and garden.

Hewitt reached the veranda and set the esky down. Boots thundered as Cressy and Denham bolted up the steps behind him. Raindrops glistened on their skin and clung to their hair, but their smiles were joyful. Hewitt looked away as Denham pulled Cressy in close for a tender kiss. Even when he'd known them years ago, the bond between them had been special. He was happy to see that after riding bulls in America, Denham had made peace with losing his father and his brother and Cressy was back in his arms. Hewitt ignored the loneliness that stirred within him.

Fliss too ran up the steps and out of the rain. But instead of laughter shining in her eyes and flushing her cheeks, her face was pale. She dragged her fingers through her hair, a deep weariness pinching her features.

Denham spoke above the drum of impatient rain on the roof. 'Hewitt, that tinny of yours might have been better for getting around the cattle than your quad bike.'

Hewitt looked out at the water already flooding the hollows in the garden path. 'True. I knew I should have brought my fishing gear.'

Fliss briefly joined in with the laughter before moving to open the screen door. 'Coffee anyone?'

Cressy walked through the doorway. 'Yes, please. I'd also love one of Meredith's brownies. They weren't ready when I left so she said she'd send some with the boys.'

Denham bent to lift the heavy esky. 'It isn't only brownies Meredith's sent over.' As he straightened he grimaced and rubbed his stomach. 'Say goodbye to that six-pack.'

Hewitt's smile lingered as Denham strode inside. It was a running joke they'd have to let their belts out when they left the rodeo circuit for an easier life. But so far they'd needed to pull their belts one hole tighter. He glanced at Fliss and his amusement ebbed.

Her wet hair showcased the delicate jut of her cheekbones and the symmetry of her features. But it wasn't her beauty that held him still. Wariness again shadowed her eyes, along with an intense seriousness. It was as though she could see straight through his defences to the pain that went far beyond any physical injury.

'Coming inside?' she asked, voice quiet.

He didn't immediately answer. Above him the hammering rain echoed the pounding of his heart. If he had any sense he'd heed the calls of his self-preservation. Living in close proximity with a strong, beautiful and perceptive woman like Dr Felicity Knight was a bad idea.

He glanced at his ute before taking a step towards the door. 'Yes.'

He couldn't back out now. He might be many things but he wasn't a coward.

Fliss needed help and he needed a place to stay, somewhere other than the family farm, where memories didn't taunt him every morning. A place where he could lie low while his body healed. His chest tightened. A place where he could grapple with the grief and the guilt he'd buried so deep he thought it would never resurface.

CHAPTER

2

What a difference three days and a cooperative lawnmower made.

Fliss sat her clean mug in the drying rack and gazed out the kitchen window. Her control-freak side rejoiced. Her wild, rampant garden had been tamed.

A short, velvety lawn stretched between the house and the turn-of-the-century bluestone stables. If a snake even looked like making a dash for the gap below the back door, she'd see it. Mauve, yellow and white blooms swayed in the neat garden beds. Who knew she'd had flowers amongst her weed jungle? A cloud of white butterflies hovered and flittered, making the garden look like it sparkled.

She hesitated and then leaned to her right. From this angle she had an uninhibited view of the front yard ... and of Hewitt. Her interest wasn't personal, she just wanted to check his shoulder was coping with all the mowing and weeding. She scanned the garden until she saw him over near the shed. All contact between them had to be kept to a minimum. He needed to be left alone as much as she did. For a split second, when she'd held the door open for him the afternoon he'd arrived, she was certain he'd almost turned on his boot heels and left.

Today he was tackling the tap that overnight four-legged visitors had rubbed against and snapped off at the base. She'd woken to a loud moo outside her window and to the sight of an impromptu water feature. She'd chased the two cows out, turned off the pump so the water spout subsided and headed inside to research how to repair it. Thanks to an internet tutorial she'd already replaced a cracked window pane. But when she'd returned outside, Hewitt had everything under control.

The faded red cotton of his shirt pulled tight across his back as he used a shovel to dig around the bottom of the tap. She reached for a plate to wash. She wasn't going there. Hewitt might be muscled and ripped beneath his shirt but the last thing she needed was to notice how good he looked working up a sweat. Even if the warm, reassuring clasp of his hand had made her feel like the world had stopped spinning, for just a moment.

She stared out the window again but this time focused on the injury he was determined to conceal. While he worked he used his left side as little as possible and when he bent to look into the hole, he briefly massaged his shoulder. From his limited range of movement, she guessed he had rotator cuff problems or had maybe done his acromioclavicular joint.

Sunlight glanced off the spoon she dropped into the cutlery drainer. The strength of the sun slanting through the oversized window bathed the kitchen in warmth. The handful of wispy clouds outside weren't going to deliver rain anytime soon. She'd be right to drive to town to meet an old school friend, Kellie, and her daughter, Zoe, when they called in to the local hospital on their way home from Sydney.

She dried her hands on a tea towel, not surprised to find her fingers unsteady. She might know all the theory behind her anxiety but surely she'd be capable of doing something simple without being a total wreck. A drive along the red dirt roads to the town she'd grown up in shouldn't be such a big deal. The sooner her nervous system went off high alert the better.

Deep in thought, she didn't hear Hewitt's boots on the veranda, until his knock rattled the front door. Her hands went to smooth her hair before she remembered her sleek city hairstyle was long gone. Along with her tailored clothes, hospital scrubs and the stethoscope she'd worn around her neck. She lowered her arms and tugged at the oversized navy T-shirt she wore with denim cut-offs.

Instead of knocking again, Hewitt spoke. 'Fliss?'

The sound of his low, deep voice curled through her. She sighed and left the kitchen. She'd been on her own for so long, it was natural an attractive male voice reminded her she was a woman.

'Yes.' She slowed her pace along the hallway. She didn't want to appear breathless. 'Morning.' She pushed open the screen door. 'The cows did a good job, didn't they?'

Hewitt answered with a reserved nod. 'The tap's had it. I'll need a new t-piece joiner.'

She stepped outside to join him on the veranda. Since coming in for a coffee the day he'd arrived, he hadn't accepted any of her polite offers to come inside. As much as she needed to be alone, her mother had passed on the importance of good manners. To her relief Hewitt hadn't only kept to himself but their contact had been limited to casual conversations about the garden. 'I'm heading to town today. I can get one, if you like?'

Hewitt turned to look at her bronze-coloured car that gathered dust beneath the car port. She ignored the splash of mud low on his tanned throat where his shirt opened.

His serious eyes met hers. 'Take my ute. It'll be better on the roads.'

She shook her head even before he'd finished speaking. Taking Hewitt's four-wheel drive would be the sensible thing to do. But the part of her that had broken when Caitlyn had flatlined would spend the entire drive fearing something bad would happen. All it took was a split second for a car to spin out of control.

'Thanks but I'm the first to admit driving on dirt roads isn't my thing. Your ute will stay in one piece if it stays here.'

Hewitt didn't immediately speak. Instead he rubbed his hand across his chin. His stubble rasped in the silence. 'I ... could drive.'

Fliss searched his face. His grave expression hadn't changed but his tone was deeper, quieter. 'Thanks again but there's no need for both of us to go.' She paused to choose her words carefully. 'Especially when town's the last place either of us might want to be.'

'True. But there are some things I need and if the bridge goes under it could be a while before we can get there again. I'm ready to go when you are.'

The slight curve of his lips reassured her he really was fine about playing chauffeur. Her relief at not having to drive must have shown in her own smile because something indefinable flared in his eyes.

'Let me get changed.' She reached for the door handle. 'I don't want to cause a traffic jam in Main Street. Woodlea's not ready to see me in my farm clothes just yet.'

'Take your time.' His voice followed her as she sped to her room. 'I'll have a quick shower.'

Despite his reassurance, she soon emerged wearing slim legged jeans, a sleeveless black top and black wedges. With any luck her

French twist would hold and she'd managed to slick gloss over her lips and not her chin.

From the kitchen bench she grabbed her phone, her sunglasses, a wrapped present and her favourite butter-yellow leather handbag. She locked the front door and, with the sun warm on her arms, headed for Hewitt's ute parked near the bluestone stables. Her steps slowed as she caught a flash of black and white to her left. She studied the trees that disappeared into the creek gully. She could have sworn she'd seen a dog.

The door of the stables opened and Hewitt emerged. Dog forgotten, she stared. Sunlight caught in the darkness of his shower-damp hair and spilled over the width of his shoulders. He'd changed into a crisp blue-and-white checked shirt and as she drew near she saw that he'd shaved. She concentrated on opening the ute door and not on the smooth, firm line of his jaw. It had to be her nerves magnifying her awareness of him. The sight of a good-looking, clean-shaven man didn't usually empty her head of all thought.

Hewitt slid into the driver's seat and the ute cabin filled with the fresh, cedar scent of his aftershave. Fliss took her time clicking her seatbelt into place. In the small space there was no escaping how good he smelt, or looked. The appreciative hum of her senses only confirmed how out of control she was and how far she had to go before she could even think about where her future lay.

She wasn't sure, but when Hewitt's gaze skimmed her face she thought his attention lingered on her mouth. 'So is this the Dr Felicity Knight Woodlea's used to seeing?'

'It is.' She worked hard to keep the strain from her words. 'It's not quite the version my city colleagues saw but this is who I am now.'

Hewitt nodded as he started the ute before touching the screen on the dashboard. The soft strains of country music wrapped around them, negating the need for small talk. Fliss entwined her hands in her lap and settled in the passenger seat. Silence fell between them.

The ute rattled over the cattle grid before following the red dirt road as it wound its way through the cream-trunked gum trees to the creek. When they reached the one-lane bridge, Hewitt slowed to check for oncoming traffic. Normally a sedate flow of water trickled beneath the white wooden structure. Today a fast torrent had submerged willow branches that were normally above the water line.

Hewitt voiced her thoughts as they crossed the creaking timber boards. 'Just as well we're heading to town. If the water level rises another few inches we won't be going anywhere.'

'I think I'll get some long-life milk. At the risk of sounding high-maintenance, I'm the first to admit I'm a hot chocolate tragic. My milk frother came with me from Sydney.'

A smile tugged Hewitt's lips but he didn't make any comment as he avoided a small, round shape crossing the dirt road.

Fliss turned to look over her shoulder at the freshwater long-necked turtle. 'At least someone's enjoying this wet weather. I thought I saw a brown snake the other day until I realised the small head was attached to a shell.'

Hewitt chuckled, a low, deep sound that hinted at the humour tightly contained beneath his gravity.

'Now your garden's tidy there shouldn't be any more cases of mistaken identity.'

'I hope so. My blood pressure can't take any more.'

'The geraniums you planted in the bed near the veranda will help. My mum swears they deter snakes.'

'Mine did too.'

The dirt road turned into bitumen and every so often they'd pass a car going the other way. Each time Hewitt would lift the fingers of his right hand from off the steering wheel. Out here everyone acknowledged each other, even if they were strangers.

Beyond the ute window, green pastures carpeted gentle hills that backed onto the ridge flanking the edge of the fertile valley. The first windmill appeared, then the second and then the third. There was a reason why Woodlea was called the town of windmills.

They passed the corrugated-iron tank perched upon nine wooden posts that tilted at a sharp angle. Thanks to a decades-ago flood, the tank stand looked like it would topple over at the next breath of wind. Somehow the tank continued to defy gravity and tourists regularly pulled to the side of the road to snap photographs.

When the ute topped a rise, signalling their arrival at the town limits, Fliss broke the silence.

'Perhaps we should swap numbers?'

'Sounds like a good plan.'

Once they'd exchanged numbers, she slid her phone into her bag but didn't relax into her seat. The WELCOME TO WOODLEA sign flashed past. Her hands found each other.

Hewitt's kindness had only bought her a little time. She may have been spared the stress of driving on the wet roads, but now she'd have to be prepared to deal with being out in public. Even though it was common knowledge she wasn't home to practise medicine, every town visit brought with it requests for medical advice. And with every request came a rush of uncertainty and self-doubt.

Anxiety coiled around her midriff and pulled tight. No one but Cressy and her close friends Ella and Taylor could suspect her composure was anything but a fragile facade.

Hewitt allowed the ute engine to idle as he watched Fliss walk down Main Street. With her dark hair, pretty features and curves in all the right places, she'd stop traffic even when wearing her farm clothes. She waved at the driver of a mud-covered Hilux who honked as they drove by. From Fliss's serene expression no one would know she had her game face on.

But he did. The moment they'd entered small town Woodlea, her knuckles had shone white and her lips had pressed together. Whatever hell she was going through she wasn't letting it get the better of her. Just like she would have driven her city car into town even though the prospect had etched lines of strain around her eyes. The relief and beauty in her smile when she'd accepted his offer to drive had winded him harder than any fall from a saddle.

Hewitt caught a last glimpse of her before she disappeared into the post office. The scent of gardenia lingered and the ute cabin felt strangely empty. Jaw tight, he set the ute into motion. He couldn't lose sight of why he was at Bundara.

Fliss saw too much with those large hazel eyes and she understood too much for her, and his, own good. Nobody could know the depth of his guilt or his sadness. After his brother died, when their father wept silent tears, when their mother wouldn't leave her bed and when Brody's widow, Ava, didn't know what day it was, Hewitt had shouldered their anguish. He'd cooked and stocked the pantry with food, he'd taken the twins to the play sessions when the preschool Bush Mobile came to town and he'd kept the cattle drenched and the farm machinery running.

He slowed to let a man walking a liver-coloured kelpie cross the road. He'd managed to hold everything together until, emotionally and physically exhausted, he hadn't seen a rock in the paddock he'd ridden over hundreds of times before. Instead of racing after a cow who'd made a break for the gate, he'd been thrown from the ag bike.

When Denham had visited him in hospital, he'd mentioned Fliss needed a hand if Hewitt was after a quiet place to recover. His gut had told him that until he came to terms with losing Brody, he'd be of no real use to anyone. He'd be another accident waiting to happen. So he'd organised for a neighbour to finish putting in Mayfield's winter oats crop, arranged for Ava's mother to stay the six weeks his fractured shoulder needed to heal and packed his duffle bag. And here he was in Woodlea.

The ute indicator clicked as he turned right at the historic two-storey pub. The white wrought-iron trim gleamed in the morning sun. No small town seemed complete without an obligatory watering hole. In some towns, the pub was one of only a handful of buildings.

Hewitt parked beside an old ute outside the Woodlea Rural store. On his list was the tap part as well as wood and nails to fix the gap beneath Fliss's back door. He'd also pick up some padlocks and NO TRESPASSING signs. Denham had mentioned local farms were having trouble with theft, vandalism and illegal trespassing. Fliss's remote location could make her a target. He found everything he needed and as he retraced his steps, the tension gripping his muscles eased.

This was exactly what he needed—anonymity and normalcy. No one knew him as the pickup rider who'd been too slow to reach his brother when he'd fallen from a rodeo bull. He left his purchases in the ute and crossed the road to enter a side street. A rainbow scarf, decorated with knitted lollipops, gummy bears and jelly beans, entwined the front fence of a lolly shop. Guerrilla knitters and their textured, colourful creations decorated much of the Woodlea streetscape and had put the small town on the tourist map.

The doorbell tinkled as he entered. A riot of colour filled the large glass jars sitting in neat rows along the back wall. He chose an assortment of lollies for his niece and nephew, Lizzie and Quinn, some chocolate almonds for Ava and a bag of liquorice for his father. His mother didn't have the Sinclair sweet tooth so he'd look elsewhere for a gift for her.

Back on Main Street he found a gift store and selected a linen handkerchief hand-embroidered with the initial of his mother's first name. As he left the lavender-scented shop, he checked his phone. There wasn't yet any message from Fliss saying she was right to leave.

When he looked up, he saw a woman with short, stylish grey hair, wearing a navy skirt and white blouse, staring at him from across the street. A string of heavy pearls gleamed around her neck. He gave her a polite nod before making his way to the post office. Here the secret Woodlea yarn bombers had struck again. The post box was blanketed in vibrant crocheted and knitted squares. He snapped a photo on his phone for his mother before heading inside.

He sat his presents, and the box he'd selected from the side wall, onto the bench, but made no move to pack his parcel. The well-dressed woman had followed him. The farmer beside him covered up the address on the large envelope he'd been writing on, while the teenage girl across from them quickly shoved the item she was posting into a padded bag. Whoever this woman was, his business would soon become hers.

She sailed over, her heavy perfume overpowering and her smile broad. The speculation sharpening her eyes reminded him that as well as pubs, every small town had a social queen bee. The two other customers headed for the counter.

'Well, hello there.'

The woman's exuberant voice oozed interest and excitement. If he could have he would have pulled the wide brim of his hat low over his face but he'd deliberately left it at Bundara. He was supposed to be re-engaging with the world not hiding from it.

He gave a brief, non-committal smile and glanced at the empty box. The woman ignored his non-verbal cues.

She stuck out her hand. 'Edna Galloway. You must be Hewitt. Welcome to Woodlea.'

He shook her hand, not surprised to find her grip vice-like. 'Thanks.'

'My pleasure. I wondered when you'd arrive. It's a relief for Cressy to have someone staying with Felicity. Those two girls are so close.'

Hewitt nodded. There had been a subtle hardening in Edna's voice when she'd called Fliss by her full name.

Not put off by his reserve, Edna spoke again. 'So you've known Denham since his rodeo days?'

'I have.'

'So that's how you met Cressy?'

'It is.'

When he failed to elaborate, Edna's pencilled brows rose as she looked at the bags of lollies. 'Some lucky little person will be happy when they open that box.'

'They will be.'

Movements deliberate, he packed his parcel. Edna's silence didn't fool him or the way she scanned the ring finger on his left hand. She wasn't going anywhere until she'd had her questions answered. He placed the handkerchief on top of the liquorice and closed the lid. But their conversation was over, whether she liked it or not.

A man entered the post office. Tall and tanned, with dark-blond hair, his Wrangler jeans and boots marked him as a cowboy. The stranger's blue eyes met Hewitt's and as the man sent him a quick grin, Hewitt had no doubt who he was. This had to be Tanner, Denham's cousin and Meredith's son. Hewitt gave him a nod.

'Hello, Edna,' Tanner said, as he drew near. 'We meet again.'

Hewitt was sure Edna's lashes fluttered. 'We do. That's three weeks in a row our paths have crossed in town. What a shame Bethany didn't come in today. She was only saying this morning she hasn't seen you for a while.'

'Yes, it's been a month since I was out to help with her young colt.'

Tanner threw Hewitt a glance that communicated they needed to leave. Now. It was an expression Hewitt usually saw before a cowgirl dragged a cowboy onto the dance floor. If he was a betting man he'd lay money down that Bethany was Edna's daughter and that Tanner ticked all of Edna's potential son-in-law boxes.

Edna's smile widened. 'He's such a fine looking horse but I'm certain she's still having issues. Why don't you come for lunch Sunday and she can chat to you about them?'

'I'm away this weekend but Bethany's welcome to call anytime.'

'That's so kind of you. I'll pass on that you're expecting her to call.'

'No … problem.' Tanner tugged at his shirt collar. 'Sorry to drag Hewitt away but I promised Fliss I'd show him around and no tour of Woodlea is complete without a counter lunch at the Royal Arms.'

'So true. My Rodger's always been partial to their chicken schnitzel even though he says mine's still his favourite.' Edna pinned Hewitt with a narrow-eyed stare. 'I have no doubt I'll see you again so we can finish …' She glanced at the box. 'Our conversation then.'

'Or we can start a new one.'

Edna's pink-painted lips thinned. She hadn't misinterpreted the resolve in his quiet tone. But as she played with her pearls, respect fired in her eyes instead of displeasure.

'Let's start one now. As a fundraising committee member, I'd like to personally invite you on our upcoming trail ride.' She glanced at Tanner. 'If those Ridley boys come, you'll need a strong hand to keep them in line. Denham's gone soft now he's with Cressy.'

Tanner chuckled. 'I won't mention that to Denham.'

Hewitt masked his own amusement. 'Edna, I'd like to help out but I doubt I'll be around for long.'

Before she could open her mouth to convince him otherwise, he strode over to the counter. When he turned, Tanner was already at the door, Edna by his side.

It wasn't until they'd walked half a block from the post office that Edna bid them farewell with a cheery wave and a reminder for Tanner to expect Bethany's call.

After they'd walked a few paces, Tanner looked over his shoulder and slowed. He blew out a breath. 'Okay. We're safe.'

He stopped to hold out a hand to Hewitt. 'Thanks for playing along. I couldn't get out of there quick enough.'

Hewitt shook his hand. Even if the drover hadn't been related to Denham, Hewitt would have liked him. 'No worries. Thanks for coming to find me.'

They started walking again. 'Anytime. I saw Fliss and she asked me to run an intervention if Edna tracked you down. I've never seen Edna walk so fast as she did when she crossed the road to follow you.'

'I take it Bethany's Edna's daughter?'

'Yes, and according to Edna she's single. But according to Bethany she's going out with a city bloke she met at university that her mother doesn't approve of.'

'Ouch.'

'I know.' Tanner held open the pub door and the timeless smell of beer rushed to greet them. 'One thing's for sure, I already like having you around. It isn't every day Edna makes … personal invitations.'

Hewitt only nodded as he entered the pub. He took his phone from his pocket but there was still no message from Fliss. He smothered a surge of warmth that she'd looked out for him by making sure Tanner had his back. He was maintaining his emotional distance. As he walked past the large window he turned to search Main Street. Wherever she was, he hoped she hadn't also run into Edna, and that the concerns that had plagued her when they'd arrived had eased.

CHAPTER

3

Fliss stopped at the end of Main Street and looked back to where the ancient plane trees were dressed in spring green. Their spreading, graceful branches threw shade over the dogs asleep on the back of parked utes.

Over the years Woodlea had changed very little. This had once frustrated her but now the familiarity brought with it an unexpected sense of belonging. When she was younger she couldn't wait to leave for the sophisticated city lights but now she was back, she had the unsettling feeling this possibly was where she was meant to be. She may have bought Bundara and made it her home, but the reality was she continued to have no idea where her future lay.

She sighed and adjusted her hold on the five pink helium balloons she'd bought for Zoe. Edna's white four-wheel drive hadn't moved from where it was parked between the hair salon and the charity shop. Thanks to a heads-up text from Taylor, Woodlea's local hairdresser who'd recently returned from London, she'd managed to avoid the notorious gossip. It was no secret she wasn't Edna's favourite person.

She hoped Tanner had managed to extricate Hewitt from Edna's Welcome-to-Woodlea interrogation. There was no better person than Edna in an emergency. She knew where everyone lived and how many members were in their family, along with their phone numbers. But when it came to private information, Edna's passion for gossip was only rivalled by her quest to find Bethany a husband who came with acres.

Fliss continued walking only to stop for a second time to untangle the balloons that were intent on gift-wrapping her in metallic pink ribbon. Visiting the quirky gift shop beside Woodlea's only grocery store hadn't been one of her better ideas. Keeping the balloons together was like herding cats. She unwound the pale pink balloons from around her neck and shortened the ribbon strings as much as she could.

She passed the museum with its white picket fence and headed for the Anglican stone church with its distinctive bell tower. Her calf muscles burned. The steep incline felt like she was climbing the narrow steps that led to the church bell. Last year the town had banded together to raise money to restore the worn bell mountings. The iconic bell would now ring out in celebration for another hundred years.

Her steps slowed as she bit the inside of her cheek. As hard as she'd tried to contain the ripple effect of her failure, Cressy had still been affected. Cressy and Denham were supposed to be the first couple married after the bell restoration but, since Fliss had been their chief wedding planner, and hadn't been able to continue after Caitlyn died, they'd put their wedding on hold. The bell had instead tolled when the local agronomist, Shaun, had married Brooke, a vet nurse, just before Fliss had moved to Bundara. Shaun and Brooke had then moved south to be close to Shaun's elderly parents.

Cressy had reassured her that she and Denham were in no rush and would wait until Fliss was ready to pick up from where she'd left off with the planning. She swallowed past the ache in her throat. Cressy did so much for her. When she had her life back under control, she'd do everything she could to make sure her sister had the wedding she'd always dreamed of.

This time, even when her breathing became laboured and the balloons battered her, Fliss kept walking. She reached the top end of Main Street and turned left. There was a reason why the red-brick building before her was affectionately called the Hospital on the Hill. Home owners in the city would pay a fortune for the three hundred and sixty degree view the historic hospital boasted.

The first of the canola crops in the rolling rural landscape were in flower. The intense yellow contrasted with the fresh green of oats and young wheat crops. The frequent rain had brought unprecedented growth but also the risk of waterlogging as the underground water table rose. When she'd bumped into Old Clarry at the pharmacy, he'd bemoaned the loss of one corner of his grazing oats until he changed the topic to his bunions. It was only the timely intervention of a young sales assistant that had saved Fliss from making a fool of herself. Self-doubt had stolen her words.

She stopped at the hospital door and battled the panic that accelerated her heart rate. She was the third Knight generation to walk through the doorway. Her mother had been a nurse before she'd stopped to raise Fliss and Cressy, while her beloved grandmother had been a devoted hospital volunteer. But such family connections meant little when guilt writhed inside. Her failure to preserve life undermined her mother's and grandmother's good works.

She hesitated, then pushed open the door. An onslaught of memories hit her. The beep of monitors and the scent of antiseptic returned her to the emergency ward she'd left behind. Her hands

trembled and nausea roiled in her stomach. When she'd stopped
resuscitation and had looked down at Caitlyn's lifeless face it was as
though the world had closed in. She couldn't breathe. She couldn't
process what had happened. Somehow she'd looked down at her
shoes to check there was no blood on them for when she spoke to
Karl. Somehow she'd drawn a deep breath and said the words that
would forever change his and his newborn's lives.

For a moment, Fliss stilled. The need to leave proved so strong
she half turned. Behind the sliding glass panels on her left a
young brunette gave her a wave from where she sat at her desk.
Fliss swallowed and returned Christi's wave. A second woman was
writing on a whiteboard and when she saw Fliss, her lined face
broke into a warm smile.

Fliss managed a smile in return and headed for the waiting room.
To her relief the small area was empty. Kellie and Zoe were still on
their way from Sydney. Fliss took a second to compose herself and
to remember why she'd come today. Two years ago Zoe had been
a patient at the Sydney Children's Hospital where she'd battled
leukaemia. Yesterday the seven-year-old had returned to be given
the all-clear. This morning Kellie and Zoe were calling in on their
way home to celebrate.

Fliss settled the small weight anchoring the balloons onto the
table beside the cabinet that stored handmade gifts. All proceeds
from the sale of the embroidered handtowels and pretty baby bibs
would go towards buying a portable ultrasound machine.

Janet entered the waiting room and they exchanged hugs. She'd
known the old nurse ever since she'd accompanied her mother and a
young risk-taking Cressy into the hospital's emergency department.

'So how have you been?' Janet asked as they each took a seat.

Fliss made sure that her expression appeared relaxed and her
words emerged calm. 'I'm well, thanks. An old rodeo friend of

Denham's has been helping me get Bundara into shape. I even have a proper garden now.'

'Your mother would be pleased. She loved her garden. It brought her so much peace.'

'I'm finding it brings me peace as well.'

Janet leaned over and patted her hand. 'Don't forget Dr Sam's always looking for another general practitioner if you ever find gardening isn't enough.'

'I won't. I'm still taking my time to see what I'll do next. I have some savings to tide me over for the short term.'

She pushed back a fresh swell of anxiety that was tinged with guilt. It was tough to attract, let alone keep, rural doctors in the bush. In the past month, the hospital had been without a permanently rostered-on doctor for two weekends. A visiting locum from Orange had covered the roster gaps but this was only a temporary solution as he would soon return to his family in Sydney.

The hospital didn't only suffer from a lack of staff but also from an erosion of services. Fliss and Cressy had been born in Woodlea but babies could no longer be delivered at the hospital. Mothers-to-be either had to travel to Dubbo or Orange. Fliss had heard stories about babies being born in cars and even in the car park of a fast food restaurant when parents couldn't reach the larger hospitals in time.

The hospital doors burst open and little feet pounded on the hard floor before a small body slid onto Fliss's lap. Fliss laughed and put her arms around Zoe as the seven-year-old snuggled into her embrace. They'd spent many hours in such a position over the time Fliss would visit Zoe during her chemotherapy to read to her. Fliss kissed the top of Zoe's blonde curls that always smelt like strawberries.

'I think you've grown even more since I last saw you.'

Zoe leaned back and Fliss could see the healthy roundness of her face. 'That's what Dr Martin said. He also said I'm *better*.'

'I know. He called me. And these …' Fliss shifted in the seat so she could slide the balloons to the edge of the table, 'are to celebrate.'

Zoe jumped off her lap to bat the closest balloon. The delight in her brown eyes made every balloon head-butt worth it. Fliss reached into her handbag and took out the wrapped present. 'This is for you, too.'

Zoe's grin widened as she sat next to Fliss to open her gift. Kellie walked through the hospital doorway and slipped the phone she'd been talking on into her bag. Kellie and Jason may have kept their happy news quiet but the loose lines of Kellie's white shirt could no longer hide the pronounced contours of her stomach. When Zoe had been diagnosed with leukaemia, Kellie had miscarried their second baby that she and Jason had waited years for. Now they'd been blessed with another child and Zoe would have the brother or sister she'd always wanted.

A squeal drew Fliss's attention back to the seven-year-old now hugging a book to her chest. 'I haven't read this one.'

The little cowgirl was horse-mad and her favourite series was about a group of girls who worked in the stables of a small town and solved mysteries.

'It only came out last week.'

'Thank you.'

'You're welcome, sweet pea.'

Zoe went to Kellie's side and pulled a purple envelope from out of her mother's black handbag. She passed it to Fliss. 'I drew you another picture.'

'Your other ones are on my fridge. Does this have a horse in it too?'

Her blonde head bobbed.

Fliss prised open the envelope and unfolded a drawing of two people riding horses. The person with dark hair rode a grey horse while the smaller figure, with yellow curly hair, rode a little and very round white pony. Zoe came to sit on Fliss's lap and pointed to the picture. 'This is us when we go on the trail ride.'

Fliss couldn't suppress a surge of panic. The thought of being around people for all three days of the ride made her chest tighten, while the possibility that she'd be called upon to act in a medical emergency made her feel sick.

She took a moment to speak. 'We look like we're having fun.'

'We are.'

'Don't forget, I need to ask Cressy if I can ride Jazz but she has sore knees so she mightn't be able to go.'

'You can ride Minty and I can ride Stella.'

Fliss touched the pony in the picture. 'I'm not sure if Minty would like me riding him. My feet would touch the ground.'

Everyone laughed and to Fliss's relief talk turned to the positive outcome of Zoe's appointment with Dr Martin. Zoe's yawns soon said it was time for her and Kellie to continue home. They'd left Sydney early to reach Woodlea by mid-morning. Fliss texted Hewitt to let him know she was ready to go whenever he was.

As Fliss waved and Zoe blew Fliss kisses from the car window, a diesel engine chugged as it climbed the hospital hill. It wasn't long before Hewitt's ute pulled up alongside her.

She slid into the passenger seat. 'Hi.'

'Hi.' He gave her a slow grin.

The tension tightly bound within her loosened. Just like when her fingers had rested in his when they'd met, his smile reassured her. As strong as he was, he also seemed capable of empathy and softness.

She clicked in her seatbelt. But Hewitt shouldn't make her feel ... safe. Such a feeling was dangerous. She'd spent her life being independent. She wasn't about to become needy, especially at a time when it was more important than ever to be in control.

His grey gaze swept over her face before he handed her a takeaway mug. 'I thought you might need this. Tanner and I had a coffee and Sally at the café made your regular order.'

'Thanks.'

She took hold of the cup, making sure her fingers didn't brush his. She wasn't taking any chances on chemistry blindsiding her. Thanks to the volatility of her emotions she was already far too aware of the cowboy beside her. She took a sip of the hot chocolate and savoured the sweetness.

'Home?'

'Yes, please. We can grab my groceries on the way.'

'I've already got them.' Hewitt took the road that would lead them out of town. 'The girl behind the counter gave them to me.'

'I can't believe I'm saying this, but living in a small community where everyone knows your business isn't always such a bad thing.' Fliss relaxed into her seat. 'If Tanner found you does that mean Edna did as well?'

'Yes. Thanks for sending Tanner to find me.'

'No worries. He's a good guy.'

Hewitt glanced at her. She pushed aside the impression he was gauging whether there was anything between her and the blond drover. 'So did Edna mention her daughter, Bethany?'

'She did, but not to me. I was packing a parcel to send to Lizzie and Quinn, so I'm guessing she wasn't sure if I was single or not.'

Fliss's hold on her hot chocolate tightened and she took another sip to buy time before she answered. She'd assumed Hewitt was single and hadn't even considered that he might have children. He didn't wear a ring, but men in rural areas often didn't for safety reasons when working around stock or machinery. Perhaps his relationship had broken down and that was why he'd come to hole up at Bundara? And if he had, there was no justification for feeling like something she'd been searching for had just moved further out of reach.

'You can be sure she won't rest until she finds out.' Relieved her voice sounded normal, she risked a sideways glance at him. 'Lizzie and Quinn are such cute names. Are they your kids?'

Hewitt flinched. He had no one but himself to blame for Fliss's question. He'd opened the conversation door to the one thing he didn't want to talk about. But even as he met Fliss's gaze, he knew he'd answer.

He might have made it clear to Edna his personal life wasn't open to discussion but when around Fliss his self-control went into a freefall. A stronger man might have talked Fliss into driving his ute to town so they wouldn't then spend the day together. But he hadn't been that man.

The silence lengthened. Unsure of exactly what to say, he glanced at her. Her eyes were now more amber than hazel. The colour of her irises appeared to be a barometer for her emotions. He looked back at the road. As hard as he tried, he couldn't always stop his own eyes from revealing his thoughts or feelings. He'd keep their conversation short and give her the condensed version.

'They're my niece and nephew. But … since my brother died … I'm looking out for them.'

'I'm so sorry.'

The genuine compassion in her soft words caused his jaw to harden. He couldn't let her empathy slide beneath his defences. 'Thanks.'

When Fliss didn't reply, or ask any further questions, he chanced another quick look at her. Expression solemn, she studied him.

'Hewitt ... I know you have your reasons for coming to stay and I don't want to pry, but if you want to talk you know where I am.'

Dealing with Edna's inquisition had been far less threatening than this brief, unobtrusive conversation with Fliss. Her genuine offer rattled the bars containing his emotions. She'd be someone who'd hear him out and not pass judgement. She'd be someone who'd really listen. Without thought, he rolled his shoulders to disperse the grief that never left him. Pain lanced through his upper arm and he fought to keep his expression from changing.

They passed the THANKS FOR VISITING WOODLEA sign but neither looked at it.

Fliss stared at the point of his shoulder. 'I'm also here anytime you need medical advice.'

He ground his teeth. He'd been right to think she'd realised the full extent of his injury. 'Is my bad shoulder that obvious?'

'Only to me.' She settled her takeaway mug in the ute console. 'Motorbike accident?'

'How did you know?'

'You're a country boy.'

Talking about broken bones was far easier than discussing Lizzie and Quinn. He matched Fliss's light tone. 'So I'm just a conformist?'

'Yes, I'm afraid so. I did a placement with the Royal Flying Doctors so saw that when it comes to motorbikes, most men who fall off are usually not wearing a helmet and are going too fast.'

'Just to be different, I wasn't going fast, and I'm pleading the Fifth Amendment about whether I was, or wasn't, wearing a helmet.'

'Next time, I hope you don't have to plead the Fifth.'

'There won't be a next time. I need to set a good example for Quinn. I don't want him ending up like me.'

'Exactly.' Fliss leaned over to take a closer look at his shoulder. 'Did you fracture the scapula? That's quite a hard bone to break.'

'Yes, but it's the side of my arm that gives me the most grief, especially if I lift anything.'

He thought Fliss was going to touch him but then her hands curled together in her lap. 'Was anything said about your rotator cuff?'

'No, because I knocked myself out, my arm wasn't really a priority. I also left hospital as soon as I could.'

Fliss's frown gave him a glimpse into her life as Dr Felicity Knight. He could imagine her levelling a stern look at a patient who'd failed to do the right thing. But along with her disapproval, he'd also seen concern in her eyes. Concern, he told himself, that wasn't personal. The way she'd taken his duffle bag the afternoon he'd arrived, so he wouldn't use his injured shoulder, told him that was just who Fliss was. She cared.

'So when did this all happen?'

'Six days ago.'

'Six days?' She shifted in her seat to face him. He didn't need to take his attention from the road to know she again frowned. Her words were clipped. 'And you've been at Bundara for three of those, where you haven't exactly been taking it easy. Didn't the hospital talk to you about what you should and shouldn't be doing?'

'They did but I've knocked myself out enough times to know what to keep an eye on. And as for my shoulder … I've had far worse broken bones.'

She shook her head. 'No wonder you and Denham are such great mates. His medical history would fill a filing cabinet.'

'Mine's not that long, really. Being a pickup rider is much safer than being a bull rider.'

Even before he'd finished, his voice had deepened. He didn't know if it was her offer that she was there if he needed to talk, or the way he'd felt comfortable discussing his shoulder, but words formed in his head. Words he hadn't been able to say for almost a year. He spoke before he lost his nerve.

'My twin brother ... Brody ... was a bull rider. That's how we lost him.'

He thought he imagined Fliss's light touch on his arm, until her fingers wrapped around his forearm and squeezed. Despite the comfort offered, he hesitated. He needed to keep his distance but he'd also come to Woodlea to deal with his grief. He owed it to Lizzie and Quinn to follow through. He'd start by getting to the end of his story, however much his heart broke.

'I rode pickup for the saddle bronco event, but for the bull riding my pickup partner Seth brought in a new guy to show him the ropes. Usually in bull riding it's the rodeo clown who keeps the cowboys safe. We just steer a bull out of the arena if it doesn't go quietly. Brody had drawn a rank bull so I wanted to see him ride before I stabled my mare.' He cleared his throat. 'When he came off ... no one else seemed to read the bull like I did ... I don't even remember getting the arena gate open, all I remember is galloping to get between Brody and the bull ... but I was too—'

He couldn't finish. He gripped the steering wheel so hard his shoulder burned. This time when Fliss's hand curled around his forearm, the warmth of her touch stayed.

'It wasn't your fault.'

He glanced at her, even knowing his anguish would be carved into every stiff line of his face. 'I should have realised what that bull was capable of earlier. I should have reached Brody sooner.'

Fliss's wide, dark eyes mirrored his pain. 'All of those things don't make what happened to your brother your fault. We can only do what we can and have faith that we did the best we could. And we have to hold on to that faith.'

The emotions writhing inside him made it impossible to reply. He broke eye contact to scowl at the road.

'Hewitt,' Fliss spoke again, her tone almost fierce. 'That's what we have to do. I know ... because I have to do it, too.'

Her hand lifted from his arm and as he glanced at her the skin of her throat rippled as she swallowed.

'I ... lost a patient. That's why I'm here. Caitlyn was twenty-three, pregnant with her first child, and had her whole life ahead of her. All she was doing was crossing the road to meet her husband for dinner, when a drunk driver hit her. I was able to save baby Jemma but ... Caitlyn ... didn't make it.'

Hewitt reached for Fliss's hand that was latched onto her seatbelt in a death-grip. She'd offered him physical comfort and he'd do the same, even if she didn't accept the gesture. To his surprise, Fliss released the seatbelt to link her fingers with his. Her delicate bones were at odds with the strength that tilted her chin.

'Medical training doesn't exactly teach you how to deal with loss or how to deliver news that will change a family's future forever. I've lost patients before, and while I've grieved for each of them, they were all ... expected. Caitlyn's death was unexpected and so unfair. It hit me hard.'

Hewitt nodded and, when her grip on his hand tightened, he let Fliss keep talking.

'But that's the thing, isn't it ... life isn't fair. Bad things happen to good people.' A deep resignation and sadness drained the vitality from her voice. 'The reality is, I can't control everything.'

'I can't imagine what you and Caitlyn's family went through.' He brushed his thumb across the smooth skin of the back of her hand.

'But I do know you would have done all that you could have to save your patient. Cressy and Denham both say what a committed doctor you are.' He gave a brief grin to ease the strain. 'Denham would actually say too committed a doctor. You follow up on everything.'

As he'd hoped, Fliss's fingers relaxed and a small smile shaped her mouth before she slipped her hand free. 'With Denham that usually meant at least two phone calls to make sure he even went near a hospital when he was injured on the American pro-rodeo circuit.'

'That sounds like Denham.'

'Let's just hope now he's home, and with Cressy, his hospital visits will be few and far between.' Fliss's voice had returned to normal and when she looked at him her face was composed. 'I bet Lizzie and Quinn are great kids.'

'They are. Lizzie's organised, loves animals and her bedroom's always tidy. She gives the best hugs. Quinn's a few minutes younger and while he doesn't say much he's a deep thinker. He's very busy and is happiest digging in the sandpit or riding his PeeWee motorbike.' Hewitt paused as emotion thickened his words. 'I'd do anything for them.'

'You must be missing them. They're welcome to visit anytime; there's plenty of room in the house.'

'Thanks, I am missing them, but I need to use this time while my shoulder heals to say goodbye to Brody. Then I can get back to taking care of them and Ava just like he would have.'

'I understand.'

Fliss folded her arms and stared out the side window, weariness bowing her shoulders. She didn't need to tell him that she had a similar journey. She needed to find peace after the trauma of losing her patient.

Hewitt slowed the ute as he turned off the bitumen and onto the dirt road. The drive home hadn't been as impersonal as the trip into

Woodlea. Regret crawled through him. What had possessed him to talk so much? He'd just bared his soul to a woman he'd only met three days ago and who, until today, had made sure they interacted as little as possible.

In the distance he could see the white wooden frame of the one-lane bridge but the knowledge they'd soon be at Bundara didn't bring any relief.

So much for keeping to himself and not crossing the emotional line. He hadn't just stepped over it, he'd catapulted himself across it, like the pebbles he and Brody used to fire from their homemade slingshots. And now, somehow, he had to find a way back.

CHAPTER

4

'So how's everything working out with Hewitt?'

Fliss didn't miss the curiosity in her sister's too-casual tone. She hunched her shoulder to keep her mobile beside her ear while she placed blue floral patty pans in a muffin tray.

'You were right. I did need someone out here. It's made a huge difference having Hewitt around. He's even fixed the fence so those cattle of yours don't moo outside my window at dawn. They're worse than that rooster that chased us as kids.'

'I remember Mr Red. He wasn't so bad after I cracked my stock whip at him.'

Fliss put the last of the patty pans into the tray. 'To you. I couldn't crack a whip so I was still fair game. You wonder why I couldn't wait to go to boarding school in Sydney.'

'Yeah, there were no feral roosters there, just city drivers who wouldn't give way on pedestrian crossings, and don't get me started about being suffocated at peak hour on a train. I couldn't wait to get back to the bush.'

'Actually, you're right. Mr Red wasn't that bad and he did breed cute chickens.'

'Felicity Knight,' Cressy's mock-shocked voice sounded in her ear. 'Have you finally come over to the dark side and admitted that it's not all bad out here?'

'I wouldn't go that far. Let's just say you and Grandfather weren't as crazy as I once thought you were for loving country life so much.'

'See,' Cressy said, laughter in her voice, 'there's a little bit of us in you after all. Which reminds me, when you come over this afternoon we can get Mum's things out of the attic. There should be something in her boxes that will help us with her family tree.'

'Good idea. Our DNA results should be in soon. Have you registered on the site?'

'Not yet. I'll do it this afternoon.'

Meredith had recently researched her family history and had suggested that Fliss and Cressy do the same. They'd been at university when their parents had died in a car wreck, and as they didn't know much about their mother's family, they'd each decided to do a DNA test.

Fliss had her suspicions that there was more behind Meredith's gentle encouragement than the older woman's usual thoughtfulness. Perhaps she hoped the research would rekindle Fliss's interest in genetics and eventually medicine? But while she may have been able to discuss Hewitt's shoulder injury with him, the prospect of returning to her old life still tied her stomach in knots.

'Fliss ... you still there?'

Fliss only half heard Cressy's question. Through the kitchen window she saw Hewitt leave the stables. She moved to the spot where she could view the whole garden but Hewitt only went to his ute and then back inside. A few quick glimpses was all she'd seen of him over the past two days.

'Yes, sorry. I'm just in the middle of cooking blueberry muffins. I'll bring some when I come over.'

'Have you asked Hewitt to come? Tanner's looking forward to talking horses with him again.'

'No, it's been wet. I've stayed inside.'

She didn't need to add that she and Hewitt had been avoiding each other.

'That's okay. I'll give him a call.'

'No, it's fine. I'll go across to the stables.' She glanced at the muffins turning golden in the oven. 'I was going to take him some muffins anyway to say thank you for driving me to town the other day.'

'I'm glad he drove you in. That red dirt road of yours would be a nightmare in your car.' Cressy's tone turned teasing. 'You really need to get a new one ... or just have Hewitt drive you around.'

'I'm sure Hewitt would love that. He has enough to deal with without playing chauffeur to a princess who needs to suck up her fears. My anxiety spikes even at the thought of driving in the mud.'

'You're not a princess and it's okay if you're not comfortable driving at the moment with how wet it is. I can only imagine what you've seen in your emergency ward. If Hewitt doesn't feel like coming, Tanner will pick you up. Just be kind to yourself.'

The hot prickle behind her eyelids held Fliss quiet for a moment. She might be the bossy and self-sufficient big sister but she didn't know what she'd do without Cressy.

'Thanks. I will. I'd better get these muffins out before they turn into door stoppers. Love you and see you soon.'

Fliss turned the muffins out onto a rack to cool and filled the second tray with blueberry batter. All the while she snuck glances through the window at the bluestone stables. The predicted bad weather had arrived and for two days rain squalls had blown in. The sky had become a morose grey and the harsh wind had rattled the loose window panes. The gloomy weather mirrored what was going on between her and Hewitt. It was only natural they'd want space after disclosing why they'd each come to Bundara. But as much as a part of her wanted to be alone, another irrational part craved his company.

She stood at the kitchen sink and frowned across at the stables. The distance between them had to be maintained. So she'd stick to some ground rules. When he spoke about Lizzie and Quinn and his voice softened to a tender and husky timbre, she wouldn't acknowledge the flutter in her midriff. And even though she felt emotionally invested in what he hoped to achieve by coming to stay, she'd remain professional and help him through his grief like he was any patient.

While the second batch of muffins cooked, she cleaned the kitchen and then checked her emails on her laptop. Lewis regularly checked in on how she was going.

When she'd arrived at Sydney University wide-eyed and naive, Meredith had given her the name of a friend who was an endocrinologist and adolescent physician. Professor Lewis Barclay had been expecting Fliss to call and had soon become a trusted mentor and friend. His wife, Jean, had been hit by a car in her early twenties and had suffered a brain injury that affected her vision and speech. Their devotion to each other reminded Fliss that marriage didn't always have to be a strained and tense relationship like that of her parents. Fliss replied to Lewis's latest email. Jean hadn't been well after a minor stroke.

When the last batch of muffins were cooling on the bench, Fliss headed to the stables. Sunlight splashed over the dark bluestone rock that had been hand cut on Bundara. The previous owners had lived in the renovated building while working on the main homestead. When their enthusiasm had dwindled, along with their finances, they'd put the run-down farm on the market again.

A willie wagtail played in a large puddle that had collected in the hollow of the gravel path. Despite all the recent rain, Cressy had reassured Fliss that the bridge and local roads would remain open. As Fliss drew near, the small bird hopped a few steps before flying off to perch on a crooked fence post.

The door to the stables opened before her knuckles could rap on the wood.

Hewitt greeted her with a reserved smile. 'Morning.'

Stubble shadowed his chin and his dark hair was tousled from where he'd tunnelled a hand through the front. An emerald green work shirt hugged his torso and hung loose over his faded jeans.

'Hi.' She held out the muffins. 'I come bearing gifts to say thank you for driving me to town.'

'No worries. Anytime.' Hewitt took hold of the plate. 'These smell great.'

'It's Meredith's never-fail recipe but they don't exactly look like hers do. Mine are more … blue.' Fliss broke eye contact to look at the muffins. Hewitt's eyes were such a clear, pure grey she'd forget what she was supposed to ask him if she wasn't careful. 'I also come with an invitation from Cressy to come to Glenmore for an early dinner.'

Hewitt's reaction was only subtle, but the lines around his mouth deepened. 'Tonight?'

'Yes. It's just with Cressy, Denham and Tanner.'

His eyes searched hers. 'Were you planning on going?'

She nodded. 'It's okay if you want a quiet night in. Tanner can pick me up so I don't have to take my car on the wet roads.'

'I'll drive you. A night out will do me good.'

THE RED DIRT ROAD

'Great. I'll let Cressy know.' Now was the time when she should say goodbye and return inside. But her feet refused to move.

Hewitt looked at the muffins and then at her. 'I'm about to check Cressy's cows if you'd like to come? So far there's been three calves born.'

She hesitated. She'd already be spending time with him tonight. A gentle breeze tousled her hair, reminding her she hadn't been outside in days. She'd enjoy seeing the new calves.

'Thanks ... I'd like that.'

'Okay. I'll find my boots and we'll go in the ute.'

After a moment, Hewitt reappeared with his cowboy boots on and a half-eaten muffin in his hand.

'How come we're taking the ute and not the quad bike?' Fliss asked, already regretting her decision to accompany him as they walked side by side towards his ute,

Hewitt might make her feel safe but he also made her feel unsettled in a way that had nothing to do with her usual anxiety. She had the insane urge to link her fingers with his to feel his warmth and his strength. She curled her fingers into her palms.

'This way we won't get wet if it rains. Also, the cattle are over where there's a decent track.'

His careful tone and grave expression suggested he too was conscious that things had to remain impersonal between them. There'd be no more raw conversations or physical contact to offer comfort. She slid into the passenger seat and her tense shoulders lowered.

When they drove past the timber-framed machinery shed, she made casual conversation. 'Did the muffin taste okay?'

'It did.'

'Wonderful. I'll tell Meredith they weren't an epic fail like my sponge cake that even the magpies wouldn't eat.'

They came to a double gate and Fliss reached for her door handle. Getting the gate had everything to do with being independent and nothing to do with needing space to breathe after Hewitt had shot her a slow smile.

Once again settled in the ute, Fliss gazed out the window as Hewitt made his way along the narrow road that cut through the middle of the paddock. A cluster of cows congregated on a nearby dam wall. Their sleek black coats contrasted with the vibrant colour of the rolling pastures. The hills didn't usually look so fertile and lush. It was as though she were in an English landscape where the only colour palette used was shades of green.

She laughed as two calves, their tails in the air, raced each other through the run-off that formed mini-streams. 'Look at them go. They're so adorable.'

'They are. Those two were born the day we went to Woodlea.'

He left the track to make a short detour to where a cow stood on her own, her head down. Hewitt stopped a good distance away. The cow lifted her head to stare at them.

Fliss leaned forwards to get a better look at the tiny, jet-black calf the cow had been licking. 'There's calf number four.'

'It's not even an hour old. Everything looks okay so we'll leave them in peace.'

Fliss stole a glance at Hewitt's profile. The gentleness of his tone matched the softness in his expression.

They continued to where a group of cows rested beneath the canopy of a grey box tree. Some came to their feet, while others stayed on the ground chewing their cuds.

Hewitt frowned as he swung the ute around to head back the way they'd come. 'There's a calf missing. The mothers can stash them really well in the grass but I'd like to make sure it's all right.'

'I'll keep a look out my window.'

Silence settled between them as they scanned the paddock either side of the road.

At the steel cattle yards, Hewitt slowed. 'There they are, down near the trough.'

He turned the ute and made his way to where a cow was on one side of a fence and her calf on the other.

'How did he get over there?' Fliss asked as they drew near. The calf's flanks were indented as he tried to suckle his mother through the wire.

'I'm afraid your fences have as many holes as a golf course.'

Hewitt stopped in front of the double gate. Fliss didn't leave her seat. The logical move was to get out and open the gate. She might be more city girl than country girl, but the wisdom of her grandfather's life lessons remained. Never get between a cow and her baby, no matter how placid the mother looked.

Hewitt glanced at Fliss. 'The cow's on your side, so I'll get the gate. Fingers crossed she gives us no trouble and stays where she is.' He swung the gate open and, keeping a close eye on the cow, drove behind the calf. The calf stared at the slow-moving ute before walking along the fence line. When he realised the gate was open, he bolted through. His mother ran to him before leading him away to the trough, where she stopped to nuzzle his neck. The calf made a beeline for her udder, his tail wriggling as he drank.

Fliss left the ute to close the gate. By the time she'd returned to her seat, a white milky froth had formed at the side of the calf's mouth.

'He won't be hungry for long at the rate he's guzzling.'

She barely heard Hewitt's answering chuckle as she stared through the windscreen at a group of willows that lined the far side of the creek bed. 'Did you see that? I thought I saw a dog again. A black-and-white one.'

Hewitt studied the area where Fliss pointed. 'No, but I've seen tracks.' His jaw hardened. 'Feral dogs, whether they're born wild or are pets that have been abandoned, are not what Cressy wants around her breeding herd. Let's hope we don't start seeing calves with torn or missing ears or worse.'

'I know. Grandfather had a lot of trouble one year with a pack of dogs led by a rogue German shepherd.'

Fliss again volunteered to open and close the gates. As she closed the final one, raindrops peppered her oilskin vest and hat. Once home, Hewitt parked in his usual place outside the stables. As the sound of the engine faded, he turned to her. A smile warmed his eyes.

'Thanks for the company and for getting the gates.'

'You're welcome. See you about five?'

Fliss didn't wait to see his nod before she had the door open. She couldn't get out quick enough, even though the rain was now a steady downpour. Her heightened emotions and unpredictable hormones had a lot to answer for. This time the heat in her cheeks and the swirls in her stomach weren't from nerves.

She had another ground rule to add to her list. Be at least a body-length away from Hewitt when he smiled. It would be the only way she'd remember her other ground rules.

Sunlight peeped through the heavy cloud cover, causing afternoon shadows to dapple the gravel road as Hewitt drove towards Cressy's farm. He released a silent breath when the tops of Glenmore's chimneys appeared through the thinning gum trees. He and Fliss would soon no longer be alone. Even though the drive had alternated between periods of companionable silence and casual conversation, he couldn't relax.

Fliss sat beside him smelling of flowers and wearing a white top with fitted black jeans that would have made his jaw drop if he hadn't been grinding his teeth at being near her. Ever since they'd checked the cows that morning, he'd been fighting to re-establish his reserve and to rebuild his self-control.

Fliss's soft laughter as the calves had splashed through the water had touched a place buried within him. She'd sounded so carefree and her smile had been so beautiful it had been impossible to look away. This was the side of Fliss that stayed hidden beneath the weight of her guilt.

Since their car conversation, he'd been determined to reclaim the emotional distance he'd lost. And he had for two days. He'd kept to himself. But his new neighbour had gotten under his skin. When he wasn't listening for the tread of her boots on the garden path, he was thinking about her. Her wariness, vulnerability and the fear he'd sensed that day in town now all made sense. She too had come to Bundara to heal. Even with her struggles, she'd been prepared to open her home to a stranger. If there was anything he could do to help her fight her battles, he would.

He concentrated on the flock of galahs feeding on the side of the road. But as much as Fliss shredded his control and made his testosterone hum, Ava, Lizzie and Quinn had to remain his sole focus. The day he'd let Brody down was the day he could no longer call his life his own.

He slowed as the galahs took flight in a cloud of grey and pink. The ute rattled as it crossed the cattle grid marking the entrance to Glenmore. Even though the homestead was still a distance away, the graceful lines of the wide veranda and roof line could be seen. Fliss leaned forwards to peer through the windscreen at the gentle green hills. Her loosely braided dark hair fell over her right shoulder.

'Glenmore looks so different to this time last year. It just about broke Cressy's heart when it didn't rain.'

'Denham said the drought made things tough.'

'It did. I was so worried about her. She was close to our grandfather and takes carrying on his legacy very seriously.'

Hewitt had seen firsthand the toll a drought could take in his own local community. A lack of services and a stigma concerning mental health had cost the district two well-known farming identities. But now, even in a good season, the community had become more aware of the importance of asking if friends and family were okay.

Fliss continued. 'While I was inside with my grandmother, reading and staying clean, Cressy was out mustering cattle in the heat and the dust. She'd always known Glenmore would be her destiny ... even when our father took over. He hadn't exactly shared her passion.' She cast him a brief smile that didn't reach her eyes. 'Sorry ... I shouldn't still be bitter that my father risked everything his grandfather had created, and that his youngest daughter loved, to bet on horse racing.'

'Gambling can be all-consuming. It took a mate of mine a long time to admit he had a problem.'

'It took Dad over ten years. I'd like to think he'd been committed to his recovery when he and Mum went on their trip to Tasmania.'

'That's a good thought to hold on to.'

From his friendship with Cressy he knew that it had been on this trip that their parents' rental car had collided with a logging truck and they'd never made it home.

'I think so.'

Fliss looked away as the road ahead forked but not before sadness dulled her eyes. As angry as she was, she clearly still missed her father.

Hewitt followed the driveway to the front of the house. Beneath the shade of a cedar tree, a blue ute was parked next to Denham's white Land Cruiser. Over in the machinery shed Cressy's seen-better-days ute was positioned beside the farm Hilux. Two dogs bounded across the plush lawn and bolted through the open garden gate.

'Brace yourself.' Fliss firmed her grip on the container that held her muffins. 'Here comes the welcoming committee.'

She left the passenger seat and a black kelpie, her muzzle sprinkled with grey, slid to a stop in front of her.

'Hello, Miss Tippy.' Fliss tickled behind the kelpie's ears. 'Juno hasn't driven you to drink yet?'

Even as Fliss spoke, a young liver-brown dog planted her paws on the back of Fliss's legs and yipped. The kelpie-poodle-cross's excitement was only matched by the fluffiness of her thick coat.

Fliss laughed as she glanced over her shoulder. 'Yes, Juno. I know you're there. Just let me finish saying hello to Tippy.'

While Fliss patted Juno, Tippy sidled over to Hewitt for a pat.

'I hope those rodeo cows of Denham's are behaving themselves,' he said, stroking Tippy's neck as she leaned against his legs. A loud screech drowned out his words before a white cockatoo swooped from the top of a nearby gum tree to land on the roll bar of his ute. The cockatoo then flew onto Fliss's shoulder.

She ruffled Kevin's yellow crest. 'Were you watching us drive in?'

'He would have been.' Cressy approached with a wide smile. The hem of her simple white dress brushed the tops of her pink cowgirl boots. 'He squawked as soon as you crossed the cattle grid. It still amazes me he can hear a car coming even before the dogs do.'

Kevin stayed perched on Fliss's shoulder while the sisters hugged.

Hewitt looked away, his throat raw. With his brother gone, not a day passed when he didn't feel like a part of him was missing. They'd gone away to school together, attended the same university to study agriculture and come home to run the family farm. They'd been a team until Hewitt had made a decision that changed everything. Guilt knifed inside. What he hadn't told Fliss was that his role in Brody's death had started long before his twin strapped himself onto that devil of a bull.

Chest tight, he collected the bottle of red wine from the ute. When he faced Fliss and Cressy, he didn't miss Fliss's gaze sweep over his face. Just like on the day he arrived he had the sense she was reading him like he'd read the horses and bulls in the rodeo arena.

Cressy stepped forwards to hug him. 'I'm so glad you came. The boys are out the back on barbeque duty. I had them start cooking before they disappeared into the shed to do whatever you men do over there.'

Hewitt returned her hug. 'I'll go and supervise. I know what Denham can do to a steak. He believes it's only cooked if it resembles leather.'

'Thank you. Tell Denham if he sneaks Tippy and Juno another sausage he can explain to Ella why they're looking so fat. Last vet visit there was talk of boot camp.'

Hewitt made his way through the colourful spring garden to the back of the homestead where a pergola shaded an entertainment area. As he rounded the corner, he inhaled the strong scent of grilled onion and meat.

Denham and Tanner stood around a barbeque. Both turned as his boots rang on the stone pavers.

Denham reached into the ice-filled esky beside him. 'Perfect timing.' He handed Hewitt a cold beer. 'Steaks are almost done.'

'Thanks. If they taste half as good as they smell I'm lining up for thirds.'

Denham grinned. 'I'm taking all the credit. All Tanner's done is drink my beer.'

'No, I haven't. I've fed Tippy and Juno sausages so technically it wasn't you feeding them.'

Hewitt placed the bottle of wine beside the vase of white roses in the centre of the table. 'Cressy knows exactly what you two are up to.'

Denham sighed and placed his empty beer bottle in a box beside the barbeque. 'There's no getting anything past her.' The pride and love in his tone contradicted his aggrieved expression.

Tanner added his empty beer bottle to the box. 'I'll take one for the team and do a drinks run.' Grin wide, he headed inside.

Wings flapped as Kevin flew overhead towards the horse paddock. Ignoring the buckskin that lifted his head to glare at him, the cockatoo perched on the cement trough and dipped his beak into the water.

Denham turned the sausages. 'I'd never thought I'd say this, but I think Bandit's met his match. I'm sure Kevin only drinks from that trough to tick him off.'

The bad-tempered gelding had once been a buck jumper and even now Denham was the only rider he'd let stay in the saddle.

Hewitt stared at the beer in his hand. There had been another time when Bandit had met his match. A time when he and his horse Garnet had been riding pickup. A time before all colour had been stripped from Hewitt's world. A time when Bandit would explode into the arena, throw his rider, and Garnet, with her brave, fearless heart, would know exactly what to do to make sure Bandit gave Hewitt no trouble.

'How's Garnet doing?' Denham asked quietly, as though reading his mind.

'Physically she's fine. Her injuries have healed but …' His voice trailed away. He couldn't say that until he rode her neither of them would have truly healed.

Denham clasped Hewitt's right shoulder. 'I have no doubt you and Garnet will be a team again. That's what being at Bundara's all about.'

Tanner returned with a six-pack of beer and passed one to Denham.

Hewitt touched beers with Denham and then Tanner before he took a swallow. 'Bumped into Edna lately?' he asked the drover.

'No, only because I haven't been to town. I figured seeing Edna three weeks in a row was enough.'

Denham used tongs to place the steaks and sausages onto an oval platter. 'You're a braver man than I am for visiting town at all knowing Edna thinks you're Bethany's perfect match.'

Tanner's blue eyes twinkled. 'Thanks to Hewitt here, I might soon lose the title. Edna seemed very impressed when Hewitt put her back in her box after her nosiness got the better of her.'

Denham's dark brows lifted. 'Hewitt, you didn't ... There's nothing Edna likes more than a strong man. I've taken to being a wuss round her. It's yes, Edna, no, Edna, three bags full, Edna.'

'We know,' Hewitt said, while Tanner laughed. 'She thinks you've gone soft.'

The back door closed with a bang as Cressy and Fliss joined them, their arms filled with bowls of salads. Hewitt moved forwards to help Fliss as the tomato sauce bottle pinned beneath her elbow threatened to fall.

'Something must be funny,' she asked, voice curious. 'Or you've all already had too many beers on an empty stomach.'

'I don't think there's any danger of that happening for Denham and Tanner.' Cressy eyed off the platter of steaks and sausages. 'There's no way Tippy and Juno have eaten nine sausages, even if they are now asleep in their kennels with very round tummies.'

As more laughter rippled around them, Fliss went to kiss Denham on the cheek and give Tanner a hug. Ever since Fliss had mentioned Tanner could take her to Cressy's, a strange emptiness had filled Hewitt. He took a swig of beer to hide his relief that their embrace appeared casual. They were just friends.

After seats were taken, wine poured and the steaks and salads heaped onto plates, the conversation turned to the dog Fliss had seen.

'I'm sure it was a border collie, a long-haired one,' she said as she looked across at Cressy. 'But your calves will be okay. Hewitt's keeping a close watch over them. There's four now and this morning when we drove around there was one that had just been born.'

Hewitt's hold on his fork tightened as Denham studied him. Cressy wasn't the only one who didn't miss anything. Denham understood him too well. He knew Hewitt had gone to Bundara for solitude, not to socialise. He also knew Hewitt didn't ever do anything he didn't want to do. No amount of buckle-bunny cleavage had ever distracted either of them on the rodeo circuit.

Tanner spoke and Hewitt's grip on his fork eased when Denham's attention turned to the drover. 'If it's just one dog hanging around, it might not be feral. It could have been dumped or be a pigging dog that's been left behind. Although, a long-haired border collie isn't the usual pig dog breed.'

Denham nodded. 'It could have been stolen. It isn't only fuel and quad bikes going missing lately, dogs are too, especially from in town. Ella's neighbour lost a staffie from their backyard. The gate padlock had been cut, the dog stolen and the three smaller dogs let out.'

Cressy sighed. 'Between people wanting money for drugs, or trespassing to hunt pigs, nowhere seems to be off limits. You be careful out at Bundara, Fliss. You're a long way out there.'

'Don't worry.' Fliss glanced at Hewitt. 'We'll be fine, won't we?'

Hewitt fought to keep his expression neutral. The way she included him shouldn't mean so much. He avoided Denham's gaze as he replied, 'Yes, we will.'

The conversation moved on to Reggie's calves and how Cressy still wasn't convinced that the bull she'd rescued as a calf could ever breed offspring mean enough to be bucking bulls. The resulting stories about bulls behaving badly continued through to dessert and until the pavlova topped with passionfruit and cream had disappeared.

Cressy pushed back her chair. 'Now before you boys reach for another beer and get too comfortable reminiscing about the good ol' days when you were supermen, I've some boxes to move down from the attic.'

Fliss came to her feet. She glanced at Hewitt's shoulder before she collected the empty plates near her. 'The attic isn't big enough for three cowboys to clomp around in. Hewitt, I've a special job for you.'

'Sure.'

He stood and reached for the large pavlova plate. He'd be a fool to read anything into her concern. She was looking out for him like she'd do for any patient. She was making sure he wouldn't lift any boxes, however light.

'Let me guess, it involves getting my hands wet,' he said as he followed, catching a faint scent of gardenia.

She stopped to wait for him on the veranda step. Laughter danced in her eyes and curved her lips.

'Not if you wear Cressy's pretty pink dishwashing gloves.'

CHAPTER

5

Fliss might have arrived home from Cressy's barbeque two hours ago, but she was still wide awake.

A loose flap of iron banged for a second time. The door of the garden shed must have blown open again. She really needed to use bricks to secure it closed. She kicked off the heavy bedcovers. Until it stayed shut, she'd have no hope of unwinding.

The polished jarrah wood floorboards chilled her bare feet as she crossed the room to pull an old university rugby jersey over her tank top and pyjama shorts. As she made her way to the kitchen for a torch the shed door bashed again.

In the city she'd had no trouble sleeping through sirens and fire alarms but now she needed complete silence to relax. Even the cheerful chirp of a cricket stressed her strung-out system. She wasn't proud she'd taken to standing outside her window and using the sole of her ugg boot to discourage crickets from taking up residence in the crevices of the bluestone blocks.

Once on the veranda she pulled on her boots. She straightened to massage her right temple. The speed of her thoughts said it wasn't just the flapping tin keeping her awake. A thin stream of light escaped from beneath a blind from over in the stables. The main reason she couldn't sleep was also awake.

She switched on the torch and followed the pool of strong light. Tonight she'd stuck to her ground rules. But even in the company of others, she'd been hyper aware of her cowboy neighbour. Of his slow smile, and the way he'd look at her across the table, giving her his full attention. Of the deep, husky tone of his laughter as he'd tried to fit Cressy's pink rubber glove onto his large hand.

She'd glimpsed the man he'd been before he carried the burden of his brother's death. And her mind just wouldn't let the images fade. Grave and silent, Hewitt was gorgeous. But relaxed and sociable, he was unforgettable.

She didn't know if it was his quiet strength or the steadiness of his grey stare, but something within him spoke to something within her. She felt at ease around him. He was a man who'd stand firm, whatever life threw at him, and he'd do so with humility and integrity. There'd be no ego, or grandstanding. Secure in who he was, and what he was capable of, he didn't have anything to prove. No wonder he was a pickup rider. In a crisis he'd head towards trouble, never away from it.

The branches of the cedar tree swayed and the open garden shed door caught in the wind. She stepped forwards to catch it before it slammed shut. A scrape from inside the shed had her lift her torch higher. Had the shingleback returned?

She shone the light through the narrow doorway. Her breath hissed. It wasn't a lizard whose large eyes caught in the white beam, but a black-and-white dog. Fliss swung the torchlight towards the ceiling and readied herself to quickly back away. This had to be the dog she'd seen.

But when the border collie didn't move or growl, Fliss lowered the torchlight. The dog had pulled the canvas lawnmower cover to the ground to lie on and tucked against her side were six tiny bodies.

'You're a clever mamma finding the warm and dry shed to have your babies in.' The dog stared at her, silent and unmoving. 'I think Tanner's right. You're not feral or wild. If you were, I'd have a few bite marks by now and be needing a tetanus shot.'

The dog's tension seemed to ebb and she lowered her head to lick the nearest pup.

Fliss glanced over her shoulder at the stables. It was too late to call Cressy or Ella about what she should do for the dog and her pups tonight. She was used to problem-solving on her own. But common sense told her Hewitt would possess the practical experience she wouldn't find in any online how-to article.

She headed to the stables, turning her torch off as the sensor light clicked on. This time she didn't even raise her hand to knock before the door swung open.

'Fliss, is everything okay?'

She didn't know if it was the concern edging Hewitt's husky tone or that all he wore was a pair of low-slung jeans, but her words refused to leave her throat.

She was a doctor. She knew the name of every corded muscle wrapped within Hewitt's smooth, tanned skin. She knew the function of every toned tendon caressed by the strong outdoor light. But never had the sight of a man's body made it impossible for her to focus or to think.

Her fingers curled tight around the torch handle. So much for being sceptical about sparks and physical chemistry. The desire to run her fingertips over the hard-packed planes of Hewitt's torso unsettled her. Her life was already out of control enough without her hormones running wild.

Cheeks too hot, she forced herself to speak. 'Yes, everything's fine. We have an unexpected guest.'

The intensity in Hewitt's eyes didn't dim. The tight, carved lines of his body were tense, ready for the age-old fight response to any threat.

'An unexpected snake guest?'

'No, an unexpected border collie guest. The dog I saw this morning is in the garden shed … and she's had puppies.'

'Puppies?'

Fliss fought to keep her attention on his face and not on the curl of his biceps as he rubbed his chin. 'Yes, six tiny newborn puppies.'

Hewitt swung away. 'I'll throw on a shirt and grab the leftovers in the fridge.'

'Okay. I'll get the other things we'll need from the house.'

Fliss turned before she'd finished speaking. She'd seen enough. The back view of Hewitt was just as impressive as the front. If she was going to get any sleep tonight she didn't need to know how well defined his wide shoulders were or how his tan disappeared beneath the low waistband of his jeans.

Her arms filled with soft towels and two large bowls, Fliss joined Hewitt outside the garden shed. The sensor light from the stables threw a pale wash of light over the lawn. Hewitt had pulled on a grey T-shirt but the thin cotton only accentuated the well-honed ridges beneath.

A container holding what looked like beef casserole sat by his boots. A pair of bricks now ensured that the shed door stayed open. She sat her armload of items on the ground before carefully shining her torch inside. Hewitt's arm brushed hers as he took a look at the dog gazing back at them. She remained still before her tail moved in a tentative wag.

'Hey, gorgeous girl.' Fliss glanced at Hewitt's profile as he spoke. His voice had the same tender, deep timbre as when he spoke about the twins. 'You've been living rough, haven't you?'

His gaze swept over the dog and Fliss sensed him assessing her just like she evaluated a patient.

He moved into the shed. 'This isn't your first litter, is it?' He spoke quietly as he approached. 'You've done this all before. You've also once trusted us humans as you've chosen to have your puppies here.'

This time when the border collie wagged her tail, the gesture was more certain. Hewitt slowed his steps as he drew near. The dog whined and lifted her head as though seeking his touch. He moved closer to stroke her ears.

'She's definitely not a feral dog.' Hewitt's words were just loud enough for Fliss to hear. 'But no sign of a collar and she needs a decent meal. By the looks of her, and these pups, they're purebred border collies.'

Fliss only nodded. She didn't want her reply to break the bond forming between Hewitt and the neglected dog.

'Okay,' he said, after he ruffled the border collie's neck, 'I'm going to check your babies and then we'll make you all more comfortable.'

Hewitt placed a hand on each of the small bodies tucked against their mother. 'All good. They're warm and their tummies are full.'

He gave the border collie a last pat and when he returned to the doorway, Fliss passed him the towels and the torch. After Hewitt had created a soft nest that would be cosier than the canvas cover, he placed a water and food bowl close by. The dog licked the back of Hewitt's hand before lapping at the water. Her thirsty gulps filled the silence.

Emotions close to the surface, Fliss looked away. Hewitt's magic didn't only work on anxious, displaced city girls. He had made the abandoned dog feel safe, too.

Hewitt left the shed. The stables' sensor light had clicked off and the waning torch provided the only source of light. A gust of wind engulfed her and she raked her fingers through her hair to drag windblown strands from off her forehead. A drop of rain wet her lip. She touched the spot with her tongue.

Hewitt crossed his arms. In the gloom she couldn't gauge his expression but his rigid stance told her their easy companionship had dissolved. Gone was the relaxed man who'd laughed at the barbeque and who'd bonded with the border collie. Hewitt was again the grave, guarded man who'd arrived, his emotions firmly held in check. His injury had to be bothering him.

If she had a chance, she'd run her fingers over the top of his shoulder to feel if the bones were misaligned. She was sure he'd done his AC joint. She tightened her grip on the torch handle. The idea of touching Hewitt, even in the context of assessing his injury, shouldn't make her pulse flutter.

She thought he stared at her mouth but then a jagged splinter of lightning flashed low in the sky to her left.

'Thanks for your help,' she said, as a cold drop of rain splashed her nose. 'I'll call Ella first thing. Hopefully our new mother will have a microchip to let us know who she belongs to.'

'Anytime. And I'm sure she will. Someone will be looking for her.' He unfolded his arms. 'See you tomorrow.'

'Night.'

Large raindrops splattered the hard plastic of the torch and caught in the thin beam. The heavens were about to rip open. Glad of the distraction, she jogged towards the house. She couldn't trust that the darkness would hide her expression. For a dangerous moment her face would have revealed that the prospect of seeing Hewitt tomorrow had made her feel something other than anxiety. It'd been a long time coming, but she'd again felt hope.

∽

Lizzie's excited squeal reminded Hewitt he needed to lower the volume on his laptop whenever his niece talked to him over the internet. In contrast, he had to increase the volume whenever Quinn sat still long enough to chat.

'You found six puppies in the shed?' Lizzie's auburn curls bounced as she wriggled on the kitchen chair, her grey eyes appearing even brighter through the laptop camera. 'What are their names?'

'Fliss found them and we haven't named them yet.'

'You haven't?' Shock rounded Lizzie's mouth. 'That's okay. I'll help you.'

Lizzie's sweet and generous heart never failed to make his own clench. He'd do everything he could to ensure his precious niece lived the happy and stable life she deserved. 'Thanks. You know I need all the help I can get.'

'I know. I love you, Uncle Hewy, but you can't call a kitten Tiger. Snowball's white.'

A freckled face popped up behind Lizzie as Quinn stuck his tongue out at the camera. Full of cheek and energy, what he didn't say in words, he said through actions. He shared his twin sister's red hair and grey eyes and if not for their Sinclair surnames, Hewitt would never have been picked as their uncle. A green and yellow tractor blurred on the screen as he pretended to drive the small toy above his sister's head.

'Hi, Quinn,' Hewitt said above his nephew's tractor noises.

'Hi.' Quinn replied with a single word and then disappeared from the computer screen.

Lizzie, used to talking for her brother, filled the sudden quiet. 'He's missing you and wants to know when you're coming home.'

Hewitt kept his voice light. 'I miss you guys, too. I'll be home as soon as my shoulder's okay. Has your surprise arrived yet? It should be in the next lot of mail.'

Lizzie's curls bounced again. 'Is it a pony?'

This time Hewitt didn't have to pretend to be upbeat. Lizzie's love of life always kept the shadows at bay. 'No. Dave mightn't quite be able to fit a pony in his mail van.'

'He can if it's a toy.'

'True. But this surprise is something you eat.'

Quinn appeared on the screen. From the gleam in his grey eyes, he'd worked out the parcel would contain lollies. Hewitt spoke before Quinn disappeared.

'How's your sandpit?'

'Good.'

The sandpit was the first thing he'd built in the bleak, brutal days following Brody's funeral. Quinn had never left his side and the golden sand had absorbed all their silent tears. 'Have you flooded it?'

Lizzie rolled her eyes. 'Yes. Three times. He made such a mess.'

Hewitt winked at Quinn. His flooding of the sandpit would happen anytime Lizzie pulled rank and played the bossy elder sister.

Quinn gave him a wave before the five-year-old vanished from view. A soft voice sounded and Lizzie came to her feet to allow Ava to sit on the chair. Lizzie settled onto her mother's lap. Ava smoothed her daughter's curls before resting her cheek on her head and folding her arms around her. Ava's hair might be blonde, and her eyes blue, but mother and daughter shared the same heart-shaped face.

Except Ava was half the size of what she used to be. Since she'd become a widow she'd lost all interest in anything but her children. Guilt clawed its way across his shoulders.

'Had much rain over there, Hewitt?'

'It's so wet even the ducks are complaining.'

Lizzie giggled. 'Jemima would be happy. She keeps trying to swim in the dogs' water bowls.'

Hewitt nodded. 'I'm sure she forgets she's a duck.'

Lizzie's white pet duck had a whole dam to swim in but preferred to stay close to the house where she had the company of the two silkie hens.

Ava smiled. 'I'm sure she does. Your mum's in town and your dad's ... resting.'

'That's great Mum's gone to town.'

Hewitt didn't want to say anything more in front of Lizzie but his mother had only just started leaving the house and farm again.

'It is. And I've been going in too. I've also sent my mum home.' Ava paused. 'Hewitt ... Garnet's missing you.'

He didn't speak, only rubbed the back of his neck. The thought of riding hollowed out his gut. There were too many memories associated with being in Garnet's saddle. The creak of leather and the scent of horse and dust would only take him back to the moment when Brody lay prone on the ground. A moment forever branded in his soul.

Ava spoke again. 'I know your shoulder needs to heal, but if you want me to bring her over, the kids and I could go for a road trip.'

'Thanks. I'll let you know.'

Through the stables' window he caught movement from over near the garden shed. Fliss was awake and checking on their unexpected guests.

He blew Lizzie a kiss. 'I'll sign off now and will call tomorrow to talk about puppy names. I hope your surprise arrives today.' He raised his voice. 'Bye, Quinn.' From somewhere to the left of the screen he caught a muffled, 'Bye, Uncle Hewy.'

Ava gave him a wave, while Lizzie blew kisses with both her hands, then the screen went black.

Hewitt released a tight breath. The daily internet calls didn't get easier. He missed the twins so much. But he'd sooner break another bone than not talk to them every day. He scraped a hand over his face. The morning's testing of his emotions wasn't over yet.

Last night, surrounded by darkness and the fragrance of the lemon-scented gum, his defences had weakened. When Fliss slid her fingers through her heavy hair and touched her tongue to the raindrop on her bottom lip, attraction had kicked deep within him. All he'd been able to think about was pulling her close and covering her mouth with his. It'd taken all his willpower to keep his hands jammed beneath his crossed arms.

She was so beautiful he lost all perspective. It couldn't happen again. She already affected him far more than she should. His needs, his wants, even his future, were no longer important. His focus had to be on getting himself together so he could get back to taking care of the people who depended on him. He stood on stiff legs and massaged his aching shoulder. Today was another day closer to achieving his goal.

He left the bluestone stables to the sound of a kookaburra celebrating the sunshine breaking through the thick cloud cover. The storm last night had saturated the already waterlogged ground but today promised to be fine and dry.

Fliss turned to watch him approach. The vivid cherry-red of her shirt reflected warmth into her face and showcased the glossy coffee-brown of her hair.

'Morning.' Her greeting was cheerful.

'Morning.' He stopped beside her and blanked out the subtle scent of gardenias. 'How did everyone sleep?'

'I think they slept well. Your casserole's gone and the puppies are snuggled close to their mum.'

Fliss took her phone from out of her jeans pocket. 'Cressy wants a photo to share on the lost dog social media groups and to make a flyer.' Fliss snapped some quick shots before speaking again. 'Ella's on her way and will bring a microchip scanner.'

'Great.' Hewitt looked at the container Fliss had placed on the ground near the doorway. 'Breakfast?'

'Yes. Ella suggested I mix up some porridge with raw eggs.' Fliss bent to pick up the oats. The border collie wagged her tail. 'The thought of which turns my stomach but is obviously just what our new mum wants.'

Fliss entered the shed. Trust shone in the border collie's brown eyes as Fliss placed her breakfast within reach. Instead of eating, the border collie whined and attempted to nuzzle Fliss's hand. She hesitated, then moved closer to pat her.

Hewitt watched the emotions flit across Fliss's face. Caution and worry were followed by uncertainty. When the border collie playfully batted Fliss's arm with her paw, the tight line of Fliss's shoulders relaxed. She laughed softly. 'Oh, I see. You like pats even more than oats.'

Hewitt's heart warmed. The confidence Fliss had lost hadn't only affected her professional life, it continued to erode the foundations of her personal life. Her anxiety was unrelenting and ever-present. He could see it in the way she avoided driving in the mud, in the way she'd bite her lip when looking for snakes and in the nervous intensity of her eyes when she thought he wasn't looking. But now, in this moment, as she and the border collie got to know each other, there was no self-doubt, just an uncomplicated connection.

A loud moo sounded and he turned to scan the undulating green hills. A cow had been close to calving last night and he hoped it wasn't her call he heard. Fliss came to his side, a smile still curving her lips.

'Everything okay?'

'I hope so. Otherwise Ella might find she's come to do more than scan Bundara's mystery guest.' He swung around to retrace his steps to the bluestone stables. 'I'll go check the cattle.'

'I'll come.' Fliss fell into step beside him. 'I can get the gates.'

The drive to the cattle paddock passed in silence. After the night's rain Hewitt concentrated on driving on the wet track, while Fliss kept a close eye on her phone and the cattle around them.

When they drew near to the steel yards, Hewitt didn't need to drive any further. The cow he'd seen yesterday with the full bag of milk and who had isolated herself from the herd didn't have a calf curled up in the grass beside her. Instead, as she turned, he caught sight of a calf's foot. The cow had started to calve but the second stage of labour hadn't progressed smoothly.

'I'll let Ella know,' Fliss said quietly.

Hewitt left the ute to open the gate of the cattle yards. He then drove behind a group of three cows grazing nearby. Used to vehicles driving around them, they ambled in the direction Hewitt wanted them to go. The cow having difficulty calving would be happier, and be easier to put into the yards, if she had company. When the small herd met up with the lone cow, he directed them along the fence line. He stopped when the black bodies milled inside the steel yards. Fliss went to close the gate. She checked her phone as she walked over to where he'd parked.

'Ella's not far away and said she'll come straight to the yards.'

He grabbed a bucket from the ute trayback. 'She'll need water. I'll fill this, then put the cow in the race.'

When he returned from the trough, Fliss had entered the yards and opened the internal gates leading to the circular race. Despite all the years she'd spent in the city, she still knew her way around a set of cattle yards. Hewitt nodded his thanks and avoided meeting her eyes. Even though he'd carried the water bucket on his right side, his injured shoulder burned.

Working quietly, and avoiding the calving cow's flight zone, he cut her out of the small herd. She walked up to the end of the narrow race and he secured her head in the head bail so Ella could take a look at her.

'You made that look easy,' Fliss said as he exited the yards. 'I don't remember it being so peaceful when Dad worked cattle. Cressy and I learned a whole new vocabulary when we first saw him load cattle into trucks.'

'Thank Cressy. Her cattle are used to low stress handling and this means the low stress part also applies to the people working them.'

Their conversation lulled as the Woodlea Veterinary Hospital vehicle made its slow way over the boggy ground. Ella parked beside his ute and Fliss walked over to greet her with a hug.

Ella gave Hewitt a wave before busying herself opening the canopy on the back of the vet ute. With practised movements she covered her curves and long jean-clad legs in navy overalls before filling a metal bucket with a calf puller, bottle of lubricant, gloves and other items. Even dressed in work gear, and with no makeup, Hewitt had no doubt Ella had been called out to check on the animals of many a lonely, single farmer. Not only was the blonde vet stunning, she exuded an infectious warmth.

She made her way over to him, her smile genuine as she offered him her hand.

'Hi, Hewitt. Nice to meet you.' Beneath the brim of her navy Woodlea vet cap, her brown eyes sparkled. 'I've heard great things about you from Edna.'

Hewitt shook Ella's hand. 'All of which aren't true. Edna caught me on a good day.'

'Somehow I don't believe that. Cressy and Denham also sing your praises and we both know their judgement is spot on.'

Hewitt glanced at Fliss who stood silently next to Ella. His eyes met hers. For some reason it was important he let her know that as beautiful as Ella was, he hadn't forgotten about her.

'Now, where's our first patient?' Ella turned to enter the yards. 'I'm sure she'd like to meet her new baby as soon as possible.'

The Black Angus cow stood quietly as Hewitt opened the top gate of the cattle race. Ella added a splash of disinfectant to the bucket of water and cleaned the back end of the cow. The vet then pulled on a long plastic glove and set about discovering what the trouble was.

Fliss stood quietly to the side. Hewitt kept his stance casual, making sure she wouldn't see how much his shoulder ached.

'If I had a dollar,' Ella said, voice low as she concentrated on feeling where the calf's front legs were, 'for every calf I've had to pull this spring, the hospital would have its portable ultrasound in no time. All this feed isn't just resulting in big calves, there'll be some chubby ponies who'll end up with laminitis and have to miss the trail ride.' Ella finished examining the position of the calf. 'Thankfully this is one of my easier pulls. The left foot was back a little but it's in the right spot now.'

After applying lubricant, Ella looped the calf puller above and below the calf's fetlock joints. She placed the base against the cow's rump. In time with the cow's contractions, the vet pushed the steel handle down to inch each of the calf's feet forwards. When the tip of the second hoof appeared, and then the head, Ella stopped the pressure to allow the mother to rest and for the calf to breathe.

When the contractions started again, Ella used the calf puller to help the slick, black body slide free. She unhooked the loops from around the calf's legs, inspected the cow and then nodded to Hewitt to release her.

'There's no better sight,' Ella said, tone satisfied as the cow licked her tiny calf. 'Now for patient number two. I can't wait to meet your mystery guest.'

While Ella cleaned and returned the items she'd used to the vet vehicle, Hewitt stood with Fliss, watching the mother and calf get to know each other.

It didn't take long for Fliss to speak. 'Is your shoulder okay?'

'It's just a twinge.'

'Can I take a look?'

He faced her, masking his discomfort at the simple movement. The pain from his shoulder radiated down his side. But no matter how much he hurt, having Fliss up close and personal, especially after his thoughts about kissing her last night, was not an option. It was bad enough the emotional distance between them had diminished. He couldn't allow their physical distance to be compromised. He locked his jaw and blanked out the undertow of attraction.

'No, I'm fine. Really. Why don't you head back with Ella to see the puppies? I'll keep an eye on this pair until the calf has had her first drink of colostrum.'

Fliss's lips pressed together but she didn't say anything more as she turned away. As she waved to him from the passenger seat of Ella's ute, he could see her staring at his shoulder.

CHAPTER

6

'*Men.*' Fliss sighed.

Beside her, Ella checked her rear-view mirror. 'I take it we're only talking about one man?'

'Yes. A frustrating, obstinate man who is in so much pain his skin tone would be the colour of concrete if he wasn't so tanned.'

Ella threw her a quick look. 'There's a reason why you're the doctor. I honestly never noticed. If anything, I thought Hewitt looked … good.'

Fliss fought the telltale warmth in her cheeks. Hewitt always looked more than good, especially with only his jeans on. 'That's the thing he does, until you really look at him. He's a master at hiding his pain. I've dealt with many difficult patients but Hewitt remains … unreachable.'

Water splashed as the vet drove through a pool of water across the track. 'I've only just met him but from what I've seen, he's not like the men you're used to dealing with.'

Fliss sighed again. Ella had moved to small town Woodlea five years ago and in that time her close friendship with Cressy meant that she'd been privy to Fliss's relationship disasters—the last one having involved a work colleague who was waylaid by the cleavage of his blonde intern while Fliss was in London.

'True, but even then I don't know why I feel out of my depth. I've never had any trouble making sure Denham received medical help, and he has a will as strong as cattle-yard steel.'

Ella glanced at her. The usual light in her brown eyes had dimmed. 'Take it from me, don't give up on Hewitt. Not that I'm saying you're motivated by anything other than wanting to help him, but sometimes the easy path ends up being the hardest.'

From the brief details Ella had let slip over the years, Fliss had gathered that Ella had had her heart broken while working overseas. Much to the dismay of the single men of the district, she still chose to keep her heart safe.

Fliss reached over to squeeze her hand. 'I won't. For all his stubbornness, Hewitt's a decent guy. By the time he leaves Bundara that broken shoulder of his won't give him any more trouble.'

This time when Ella looked across at her, her eyes were again a vibrant brown. 'Does Cressy know you think Hewitt's a *decent* guy? That's not a word I think I've ever heard you use to describe someone of the opposite sex.'

Fliss laughed to cover her self-consciousness. What Ella said was true. She usually described a man in terms of how well their work schedules fitted together. 'I'm sure she does. After all, Hewitt's still here.'

Ella's own laughter followed Fliss as she jumped out to open the double gates. Fliss knew Ella was thinking back to a blind date at the Royal Arms. When Cressy and Ella arrived to see how the date was going, the man had pushed past them on his way out. He hadn't appreciated Fliss's direct questions about what he expected after their date or her view that women should be heard and not just seen. Cressy's tip for any future date had been to not wear heels that could serve as a lethal weapon.

For the rest of the drive to the homestead Fliss and Ella relived memories when sky-high heels had resulted in wardrobe malfunctions and lawn aeration.

When Ella met Bundara's most recent guests she agreed with Hewitt's assessment that the dog and her puppies were purebred border collies. She confirmed that mum and all six babies were doing well.

'You're such a sweet mamma,' Ella said as she passed the microchip scanner over the border collie's neck. 'Let's see if you're microchipped.' She paused to check the small screen. 'And you are. Great.' Ella looked across to where Fliss stood at the shed doorway. 'I'll check with the national database when I'm back at the surgery and let you know what I find.'

'Thanks. I'm sure there's a logical explanation why she's out here.' The new mother nuzzled one of the puppies to make sure it stayed close against her side. 'No one in their right mind would dump her.'

Ella gave the border collie a farewell pat.

Fliss stepped away from the doorway. 'I'm already not looking forward to seeing them go. I've forgotten how nice it is to have a dog.'

'Anytime you're ready for a furry friend just let me know.' Ella joined Fliss outside. 'Unfortunately, I know of some dogs in need of a loving home.'

Fliss nodded and turned away. She couldn't let Ella see how much the thought of taking on the responsibility of a pet overwhelmed her. She wouldn't be ready for a fur-kid of any kind until anxiety no longer controlled her. She couldn't spend a summer fearing the worst every time a dog barked.

As a child she'd lost her beloved Jack Russell to a western brown snake. The trauma still haunted her. Midge had been bitten while protecting Fliss and Cressy as they'd played in the sprinkler. She'd returned to check they were okay and when Fliss had hugged her, she'd collapsed. The brave Jack Russell had received a lethal dose of venom and no amount of anti-venom or prayers had saved her.

Once Ella had headed off to see her next client, Fliss went inside. The hum of the electric kettle grew louder as she settled herself at the table to check her emails. The screensaver on her laptop was a picture of her and Cressy with their mother, taken before her parents' Tasmanian trip. Normally the sight of the three of them hugging triggered happy memories. But today only thoughts of Hewitt filled her head.

Hewitt wasn't technically her patient, but as she'd said to Ella there was no way she'd give up on him, no matter how much he continued to weather his pain or refuse her help. When he came back she'd take over her first-aid kit and see if he needed anything.

The kettle clicked off and still Fliss stared at her laptop screen. She was used to the way men behaved around Ella. Their voices deepened and they hooked their thumbs in their jeans pockets. Yet Hewitt had appeared unaffected by the vet's blonde beauty. When he'd glanced at Fliss as though to say he hadn't forgotten she was there, she'd felt a bone-deep relief. The man she'd been spending time with was the man she thought he was. Honourable and level-headed, Hewitt wouldn't be distracted by a pretty face, even one as lovely as Ella's.

Fliss opened her inbox. There was an email from Lewis, letting her know Jean had been admitted to hospital and that he'd call tonight with an update.

Hewitt's ute engine rumbled and tyres crunched on gravel. Fliss finished off her email to Lewis, then, with the first-aid kit in her hands, headed across the garden to see Hewitt.

This time when she knocked, the wooden door didn't immediately open. When it did, deep lines were carved beside Hewitt's mouth. 'Is this a house call?'

'I know you said you were fine, but in case you've run out of painkillers, I've brought some over.'

For a moment she thought Hewitt would insist he was okay, but then a muscle flicked in his jaw and he stepped aside to let her in.

'I haven't exactly run out. I can't find any. I'm sure I threw a box in my bag when I left hospital.'

Fliss shook her head as she walked past him into the stone stables. 'How did I know you hadn't been taking anything?'

'Because I'm male and a conformist, remember?'

She smiled and sat the first-aid kit on the kitchen bench.

What the stables lacked in space, it made up for in charm. A small window in the fully-equipped kitchen looked out over the paddocks, while overhead thick beams paid homage to its practical past. Exposed bluestone walls added colour and texture and a wooden staircase curled its way up to the bedroom and bathroom on the second storey.

When she'd bought Bundara she'd originally planned to live in the cosy stables, but there was something about the vast, unfinished main house that spoke to the emptiness within her. She too was a work in progress.

Fliss rummaged through the first-aid kit. She placed a small box on the bench and turned towards Hewitt. He leaned against the table, his arms loosely folded. His casual position didn't fool her. His mouth was set and his jaw tight.

'Okay, Mr Conformist, can I please take a look at this shoulder of yours? I'll need you to take your shirt off.'

Again his response surprised her. He tensed but unfolded his arms. As his fingers flicked open the first button of his blue shirt to reveal the strong, tanned column of his throat, she made the mistake of looking into his eyes. Sometimes a clear grey, other times a dawn-grey, they now shone like polished pewter.

Reality fell away. All she could feel was the pull of attraction. All she could hear was the drumbeat of her heart loud in her ears. Hewitt's fingers stilled on the second button. His attention fastened on her mouth. Her lips parted and she readied herself to lean forwards to meet him halfway.

As if from a great distance away, an electronic gurgling sound brought the world back into focus. She blinked, her bearings disoriented and her breathing shallow.

Hewitt moved to touch the screen of the laptop resting on the table behind him. The bubbling sound subsided to be replaced by a child's voice.

'Hi, Uncle Hewy. Were you with the puppies? I tried to call earlier. I've thought of some names.'

Hewitt flashed Fliss a look so raw and intense her breath caught. He too had been thrown by what had surged between them.

He eased himself into the seat in front of the computer. 'Hi, munchkin.' He cleared his throat. 'Sorry. I was out helping deliver a calf.'

'That's okay. Quinn said you'd probably got your ute bogged.'

The husky depths of Hewitt's chuckle strummed across Fliss's tightly drawn senses. She swung away to pick up the box of painkillers from the bench. The tenderness and affection in Hewitt's voice reached a part of her she always kept off limits.

She collected a glass from a low cupboard and filled it with water. After pressing out two tablets, she sat the glass and painkillers on the corner of the kitchen table. She thought she'd stayed out of the camera's range until Lizzie's voice questioned, 'Who's that?'

Fliss backed away and mouthed, 'Sorry.'

Hewitt carefully shifted his chair back and motioned for her to come closer. He spoke, his voice low. 'I'm the one who's sorry. Edna has nothing on Little Miss Lizzie. You're about to be interrogated.'

Fliss bent so Lizzie would see her face and not just the red of her shirt. 'Hi, Lizzie. I'm Fliss.'

Lizzie stared at her. Big grey eyes, similar in colour to Hewitt's, assessed her. 'You're pretty.'

'Thank you.'

Lizzie continued to examine her. 'Quinn, there's someone here with Uncle Hewy. It's a lady. So do you like the name Poppy for a puppy?'

'Yes, I do. Especially if the puppy is a girl. It'd be a bit strange for a boy.'

Lizzie giggled and her red curls danced as she turned to speak to someone on her left. 'Quinn, hurry up. Come and meet Fliss. She's nice. Not like that other lady Uncle Hewy brought home who hated cats.'

Hewitt groaned softly. 'I learned the hard way that Lizzie and Quinn don't always approve of my dates.'

Fliss smiled at the camera. She already liked bossy Little Miss Lizzie. A boy's face appeared. He shared his twin's pale skin and auburn hair, but worry overshadowed the brightness of his grey eyes. Fliss's heart melted.

'Hi, Quinn. I'm Fliss. Thanks for letting your uncle come and help me on my farm. He'll be back home soon.'

Quinn nodded but didn't speak. The furrow of concern between his brows eased.

'So what other puppy names do you like?' asked Lizzie.

'I like lots of names, but not Gertrude or Percival or Rufus.'

Lizzie laughed and Quinn gave a slow smile.

Fliss continued. 'But I'm not a name expert so I'll leave it up to you and Quinn to choose. I'd better go check on the puppies and let you keep talking to your uncle.'

With a wave, Fliss stepped out of camera range. Hewitt's dark eyes held hers before he leaned forwards to answer Lizzie's question about how many girl and boy puppies there were.

Once outside the stables, Fliss paused to let the cool breeze strip the warmth from her face. She wasn't sure what had just happened between her and Hewitt. But whatever it was, no amount of ground rules were going to keep her safe. They gave her as much protection as a saline placebo injection. Restless and on edge, she headed inside the main house and flicked on the kettle. She was well past having a cup of tea. It was chocolate and sugar she needed.

While the water boiled, she checked to see if Lewis had replied to her email. But the only message in her inbox was from the company she and Cressy had tested their DNA through. Cressy's results had already arrived and hadn't contained any long-lost relatives. Fliss followed the link to her own results. As expected, Cressy was the only match listed as an extremely high chance of being close family. Now it would be a matter of sifting through the other matches and compiling a family tree to identify the unknown links on their mother's side.

As Fliss sipped her hot chocolate, she searched for another DNA site she remembered from her university days. While the raw data from her DNA results uploaded, she looked for puppy names to keep one step ahead of Little Miss Lizzie. Once her DNA was processed she scanned the list of results. She now had more in-depth numerical data and could switch between autosomal and X-DNA matches.

She suddenly lowered her mug. Attention never leaving the list of matches in front of her, she opened another webpage to find a centimorgan chart that showed the average number of centimorgans shared between relatives. She hadn't even finished reading the first two boxes when she reached for her phone. Breathing fast, she waited for Meredith to answer.

After three rings, her well-spoken voice sounded. 'Hi, Fliss. I was only just thinking about you.'

'Hi.' Fliss swallowed. 'My DNA results are back.'

The almost imperceptible intake of breath at the other end of the phone confirmed that Meredith's gentle encouragement hadn't been to rekindle Fliss's interest in medicine. Meredith had suspected that their DNA results would contain a secret.

'You knew?' Fliss's pained words were little more than a whisper.

'I'm so sorry, sweetheart. I was hoping it wasn't true. I didn't know. Not for sure. Every time I see the son I thought I'd lost, I'm reminded that secrets only ever bring heartache. Your mother always believed in the truth and if she hadn't died when she did, I've no doubt she would have told you. How did Cressy react?'

'She doesn't know. Not yet. She's only glanced at her results and wouldn't know the significance of the centimorgans.' Fliss's voice cracked as shock hit her square in her midriff. 'She wouldn't know that we share the same mother ... but not the same father.'

Hewitt closed the lid of his laptop and took his time easing himself out of the chair. He swallowed the two tablets Fliss had left and as he placed the glass on the table a car engine started. Ignoring the fire in his shoulder, he tugged on his boots and headed outside. Guilt weighted his steps. He only hoped that their almost-kiss hadn't rattled Fliss as much as it had him. And if it had, he needed to make things right. He couldn't have her driving out on the slick back roads just to put some space between them.

He caught a glimpse of her grim expression and his gut clenched. But as she drove alongside him, she stopped and wound down her window.

He spoke first. 'Is everything okay?'

She didn't look at him. 'I need to see Cressy.'

'Fliss, I'm sorry about earlier. The last thing you need right now are complications, and we both know I was about to kiss you.'

'I'm sorry too.' She briefly glanced at him. 'We both know I was going to kiss you back. But I'm not leaving because of what almost happened between us.' This time her eyes met his for longer. 'And what wasn't the most well-considered of plans.'

He nodded, fighting hard to keep his expression from changing. Even though Fliss was right, his testosterone wasn't so eager to agree. Hair had escaped her ponytail and fallen across her cheek. He curled his fingers into a fist to stop himself reaching through the window and tucking the silken strands behind her ear.

She again stared through the windscreen, her back straight and shoulders hunched. 'It's … family stuff.'

'Okay. Take my ute. It can handle the mud.'

She bit her full bottom lip. Indecision flashed across her face, quickly followed by apprehension. 'I'd … forgotten the roads will be wet.'

Hewitt didn't reply. He needed to give Fliss space. Something had upset her, and it hadn't been a minor thing. But at the same time his need to make sure she arrived at Cressy's safely hammered at his temples. The thought of anything happening to her made the blood rush too fast through his veins.

'I'm really not comfortable driving your ute. I know your shoulder's not great but you don't want to come and see Denham, do you? It's really important I see Cressy as soon as possible.'

'I'll come. There's a plough Denham needs help fixing.'

The relief that relaxed her mouth thanked him even before her quiet 'Thank you.'

It was no surprise that the trip to Glenmore started without any conversation. Fliss appeared deep in thought and he didn't want to pry. He also needed a chance to get himself under control. The need to reach for her hand to comfort her had him clamping his fingers around the steering wheel. There'd already been one close call today.

After they'd crossed the white wooden bridge, she spoke in a low voice. 'I thought life was done messing with me.'

He glanced at her drawn face. 'It will be soon. Life just seems incapable of delivering a single hit.'

She sighed. 'So I'm not the only one.' Compassion softened the tense line of her mouth. 'Anything I can help with?'

He shot her a smile to lighten the mood. Now was the worst possible time to go into the guilt keeping him awake at night. 'You've already done more than enough by letting me stay.'

She didn't return his smile. 'Does this other thing have anything to do with Brody?'

Hewitt chose his words carefully. 'Life can deliver hit after hit, but it can also deliver good thing after good thing. Brody may no longer be here but his memory lives on in Quinn and Lizzie.'

Fliss nodded but didn't look away. 'Hewitt ... talk to me.'

'You've enough to deal with today.'

She rubbed her temple. 'Trust me. There's never been a better time. I need something else to think about.'

'If it'll help, it's my turn to listen.'

'It would but I need to see Cressy first.' She twisted in her seat to look at him. 'Is why you don't ride another of life's hits?'

He briefly met her gaze.

She answered his unspoken question. 'You're a pickup rider, horses are a huge part of your life, and yet you brought a quad bike to ride around Cressy's cattle on.'

He passed a hand around the back of his neck. Fliss's stare was fixed and intense. He'd talk, but he'd make sure this conversation was all about distracting her and not him baring his soul.

'I haven't ridden in a year. It wasn't only Brody the bull went after. When I was on the ground with him, he gored Garnet. I almost lost her. All she'd been doing was protecting me.'

'You're not to blame, remember?'

'Actually, I am.' He worked hard to keep his voice casual. 'The reality is not only didn't I get to Brody in time, I was the reason he was on the bull. When Lizzie and Quinn were born, he gave up competing. He was only riding because he needed money to buy out my share of the family farm.'

He ground his teeth as the hold on his emotions weakened. Fliss's hand curled around his arm. She stayed silent.

'Not only did I put Brody on the bull, I was the reason why Seth rode with a new and inexperienced partner.' Despite his best intentions, bitterness rasped in his words. 'Even with two farms, supporting three families was going to be a stretch, so I was leaving to do my own thing.'

'It's not a crime to want to make your own way.'

'No, but putting your needs before others isn't exactly admirable. The truth was the main reason I was leaving was because I was lonely. If I stayed I'd have ended up like our neighbours on the eastern side. You'd never meet more hardworking or humble men but they've never married. The farm is their life.'

'I've seen the same thing happen. I know wonderful women where medicine has become their whole world and they've never partnered or had children. You wanting to leave is a completely normal and unselfish thing to do.'

'But my selfishness had consequences. What happened to Brody is my fault, on so many levels.'

'No, it's not. People move away all the time, for a variety of reasons. Look at me, I wanted things that couldn't be found here.' She lifted her hand from his arm. 'I've always been ... different to Cressy.'

It was just a raw note, a vulnerable quiver that had him give in to the urge to comfort her. He reached for her hand. Her fingers linked with his before she sighed and shifted in her seat to look through the windscreen. Silence filled the cabin as the tops of Glenmore's chimneys appeared through the trees.

Fliss's fingers stayed entwined with his until he pulled up outside the front garden gate. Then she slipped her hand free, unclipped her seatbelt and leaned in close to brush her soft lips across his cheek. 'Thank you.'

Then she was gone, leaving behind a faint floral scent and an emptiness within him. He stayed in his seat, giving her the space to find her sister alone. Cressy appeared from around the side of the wide veranda. Dressed in jeans, a green work shirt and boots, she met Fliss across the lawn. Hewitt saw the exact moment Cressy realised this wasn't a social call. Her expression sobered and she looped her arm through Fliss's before they climbed the front veranda steps and disappeared into the homestead.

Kevin squawked and swooped down from a gum tree to perch on the bull bar. Hewitt left the ute and the cockatoo flew onto his uninjured shoulder.

Hewitt ruffled his yellow crest. 'Looks like it's just you and me, buddy.'

'Get a six-pack of beer,' the cockatoo said.

'I think you might be right.'

Gravel crunched beneath hard boot soles as Denham walked over from the cluster of sheds to Hewitt's right. Tippy and Juno ran by Denham's side before bolting over to sniff the mud-covered tyres on Hewitt's ute.

'I thought it was you. The trouble with all this rain is there's no dust to confirm which direction anyone comes from. Fliss with you?'

'She is. Kevin here said we need a six-pack of beer but, just a heads-up, I think it's the girls who'll need a drink. Fliss was desperate to see Cressy.'

Concern sobered Denham's blue eyes. 'Fliss is always so self-reliant it takes something major for her to even admit there's a problem.'

Hewitt stood still as Denham started towards the house. He didn't want to intrude upon whatever the sisters needed to discuss. Denham looked back and stopped.

'It's okay. Cressy won't mind you coming inside and neither will Fliss. Besides, I might need backup.'

They fell into step beside each other as they headed into the house. Denham pushed open the kitchen door and they walked into the large and homely room. Over by the bench Fliss draped tea bags into two mugs while Cressy collected milk from the fridge. Fliss's preoccupied expression revealed that whatever she'd come to see Cressy about was still on the agenda.

She glanced across at him. 'Coffee? Tea?'

'I'm good, thanks.'

'I'm good too,' Denham said as he walked over to where Cressy now sat at the kitchen table. He seated himself beside her and wrapped an arm around her shoulders. The tight press of Fliss's lips eased. She'd waited to talk to Cressy until Denham had arrived. She took a seat opposite her sister.

Hewitt sat to the right of Denham, careful to avoid his gaze. The need to comfort Fliss and make sure she was okay hadn't diminished now they'd arrived. Denham wouldn't miss his deep concern.

For a moment Fliss didn't speak, just stared into her tea. Then she cleared her throat. 'Cressy ... you know how our DNA results are back? Well ... the results have revealed something ... unexpected.'

'You're related to Edna Galloway?'

Denham's dry remark brought a brief smile to Cressy's face but Fliss's mouth didn't curve.

'Not quite.' Fliss swallowed. 'Cressy ... I'm so sorry to have to tell you this but ... you and I are only half-sisters.'

Cressy remained intensely still. The only movement in the room was Denham's arm tightening around her shoulders.

Hewitt exchanged a look with Denham. The shock on Denham's face would be reflected on his own. He glanced at the silver-framed photographs on the wooden hutch. When he'd helped Fliss wash up the night of the barbeque, he'd snuck a look at the snapshots that had captured a young Fliss's life. He remembered thinking how much Fliss and Cressy, with their high cheekbones, hazel eyes and dark hair, resembled each other.

Fliss spoke again, her hands clasped tightly together on the table. 'Even though Dad's name's on both of our birth certificates, our DNA results say we don't share the same father.'

Cressy blinked then reached across the table to take hold of her sister's hands. 'This changes nothing. You are my *sister*.'

Fliss nodded, her eyes overbright. 'I feel the same way.'

Hewitt looked away, throat raw. The unconditional love between Fliss and Cressy underlined how empty his life was with his twin gone.

'Do we know ... why or how?'

The only other time he'd heard Cressy's tone so subdued was when she'd called to say Denham had left for America.

Fliss's sigh sounded like it came from a place deep inside her. 'No. I spoke to Meredith before coming to tell you. She has no idea. I know Mum and Dad's marriage wasn't easy but there was no one else in Mum's life but ... Dad.'

Cressy released Fliss's hands and dragged her fingers through her loose hair. 'I don't know about anyone else but I need to go for a ride.'

Denham pushed back his chair. 'I'll come with you.'

Cressy stood and slipped her hand into Denham's. She studied Fliss's face. 'We have no idea which one of us isn't Dad's daughter, do we?'

'No.' Fliss came to her feet and walked around the table to Cressy. 'We don't.'

The sisters exchanged a long and tight embrace. But as Fliss stepped away, the bleak darkness of her eyes suggested she already knew which one of them wasn't their father's biological child.

Everything she'd believed about herself was a lie.

Fliss stared out over the garden beds beyond the veranda that rippled with purple and white colour. A cup of tea sat to her right, the steam curling into the air. It had become her breakfast ritual to sit on the veranda steps. She stroked the ears of the border collie resting her head on her lap. The six puppies hadn't opened their eyes but the new mum now left them for short periods of time.

'You know we're just the same, you and I. We still don't know your name and the truth is I don't know my real name either.'

Ella had searched the national database but hadn't found a match with the border collie's microchip number. She was now hoping the owners had registered their dog's number on a smaller database, but it was taking time working through them state by state. The vet had also notified the pound to pass on the dog's details in case anyone contacted them. As Ella was involved within the legal timeframe for lost dogs to be taken to a vet or council animal shelter, the dog and her newborn pups were right to stay with Fliss for a fortnight. The owners had until then to claim them.

From over in the paddocks a cow mooed and a calf answered. In the past few days there'd been five new babies. Not that she'd seen them. She hadn't checked the cattle again with Hewitt. She'd been obsessed with her DNA matches and looking for clusters of similar names or DNA segments. Lewis would be the best person to ask about what she could do next to evaluate her results. But with Jean still in hospital, now wasn't the time to pick his sharp, analytical brain.

She picked up her tea and wrapped her hands around the warmth of the mug. The aftershocks of only being Cressy's half-sister continued to rip through her. She now questioned every truth she'd ever known. No wonder she'd never shared Cressy's passion for Glenmore. No wonder she was taller and her skin wasn't so fair. No wonder she couldn't wait to head to the neon lights of the city.

Filled with uncertainty and loss, she'd harnessed her pain in a quest to find answers. It had taken two days and many family trees, but she'd found the evidence to confirm she wasn't a direct descendant of the Knight ancestors who'd carved out a life in the Bell River valley. She bit the inside of her cheek. She wasn't even a blood relative of her beloved grandmother. But she didn't care, she was still her grandmother and she was the reason behind her decision to study medicine. Complications after a routine hip surgery robbed them all too soon of the generous and kind woman they'd all loved.

As for her father, she wasn't sure if he'd known she wasn't his daughter. He'd never treated her and Cressy any differently. But he'd always been in the background of their lives. After being an only child, and almost dying from pneumonia as a toddler, she could understand why he'd been overindulged and not always held accountable for his actions. It had been her mother who'd sat by their grandfather's hospital bed when he'd fallen from the grain silo. And it had been her mother who'd held Cressy and Fliss close when she told them he wasn't coming home.

She took a sip of tea to ease the ache in her throat and concentrated on absorbing the peace around her. Wings whooshed overhead as a group of cockatoos landed in the old cedar tree. The last couple of days had brought nothing but sunshine and today the sky was a pure blue. One cockatoo settled on the roof of the stables, its feet clicking as it walked over the tin.

The stables door opened and Hewitt emerged. His easy, loose strides belied his understated power. Only a fool would underestimate him. Even with a broken shoulder, he'd be the last man standing. No wonder Edna was impressed. The border collie raced over to him and the gentleness of his smile triggered a flurry in Fliss's stomach. But it was what lay within Hewitt that impressed Fliss the most.

When he'd driven her to see Cressy she'd fully understood the depths of his empathy as well as his inner strength. She knew he'd spoken about the additional layers of his guilt not to help himself gain closure, but to distract her. He'd put her needs first. In the days afterwards he'd brought her dinner when she'd been too distracted by DNA to cook and said he was there if she needed to talk. He'd called himself selfish for wanting to leave the family farm. She'd never met a more unselfish or honourable man.

She came to her feet and resisted the urge to dust off the seat of her jeans. But while she finally might have found someone who interested her, the timing couldn't be worse. For both of them. The intensity of their almost-kiss in the stables warned her the sparks she felt weren't only on her side. As inevitable as summer leaching the colour from the hills, Hewitt would return to the family who needed him. She had enough to deal with without missing him when life resumed its solitary pace. And he had enough to deal with as well. They couldn't let the chemistry simmering between them blind them to reality again.

'Morning,' she said, when he stopped in front of her.

'Morning.'

Today he wore a royal blue shirt that made his eyes appear a blue-grey. His dark hair was tousled and stubble shadowed his jaw. She firmed her hold on her mug to stop her fingers from feeling the rough scrape of his whiskers.

'How's Lizzie and Quinn?'

'Good. I just spoke to them. They were making chocolate-chip cookies. Going by Quinn's wombat-sized cheeks and Lizzie's stormy face there wasn't much mixture left.'

'I know exactly how Lizzie feels. Cressy was always eating the cookie dough and I was always rousing.'

Hewitt's expression turned serious. 'Any DNA news?'

Fliss sighed. 'No, nothing new. It will take time to work out which matches could be from my father's family tree.'

'How does cannelloni for dinner sound?'

'You know you don't have to cook for me ...' She smiled. 'But it does sound wonderful.'

Hewitt's focus only dipped to her mouth for a second but it was enough for her breath to catch. Her hormones hadn't heeded the message he was off limits.

He slid his hands into his jeans pockets and took a step away to study the front of the run-down homestead.

'So ...' He cleared his throat. 'The cattle troughs are clean, I've straightened the clothes line after the branch fell on it and the fences have been re-strained, which just leaves the jobs on the house to get done.'

Fliss examined the faint hollows below his cheekbones. The first day Hewitt had worked in the garden, she'd made it clear he was at Bundara to rest and recover. Now was her chance to repeat the message. But a low growl from the border collie beside her held her quiet.

Hewitt swung around to look at the drive into Bundara before lowering his hand to touch the dog's head to reassure her.

'Are you expecting anyone?' His too-quiet voice reminded her of the NO TRESPASSING signs and padlocks he'd attached to her boundary gates.

She squinted into the bright morning light as a familiar vehicle appeared on the red dirt road. 'No, but I should have known we'd have a visit from a certain prominent Woodlea local sometime.'

'Really?'

Fliss couldn't hide her smile as she walked down the veranda steps. 'Yes, really. I'm not the only one who makes house calls. Edna does too. She's apparently found out you're single.'

Hewitt groaned.

The border collie headed to her puppies while Fliss and Hewitt walked along the garden path. Edna pulled up in front of the small wrought-iron gate. Mud streaked her white four-wheel drive.

Fliss held the gate open for their visitor. 'You're out and about early.'

Edna enveloped her in a hug that had Fliss holding her breath to avoid inhaling her strong perfume.

'It's never too early to come and see you, Felicity.'

From the corner of her eye, Fliss caught Hewitt's wry grin.

Edna took a step back and gave Fliss the once-over. 'I must say you're looking ...'

'Rural,' Fliss filled in sweetly before Edna could label her casual farm clothes and windblown hair as something far less complimentary.

'Ah ... yes ... rural.'

Edna swung around. 'Well hello, Hewitt.' She closed the distance between them. 'Can I give you a hug? My husband Noel says I've always been a hugger.'

Edna enveloped Hewitt in a swift embrace. Fliss stifled a flinch. She only hoped Hewitt's shoulder survived Edna's exuberance.

Fliss spoke as Edna's hug passed the socially acceptable three seconds. 'Would you like a cuppa, Edna? The kettle's just boiled.'

Edna released Hewitt and barely glanced at Fliss. 'That would be lovely. Hewitt and I didn't have much of a chance to chat when we met in town.'

To Hewitt's credit his expression remained neutral while Edna accompanied him to the house. But after he'd opened the door and let Edna walk through, he flicked Fliss a 'shoot me now' look.

Once Hewitt had his coffee and she'd sat the teapot in its crocheted tea-cosy on the table, she took the seat closest to Hewitt. For some reason it was important she let him know he had her support.

From across the table, Edna's gaze sharpened. 'Felicity, do you have anything sweet? You know how my blood sugar dips this time of morning.'

Fliss poured tea into two floral mugs. 'I thought you said you were watching what you ate?'

'I am.' Edna smiled her best smile at Hewitt. 'My sister has high cholesterol and so nice Dr Sam's concerned about me. But as I told Fliss and Dr Sam, I have big bones and am simply not meant to be reed thin.'

Fliss pushed back her chair. What Edna had failed to mention was that she'd been warned by Dr Sam that unless she lost weight and exercised to lower her LDL cholesterol, the next step would be medication. 'How about I rustle up something?'

'That would be fabulous. Hewitt and I can get to know each other a little better.'

Fliss collected two carrots from the vegetable crisper and a tub of hummus dip.

'So, Hewitt,' Edna said, tone smug. 'You're still with us.'

'Yes. I am.'

As she peeled the carrots, Fliss snuck a look at Hewitt. His dry tone matched his closed expression.

Edna continued unfazed. 'My personal invitation still stands to attend the trail ride. As much as I have faith in Tanner, there are *three* Ridley boys to keep an eye on.'

'I'm flattered you believe I'll be of use, but unfortunately I came off second best with a motorbike and am not as fit as I should be. I've no doubt Tanner will have everything under control.'

Fliss stopped slicing. Hewitt's words were genuine but a note of steel was embedded in his tone. She took a better look at him. She also could have sworn self-disgust had rasped in his voice when he'd mentioned his accident.

'Oh dear.' Edna's formidable frown would have made a lesser man reconsider his response. 'You don't look like you're injured.'

Fliss spoke. 'Hewitt has a fractured scapula.'

Edna barely glanced at her. 'Thank you, Felicity.'

Fliss sliced another carrot. One day Edna would forgive her for dumping her precious Rodger when they were thirteen. Rodger had had a crush on another girl so they'd pretended that Fliss dumped him to give him some street cred. He'd won the girl of his dreams only to have his heart broken for real two days later.

Fliss placed the platter of carrots and hummus on the table and returned to her seat. Edna's lips pursed before she selected the thickest carrot stick.

She again focused on Hewitt, eyes narrowed. 'We're also having a ball to raise money for the hospital's portable ultrasound. I'm sure you'll be able to dance with a broken shoulder, especially if you have a partner like my Bethany; she's so light on her feet.'

Hewitt took a slow swallow of coffee. 'I'm sure your daughter's very light on her feet. But I'm not willing to commit to anything. I've a family farm to return to.'

'That's most ... inconvenient.'

Fliss caught the deflated note in Edna's reply and almost felt sorry for her. It wasn't often Edna had her wishes thwarted.

Her phone vibrated and she took it out of her pocket. When she saw the caller was Lewis, she looked across at Edna and Hewitt. 'Sorry, I need to take this.'

She left for the privacy of the sparsely furnished dining room.

'Hi, Lewis.'

'Hello, Fliss.'

Her stomach dropped. Lewis's refined voice sounded ragged and rough.

He spoke again. 'Jean's gone. This time it was an irreversible stroke, not a transient ischaemic attack.'

Fliss closed her eyes against the sting of hot tears. 'I'm so, so sorry.'

'I knew this day would come. Jean's battled on so many fronts, but now she's not here ... it's harder than I ever imagined.'

Fliss dashed a tear from her cheek and turned towards the door. 'If Meredith and I leave soon, we'll make it to Sydney by dinner.'

'Meredith said the same thing but I feel bad you both dropping everything.'

'Don't be silly.' Her hurried footsteps echoed in the hallway as she made her way towards her bedroom to pack. 'I'll pick up Meredith and we'll be there to stay and to keep you company as soon as we can.'

Hewitt took a seat on the top veranda step where the border collie had waited since breakfast, her head on her paws and eyes on the front door. It hadn't even been two days since Fliss had left, and they both missed her.

He hadn't realised how much she'd become part of his life at Bundara. Her ready laughter and quick wit made him smile. Her beauty, even when dressed in gardening clothes, stole his breath. Her strength and determination humbled him. She continued to fight her self-doubts and fears with a resolute single-mindedness.

It hadn't only been sadness tensing her mouth when she'd driven away. Her hands had been unsteady as she'd loaded her car. Even though she'd channelled her shock at not being Cressy's full sister into the search for her father, loss continued to add a distant look to her eyes. But ever since Lewis's call her only focus had been on helping her university mentor through his grief.

Hewitt stroked the border collie's nose as she rested her head on his lap.

'We need to keep busy, otherwise the five days Fliss is away will feel even longer.'

He came to his feet and walked around the homestead, taking note of what needed to be done. The border collie stayed by his side until a chorus of hungry yips drew her back to her puppies.

The sun put in a brief appearance as he climbed over the rusted roof to inspect the gutters and to clean out the accumulated leaves and twigs. Just as well it was a wet spring and not a hot summer—Fliss's home was far from bushfire ready even if her garden was no longer choked with weeds. Since she'd been gone daffodils had flowered beside the veranda steps and the camellia tucked next to the water tank had burst into brilliant red blooms.

He stepped off the bottom rung of the ladder when his phone rang. He ignored the kick in his pulse and took his time to answer. Fliss had texted several times and said she'd call when she got a chance to see how the dogs were doing. If this was Fliss, he didn't want to appear eager to answer. She didn't need to know how much he missed hearing her voice.

When he checked the screen, he recognised Ella's number.

'Hi, Hewitt.'

Frenzied dog barking sounded in the background.

'Hi. Someone sounds happy?'

'Sorry, that's little Goose. She loves coming in. Thankfully she's only here to have her yearly shots. Last time she had a grass seed in her ear and it was impossible to keep her still.'

Whatever breed little Goose was, from her high-pitched barks, he had no doubt it was an excitable one.

'Hang on ...' Ella spoke again. 'I'll shut the door. There, that's better. So how are you going holding down the fort?'

'So far, there's been no dramas. But by the time Fliss returns, the puppies will have their eyes open.'

'Which means the days of leaving boots on the veranda are numbered.'

'Along with the washing staying on the line.'

Ella chuckled. 'For all their mischief nothing melts hearts faster than a gaggle of fluffy border collie puppies.'

'True.' He looked to where the border collie lay beside his boots, watching him with her bright brown eyes. 'Any hits on the interstate databases?'

'That's why I'm calling. I don't want to bother Fliss right now, so can you please pass on I have both good and bad news?'

'I will. So does our mystery guest have a name?'

'Yes, I finally found a match on a Victorian microchip database. Her registered pedigree name is Bonnyrigg Golly Miss Molly and it's no surprise her name's Molly for short.'

'Molly ... it suits her.'

'The bad news is I've left three messages with the contact numbers with no response. At least she's microchipped, which gives us another week to find her owners.'

'They could be away?'

'I'm thinking that as well. She comes from a property in the high country, so I've called in a favour from a university friend who works down south and he'll visit the farm on his day off.'

'The neighbours could know something.'

'Fingers crossed. I'll keep you and Fliss posted.'

'Thanks.'

'Anytime. Enjoy those puppies and guard those boots of yours.'

'Will do.'

Hewitt ended the call before sending Fliss a text. He returned the phone to his shirt pocket.

'So Miss Molly ... you have a name. I've no doubt if your owners knew you were missing they'd be looking for you.' He rubbed behind her ears as she leaned against his jeans. 'You wouldn't have just been a working dog, you would have been their best mate.'

He returned to the roof to remove the debris from the front corner gutter. With the original bluestone stables now being living quarters, alternative stables had been built beside a round yard. From where he was, he could see straight into the three stalls. On his farm, whenever Garnet would see him, she'd hang her head over her stable half door and whicker.

He braced himself, but the usual cold ball of tension at the thought of Garnet and of riding didn't lodge in his stomach. Instead a yearning to see his blood-red bay mare coursed through him.

He went back to cleaning the gutter, every so often glancing at the empty stables.

Once the ladder had been returned to the shed, he made a coffee and sat on the top veranda step to keep Molly company. He checked his phone and there'd been a text from Fliss.

He tickled behind the border collie's ears. 'Fliss thinks your name's perfect. She reckons Lizzie would approve.'

He hadn't started on his coffee when Molly's ears pricked and she stared at the road into Bundara. A growl rumbled in her throat as a white Land Cruiser ute negotiated the narrow causeway that was now free of water.

'It's okay. It's only Denham. You'll like him. He's not a threat to you or your babies.'

As Hewitt had predicted, when the border collie met Denham, she took to him straight away.

Denham grinned as he patted her. 'No wonder you have Fliss wrapped around your doggy paw, you're a sweetheart.'

Denham passed Hewitt a cold six-pack of beer. 'These are from me and this esky full of food is from Cressy. Anyone would think you were out here by yourself for a year.'

'Thanks.' Hewitt accepted the beer and fell into step beside Denham as they made their way to the bluestone stables.

With a beer in hand, they returned outside to take advantage of the sunshine. Next week the heavy cloud cover and rain squalls would return.

Hewitt settled himself on the veranda steps. 'Fliss needs some outdoor furniture. I found an old door that would make a decent-sized table.'

Denham too sat on the steps and rubbed Molly's tummy as she lay beside him. 'I like your thinking. I happen to know of a shed that has all the boy's toys you'll need.'

Hewitt chuckled. 'I bet you do. How's that offset plough coming along?'

'Slowly. I've had to replace the axles and bearings.'

'When I come round to make the table, I'll help speed things up.'

'Thanks.' Denham took a swig of beer and looked out over the tidy garden. 'This place is unrecognisable. Cressy sleeps easier knowing Fliss isn't sharing her garden with any snakes.'

'Being here has helped me sleep a little easier too.'

'You do seem more relaxed.'

'I'm working on it. I still need to deal with losing Brody but you're right … I'm not in the same place I was before I fell off the bike.'

'You look like you're moving easier … your shoulder must be healing?'

Hewitt stilled, his beer halfway to his mouth. Even with Denham, he hadn't gone into detail about the extent of his motorbike injuries.

Denham shook his head. 'Don't think I didn't know how much pain you were in.'

'Not you too. Fliss picked it the moment I got here.'

'Welcome to my world. I'm not sure what the hardest thing was, falling off a bull or taking the call when Fliss knew I'd been injured.'

'I can only imagine Fliss's reaction. I thought Cressy had a strong will …'

'She does. They both do.'

Denham's intent blue stare confirmed he hadn't missed Hewitt's awareness of Fliss at Cressy's barbeque or when Fliss had visited last week. But instead of making any further comment, he lifted his beer and clinked the bottle against Hewitt's.

'To strong Knight girls.'

It wasn't Denham's words that stayed with Hewitt that night and the following day as he kept himself busy but the memory of his tone. When Denham had toasted Fliss and Cressy his voice had been tender and solemn. His meaning had been clear: both women were special.

The message hadn't been lost on Hewitt. Since he'd arrived he'd struggled to repress the realisation he'd never again meet a woman like Fliss. But it didn't matter how much she affected him, or how much he was drawn to her. Ava and the twins were counting on him. Even after coming clean to Fliss about his true role in Brody's death, the weight of his guilt hadn't lessened. With Fliss away he now had a chance, and the space, to regroup and to refocus. Somehow he had to find a way to say goodbye to his twin and to move on.

He threw himself into sanding the old door so it would be ready for when he worked on it in Denham's shed. Then he drew up plans for a fire pit to weld before finishing the empty garden bed along the side of the stables. He dug up the agapanthus filling the overgrown bed at the back of the house, split them into clumps, and repositioned them. When the last of the plants had been watered in, he gave in to the ache in his shoulder and sat on the veranda to watch the sunset.

A tiny black-and-white face appeared at the garden shed. The puppies had opened their eyes and every day grew more adventurous. Molly licked his hand before returning to her babies. The puppy, who Quinn had named John Deere after his favourite tractor, scampered out the shed door on chubby legs to meet her.

It wasn't only the puppies that had changed. He felt himself changing as well. With its serenity and its rugged beauty, Bundara had drawn him in and held him tight. Bringing the derelict farm back to what it had once been filled him with a sense of peace and achievement.

He stared at the pastures beyond the post-and-rail fence that had become as familiar as his family farm. He didn't know if it was because it was spring and he was surrounded by new life, but he felt a renewed sense of hope.

After the grey hues of the overcast weather, tonight's sunset proved spectacular. Vivid yellows, crimsons and oranges splashed across the sky in bold streaks of colour. He traced the jagged silhouette of the western ridge that would only be accessible by horseback. From the high granite slopes the sunset would prove even more brilliant. Something unravelled deep inside.

When they'd been young, and life had been simple, he and Brody would ride their ponies to the highest point on Mayfield to watch the sun descend. They'd used to feel like they could touch the sky and as though they too had been painted in colour. A breeze brushed over his skin as if offering encouragement. He stared at the ridge and acknowledged the emotions thrashing within him. He needed to feel the chill air as he and Garnet climbed the timbered slopes and looked down on a still and silent world. He needed to sit in silence and to watch the sun slowly sink in the sky.

He came to his feet and slid his phone free from his shirt pocket to call Ava. Bundara's stables would no longer stand empty. It was time to reclaim what he'd lost.

CHAPTER

8

Mid-morning sun streamed through the kitchen window of Lewis's city home and bathed the minimalistic room in light.

'How does this look?' Fliss asked Meredith, as she smoothed melted chocolate over a creamy layer of caramel that covered a biscuit base. It was her second attempt at melting the chocolate as the first packet had congealed into a crumbly mess in the microwave jug.

'Wonderful. Caramel slice always goes down a treat.'

Fliss and Meredith had helped with the funeral plans and had sorted through Jean's clothes and personal items. With the funeral on tomorrow, they were now spending the day preparing for the wake. Jean had only wanted a simple affair so family and friends were to be invited back to Lewis's home after the church service.

Fliss ran a sink full of hot water to wash up the latest round of cooking utensils. She glanced to where Meredith was assembling the ingredients for her famous sponge cake that Fliss's mother had included in her own recipe book.

'I know we talked about this on the way down here, but why did you suspect I wasn't a honeymoon baby? I've looked at the dates on my birth certificate, and on Mum and Dad's marriage certificate, and the timeline is plausible.'

'It wasn't anything specific your mother said or did, it was more a result of my own situation.'

Fliss nodded. Many years ago, Meredith had been forced by her family to give up her precious son that she'd had with the jackaroo she'd loved and lost to a riding accident.

The older woman's expression grew pensive as she sifted flour into a large glass bowl. 'Those early years after losing Simon and giving up Tanner, I was consumed with grief and guilt ... and I was sure sometimes I'd see a similar expression in Ruth's eyes when she'd look at you. Which made no sense. But after Cressy was born I started to believe something wasn't right. It was always assumed you'd been in a hurry to enter the world. You also were a small baby so this fitted in with you being early. However, when Cressy arrived she went full term and was still smaller than you.'

'Mum always said I wore her out so she didn't put on as much weight with Cressy as she did with me.'

'Which made perfect sense as you were a very ... energetic toddler.'

'Which is your nice way of saying I was a horror.'

'Let's just say Cressy slept more in her first month than you did in your first two years and I suspect more than you sleep even now.'

'Sorry, did I wake you?' She'd hoped Meredith hadn't heard her walking around last night. 'I tried to be quiet when I went downstairs for another book but that first floorboard always squeaks.'

'It's no problem, I was reading too. I know I once lived in Sydney, but the traffic noise still keeps me awake.'

Fliss finished the last of the dishes and wiped her hands on a red tea towel. 'I'll see if Lewis wants a cuppa and then I'll walk to the shops for some more eggs.'

'Thanks.' Meredith opened the egg carton she'd sat on the bench earlier to allow the eggs inside to reach room temperature. 'I'll need all of these ones and we still have banana bread to make.'

Fliss quietly rapped on Lewis's study door. Since they'd arrived, Lewis had been a silent and sombre presence, spending hours on his computer writing Jean's eulogy and selecting photos for the funeral programme. When his voice sounded, Fliss opened the door and entered the sun-drenched room that overlooked an immaculate garden. Jean had loved birds and would sit for hours in the bay window of the living room listening to their songs.

Lewis stopped typing on the computer to turn towards Fliss. Despite the grief thinning his cheeks, his eyes warmed. Tall, with his dark hair liberally sprinkled with grey, Fliss had never seen him anything other than clean-shaven.

'How's the programme coming along?' She slid into the leather chair close to his desk. Many of her university issues had been resolved while sitting in this chair and chatting to her wise mentor.

'It's taking shape.' Lewis removed his glasses to rub at his eyes. 'I just have to finalise the last piece of music. How's everything going in the kitchen?'

'Let's just say Meredith's a saint for being so patient. This time I only burned the chocolate.'

A brief smile moved his lips. 'I thought it was a little quiet without the smoke alarm going off.'

Fliss groaned. 'Sorry again about yesterday. Who knew if you opened the dishwasher too early the steam set off the alarm?'

Lewis's grey gaze flickered over her face. 'I know we're all …
missing Jean … but is there anything else going on with you?'

Fliss kept her expression unchanging. She should have known
Lewis wouldn't miss how distracted she was. She'd never been able
to hide anything from him. But she couldn't have him know that
as well as grieving for Jean she was still coming to terms with her
DNA bombshell. This trip to see Lewis was about him, not her.

'Nothing that some more time at Bundara won't fix.'

'Living there has been the best thing for you.'

'It has. You'll have to come and visit. It's so quiet and peaceful.'

'I'm sure it is. I will come and stay … sometime.' Sadness dulled
his words and he paused to settle his glasses back on his nose. 'So
tell me about this Hewitt who's been helping you in the garden?'

'There's not much to say. He's an old rodeo friend of Denham's
who needs some time out after losing his twin brother and injuring
himself in a motorbike accident.'

'Does he like vectors more than people?'

'No, he doesn't. Not that this is where I'm heading with Hewitt,
but you're never going to let me forget my lapse in judgement when
I dated that physics PhD guy, are you?'

Lewis's lips twitched. 'No, or the guy who preferred vodka shots
to vectors.'

'Of course there was also the surgeon whose ego was triple the
size of his attention span.'

Lewis chuckled. It was a relief to hear him laugh. 'No, let's not
forget him. He was charming, though. I'll give him that much.'

'You can say that again, especially if you're a curvy blonde intern.'

'Life was never dull when you brought someone around to
meet … us.'

Fliss's heart clenched as loss erased the amusement relaxing
Lewis's face.

'Lucky for you there won't be anyone for quite a while. I need to work out where I'm heading before I can even think about looking for my next dating disaster.'

She hoped it was her imagination that Lewis's gaze rested on her a moment longer than usual. 'I have every faith that not only will you work out where you're heading, your next dating disaster won't be a disaster at all. The right man is out there. Jean always said it would take a fearless man to be worthy of you.'

'I'm not sure such a man exists, but that's okay. I'm going to be the best spinster aunt ever when Cressy and Denham have their little cowgirls and cowboys.' She stood to rest her hand on Lewis's shoulder. 'Would you like a cuppa or some of those Belgian chocolates before I head to the shops?'

He covered her hand with his. Despite all his academic achievements and distinguished medical career, his callused palm spoke of a lifetime love of gardening.

'No, thank you.' He squeezed her fingers before turning back to the computer. 'I'll keep working on Jean's programme.'

Fliss shifted the grocery bag from one hand to the other. Between the city humidity and the afternoon sun, she was working up a sweat walking home. On her right cars passed by in a constant stream of peak-hour noise. Lewis's suburb was in a quieter neighbourhood but she'd still seen more traffic in one hour than she'd see in a month in Woodlea.

She moved to the side of the footpath as a lean woman in black lycra power-walked towards her, leading a fluffy white dog. A wave of longing washed over her. She missed her morning routine of sitting on the veranda step with Molly. Now that Ella had discovered the border collie's name and address, it wouldn't be long before her owners were tracked down. A part of her already mourned that the garden shed would soon only be home to the temperamental lawnmower. The white dog trotted past, giving her a cursory, disinterested glance. Its owner didn't acknowledge her or thank her for moving aside to let them pass.

She sighed. She was in the city now, not in the close-knit outback community of her childhood. She returned to the middle of the footpath only to stop to allow a sleek black car to turn into a driveway. The suited driver didn't appear to know she was there. She continued walking.

Clipped garden hedges, manicured lawns and stately old homes marked the suburb as an affluent one. But despite the fresh greenery and sense of space, the breeze retained the scent of fumes. This was the bright city life that had lured her from the bush. As hard as she now looked, she couldn't see its appeal. Once this was the only world she'd wanted to inhabit and now she found it somehow lacking.

When she returned to Lewis's house she poured a glass of iced water and took her laptop into the garden. Leaves whispered overhead as she sat at the table beneath an old liquid amber tree. Since she'd left Bundara she'd texted Hewitt and made a quick phone call. But it hadn't been enough. The need to see him had almost become a physical ache.

Before she lost her nerve, she opened her laptop and activated the call button. The electronic gurgling sound gave way to Hewitt's voice before his face filled the screen. 'Hi, Fliss.'

'Hi.' She gripped the edge of the table to stop her words from sounding breathless. 'I was going to text to ask about the puppies but had my laptop open …'

Hewitt's grin flashed. 'Hold on.' He stood and the screen moved as he carried his laptop outside and sat it on the lawn. Tiny black-and-white bodies waddled in front of the camera before a pink tongue licked the lens.

'They are *so* cute. I want to come home right now and hug them.'

The screen moved again as Hewitt returned inside. 'They're already up to mischief. I'm down one leather glove.' He paused and when he spoke Fliss thought his voice had deepened. 'When do you think you'll be home?'

'The funeral's tomorrow, so maybe the day after. It just depends how Lewis is going.'

'Stay as long as you need. Everything's under control here.'

'Thanks. I'll let you know what's happening. How's Lizzie and Quinn?'

'Going well. Ava said there's only been one recent sandpit flooding incident.'

Fliss nodded and hoped the screen didn't reveal how much her attention fixated on his mouth. His smile, even onscreen, had the power to stir her senses. 'Everything sounds … good.' She couldn't strip the wistfulness from her voice.

'It is, but you're not here. Molly still waits for you on the veranda step every morning.'

'Does she? Please tell me there's been no word about her owners. I know she already has a home but is it wrong of me to hope she can stay as long as possible?'

'No, there's been no word, and it isn't wrong to want time with her.' She thought he was about to say something more but then he stopped to run a hand over his jaw. 'I'd better go, it's starting to rain and the puppies will need to go into the shed. I hope all goes well tomorrow.'

'Me too. See you soon.'

When the screen went black she couldn't suppress a sudden sense of emptiness. She had never experienced such homesickness, even when away at boarding school. Seeing Hewitt and hearing his voice shouldn't affect her so much. She dragged her fingers through her hair. Never before had she felt such an intense pull towards someone or felt such a need to be around them. But falling for Hewitt, even just a little, was an even worse idea than keeping her city car. He'd soon be gone.

She stared at the lifeless laptop. Being back in the city hadn't made her wish she still lived within its sophisticated embrace. All it had done was reinforce that she'd changed and now wanted different things. It wasn't only her origins she now questioned, but who she was.

When Hewitt entered the Woodlea town limits, the heavy clouds that had hovered over him since he'd left Bundara disappeared. Sunlight caught in the white puffs of blossoms and in the cheery yellow of daffodils growing in neat front gardens.

Over in the city, Fliss would be saying farewell to Jean. He hoped the funeral didn't prove too tough. There'd been a renewed vulnerability in Fliss's tone and the dark shadows beneath her eyes had returned.

When she'd called yesterday, he'd been glad the puppies had provided a distraction. Thanks to Garnet arriving today, and the ride they had to make that evening, his emotions were already volatile. Seeing Fliss again, and experiencing the warmth and beauty of her smile, only made him feel more on edge. No matter how busy he'd kept himself, he continued to miss her with a depth he'd never imagined possible.

He rolled his good shoulder before checking his watch. He still had an hour before Ava, his mother and the twins met him at the local park. Ava had offered to bring Garnet out to Bundara but by Hewitt meeting her in town it would shorten her already long trip. It was only his father who'd refused to come. Hewitt would make sure he sent home a large bag of the liquorice he liked.

He pulled into a space a few spots down from the only hair salon in town. His mother had put up with him looking rough for long enough. He also needed to set a good example for Quinn. The five-year-old had started resisting having his hair trimmed by Ava as he wanted to look like Hewitt.

He entered the hair salon and a slim blonde looked up from where she was blow-drying a lady's long silver hair.

'What can I do for you?' A faint accent overlaid the hairdresser's cheerful words.

Behind him, a man chuckled. 'From the looks of him, he needs the same as me.'

Hewitt turned to see an older man whose salt-and pepper hair hung past his collar. He nodded at the man before facing the hairdresser. 'If you have time, I do need a trim.'

'No problem. I can squeeze you in after Arnold. I'd say grab a coffee from next door but I have a feeling once you leave you mightn't come back.'

'I'll wait.'

He sat in a spare seat and shook Arnold's hand. 'I'm Hewitt.'

'Nice to meet you. Taylor said the same thing to me and she was right. If I didn't plant my butt in this chair, I wouldn't have been back.'

'That makes two of us.'

'You're not from around here?'

'No, further out west.'

To their right Taylor held up a mirror so her client could see the back of her styled hair.

Arnold frowned. 'I've got a family reunion on. I hope Taylor doesn't take much off. My old dog disowns me whenever I come back from town shorn.'

Taylor signalled to Arnold that it was his turn in the chair. With a deep sigh the man took his time walking across the room. Taylor riffled through a pile of magazines and handed Hewitt an edition with a header on the front.

'Just in case you don't want to know about the latest hair extensions or contouring techniques. Fliss back?'

'Not yet.'

The hairdresser answered his unspoken question. 'Fliss and I grew up together. My mum, Sue, was the local librarian who'd keep Cressy in horse-book heaven and make sure Fliss found a book to answer every one of her thousand questions.'

He could see a little Cressy with her nose in a horse book and imagine how a young Fliss would have had an infinite thirst for information. She and Lizzie had much in common.

Taylor reached for a broom. 'Please tell Fliss I'm sorry to hear about Lewis's wife and that we must catch up soon.'

'Will do.'

Hewitt passed the time flipping through the farm machinery magazine and listening to Arnold's stories about the elusive white kangaroo that lived near his bush block two hours from town. All too soon, a neat short-back-and-sides Arnold left the chair and it was Hewitt who sat cloaked in the black cape.

'Good luck,' Arnold said as he rubbed his bare neck. 'That breeze out there's going to feel a bit nippy.'

Arnold's prediction proved true. As Hewitt left the hair salon, cool air rushed over the exposed skin of his nape. He turned up his shirt collar and gave Taylor a final wave through the shop window.

Ava's most recent text confirmed she'd passed the WELCOME TO WOODLEA sign, so he had time for a last errand. He crossed the road to the gift shop.

With two large wrapped boxes on his passenger seat, he drove through the wide gates of the Woodlea park. A row of thick poplars sheltered the picnic tables and barbeque areas. The children's play area backed onto a large oval that was surrounded by a white picket fence. Over the years the historic sportsground would have been home to many cricket and rugby matches, market days and sheep dog trials.

Hewitt parked near a climbing spinner draped in a heavy, thick web. The rattle of a horse float had him look to his right. Tension clamped his shoulders but then receded. Today wasn't about regrets and guilt, but about moving forwards and accepting the new direction their lives had taken.

Quinn was the first out of Ava's steel-blue four-wheel drive. Emotion flooded Hewitt as Quinn flew into his arms and strangled his neck in a fierce hug. Lizzie quickly followed and made do with hugging his leg. When he lowered Quinn to the ground he drew Lizzie close. She rested her head in the curve of his neck like she'd done since she was a baby. She smelt of sunshine and the sweet scent of the pink soap she liked.

Quinn raced away to clamber to the top of the spinner. Lizzie joined him, climbing at a slow and cautious pace.

Ava came over to give Hewitt a hug. 'That last half-hour took forever. Quinn isn't wired to sit still.'

Hewitt grinned, relieved that the jut of Ava's cheekbones wasn't quite so pronounced. 'Don't worry, I'll wear him out.'

Ava's blue eyes sparkled with a light he hadn't seen in a long time. 'Does it sound bad if I said I was hoping you'd say that?'

Hewitt turned to the elegant, grey-haired woman who he was sure used to reach his chin and who he could now tuck under his arm. 'Hi, Mum.'

'Hi, dear.'

She clung to him and he let the hug last as long as she needed it to. When she pulled away a smile erased years from her face. 'It's about time you listened to your old mother and got rid of all that hair.'

Hewitt kept his arm around her thin shoulders. 'I always listen to you.'

'Ava, do you want to help me remind Hewitt of all the times he hasn't listened to me or anyone else?'

Ava laughed from where she was unlatching the front door of the horse float. 'If I had all day I would, but there's someone else desperate to see Hewitt.'

Hewitt dropped a kiss on his mother's head and went to see Garnet. Her soft whinny greeted him as he entered the front of the horse float.

He stroked her velvet-soft muzzle. 'Hello, Garnet girl. I'm sorry it's taken me so long to get my act together.'

She blew against his cheek as he rubbed her favourite spot high on her neck.

'We've got a special ride to make tonight.'

Lizzie's voice sounded behind him. 'Uncle Hewy, have you got more photos of the puppies? I want to see how big Delilah is now.'

'I do.' Hewitt ran his hand over Garnet's blood-red-bay neck before leaving the float.

He handed Lizzie his phone. 'If everyone's happy, I'll take Garnet around to the vet stables and be back soon.'

'Take as long as you want.' Ava handed him her car keys. 'I don't even think the sight of a digger driving past would get Quinn off the play equipment.'

When Hewitt returned, Quinn was exactly where he'd left him, clinging to the webbing near the top of the spinner.

Hewitt lifted his arm to catch Quinn's attention. 'Lunch time.'

Quinn scrambled straight down.

Ava sighed. 'You have no idea how glad I'll be when you're home. I would've had to call him at least three times.'

'Be careful what you wish for. Don't forget when Quinn and I are in the shed you have to call me at least three times.'

Ava's lips swept into a smile. 'Make that five times.'

Hewitt opened the car door for Lizzie and Quinn to climb into their seats. Noticing Ava rubbing at her lower back, he offered to drive.

Once at the Windmill Café, Lizzie and Quinn deliberated over what to eat before ordering their usual vanilla milkshakes and cheese sandwiches. The next stop was the lolly shop. Hewitt snapped a picture of the twins' faces when they realised how many lolly-filled jars there were on the shelves. His mother stayed outside taking photos of the yarn-bombed front fence. All too soon it was time for Ava to head home in order to avoid the kangaroos that would graze on the roadside verges at dusk.

They returned to the park for a last play and to drop Hewitt off at his ute. After Hewitt had pushed both Quinn and Lizzie on the swings, he gave them a final hug. When they were settled in Ava's four-wheel drive, he passed them their presents.

'Here's a surprise to open when you're home.'

Quinn gave a sleepy nod while Lizzie blew him a tired kiss.

Ava's expression was thankful as she hugged Hewitt goodbye.

He held his mother close. 'Say hi to Dad and tell him I'll be home in about a month.'

She nodded, tears welling in her eyes.

Hewitt waved them off, a cold weight constricting his chest. But as he left town, with Garnet in the horse float behind him, a growing sense of hope eased his strain. For the first time since they'd buried Brody, he'd had time on his own. For the first time since a part of him had also died in the rodeo arena, he'd had space to truly grieve.

The lightness and anticipation within him intensified when he reached Bundara and unloaded Garnet into the round yard. Even though afternoon shadows cast long shapes on the lawn, there was still time to climb the ridge before sunset. When the mare realised the saddle and bridle Hewitt carried over were for her, she tossed her head and side-stepped.

'This will be a slow and steady ride,' he said as he sat the saddle on the top rail, 'so don't get too excited.' As he entered the yard Garnet came straight over to him. He slipped the snaffle bit into her mouth and eased the leather headpiece into place behind her ears. He smoothed a hand along the scars on her shoulder from her battle with the rodeo bull. 'But it will be the first of many.'

Any doubts that he was doing the wrong thing dissolved the moment he slid into the saddle. The creak of leather and the happy flicker of Garnet's ears confirmed he was where he should be. He could feel the tense, tight line of his shoulders easing.

Curious cows raised their heads as they rode through the carpeted paddocks to where the pastures ended and the gum trees thickened. Hewitt allowed Garnet to pick her own pace as they negotiated the steep slope that would take them to the top of the ridge.

The valley fell away, the blue of the sky faded and when the first blush of the sunset painted the horizon, Hewitt pulled Garnet to a stop.

He rubbed her neck. 'We're here.'

He slid to the ground and took a seat on a hewn piece of granite. Garnet came to stand beside him. The cold of the rock chilled him and the air nipped at his skin, but he stayed still.

Silence shrouded them. Colour embraced them. Light burst across the sky in brilliant swathes of gold, orange and pink. The sun slowly descended.

Hewitt filled his mind with happy memories of his twin. As the sun lowered from sight, he rasped the words, 'Goodbye, Brody.'

CHAPTER

9

The cheerful warble of a magpie perched in the old fir tree at Claremont welcomed Fliss back to the bush.

'Meredith, you make the best hot chocolate.' She took an appreciative sip from her mug decorated with cheerful red poppies. A gentle country breeze blew around her, untainted by city fumes.

'Thanks.' Meredith lowered herself into the wrought-iron seat opposite Fliss and sat a plate of coconut and lemon slice on the outdoor table. 'Sorry I don't have any more jam drops. I was sure I'd left some in the freezer before we left for Sydney.'

'I'm sure you did, but if Phil or Tanner are addicted to them like I am, it's no wonder you can't find any.'

Meredith's blue eyes grew soft. For years she had baked for everyone but the son she never knew and the man she'd loved from afar. Now that Denham lived at Glenmore with Cressy, Claremont was the home of Meredith and Phil and sometimes Tanner, when he wasn't out droving.

Fliss looked around the extensive park-like garden that had weathered drought, fire and locust plagues. Many of her mother's cuttings, which she'd shared with Denham's mother Audrey, continued to flourish in the carefully tended beds. Meredith, Audrey and her mother Ruth had met in their early twenties in Sydney and their bonds had deepened when they'd moved out west. Fliss still remembered the laughter that would come from the tennis court when the three friends would spend the morning playing tennis.

She reached for a piece of slice. 'This is just what I need before I head to Bundara.'

'It's been a busy and emotional time. It was a huge job going through Jean's things but I'm glad we did as it would have been too much for Lewis.'

'You're right. I've never seen him so quiet and withdrawn. Do you think he'll be okay?'

'It'll just take time. He's a strong man but he's been by Jean's side for over thirty years.'

'And you've known him for that long too?'

'Longer.' Meredith took a piece of slice. 'He was one of the first people I met when I lived with Audrey's family. He used to mow their lawns as a way to put himself through university.'

Fliss examined Meredith's beautiful, ageless face, a face that had once earned her the title of Miss Woodlea Showgirl. 'Didn't you also meet my mother while you were in Sydney?'

'I did but not until I'd been there for quite a while. Her family had a house on the beach that I used to walk along. One day her cocker spaniel escaped and I found him down by the rock pools. I never really got to know her well until she married your father and moved to Glenmore.'

Fliss took another sip of her hot chocolate.

'I've been through all of Mum's scrapbooks and photo albums and there isn't anything to link her to any man other than Dad.'

Meredith sighed. 'I know. I've been racking my brain to think back but she never mentioned anything about seeing anyone in Sydney. Her parents were very strict and that was something we had in common.' Meredith paused. 'Actually, perhaps she *was* seeing someone. I think your mother knew I was pregnant even though I didn't show for a long time. Sometimes, when we'd walk along the beach, she'd have this intense look on her face when she'd glance at my stomach. I used to think she was shocked but maybe there was another reason. Maybe the look was one of ... longing?'

Fliss leaned forwards to cover Meredith's hand with hers. 'Thank you. This is the first clue, or even half a clue, I've had. Mum moved out here after she was married and since she must have only just been pregnant with me before her wedding, my father had to have come from her Sydney life.'

'Exactly.' Meredith squeezed Fliss's hand. 'You keep working with your DNA matches and I'll keep thinking.'

The white wooden bridge rattled as Fliss drove over the timber planks. The water flow below remained swollen and elevated but no longer was the bridge in danger of being flooded. Every morning at Lewis's she'd checked the Woodlea weather forecast. Her worry would spike until she saw there would be no rain. The prospect of driving home on the wet red dirt roads had made her stomach churn.

The mailbox flashed by and she was over the cattle grid, through the now dry dip in the road and driving up to the farmhouse. A farmhouse she no longer considered as merely a place to live but as … home. Somewhere along the way, it had stopped being just a haven and a place to heal, and had perhaps become her future.

She slowed to appreciate the last of the sunlight as it streamed over the purple wisteria that climbed the tank stand. The white blossoms on the tree near the car port had almost finished and as she watched a breeze dispersed the tiny petals so they floated to the ground like snowflakes. She left her car and headed straight for where Molly sat at the garden gate surrounded by six plump puppies.

She eased herself through the small gate, making sure no one escaped. 'Hello, Miss Molly.' She patted the border collie who wriggled closer. 'Look how much your babies have grown.'

Then, uncaring of her tailored black trousers, Fliss sat on the lawn. Molly lay down beside her. Soon puppies were clambering over Fliss's legs, chewing the bottom of her heels and burrowing under her arms. She laughed as a small wet nose kissed her chin.

'You guys are going to be the biggest time wasters. How am I going to get any DNA stuff done with you to play with?'

Hewitt's deep chuckle sounded. 'Now that's what I call a welcome committee.'

She went to reply but quickly closed her mouth as a puppy licked her face.

He spoke again. 'Maybe welcoming committee wasn't the right description, maybe assault team would be better. Here …'

She focused on the tanned hand he extended to help her. With a puppy trying to eat her hair, she wrapped her hand around Hewitt's strong wrist and he pulled her upright.

Their eyes locked. It wasn't the heat of his skin, or how effortlessly he'd hauled her to her feet, that held her still, but how different he looked. With his hair cropped short, she had an uninhibited view of his moulded cheekbones, the firm angle of his jaw and the pure grey of his eyes.

Realising she was staring, and still holding on to him, she slid her hand free. He couldn't have missed how fast her heart was racing.

'Thanks. Sitting on the ground wasn't one of my better ideas.'

'The puppies thought it was.'

There was a raw huskiness to his words but that could have been wishful thinking.

Hewitt picked up a second puppy that had latched onto Fliss's hem. 'I'll take everyone to the shed so we can get your bags to the house in peace.'

Fliss rubbed Molly's ears in farewell before the border collie and her pups followed Hewitt to the shed like he was the pied piper.

Fliss returned to her car. Over in the machinery shed a silver-and-white horse float was parked next to the quad bike. She looked around. A glossy bay horse grazed near the cluster of yellow wattles in the creek paddock.

She turned to Hewitt as he joined her at the boot of her car. 'You're a pickup rider with a horse again?'

'I am. Ava, the twins and my mother brought Garnet over yesterday.'

'Have you been for a ride?'

'Yes, last night to the top of the ridge.'

Fliss studied the rugged granite outcrops rising above the timbered hills. 'The view must have been spectacular.'

'It was.'

Her attention returned to the man beside her. The seriousness she associated with Hewitt appeared to have lessened. There was a lightness to his smile and the lines beside his mouth weren't so defined. Seeing his family, and riding Garnet again, seemed to have taken the edge off his grief and made him happier. The life he'd once had was slowly being pieced back together. As pleased as she was for him she couldn't stifle a surge of loss.

'Do I need to put my Dr Fliss hat on? Just because your shoulder feels better doesn't mean it isn't still broken. If I sent you for an x-ray there'd still be a visible fracture line.'

'I'll be fine.'

Hewitt reached for her bag. The amused glint in his eyes did more damage than if he'd flashed her another grin. It was impossible to be around him and remain unmoved. It wasn't just her exhaustion rendering her vulnerable. The emotions hovering close to the surface made her realise just how glad she was to see him and how empty Bundara would feel when he was gone.

'I'm serious, Hewitt.'

Her words emerged sharper than she'd intended. Embarrassed heat flooded her face.

His fingers touched her hair. 'It's okay,' he said, tone gentle and eyes dark. 'I'll be careful.'

His hand lowered and she saw a small white petal that blew away in the breeze.

Hewitt bent to pick up her bags and she lost sight of his face. 'How about we take these inside and I'll fill you in on all of the news. Cressy's coming over for an early dinner. You're now the owner of a fire pit and we thought we'd christen it tonight.'

Fliss nodded and relaxed. Hewitt had given her exactly what she needed: something to focus on other than what was going on between them.

When they walked through the garden she discovered more changes than just the metal fire pit sitting on the paved area in front of the old brick wall. New window panes gleamed and the front screen door no longer drooped.

'Thanks for everything you've done,' she said as Hewitt held the door open. 'I really appreciate your help getting Bundara in shape.' She pressed her lips together before she said something more personal. It wasn't only her home he'd had a profound effect on.

The corners of his eyes crinkled as he smiled. 'Anytime.'

She walked through the doorway to hide how much she'd missed seeing the white flash of his grin.

'Would you like a cuppa?' she said over her shoulder as he followed her inside.

'Thanks.' He set her cases down in the hallway. 'I spent the day in Denham's shed and missed my usual afternoon coffee.'

As he accompanied her into the kitchen, Fliss drew a silent, steadying breath. This was the first time they'd been alone together in her home. But instead of feeling anxious or awkward, having Hewitt in her personal space felt comfortable, safe. She busied herself making a coffee and a pot of tea. When they were seated on opposite sides of the kitchen table, Hewitt filled her in on what Ella had discovered.

'It turns out Molly's owners were away. Their daughter and her young family had been looking after Molly and the other dog, Max. Three weeks ago, when they went to let them off, they were gone. Apparently there's been a few thefts of valuable working dogs.'

'Please tell me Max has been found? Is he the father of the puppies?'

'No, he hasn't been, and yes, he's their father.'

'Could Max be around here somewhere?'

'The police believe so. The theory is that Molly escaped from wherever she was taken and Max is still there.'

'I hope they find him soon.' Fliss paused and stared at her untouched tea. She dreaded knowing the answer to what she was about to ask. 'So now Molly's owners have been located, when are they coming to get her?'

'The daughter has passed on photos of Molly and the puppies to her parents who are still overseas. They've completed the paperwork to prove Molly's their dog but have asked if we could keep them all a little longer so the puppies will be better able to travel.'

Fliss smiled. 'That's more than okay with me.'

'That's what Ella thought. They'll be here for at least another three weeks. If Max is still missing, the owners plan to come and search for him.'

'Three more weeks …'

Even though it was a relief not to be saying goodbye to Molly and her babies straight away, Fliss couldn't keep the sorrow from her voice.

'That will give you plenty of time to be mobbed.'

She thought Hewitt was going to say something further but then he came to his feet, his coffee unfinished. The line of his shoulders appeared rigid. 'That's Cressy's ute. I'd better rustle up some dry firewood.'

Hewitt fed the fragile flames in the fire pit with thin pieces of kindling. Never had he been so pleased to see Cressy than when she bounded up the Bundara veranda steps. He couldn't trust himself alone with Fliss.

The simple act of helping her to her feet when she'd arrived had been a mistake. He should have known better than to touch her. He'd felt far more than a physical connection when they'd joined hands. He'd felt her fragility, strength and the beat of her pulse down to his bones. Even with shadows of exhaustion beneath her eyes, he'd never seen her look more beautiful.

He'd thought the worst was over. He'd seen her and could now let the intensity of her homecoming fade to a safe and casual companionship. Then she'd sat across the kitchen table from him, sadness at the thought of saying goodbye to Molly dimming the warmth in her smile, and he'd been just as lost. He'd had to leave the kitchen before he said or did something he and Fliss would both regret.

He stared at the growing fire. Like the flames engulfing the wood before him, his feelings for Fliss continued to incinerate his self-control. So until he could refocus and get himself back behind the line he shouldn't ever have crossed, he had to somehow stay strong.

'Your fire pit looks fabulous. Can I put in an order for one?'

He turned at the sound of Cressy's voice. He hoped the twinkle in her eyes wasn't because she'd twigged he'd spent the day welding in Denham's man-cave to distract himself from wondering when Fliss would be home.

'Thanks. Tell Denham I owe him some checker plate next trip to Woodlea. I'll get double so I can make you one.'

Cressy sat a basket of fresh bread rolls and a bottle of tomato sauce on the new outdoor table that sat on a stand he'd also welded.

'I'll put in an order for one of these too,' she said, running a hand over the recycled old door.

'Order taken.' Hewitt unfolded three camp chairs and placed them in a circle in front of the fire pit. 'I just need to work on the seating part of Fliss's outdoor entertainment area.'

Cressy sat in the closest chair and Molly came and flopped beside her. Fliss walked across the lawn carrying a tray of sausages and three long metal forks. She wore jeans, boots and a long-sleeved pink shirt. Her hair had been twisted on top of her head, but wisps escaped to fall around her face.

Cressy smiled at her sister. 'Enjoy your neat garden while it lasts. You'll have nothing but chewing, noise and wrestling ahead of you for the next three weeks.'

Fliss sat the sausages and forks on the table. 'I can't wait.'

Cressy took a long look at Fliss. 'You know you'll get covered in dog hair, puppy slobber and everything will be annihilated, from your garden pots to your shoes.'

Fliss sat in the middle chair. 'I still can't wait.'

'Who are you? And where's my real sister?'

Fliss's soft, contented laughter rippled across Hewitt's arms like goose bumps. 'The neat control freak is still here ... I'm just taking a step outside my comfort zone.'

'Good on you.' Cressy's words were heartfelt.

Darkness wrapped around them and glimmers of starlight appeared overhead. The sausages were cooked, followed by the marshmallows. An easy silence settled amongst them, only broken by the pop of wood and the chirp of crickets.

'Remember how we'd camp down at the creek and have a fire?' Fliss studied the flames while her marshmallow roasted. 'Mum would leave the laundry light on so we could find our way inside if we got scared.'

'Those were the days. Remember how Midge used to sleep with us and would snore so loudly you'd have to go back to the house to get cotton wool to block our ears?' Cressy lifted her marshmallow out of the fire and glanced at Fliss. 'You know what we should go on, except I'll be away up north with Denham, is the trail ride. There'll be campfires every night.'

Fliss didn't look away from her own marshmallow. 'Taylor wasn't sure if it would be on after all the rain.'

'It will be.' Cressy popped her roasted marshmallow into her mouth. 'I hope no one's counting how many of these I'm eating. The officials have done a pre-ride inspection and it will definitely go ahead.'

'Zoe will be pleased. She's so excited. She really wants to take Minty and for me to come with them.'

Hewitt used the excuse of putting another marshmallow on his stick to observe Fliss's face. Her tone had lowered and her words had tensed.

'Why don't you?' Cressy asked. 'Jazz's arthritis is playing up so her knees wouldn't cope, but you could take Flame. I have a young horse I'm training so she doesn't get ridden as much as she should.' Cressy paused as her tone grew teasing. 'Or you could take Bandit.'

'Bandit? No thank you. Don't forget I've patched Denham up enough times to know just what that horse is capable of. Besides, he'd have Zoe's sweet little Minty shaking in his tiny horse shoes with those death stares of his. I'd spend the whole ride by myself.' The mirth ebbed from Fliss's eyes. 'I know it's a really worthwhile cause, the hospital needs a portable ultrasound machine ... but I'm not sure it's a good idea I go.'

Hewitt sensed an undercurrent of unspoken words between the sisters.

Cressy leaned over to squeeze Fliss's hand. 'There's always next year.'

Fliss didn't answer. Instead she stared at the fire coals with a desperate intensity.

Hewitt spoke into the quiet before his self-preservation could tell him to keep his mouth shut. 'I'll go, if you go. Garnet would enjoy the ride. After the year she's had, she deserves some fun.'

Fliss looked at him. Hope flared and then faded in her eyes. 'I'm sure she would but you really shouldn't be doing too much riding.' She rescued her charred marshmallow. 'You were right to tell Edna you weren't fit enough to ride.'

Hewitt sensed Cressy looking between the two of them.

'Perhaps ... but things change. Like you said, it's for a worthy cause and it would be an enjoyable few days. Brody and I used to camp and trail ride in the Snowy Mountains.' Hewitt saved his marshmallow before it burst into flames. 'Besides, if you came, I wouldn't have a chance to do anything risky.' He lightened his tone. 'Just think of what I could do if you weren't there to read me the riot act.'

He thought Fliss's lips would curve but instead worry furrowed her brow.

'Go, Fliss.' Cressy's voice was gentle. 'I'll look after Molly and her babies and check on the cows. Then when I'm away, I'm sure Phil will come out.'

The silence lengthened and then Fliss spoke. 'Okay ... I'll go.' She cast Hewitt a stern look. 'You'd better be prepared to ride as if you were on the lead rein. There'll be no fast riding for you.'

'Understood.'

Cressy laughed. 'Hewitt, are your fingers crossed behind your back? I know for a fact you do low risk about as well as Denham.'

The firelight caught the flicker of alarm in Fliss's eyes. 'One fall and you could undo all these past weeks of healing.'

'I'll be sensible. You have my word.'

He reached for another marshmallow to conceal how much her genuine concern moved him. He was also wise as to what Cressy was doing. In his rodeo days he mightn't have always played it safe, but Cressy knew once he gave his word, his promise was binding. She'd now planted the seed in Fliss's mind he mightn't be sensible. Fliss's strong desire to help people would ensure she'd not only keep a close watch over him, she'd also not change her mind about attending the ride.

While Fliss bent to pat Molly, Hewitt gave Cressy a nod signalling he'd have Fliss's back.

A smile shone in Cressy's eyes before she turned to Fliss. 'I'll drop Flame around tomorrow. Five days will be plenty of time to get used to being back in a saddle.'

'Even after one ride I won't be able to walk straight. It's been years since I was on a horse.'

'All the more reason to ride Flame as much as you can. Five days will also be long enough to work out a costume.'

Fliss groaned. 'I'd forgotten about the parade that rides through town. You know I hate dress-ups.'

'I do—you're the only person I know who has worn jeans to a university toga party. Just look at wearing a costume as taking another step outside your comfort zone.'

'I'll just wear my scrubs … if I still have some.'

'You will not.' Cressy glanced at Hewitt. 'You're not wearing your rodeo chaps, either.'

'I won't. Just as well I know someone who enjoys dress-ups as much as she does deciding on puppy names.'

Fliss covered her face in her hands. 'That's it, I'm doomed. I'm going to end up with fairy wings and covered in pink glitter.'

CHAPTER

10

The Woodlea rodeo grounds were already teeming with colour and life when Fliss and Hewitt drove into the pre-ride hustle and bustle. Fliss looked around the rodeo grounds that would be her home for the next two nights. Each day they'd ride in a different direction and by nightfall return to a campfire and the comfort of swags, tents and horse trailers or trucks.

She uncurled her hands that were fisted in her lap. She could do this. She'd gone through each day and prepared herself for what might happen. She had her first-aid kit packed in her saddlebag and had compiled a mental list of issues she might be asked to give medical advice on. She'd also rehearsed conversation starters for when she met new riders or caught up with old acquaintances. She wasn't going to let anxiety stop her from enjoying what should be a fun event.

She glanced beneath her lashes at the man beside her. Most of all she'd rewritten her ground rules. As her previous rules had proven ineffective at controlling how she responded to Hewitt, she now only had one. Keep the status quo. Things couldn't progress any further between them.

Yes, just seeing him made her breath rush faster. Yes, any physical contact, however brief, made her want more. And yes, his steady strength and empathy anchored her in an uncertain world. But that's as much as she could allow herself to feel. Anything more and the day he left would be the day her heart would break. Getting her life under control didn't include loving a man whose sole focus could only be the family of the brother he'd lost.

'Everything will be okay.' Hewitt's quiet words filled the ute cabin. 'Both on the ride and at Bundara. Cressy will look after Molly and the pups.'

Fliss relaxed into her seat. 'You're right, everything will be fine.'

She waved as they passed a horse float with a white pony tied to the side. Zoe, dressed in purple jodhpurs, waved back at her with both hands.

'Zoe's so excited. I must take a photo of her to send to Dr Martin.'

'She's not the only one.'

Hewitt slowed as a group of older children raced each other along the road and then disappeared amongst the goosenecks and trucks congregated around the arena.

'I think Taylor's float's over there.' Fliss pointed towards a white dual-cab ute at the far side of the rodeo ground. 'She was going to find somewhere where there'd be enough room for us all to roll out our swags.'

Hewitt parked alongside where Taylor's paint gelding stood in a small portable yard. The gelding briefly opened his eyes when Flame's and Garnet's hooves rang on the float ramp as Hewitt led them outside. He then returned to sleeping. There was a reason Taylor rode the seasoned gelding—he was bomb proof.

To Fliss's relief Flame appeared unfazed by the noise and fuss. The chestnut mare gazed around, her brown eyes bright but her breathing even. In contrast, sweat darkened Garnet's flanks and her breaths emerged as loud snorts.

Hewitt tied her to the side of the float and smoothed a hand over her neck. 'I know. This is far more exciting than being in your paddock. But we're not riding pickup, we're here to have a quiet and relaxing trail ride as per Dr Fliss's orders.'

Hewitt stayed by Garnet's side until the mare calmed. Then with a last soft word to her, he helped Fliss unload their gear from the front of the horse float. Fliss watched him carry over their saddles, relieved he didn't appear to be in any discomfort. She carefully bent to collect a brush from the grooming kit next to her boots. If only she could say the same thing about herself.

Even after the short rides she'd taken with Hewitt to check the cattle she felt muscles she hadn't used for over a decade. She didn't want to think about how stiff she'd be after the upcoming days of intensive riding.

She brushed Flame's chestnut coat and over the mare's withers saw Taylor approach. The hairdresser was no longer a dancer but she retained her graceful poise and her toes pointed outwards when she walked. Her straight chin-length hair was again a pale blonde. When Fliss had caught up with her in London last year, the colour had been a dramatic black.

Taylor stroked Flame's nose. 'Hello, old girl, remember me? I used to come with my mum to visit Audrey.'

Before Flame had lived with Cressy, the mare had been a rescue horse Denham had bought for his mother to care for. The first time Fliss had seen the mare she'd been nothing but a gaunt skeleton.

Taylor handed Fliss a plastic pink tag bearing a number and the silhouette of a horse. 'Ella's at the registration desk and says hi. She's drawn the short straw and has to work.'

Taylor went over to where Hewitt brushed Garnet and handed him his tag before saddling her paint gelding. Soon all three horses were ready and the registration numbers attached to the front of each saddle. Fliss tightened Flame's girth one more hole when Tanner rode up on a glossy palomino.

Arrow had been a mustang the drover had trained while he'd lived in Montana. The golden gelding was as headstrong as Denham's Bandit but without his bad temper and intolerance. The palomino nickered at Flame who'd been his old paddock buddy at Claremont.

Tanner dipped his felt hat at Fliss and Taylor before grinning across at Hewitt. 'Just a heads-up, Edna's heading your way. She spied you the minute you drove in. Apparently Bethany's young horse isn't fit to ride so she's been a late withdrawal. Edna's devastated Bethany's not going to meet you.'

Hewitt swung into Garnet's saddle. 'I was hoping to meet Bethany … just to reassure her I don't share her mother's matchmaking vision.'

Fliss made no effort to mount. She watched Hewitt as he rode over to Tanner. Even after the days spent riding together, seeing him on Garnet still moved her. It was as though horse and rider were a single entity. Hewitt didn't seem to move in the saddle and the mare understood exactly what to do. Hewitt's scars weren't visible like the one's marring Garnet's chest and shoulder but they still existed. The two of them had been through so much and yet their trust and connection remained.

Edna's four-wheel drive crawled towards them. Fliss grasped her left stirrup and, smothering a groan, hoisted herself upwards. Hewitt's gaze rested on her before he turned Garnet towards the marshalling area. Taylor and her paint gelding rode alongside and together they followed Hewitt and Tanner. As they passed Edna, they waved. Edna's face hardened before she lifted her hand off the steering wheel in a brief greeting.

Taylor glanced at Fliss. 'You know I'm still guilty by association. Just because I was your friend when you dumped Rodger, I'm also a pariah.'

Fliss focused on the blue width of Hewitt's back as he rode ahead. 'There's only one thing worse than being on Edna's naughty list and that's being on her nice list.'

'True. Poor Hewitt and Tanner. Even without Bethany it's going to be a long trail ride. Edna will be dropping by every chance she gets.' Taylor paused as she too considered the back view of the two cowboys ahead. 'Not that I'm in the market—Rory and I are trying to make this whole Irish-Australian long-distance thing work—but Edna does have impeccable taste.'

Fliss merely nodded. Taylor had sent her a thoughtful look. As hard as she tried, she couldn't hide that she agreed with Edna's glowing opinion of Hewitt.

Once the riders had gathered and a committee member had run through the safety and logistical requirements, the lead riders headed off. Hewitt and Tanner allowed the bulk of the riders to pass. When three red-haired teenagers on nervy horses jostled by, Tanner and Hewitt exchanged glances before following them. They'd found the Ridley boys.

Fliss could see Zoe in an approaching group. Minty's short legs worked twice as hard as the other horses but his little ears were pricked forwards. Zoe stopped beside her and Fliss leaned over to give her a hug. 'I think Minty's already having fun.'

Zoe's black riding helmet bobbed. 'So am I.'

The tall man beside Zoe smiled. 'She's been counting down the days. Great to see you, Fliss. It's been a while.'

'It has. Kellie looks well and it's wonderful there'll soon be another little Swain.'

'We wanted to tell you earlier but after everything that happened it felt ... safer to wait.'

'I understand.' She'd been the first person Kellie had called when she'd started to miscarry and Fliss had been privy to the depths of their heartbreak. 'Please tell Kellie I'm here anytime she needs me.'

'Thanks. I will.'

Minty let loose a loud ear-piercing neigh.

Fliss nudged Flame into a walk. 'I think that's our cue to stop the small talk and get going. Minty doesn't want to be left behind.'

As the sun climbed and pushed aside the clouds, Fliss and Taylor stayed with Zoe before riding ahead to allow Zoe to be with her friends. When Taylor fell behind, deep in conversation with a teenage cowgirl, Fliss let Flame pick her own pace.

Leather creaked and Flame's hooves continued their rhythmic clip-clop. The warm breeze carried the scent of honey and bees buzzed as they congregated around the hollow of a nearby gum tree. To her left, a sea of brilliant canola yellow stretched to a distant pair of silos that glinted in the sunlight. To her right, gentle hills rolled into the steeper slopes of the valley edge that they'd soon be climbing.

Over the past few days she'd rediscovered her love of riding. As a child, she'd ridden as much as Cressy had, but the older they grew the more Fliss had seen how passionate Cressy was about the bush. It hadn't been a conscious decision to step aside and let Cressy live the only life she'd ever want. There was only one Glenmore and Cressy wouldn't be happy living anywhere else, whereas Fliss hadn't yet known where she belonged.

She gazed around at the rural landscape she'd swapped for a city skyline. But here she was, back in the bush and once again a blank canvas trying to work out who she was and what she wanted. She'd reconnect with what once brought her peace and pleasure and see where it took her. She patted Flame's warm, velvety neck. She'd start by asking Cressy if Flame could stay at Bundara. The thought of being responsible for Flame didn't fill her with the expected anxiety. She was beginning to feel like she had control over her life.

'Enjoying yourself?'

Hewitt's deep voice slid through her. She hadn't realised he'd stopped ahead on the trail and waited for her.

'Yes, thanks. How are you going? Enjoying your slow lead line pace?'

'I am.' Garnet fell into step beside Flame. 'The only fast and furious riding is being done by the Ridley boys. If there's a fallen tree, all three have to jump it.'

'No surprises there. They didn't just inherit their father's red hair.' Fliss concentrated on the view between Flame's chestnut ears. Hewitt's wide-brimmed felt hat and dark sunglasses meant all she could focus on was his mouth and the firm line of his jaw. 'They're actually great kids. They're just full on, like Denis was. We used to do pony club together.'

The horses' steps slowed as the flat trail wound upwards through rocks and smooth-trunked gum trees. Fliss let Garnet and Hewitt lead the way. When they reached the ridge top, the spreading panoramic views of the valley below made the climb worth it.

Riders were already off their horses and clustered around two trestle tables covered in blue-checked tablecloths and laden with morning tea. Fliss headed Flame over to where Taylor sat on a large rock, a mug of tea cupped in her hands. Hewitt followed on Garnet.

Fliss couldn't hide her groan as she slid from the saddle and her boots took her weight. Hewitt flicked her a look but didn't say anything. Once Garnet's and Flame's reins were secured on a tree branch and their girths loosened, Hewitt strode away with his usual lithe stride. Fliss hobbled over to Taylor.

'I'd offer you a seat,' the hairdresser said, rubbing her knee, 'but if you're feeling anything like I was five minutes ago, standing is all you can think about.'

'Standing, plus a hot bath, plus a massage.' Fliss stretched to iron out the kinks in her lower back.

'Now you're talking. I can see a girls' weekend away in Dubbo very soon.'

Hewitt returned with two mugs and a plate of scones and apple slice. He'd removed his sunglasses and placed them on the front of his hat.

He handed Fliss a mug. 'Sorry, there's no hot chocolate.'

'Tea will be perfect. Thank you.'

She accepted the mug, conscious that two cowgirls sitting on a nearby slab of granite were scrutinising them. She took a cream-topped scone and stepped away. She didn't want to start any rumours that would be sure to reach Edna's ears.

Fliss was finishing her second scone when Zoe walked over accompanied by a small girl in green jodhpurs. The child held her right hand close to her chest and tears streaked the dust on her cheeks.

'Here's Dr Fliss, Alice, she'll make your hand better.'

Fliss set her mug on the ground. Should her hands shake she didn't want her tea to spill. 'What's happened, Zoe?'

'Alice was feeding Pudding his apple and he bit her finger.'

Fliss ignored the tightening of her nerves and bent to examine the girl's grubby hand. 'Can I take a look?'

She watched for a reaction as she inspected Alice's tiny fingers. But the little girl's shy expression didn't change. Alice wasn't in pain, just shocked and uncertain.

'Nothing's broken but I can see from the red mark here that's where Pudding's teeth nipped you. Don't forget next time to hold your hand out flat when feeding your greedy pony.'

A solemn smile shaped Alice's lips. 'Okay.'

'It just so happens I have the perfect thing for sore fingers.'

Fliss went to her saddlebag and came back with two round lollipops. She and Hewitt had made a stop at the lolly shop before they arrived at the rodeo grounds.

The two girls' faces broke into huge grins as Fliss handed each of them a treat.

'See, I told you Dr Fliss was the best doctor ever,' Zoe said as the girls walked away unwrapping their lollipops.

Fliss released a silent breath. The fear of failure still gripped her but dealing with Alice's injury hadn't been too nerve-racking. She glanced around. No one seemed to have noticed she'd temporarily put her doctor hat back on, let alone how anxious she'd been. Taylor was over talking to the cowgirls, and groups of riders had their backs to her as they chatted around the trestle tables.

Then grey eyes met hers. Grey eyes that were dark with an indefinable emotion. Hewitt hadn't missed a thing.

And for the rest of the day's ride, whenever she rode beside him, gravity shadowed his gaze.

Hewitt took a swallow of coffee as he stared into the flames of the campfire lighting up the rodeo grounds. Conversations surrounded him as riders reminisced about past rides and renewed friendships.

Fliss and Taylor sat to his right, their camp chairs close together as they chatted. He could see why Fliss and the friendly hairdresser were friends. Taylor shared Fliss's curiosity and had spent the past four years travelling the world. Nowadays she said the only travel she'd be doing was by horseback on the trail ride.

Tanner sat a few empty chairs around to his left, his attention on the Ridley boys across from him. The three teenagers had collected a posse of other boys and their boisterous laughter confirmed that after a day's riding they still had energy to burn. Tanner and Hewitt had already had a quiet word to them about not letting any of the horses out of their yards. Hewitt had repressed his amusement at the eldest Ridley boy's disbelief that they had guessed their plan. The Ridley boys were yet to work out that Tanner and Hewitt had once been young and high-spirited.

Edna had been and gone. She'd arrived to much fanfare as she brought two huge chocolate mud cakes and tubs of ice cream for dessert. Apart from coming over to where he and Tanner sat for a quick interrogation about how the first day had gone, she hadn't otherwise approached him. As soon as the barbeque dinner had ended she'd made her farewells.

Fliss laughed at something Taylor said. Hewitt risked a look sideways to where the firelight played over Fliss's face. There'd been no mistaking the worry that had etched lines of strain on her brow or her subtle breath of relief when the sore-finger crisis was over. Her professional confidence remained fragile.

He could see why it had been important to Cressy that Fliss go on the ride and that she step outside her comfort zone. Re-engaging with people in a relaxed context was just what Fliss needed. Although tired, her laughter came readily and her eyes were lively.

Hewitt shifted in his camp chair to ease the ache in his shoulder. He'd enjoyed the day too. Riding Garnet had eased an emptiness within him, while being on a trail ride had triggered many fond memories of time spent with Brody. Seeing the companionship and comradery around him reminded him of the bonds of community and belonging. But after witnessing Fliss's concern about treating little Alice, unease undermined his contentment.

He was supposed to be in damage control and containing his emotions. And yet the need to help and support Fliss beat inside him with an insistency he couldn't ignore. Add a heady attraction into the mix and he was a man in quicksand and sinking fast.

He gave in to the restlessness inside him and came to his feet. He spoke with what he hoped passed as a casual tone. 'I'll check the horses and call it a night.'

Fliss's attention briefly focused on his shoulder before she stood. 'I'll also call it a night.' She held out her hand for his coffee mug. 'I'll take this to the kitchen and grab some water bottles.'

Taylor left her chair. 'I'll come with you.'

With no sign of overnight rain there was no need to sleep in the back of the float or over in the covered area. Hewitt made sure he laid his swag out on the edge of the open space between the two floats. He'd get no sleep having Fliss close by. She'd washed her hair and the scent of gardenia overlaid the smell of wood smoke whenever she walked by.

To his relief, she set up her swag a body-length away and close to Taylor. Hewitt lay on his back, his uninjured arm beneath his head, and considered the stars. An owl hooted, horses stamped and Taylor's soft breaths signalled she was soon asleep. Canvas rustled as Fliss tried several times to get comfortable. After five minutes, her deep sigh said it all.

'Hewitt …'

'Yeah.'

'I'm wide awake.'

He chuckled softly. 'I thought so. You fidget more than Cressy does. I once had to double her after her horse went lame and she wriggled the whole time.'

Fliss's laughter was low. 'Tell me about it. I used to have to share a seat with her on the school bus. I'm not that bad. I'm just wired after Meredith's chocolate cake.'

'I thought Edna made the cakes.'

'Our Edna excels at many things, like knowing everyone's business and being efficient in a crisis, but baking isn't her strong point. Mum, Meredith and Audrey once did a cooking class with her and she talked so much she missed all the instructions.'

'That doesn't surprise me.'

'Edna hasn't changed over the years.' Fliss paused. 'Neither has Meredith except … she's the only one left now.'

Hewitt turned his head to look at Fliss. In the darkness all he could see was the shape of her swag. A sombre note had crept into her words. After the shock of discovering she wasn't her father's daughter, and attending Jean's funeral last week, Hewitt could understand how the losses in Fliss's life were on her mind.

'Just because those we love aren't physically with us doesn't mean they're not with us in other ways.'

'I hope so.'

'I know so. Whenever I lead Quinn or Lizzie on Brody's horse, it's as though I can feel Brody there with us.'

Canvas rustled as Fliss moved and he sensed her staring at him. 'I still go into the music room at Glenmore and sit at my grandmother's piano. If I close my eyes I can feel her sitting next to me helping me play.'

'See … she's still with you.'

'I guess.'

'She is. The bonds that bind us won't fade or weaken, they endure and strengthen us so we can live the best lives possible in their memory.'

Fliss didn't answer immediately. 'Hewitt ... thank you.'

'You're welcome.'

The dawn birdsong came too early. Hewitt scraped a hand over his face and looked beyond his swag to the pale wash of pink across the sky. Grit rasped his eyelids and his shoulder hurt like hell. He'd been prepared for his injury to flare up after a day of riding but he hadn't expected to be so sore. After he'd unsaddled Garnet, she'd swung her head around to sniff his shoulder. The perceptive mare sensed something wasn't right.

He braced himself and flipped open the dew-wet canvas on his swag. The morning chill rippled over his bare chest, leaving goose bumps in its wake. He'd have a hot shower to ease his pain. He made no sound as he walked past a still sleeping Fliss and Taylor.

As he returned from the amenities block, smoke curled from the stoked campfire and the scent of bacon clung to the breeze. Muted voices sounded and horses shuffled as the camp came to life. He waved to Tanner who was carrying a bale of hay over to a row of yarded horses with their heads hanging over the front rail.

Hewitt reached his float and saw that Fliss's and Taylor's swags were rolled up and stacked inside. The girls had to be in the showers. Knowing he didn't have an audience, Hewitt used his left side sparingly as he assembled what he needed for another day of riding. He'd fill up on coffee and greasy bacon and eggs and all would be good.

Garnet nickered as he entered her makeshift yard. He rubbed her forehead.

'Morning, Garnet girl. You're looking far too bright-eyed for this time of day. Let's take a look at these feet of yours to make sure you're right for today.'

It wasn't until he'd checked her two front feet and lifted her hind foot that he realised Fliss was standing over at Taylor's float watching him. She gave him a brief smile before turning to riffle through the duffle bag that sat open on the float ramp.

Hewitt finished checking Garnet's feet and then moved on to check Taylor's gelding and Flame. All the horses' hooves were stone free and their steel shoes were in place. After he'd lowered Flame's hind hoof he carefully straightened. Fliss stood over by Garnet, stroking her neck.

The strengthening light picked out the red in Garnet's bay coat and revealed Fliss's solemn expression. He left Flame's yard. Fliss walked towards him.

'Okay, Mr Pickup Rider, it's your turn to be given the once-over. Don't think I missed the way you're favouring that shoulder of yours.'

Hewitt didn't attempt to hide his sigh. He folded his arms. 'I'm fine.'

'You'd better do what Dr Fliss says.' Laughter threaded Taylor's words as she came over drying her hair with a towel. 'I'm not picking sides, but there's a reason why Fliss was the stare-down champion in primary school. She never gives in.'

Hewitt unfolded his arms. 'Okay. The sooner we get this over with the sooner I can have my first coffee for the day. Shirt on or off?'

'Off,' Taylor said with a wide grin.

Fliss gave her a long look. 'On. Well, half on. I just need to see your left shoulder.'

He flicked open the top button on his red-striped shirt. A tinge of colour entered Fliss's cheeks. He slipped open another button. Fliss stepped in close and he breathed in her fresh floral scent.

'Right.' She slid the shirt off his shoulder and he lifted his arm from the sleeve. 'Let's take a look.'

The crisp, professional edge to her voice reassured him that the situation would remain under control. This time the chemistry between them wouldn't spark into life. They were in public and had a very attentive audience. Taylor continued to watch them, laughter twinkling in her eyes.

Fliss's hand touched his shoulder, her fingers taking their time to learn the landscape of his skin. He ground his teeth. This was worse than the intense moment in the stables. Far worse. She was so near he could see her thick lashes and the green flecks in her hazel eyes. So close he could see the satin softness of her full bottom lip.

She spoke without looking at him. 'The bones at the top of your shoulder have separated so you've definitely done your AC joint. It's nothing to worry about. It's just that the bones won't ever be flush together.'

He nodded, barely registering her words.

Her fingers slid down the slope of his shoulder blade. 'So where was the scapula break?'

He took a second to speak. 'Almost ten centimetres down …' He lifted his arm to indicate where the fracture was.

Fliss's fingertips grazed his before she pressed around the area. 'Any pain?'

He shook his head until she found a tender spot. Jaw tight, his flinch said all that he needed to.

She moved away and, her eyes still not meeting his, ran her hand over the top of his arm. 'Still sore here?'

He went to say no but pressed his mouth shut when she found a sensitive area.

'Your rotator cuff still needs time to heal.' Fliss stepped back. 'Arms up. Don't let me push them down.'

The heat of her palms pressed into his forearms as she tried to force his arms lower. She searched his face, her preoccupied expression reassuring him that she wasn't looking for any reaction other than pain. He held his arms firm.

The warmth of her touch lifted. 'There's nothing wrong with your strength even though I suspect that's down to your high pain threshold.'

She reached for his shirt and he fought to hide his relief that the examination was over.

'Did you bring that box of painkillers I gave you?'

He shook his head, not trusting that his voice wouldn't sound hoarse, and tugged his shirt over his shoulder.

Fliss looked skywards before glancing at Taylor. 'Men.'

Taylor only grinned.

Fliss watched his hands as he slid his shirt buttons in place.

As his fingers hovered over the final button, her eyes flicked to his. In the hazel depths, he caught a shimmer of the same intense need that burned inside him. But the knowledge didn't bring him any satisfaction. For both their sakes, neither could give in to what flared between them.

He rolled both shoulders. Physical pain was nothing compared to the torment of Fliss being within kissing distance and being unable to touch her. For the rest of the morning he was hanging out with Tanner and the Ridley boys.

CHAPTER
11

'This is my worst nightmare come to life.'

Fliss looked down at her hot pink jodhpurs and matching tank top that had two fairy wings attached to the back. Somehow she'd escaped wearing glitter but over where Minty stood next to Flame, the pony's hooves sparkled with candy-pink hoof polish.

Taylor touched Fliss's shoulder to hold her still. 'It's about to get worse. Close your eyes.'

Fliss closed her eyes and her mouth as a cloud of hairspray smothered her.

'I'd forgotten about your hairspray obsession,' Fliss said when it was safe to speak.

Taylor tucked Fliss's hair into place. 'Too bad you have to put your riding helmet on, but you're still going to be the best sexy fairy.'

'Hang on. I'm just a plain, boring fairy. There was nothing in Lizzie's costume brief that said I was supposed to be a sexy fairy.'

'There is now.' Taylor ran a practised eye over Fliss's face and hair. 'And I might have given you a shirt that's a size too small.'

Fliss groaned. Taylor's similar purple top covered far more of her cleavage. 'So I take it I'm the only sexy fairy?'

'Yes, I'm a taken fairy, remember? I've already sent Rory a picture to show how unsexy I look.'

Fliss closed her eyes as worry hit. With her tousled bedroom hair and skin-tight clothes there was no way she could easily blend into the crowd.

'Relax, Fliss. I know how you hate dressing up and being in the spotlight, but this will be fun, you'll see. Besides …' Fliss opened her eyes to look at her childhood friend as her voice grew teasing. 'Riding in the parade will be nothing compared to running your hands over a half-naked Hewitt. If you can touch a man built like that and keep your composure, you're a stronger woman than I am.'

Fliss narrowed her gaze. Taylor's grin was far too mischievous. 'This whole sexy fairy thing had better not be for Hewitt's benefit?'

Taylor's blue eyes rounded. 'Of course not. This is all for you. I might have promised Cressy you'd have a fun time.'

Taylor raised the hairspray and blasted the back of Fliss's hair. 'But now I've seen you with Hewitt, this is actually for the both of you. You need an incentive to stop fighting whatever it is between you. I could have burst into flames this morning and neither of you would have noticed.'

Fliss tugged the front of her snug tank top higher. What Taylor said was true. She had forgotten the hairdresser was there while her fingertips had memorised the shape and texture of Hewitt's bare shoulder. 'That's because I was being professional and assessing a patient.'

'What about when you'd finished assessing your patient?'

Fliss didn't reply. The heat and intensity of the brief look she and Hewitt had shared still made her toes curl.

Taylor spoke again. 'Just be ready for the thud when Edna and every other woman here faints seeing Hewitt and Tanner in their costumes.'

Before Fliss could question Taylor further, Jason walked over with Zoe. Fliss had invited the seven-year-old to also dress up as a fairy. She too wore all pink along with a tutu and a pair of glittery fairy wings.

Fliss touched the frothy pink tulle. 'I love your tutu.'

'Minty does as well. He's always trying to eat it.'

While everyone laughed, Fliss stared with envy at Jason's jeans and faded khaki work shirt. 'You're not dressing up?'

He grimaced. 'Not on your life. It's not compulsory.'

Fliss speared Taylor a sharp look but her friend only mouthed the words, 'sexy fairy'.

Talk then centred on how wonderful the horses looked. Minty sported a white felt unicorn horn attached to the brow band of his bridle. Taylor's mother, Sue, had put all her years of sewing sequins on dance costumes to good use by designing three floral horse wreaths. Minty's and Flame's wreaths had a pink floral theme while Taylor's gelding was decorated in purple and white. All horses had more flowers braided into their manes and tails.

Before everyone put on their helmets, Jason snapped photos on his phone. Fliss made sure she had a special one taken with Zoe. Zoe's tight hug and joyous smile made dressing up in fairy wings worth it.

Fliss slid on her helmet and grimaced while Taylor fussed with her hair to make sure it hung down her back in exactly the right way. Once in the saddle, she battled with her fairy wings that were determined to dig into her back. While she waited for Zoe and Taylor to mount, she looked around for Hewitt.

It was no surprise she didn't know where he was. Ever since her up-close-and-personal shoulder assessment he'd hung out with Tanner. While she'd missed him on their morning trail ride, their time apart had given her much needed space to collect herself. She was supposed to be making sure things didn't progress between them. Her grip on the reins tightened. Even if her fingers could still feel the hard ridges packed beneath his smooth, warm skin.

The hum of conversation around the rodeo ground quietened down. Fliss looked across to where two riders appeared from behind the kitchen block. Arrow's palomino coat gleamed in the afternoon sunlight but it wasn't the gelding that held her attention or his rider. Fliss could only focus on one man … Hewitt.

The cowboys rode bareback, dressed in white linen shirts and green-plaid kilts. But it wasn't only what they wore that held everyone silent, it was the way they carried themselves, broad-shouldered and proud. It wasn't hard to imagine either Hewitt or Tanner as real Highland Scottish warriors.

Taylor sighed. 'Now that's what I call an entrance … and a to-die-for costume.'

Fliss could only nod.

'I wonder …'

Fliss cut off Taylor's question about what they'd be wearing under their kilts.

'It would be rugby shorts. That's what Hewitt wore in his swag last night.'

Taylor arched a delicate eyebrow. 'To think all I was doing was falling asleep. Remind me to stay awake tonight.'

Fliss changed the subject. 'No wonder you said Edna would be impressed.'

Even as Fliss watched, Edna rushed forwards with Bethany following more slowly behind. The pair had come to see the parade costumes but Edna didn't seem to be looking at anyone but Hewitt and Tanner. She couldn't hear what was being said but when Edna introduced Hewitt to Bethany and he gave her a slow smile, the tall girl smiled in return. Edna spent the conversation looking between Hewitt and Tanner and fanning her face with her hand.

Fliss frowned across at Taylor. 'Those costumes should come with a health warning. I hope Edna doesn't actually faint.'

'We both know Hewitt and Tanner could wear sacks and the effect would be the same. Just as well Denham isn't here too.' Taylor grinned. 'Don't look so worried—once Hewitt sees you I guarantee he won't be looking at anyone else.'

Fliss didn't comment. The normally moody and withdrawn Bethany stood beside Hewitt. Had she actually just flicked her long blonde hair?

Fliss swung Flame around so she could no longer see Bethany or Hewitt. Zoe rode over, her tutu flouncing as Minty trotted.

'Dad says we'll head off now and meet you in town. Mum's there with Janet and I want to show them Minty's costume.'

'Okay. I'll see you and your very cute unicorn soon.'

They blew each other a kiss.

A horse walked up beside Flame. Fliss turned, expecting to see Taylor. Instead it was Hewitt. Behind him, Taylor gave a cheeky wave as she rode away with Tanner.

Mind blank, Fliss could only stare. The white ghillie shirt showed off the deep tan of his skin while the lace-up front did little to hide the strong contours of his collarbones.

Apart from the flicker of a muscle in his jaw, he didn't appear to notice the way she was dressed. His grey gaze met hers.

'So how are you holding up?'

'Good, but I'm not sure how I'll go with these wings if the breeze gets any stronger.'

He smiled and reached into his saddlebag for his phone. 'Can I get a picture for Lizzie? She's been pestering me for the last hour.'

Fliss nodded. Feeling a little self-conscious, she turned Flame sideways so she wouldn't have to look directly into Hewitt's eyes or the camera. She patted Flame's neck and heard the click of Hewitt's phone.

'You make a beautiful fairy, Fliss.'

She swallowed. Hewitt's compliment shouldn't mean so much. 'Thanks. It's all Lizzie's idea. Even though Taylor went rogue on my hair and must have used a can of hairspray.'

Hewitt's attention briefly rested on her hair and the loose curls Taylor had created with rags. Fliss thought she caught a flash of something in his eyes before he looked down to slip his phone inside his saddlebag. He dipped his head towards the stream of costumed riders that were leaving the rodeo ground. 'Shall we?'

'So how did you avoid being an elf?' she asked as they rode side by side. 'I thought that was what Lizzie had planned?'

'It was, until Quinn flooded the sandpit. He hated the idea and thought it too babyish.'

With each step the horses took, the early morning's awkwardness dissolved. Even though Hewitt didn't quite meet her eyes, their conversation flowed. They joined the other riders and became part of the riot of colour around them.

The three tearaway Ridley boys were dressed as ghoulish pirates and dashed around on their horses, brandishing plastic swords. Tanner followed more slowly, his pace hampered by a group of laughing cowgirls dressed in wedding dresses. A nearby group of riders wore animal onesies and another group were dressed as superheroes. A white horse had large black dots painted on her to look like a dalmatian, while a chestnut gelding had yellow markings to resemble a giraffe.

To Fliss's surprise, she enjoyed the ride through Woodlea's Main Street. People gathered on the footpaths and came out of the shops to see the parade. She waved to Will and Judith, old family friends who'd given a home to Juno's brother. Their farm had been hit by a mini tornado last summer but they now had a new garden growing in memory of the son they'd lost in an overseas skiing accident.

Tourists who'd come to see the town's yarn-bombing took photos of the riders as they passed. Toddlers sitting in prams clapped their hands while dogs barked from where they were tied around lampposts or stood next to their owners. Fliss gave a special wave to where Kellie and Janet sat on a bench. Kellie waved in return as she rubbed her pregnant stomach. Zoe had already ridden past in a group of excited little riders.

Hewitt left Fliss's side to help a woman whose horse spooked at the flap of the flag outside the craft shop. While the young horse fussed and shied, Garnet stayed calm, even when the horse cannoned into her. Fliss could see why Hewitt and Garnet made an effective pickup team when the rodeo action went from fast to hairy in under a second.

The two elder Ridley boys took Hewitt's place beside her. From the glances they snuck at her shirt, they weren't checking out her fairy wings. By fair means or foul, now she had their attention, she'd talk to them about quad bike safety. Last night around the fire she'd overheard their conversation about doing circle-work in the mud. She'd almost completed her safety talk about wearing helmets when Hewitt appeared. One look into his steel-grey eyes and the two teenage redheads moved on.

Hewitt didn't say anything as he resumed his place next to her. But as she snuck a glance at his profile she noticed the tight line of his jaw. The leather lacing on his shirt had loosened to reveal more of his tanned throat. She looked away before he could catch her staring. She was as bad as the Ridley boys.

All too soon the lead riders turned towards the rodeo ground and the parade through town ended. Once back at camp, Fliss slid from Flame's saddle. As her feet touched the ground, her fairy wings snagged on the saddle. She twisted, trying to see where she was caught.

'Hold on.' Hewitt dismounted and came to her side.

She stayed still. She'd planned to send the fancy fairy wings home with Hewitt for Lizzie and didn't want to tear the delicate pink fabric.

Hewitt stepped in close and she breathed in the faint scent of cedar. 'You're hooked on the saddlebag clip.'

'Maybe the safest thing to do is to take them off.' She removed her helmet and dragged a hand through her stiff hair that had begun to itch. 'They're pinned on the inside of my shirt.'

She didn't know for sure but she thought Hewitt hesitated before he gathered her hair and draped it over her shoulder. The simple action rekindled the intense need that had flooded her when she'd inspected his shoulder. Her nails bit into her palms as she readied herself for his touch.

But he removed the first pin without brushing her skin. 'One done.' His deep voice sounded close to her ear.

'Thanks.' She sought for something to say. 'Edna finally introduced Bethany to you.'

'She did. Bethany wasn't quite what I was expecting.'

Fliss wished she could see his face. His casual tone didn't reveal if this was a good or bad thing. For some reason it mattered if he'd felt a connection to the willowy blonde. 'People often say that since she looks more like Noel than Edna. She's quite pretty.'

Hewitt didn't answer straight away. 'I guess she is, if I was a blondes man.'

Fliss felt the wings detach from her shirt. As she turned, Hewitt handed them to her.

His smile was relaxed as he lifted his arm and brushed her hair from her shoulder. As it slid to fall down her back, he trailed a curl through his fingers. 'I happen to be partial to brunettes, even if their hair does feel like Garnet's hay.'

Fliss reined in the surge in her hormones. Hewitt didn't mean anything by his teasing words. He was relaxed and having fun on the trail ride, just like she was. He knew nothing could start between them. 'Taylor will be most distressed to hear her best work compared to a horse's breakfast.'

'I'm sure she'll survive.'

His husky chuckle lifted the hairs on Fliss's nape and she fought to keep her breathing even.

His thumb brushed her cheek. 'There'll be a rush for the showers, so if you want to de-fairy now's the time.'

His fingers lingered on her skin. Their lighthearted banter had ended. Eyes slate-grey and hooded, he stared at her with an intensity that fuelled her own deep needs. It was either leave now or kiss Hewitt in the very public rodeo ground where rumours could build faster than a bushfire.

She swallowed and slowly nodded. 'I do.'

The corner of his mouth curved before his arm lowered and he took a step away. 'Sensible choice. I'll unsaddle Flame.'

For the second day in a row, Hewitt awoke to the chorus of dawn birdsong but, unlike yesterday, he'd had a restful night's sleep. The pain in his shoulder had dulled to an ache.

In the gloom he could just make out Fliss's tousled dark head as she slept to his right.

Yesterday, after she'd examined his shoulder, he'd kept his distance. But he may as well have stayed glued to her side. Tanner had noticed his preoccupation with her whereabouts. At lunch the drover had brought him a coffee and sat on the fallen tree beside him. He'd looked across to where Fliss was chatting with a grey-haired farmer and his wife.

'Fliss and Cressy are the sisters I never had. I'd do anything for them and I'm not the only one. No one wants to see Fliss hurt. She's been through a lot these past six months.'

Hewitt didn't misunderstand the message. 'I'm not here to hurt her.'

'I know … but the way you two look at each other will either bring happiness or heartbreak. People already think highly enough of you to not want you hurt either.'

Hewitt had only nodded. Knowing people watched them was both stifling and liberating. Fliss hated dressing up and drawing attention to herself so the last thing she'd do in public was anything inappropriate. The knowledge had reassured him and sent him straight back to her side. His self-control would hold as long as it wasn't under threat.

Fliss stirred. Light crept across the sky and he could now see her features and the curve of her lashes while she slept.

When he'd caught sight of her in her pink jodhpurs and top that fitted like a second skin, he couldn't have stayed away if he tried. The memory of the Ridley boys admiring her curves still triggered a rush of possessiveness and protectiveness in him. He felt things for her that he'd never felt for another woman.

It'd been a huge risk to remove her wings. But he made sure he didn't touch her and kept the mood light for as long as he could. And it had worked. They'd shared a moment, but it hadn't escalated into something beyond their control. He'd meant what he said to

Tanner. He was serious about not hurting her. He dressed in the clothes he'd put inside his swag to keep dry from the dew and, after a last look at a sleeping Fliss, headed off to help with breakfast.

As the bacon and eggs queue shuffled past he kept a close watch until he saw her. From where she stood next to Taylor, she looked over to the barbeque area and gave him a quick wave. As soon as he lifted a hand in return, she glanced away. He too felt the stare of curious eyes. He laughed at the joke of the farmer cooking beside him, making sure he didn't look at her again.

Today offered a rare opportunity. While on the trail ride, he and Fliss existed in a bubble. Surrounded by people, nothing could happen between them. So for now he could relax and lower his guard. They could simply hang out and enjoy each other's company. Tonight it would be back to Bundara, where it would just be the two of them, and his control would have to be watertight.

Once the breakfast area had been tidied, the horses were saddled for a final time. The last activity of the riding fundraiser involved a trek along the stock routes to a creek where both horses and riders could swim. The weather had cooperated. The sun shone steady and bright and humidity hung heavy in the air. Thanks to the unseasonal rain, a usually small watercourse now provided a series of safe and sedate waterholes.

Fliss and Taylor rode slightly ahead of Hewitt. They looked more comfortable now, their muscles having grown accustomed to being in the saddle. Beneath the collar of Fliss's blue cotton shirt, he glimpsed thin black straps tied around her neck.

Today Taylor had brought her camera to take photos to send to Rory and her London friends. When they reached the yellow canola crop they stopped to allow Taylor to take a photo. Three riders overtook them. The end rider's horse had a red ribbon on its tail, signifying that the horse could kick. While they waited to let a safe distance open up between them and the group ahead, Fliss smiled across at him. Warmth that had nothing to do with the spring sunshine settled into his chest.

They continued to follow the stock route only to stop while Taylor snapped a shot of grey kangaroos resting beneath the spreading canopy of a gum tree.

She flashed Fliss and Hewitt an apologetic grin. 'I promise this will be the last photo.'

It was, until she saw an echidna walking on stubby legs around the edge of a clearing.

'I *have* to get this picture.'

Hewitt and Fliss swapped looks and followed. At the back of the clearing, parked between two yellow-tinged wattle trees, was a white ute with a dog crate on the back. An assortment of small and large dogs were packed inside. It wasn't unusual for hunters to have a variety of pigging dogs.

The closer Taylor rode to get a photo of the echidna, the more frenzied the dogs' barking. Hewitt looked around for the driver but there was no sign of anyone nearby. The echidna disappeared into the undergrowth and Taylor left the clearing. As they rode away, Hewitt turned to take a final look at the ute.

The sound of the pigging dogs was soon replaced by the rush of water.

'I've never seen this creek so full,' Fliss said, as Flame walked into the steady flow. Her hooves clattered on the smooth, round pebbles before she lowered her head to drink.

Garnet and Taylor's gelding also took a drink before they continued on to find a suitable place to swim. When they arrived at the first waterhole, the younger riders were already in the water with their horses. Close to the bank, Jason stood holding Minty and another grey pony. Water reached up to their withers. Both ponies appeared content and Hewitt suspected it was because their stomachs were full of carrots.

Zoe waved to Fliss and called out, 'Look at me!'

They watched as Zoe and Alice climbed onto the ponies' rumps and, holding hands, jumped into the water together. Minty tossed his head at the brief splash before turning his head to see where his little rider was.

Fliss laughed. 'That looks like so much fun.'

Hewitt led the way along the willow-lined creek to a wider waterhole. Here horses dozed beneath gum trees or grazed on the creek bank while their riders swam or sunbathed.

A rope had been tied to a low, strong branch and the Ridley boys were at the head of the line of teenagers waiting to swing out over the creek. Tanner stood with a group of committee members supervising.

'I can't look,' Fliss said, voice strained as the eldest Ridley performed a somersault into the water.

Hewitt slowed Garnet so Fliss drew level with him. 'It's okay. Tanner would have checked the water for any submerged logs or rocks.' Hewitt paused as Tanner frowned and shook his head at the Ridley boy as he surfaced. 'See ... Tanner's saying no somersaults.'

Fliss nodded but her tense shoulders didn't relax. She turned Flame away from the waterhole.

Taylor glanced at Hewitt. 'You two go on to where it's a little quieter. I'll work on my tan here with the girls.'

Hewitt followed the fresh hoof prints of others who'd gone in search of a more peaceful place. Fliss rode behind him. But when the creek widened and the water deepened, there was no one else to be seen.

Flame seemed to know why they were there and headed straight for the waterhole.

A smile broke through Fliss's seriousness. 'Just a second. We have to check it's safe and I have to get your saddle off.'

While Fliss unsaddled Flame, Hewitt busied himself removing Garnet's tack. He didn't need a bridle and a bit to ride. He stripped off his jeans down to his board shorts and, using his good arm, tugged his shirt over his head.

Fliss removed her jeans and shirt and draped them over Flame's saddle she'd sat on the creek bank. Sunlight played over the lightly tanned skin of her toned arms and back. She added her pink trail ride cap to her pile of clothes. Her ponytail swung between her shoulder blades as she moved. Hewitt thought the black halter-neck swimmers she wore with black shorts were conservative, until she turned.

His mouth dried. Instead of being a solid colour, her swimsuit was a combination of opaque and sheer panels that did little to hide her full curves. He scanned the creek bank for a sign of other riders. Suddenly, being alone with Fliss didn't feel so safe.

She barely glanced at him before she led Flame over to a hollow. Using the bank for leverage, she jumped onto Flame's bare back.

Garnet followed him to the water's edge and he focused on assessing the waterhole for any obstacles or hazards. The creek bed gently sloped and didn't fall away into a sudden drop. The stony, sandy bottom was also free from mud.

'Everything look okay?' Fliss asked to his left.

'Yes, in you go. Garnet and I'll follow.'

Flame walked into the water. When she stopped to splash with her front hoof, Fliss smiled and urged her forwards. 'No, you don't. Thanks to my old pony I know exactly what that means. We're here to swim together, not for you to roll and ditch me.'

Flame continued into the creek. When Fliss's legs and waist disappeared below the water line, the mare began to swim. With her head above the surface, she slowly circled until she found her footing in the shallow depths. As soon as Fliss's waist and legs came into view, Flame swung around ready to go swimming again.

Fliss called over her shoulder. 'It's lovely in.'

Hewitt swung onto Garnet and they headed into the water. Soon she was swimming, her ears forwards and movements sure. He made sure they kept to their section of the creek. Horses' hind legs stretched backwards when they swam and he didn't want either Flame or Fliss to be kicked.

Fliss's laughter carried over the waterhole as Garnet blew bubbles before sticking out her tongue to lick the water. 'She loves it.'

'She's always been a water baby.'

He wasn't surprised his voice sounded hoarse. He glanced at the empty creek bank. A dry and fully dressed Fliss pushed his self-control to the brink. A wet, semi-naked Fliss was guaranteed to send him over the edge.

A splash sounded. He swung around. Fliss was in the deeper section of the waterhole while Flame headed to shore. He turned Garnet towards where Fliss treaded water and glanced over his shoulder to check Flame wouldn't bolt. But all the chestnut mare did was leave the creek to graze on the spring grass at the top of the bank.

He reached Fliss and offered her his right hand. 'Like a ride back?'

'Thanks. This water's colder than it looks.'

Just like when he'd pulled her to her feet when she'd been mobbed by the puppies, her hand settled around his wrist. He took her weight and drew her up behind him onto Garnet.

Fliss's hands rested lightly on his waist. Her warm breath fanned his shoulder as her laughter wrapped around him. 'I don't know what happened. Flame went one way and I went the other.'

The creek level deepened. Garnet sank as she swam, the movement causing Fliss to slide into him. He didn't miss her gasp or the way her chest pressed against his back. The water dragged at them, causing her grip to tighten on his waist.

Every breath she took increased the contact between them. Every breath he took eroded a little more of his self-control until there was nothing left but the desperate need to kiss the woman behind him. It wasn't even a conscious thought that prompted him to loosen the grip of his knees and turn towards her. Garnet surged forwards, sending them both into the water. His feet hadn't touched the creek bed before Fliss was flush against him, her hands in his hair and her mouth on his.

Nothing had prepared him for the feel of holding her. Nothing mattered more than kissing her. Never had a woman fitted so perfectly against him. Never had the world seemed so complete. There was no more guilt, loss or pain. All he could feel was heat and a connection so intense it consumed them both.

It took Hewitt a moment to realise their ragged breaths weren't the only thing he could hear. Words carried on the breeze, along with the sound of horses' hooves.

He spoke against Fliss's lips. 'We're about to have company.'

She stiffened and he thought she'd move away, but instead her fingertips traced the whiskered line of his jaw. She kissed him, a swift, molten kiss, before moving backwards to stand an arm's length away. Without her warmth, the chill of the water seeped into his skin.

He saw the moment when reality returned. Her hazel eyes lost their dazed look and their golden lustre dulled.

'Did I hurt your shoulder?'

'No.'

Three riders stopped on the creek bank to remove their saddles. Fliss didn't head for the shore where Flame and now Garnet were grazing.

Fliss stared at him. Then, under water, out of sight of the newcomers, her hand linked with his. In the tremble of her fingers he could feel the same yearnings and the same riot of emotion that shook his own hands. He ran his thumb over her palm to comfort her.

'Hewitt, that wasn't … a good idea.'

'I know.'

'It can't happen again.'

'I know. It won't.'

A horse and rider entered the creek. It would soon be obvious that he and Fliss were not having a casual chat between friends. Still she stared at him, her lips parted and eyes overbright. Then, at the last possible moment, she slid her hand free.

CHAPTER
12

'So how was the trail ride?' Cressy's curious voice sounded down the phone line.

Fliss silenced a sigh. What her sister really wanted to know was how things went with Hewitt. Edna's matchmaking was proving contagious. The Woodlea grapevine had been buzzing about how gorgeous Hewitt and Tanner had looked in their Highlander costumes.

'It was … fun.'

Heat suffused her cheeks. 'Fun' didn't come close to describing her kiss with Hewitt. Until now she'd been living a lie. She wasn't a slow-burn girl at all. If they ever went on a first date, she was ditching her no-kissing rule. She was kissing him *before* they left for the date.

'That's great. Tanner said everyone enjoyed themselves and the Ridley boys didn't cause much trouble. The committee also reached their fundraising target.'

'Yes, Janet's thrilled. She's hoping the upcoming ball will raise the final amount needed for the portable ultrasound. Thanks again for looking after Miss Molly and her babies.'

'No worries. Phil did most of the feeding and puppy playing. Denham and I ended up staying a second night up north. Between Denham buying cows with bucking blood and Tanner buying young horses to train, there soon won't be any room left on either Glenmore or Claremont. Reggie will have to come and live with you.'

'I'd love to have him. I'm planning to put in a veggie garden so he'd never miss his daily carrot-fix. I'm with you … I don't know what all the fuss is about. There's not a mean bone in that massive body of his.'

'Try telling Denham that. He has no doubts that Reggie's genetics will produce champion bucking bulls. Speaking of Reggie … as gorgeous as Hewitt might look in a kilt, he still has to pass the Reggie test, otherwise he's not man enough for you.'

'Just as well I'm not looking for a man because Hewitt will never meet Reggie let alone feed him carrots to pass the test.'

'I wouldn't be so sure about that. Denham and Tanner are itching to see Garnet and Hewitt in action in their rodeo yards. Reggie's paddock's only the next one over.'

'Hewitt riding in the boys' yards will never happen. A slow trail ride was okay but fast and high-risk riding … Hewitt would have to see that as a bad idea.'

Fliss realised the foolishness of what she'd said and joined in with Cressy's laughter.

'Okay,' she added. 'I take that back. Hewitt's male and a cowboy so he probably wouldn't think it was a bad idea. I would.'

'So would I. His body's been through enough. So how's the DNA sleuthing coming along? Do you need any more of Mum's boxes?'

'No. I already went through the boxes you have and there wasn't anything but old books. The sleuthing's going slowly. I'm hoping there'll soon be some unknown names that keep cropping up. The answer to who my father is has to be in there somewhere. I'd love to pick Lewis's brains but he still has enough on his mind.'

'If you want any help or want to run names by me, you know where I am. I'll still give you Mum's books. You were always the reader.'

'Thanks. I'd like to have them. And Cressy ... thanks for not letting all of this ... come between us.'

'Don't mention it. You are my sister and always will be, no matter who your father ends up being. Mum would have had her reasons for things working out the way they have. I just hope one day we'll have some answers.'

'So do I. I'd better go. I can see Hewitt heading over.'

'Can you now?'

'Yes.' Fliss shook her head at her sister's intrigued tone. 'Have you been talking to Taylor? She's determined to push Hewitt and me together. I'm never borrowing her clothes again or letting her near me with hairspray.'

'She was very proud of her sexy fairy creation. But no, it was Ella.'

'As you know better than anyone, any sort of relationship is the last thing Hewitt and I need right now.'

'I do know,' Cressy's words sobered. 'But I also know the two of you deserve to find happiness.'

Hewitt's knock sounded on the front screen door.

Fliss swallowed. She lived in hope she'd one day find the happiness Cressy and Denham shared. 'Maybe. I'll talk to you tomorrow.'

She ended the call and ran her hands through her loose hair. It was a little late to be self-conscious about what she wore and how she looked. Hewitt would be used to seeing her at her rural best, even if Edna wasn't.

Fliss had spoken the truth to Cressy. Allowing emotion and attraction to lead her down a road she wasn't ready to travel was only asking for trouble. As for Hewitt, he needed to heal so he could get back to being there for the twins and family he cared so deeply about. So she'd done the sensible thing after their kiss and established that giving in to the chemistry between them hadn't been the best idea. Hewitt had agreed. He wasn't a man to go back on his word. There'd be no more heady kisses. So why did she feel so unsettled?

She opened the screen door and hoped her smile wasn't strained. Her senses registered the clean scent of Hewitt's skin and the fitted stretch of blue across his chest even before she'd stepped outside. What she hadn't noticed were the puppies milling around his boots. Tiny nails clipped on the polished floorboards as two fluffy bodies ran past her.

'Not again. I've only just cleaned up the last lot of puppy piddle. You two stop right there.'

Hewitt's husky laughter followed her as she sped down the hallway to scoop up the runaways. Once back outside, she put the puppies on the veranda floorboards. They started growling and wrestling over the top of her bare feet.

Hewitt's laughter deepened. 'All we need now is for Juno to visit.'

'I think even Juno would have met her match with these two. Whereas this one'—Fliss bent to pick up a smaller puppy sitting on her haunches looking up at her—'is a sweetheart.'

Hewitt stroked the puppy's tiny head. 'Yes, Poppy isn't as high-maintenance as her two brothers.'

Fliss looked at Hewitt's tanned, well-shaped hand. A hand that only yesterday had trailed heat over the sensitive skin of her lower back.

Breathing uneven, she waited for Hewitt to finish patting Poppy and then took a step back to set the pup down. Now she knew what it felt like to have Hewitt's mouth on hers, she wasn't sure she could trust herself when around him.

Hewitt put his hands in his jeans pockets.

'Ava asked if it was okay to bring the kids to stay this weekend? Lizzie's desperate to see the puppies and to meet you. Quinn apparently also needs some Uncle Hewy time.'

'That sounds wonderful. Tell Ava she can stay as long as she wants. I've plenty of room.' Fliss paused to look over her shoulder at the long hallway. Her drafty guest bathroom was stuck in a time warp and the bedrooms only partially renovated. 'Actually, maybe you should stay over here? Ava and the twins would be much more comfortable in the stables.'

Hewitt's gaze briefly dropped to Fliss's mouth and when his eyes met hers they were a gunmetal grey. 'That mightn't be such a sensible plan.'

The trip in her pulse at the thought of Hewitt sleeping across the hall confirmed it wasn't one of her better ideas. But her anxiety didn't listen. She bit her bottom lip. 'Maybe not ... but you've seen what state the house is in. At least Ava will have reliable hot water over in the stables.'

'True. I'll let Ava know. The twins will be excited.'

'It will be great to meet them all.'

He slid his hands free from his pockets and half turned. 'I'll get back to working on the chook pen.'

'Thank you. Cressy has some hens I can have, and Meredith has a rooster, so it might be fun to get them while the twins are here. Lizzie and Quinn can help with the names.'

The warmth of Hewitt's smile stayed with Fliss as she settled into her chair in her home office. She soon lost track of time as she concentrated on coloured DNA segment comparisons and tables of common matches. After printing out and adding another family tree to her pin board, she stood to relax her tight muscles. She eyed off the neat piles of photo albums that were stacked on the bookshelf along with her mother's scrapbooks. She'd been through everything, twice, and there was nothing to connect her mother with a man from her Sydney life. She and Cressy had also taken out all the family photographs from their frames to check there wasn't a photo tucked behind them. What had she missed?

In a perfect world she'd have known more about her mother's family. But her mother's parents hadn't ever enjoyed travelling past the Blue Mountains so had been shadowy, remote figures in Fliss's childhood. When Fliss had gone away to Sydney to boarding school, they'd no longer been alive. Her mother had had an older sister but she'd lived in New York and had never had children. Aunty Kath had passed away while Fliss had been in her final year of school.

Filled with a sudden thought, Fliss headed for the kitchen. Her mother and Aunty Kath had often swapped recipes. Fliss switched on the kettle before going into the pantry where cookbooks were lined in a neat row on the middle shelf. When her mother had taught Fliss and Cressy to cook, she'd had an old family cookbook she'd often made notes in. The well-loved book was far more than a collection of handwritten and pasted-in recipes she'd started before her married life. Her mother would make notes about where a dish might have been eaten and who had cooked it.

Fliss ignored the kettle as it clicked off and opened the dog-eared pages. The recipes were all categorised in different sections. Soon she was lost in the memories of birthday breakfasts, campfire dinners and the feel of her mother's arm around her while she licked cupcake batter off the beaters. On the second page of the cake section, Fliss skimmed the recipe for an orange and poppy-seed cake. Heart racing, she re-read her mother's note at the bottom.

Valda Ryan's never-fail recipe. Beach picnic. Patrick's mother.

Leaving the cookbook open, Fliss sped into her office. This was the first male name she'd come across and she was sure she'd included Ryan in the list of unfamiliar names. The recipe was early on in the cake section which indicated it was recorded in her mother's younger years. A beach picnic was also highly likely to have taken place near where her mother had lived in Sydney. Fliss scanned the list on her pin board and discovered the Ryan name near the top.

Filled with a new sense of purpose, she searched her matches on the DNA website for the names Patrick Ryan and Valda Ryan. When no matches appeared, she wasn't surprised. It would be too lucky to have their personal DNA in the system. Next she plugged in the more general Ryan surname. Three pages of matches who had the Ryan surname in their family tree appeared. The closest match was an extremely high fourth to sixth cousin connection.

Fliss's excitement waned, but her determination grew as she worked her way through the names. Some matches she could eliminate as there were exact family tree matches but under a different surname. She ruled out any match she shared with Cressy. Some matches were also American based so weren't relevant. But as Fliss progressed, her list of possible Ryan links grew.

Back stiff, and in need of a sugar fix, Fliss investigated the final Ryan connection on the first page. Once done, she made her way into the kitchen. While the kettle boiled for the second time, she tilted her head and dug her fingers into the knot in her neck. The trigger point in her trapezius muscle refused to release.

Beyond her kitchen window her once neat garden resembled a battle zone. Cressy had been right. The puppies had wreaked havoc.

Discarded and chewed sticks littered the ground. Tennis balls lay scattered amongst the black plastic garden pots she'd need to put away on a higher shelf. But the mess and disorder didn't fill her with worry. The chaos outside reminded her that life was to be lived and enjoyed.

Two fluffy bodies played tug of war with a rag rope she'd plaited after watching an internet tutorial, while three other puppies had claimed a veranda step each and were stretched out so the sun could warm their bellies. Molly was at the back garden gate keeping Hewitt company while he rebuilt the chook pen.

Beyond the post-and-rail fence was a path that led to a small shed and wire-enclosed pen. The farmer's friend weeds inside the chook pen had been up to Hewitt's chest when he'd dragged them out. At the door of the chook pen grew low clusters of yellow and black weeds. Her mother used to swear that the capeweed flowers would lie down beneath the lawnmower to avoid being cut. The next day the daisy-like blooms would wave to her as cheerful as ever.

The electric kettle came to a boil. She went to make her tea when something caught her eye. Uncertainty held her still. A longish stick hadn't been at the edge of the garden earlier. Even as she stared, trying to decide if it was a snake, a black-and-white blur raced across the garden. Eyes fixed on the object, Molly's tense body remained low to the ground.

Hands shaking, Fliss reached for her phone on the kitchen bench. *Please let Hewitt have his mobile on him.* A text would be quicker than running over to him. Fingers refusing to cooperate, she misspelt snake and then managed to type where it was.

She grabbed the snake kit from her emergency shelf and ran down the hallway. The screen door banged behind her as she gathered the sleepy puppies and placed them safely inside. It wasn't until she pulled the front door closed that she realised one puppy was missing.

Hewitt was already through the back garden gate and following Molly when his phone chimed. There was only one explanation for the border collie's deep growl and dash across the lawn. He didn't bother to check his phone. The relief in Fliss's strained face when she saw him confirmed what had been in the message.

He quickly assessed the yard. Fliss had already taken the puppies that were near the house inside. With her babies no longer under threat, he could only hope Molly would maintain the distance between herself and the snake. He glanced at Fliss, hoping she wouldn't call the border collie away. Any sound could distract her. But Fliss stood on the veranda edge, her hands around the white post and her lips pressed together. A plastic box sat near her feet.

The snake faced Molly, its upper body lifting off the ground in an S-shaped coil. Small and flattened, its head was poised to strike. Molly growled but didn't move closer. After what seemed like a lifetime, the snake's head lowered. Sunlight glanced off glossy, scaled skin as it turned and slid away in burnished ripples across the yard. The tension aching in Hewitt's shoulders eased. The reptile would soon reach the undergrowth on the other side of the wooden fence.

A flash of black-and-white kickstarted his adrenaline. Poppy ambled along the fence line, cutting off the snake's escape route. The snake slowed, assessing the new risk. Molly lowered herself to the ground and slunk forwards, readying herself to protect her baby.

Poppy needed to be distracted long enough to allow the snake to pass. He whistled softly.

The sound was enough. Poppy stopped to look at him. The snake took advantage of the gap that opened up between them and slithered beneath the fence and towards the creek.

Molly raced over to Poppy and after sniffing her to check she was okay, led her over to Hewitt.

He ruffled the top of Molly's head. 'Everyone's okay.'

Fliss opened the screen door and puppies spilled down the veranda steps. Molly went to assess each one before lying on the lawn, her attention fixed on where the snake had disappeared.

The sight of the puppies climbing all over their mother didn't bring the usual smile to Fliss's face. Instead she glanced at him, face pale. 'I think I need to sit.'

She sank onto the top veranda step.

He collected two camp chairs from near the fire pit and set them up in the veranda shade not far from Molly and the puppies. 'You'll be more comfortable here.'

'Thanks.'

After Fliss slid into the closest chair he scooped up two puppies and settled them into her lap. As if sensing her tension the puppies snuggled into her arms instead of making it their mission to chew her fingers. The strain in her eyes faded as she ran her hand over their soft coats.

'Box ticked,' she said, words tighter than usual. 'The first snake of the season.'

'Believe it or not, they want to avoid us as much as we want to avoid them.'

Fliss shuddered. 'At least no one was bitten ... I've seen what a snake bite can do. One summer Cressy and I lost our childhood Jack Russell to a snake bite.'

Hewitt picked up a puppy who was gnawing on the toe of his boot. With the puppy wriggling in his arms he wasn't so tempted to reach over and draw Fliss against him. He now understood the personal reasons behind her aversion to snakes.

'I'm sorry to hear that.'

'Thanks. It was a long time ago now but I'll never forget how fast it happened and how brave little Midge was.' She scanned the garden beds. 'I think I'll plant more geraniums.'

'You could get some guinea fowl. They're supposed to deter snakes.'

'I'll ask Ella—she'll know where I can get some.'

'With your lawn now mowed and the garden beds tidy, the snakes will realise Bundara isn't as inviting as it once was.'

'I hope so.' She paused while one of the puppies in her arms jumped to the ground. 'I'd better get back to my computer. Analysing DNA is like going down a rabbit hole. I have to remember to come out to eat.'

'Come over to the stables for dinner. I'll cook.'

Brow furrowed, she studied him. 'I thought we were making sure what happened at the river doesn't happen again?'

'We're both mature grown-ups. Fliss … I promise I've not come here to cause trouble or hurt you.'

'Okay.' Her eyes searched his. 'Dinner does sound nice. Can I bring anything?'

'No. I'm all sorted thanks to the shop we did on the way home from the trail ride.'

The puppy in Fliss's arms yawned and wriggled until its little head rested in the crook of her arm.

Hewitt stared at the tiny face that was all white except for a black eye that had earned him the name Patch. Still looking at the distinctive black marking, he put the puppy he was holding onto the ground.

'Hewitt, what is it?'

'Just a thought. Hold still while I take a photo of Patch's face to send to Ella.'

After he sent the photo to the vet, he glanced at Fliss. 'Who does that little face remind you of?'

'No one.'

'What about a dog we've seen lately?'

'But we haven't seen any border collies, have we? The only black-and-white dog, and I'm not even sure if it was that colour, was the one in the pigging ute we saw on the trail ride.'

'Exactly. It had a black patch around its right eye, too.'

Fliss shifted in her camp chair to take out her phone from her jeans pocket. 'Taylor took photos of that echidna. I wonder if she took one of the dogs?'

While Fliss talked to Taylor, Hewitt texted Ella to see if there were any photos of missing Max.

Fliss ended her call and then her phone whooshed as pictures came through. She placed Patch beside Molly, left her chair and leaned over Hewitt to show him her phone. She appeared unaware that her heavy hair slid over her shoulder to touch his shirt.

'You're right.' She examined the photo, voice excited. 'Look, there he is. Right up the back. You can't see much but that's a marking just like Patch's.'

Hewitt touched the photo to move it higher. 'And there's the ute's rego number.'

Fliss met his eyes and smiled. 'This dog could very well be Max.'

'It could be.'

Hewitt forced his hands to rest on his thighs. All he could smell was gardenias and all he could think about was how soft and sensual Fliss's lips were. She was so close all he had to do was thread his fingers into her hair and turn her mouth to his.

Fliss spoke again. 'I'll send this photo to Ella. She can pass it on to the owner's daughter and the police they've been dealing with. I'll send it to Daniel at the police station here.'

As if suddenly conscious of how close she was, she straightened. Colour painted her cheeks as she moved away. Hewitt took a deep, silent breath of relief.

'Hey, Miss Molly,' Fliss said as she bent to pat her. 'Hewitt might just have found your missing Max.'

Fliss's phone whooshed again and she read the text aloud. 'Ella says thanks and she'll keep us in the loop. I'd better head inside. DNA sleuthing calls. I'll look forward to dinner tonight.'

For the rest of the day Hewitt focused on rebuilding the chook pen as well as his self-control. If he was going to survive dinner with Fliss the emotions simmering inside him had to be tightly contained. Not only would they be alone, he now knew exactly how it felt to have her pressed against him. Holding Fliss once would never be enough.

Once the afternoon shadows had lengthened, he showered and made his mother's signature spaghetti bolognaise. When the garlic bread was almost cooked and the rich aroma of spaghetti sauce filled the kitchen, he checked the wall clock. Fliss would be here soon.

Movement flickered in the living room window as Fliss left the main house. But instead of descending the veranda steps, she stopped to sit on the top one. Molly came to her side and Fliss slipped an arm around her.

Hewitt's first instinct was to stay where he was. Fliss wore a loose floral dress that left her smooth shoulders and arms bare.

One glimpse of her was all his testosterone needed to lurch into overdrive. But his second instinct was to sit with her. He took down two wine glasses and filled them with red wine. This dinner was all about proving that things could remain relaxed and easy between them. And he'd start now.

He collected the small antipasto platter sitting on the bench and headed across the garden.

Fliss greeted him with a smile. 'Lucky for you and that platter a certain six little ratbags are in the shed.'

He handed her a glass of wine before setting the antipasto platter between them. 'Yes, it would have been the shortest pre-dinner drinks in history.'

He sat on the top step, making sure a careful distance existed between them.

'This all looks great.' She cut a piece of soft cheese. 'I was coming over but ... this sounds silly ... I just wanted to spend as much time with Molly as I can.'

'That doesn't sound silly at all.'

'So where did you learn to be so handy in the kitchen?'

'My mother. She was determined Brody and I learn to cook. Brody wasn't interested but I enjoyed learning the recipes that had been passed down by her mother and grandmother. Also, I live by myself so if I don't cook, I starve.'

'You mustn't live far away from your parents and the twins?'

'I don't. Ava and the twins live in the cottage on Mayfield. Mum and Dad live in the main house. Years ago they bought the neighbouring farm and I live there.'

'Have you spoken to Lizzie and Quinn about visiting?'

'I have.' He took a swallow of wine. 'Lizzie's already told me what she's packed.'

'I'll need to think of some fun things we can do.'

'They'll be fine. Lizzie will play with the puppies and ask you dozens of questions while Quinn will follow me around like he used to do with Brody. The two of them were always in the shed fixing things.'

'It's nice to hear you talk about your brother. You seem more … at ease now.'

'It's still tough to talk about him but I am feeling a little more comfortable.'

He stared at the ridge he and Garnet had climbed. 'I've been able to say goodbye and to let go of some of my grief.' While the weight of his grief had lessened, the guilt that hounded him remained. 'Being here hasn't just been good for me. By not being at home to keep everything together it's allowed Mum and Ava to regain a sense of purpose. Mum's knitting again. Ava has put on weight and has been going to town at least once a week.' Hewitt frowned. 'The only person who hasn't benefited from me not being there is Dad. He refuses to leave the house.'

'Grief's a very personal thing. Everyone will have their own timetable.' She sipped her wine. 'It's also been good for me to have you here. I've left Bundara more times since you arrived than I had in the past six months. I have a garden littered with puppy toys that I couldn't have tolerated earlier and here I am looking forward to visitors.'

Hewitt grinned. 'Are you blaming me for your messy garden?'

Fliss returned his smile. 'Only for giving me the confidence to cope with chaos.'

'You don't need me to give you confidence. You're one of the most competent and knowledgeable people I know.' He hesitated, not wanting to ruin the relaxed mood between them. But the need to help her wouldn't let him remain silent. 'I know how hard it was for you to deal with Alice's finger. But the Fliss you were before

Caitlyn died is still the Fliss you are now. You can more than handle anything that comes your way. Not only that, you can handle it well.'

She stared at him, expression wary. 'You notice far too much.'

He matched her wry tone. 'I'm afraid it comes with the territory. I need to know what a rider, a horse or even a bull will do before they even think about doing it.'

Her lips tilted. 'It's nice to know you can read my body language as easily as you can a bull.'

'If it's any consolation, you're much easier to look at than a bull.'

Fliss raised her wine glass to his and clinked. 'Nice save, cowboy.'

Peace flowed through him. Sitting next to Fliss and just talking felt right. It wasn't only being at Bundara that was good for him. The beautiful woman beside him was, too.

CHAPTER

13

'Uncle Hewy,' Quinn called before he catapulted himself into Hewitt's arms and hugged his uncle as hard as he could.

Fliss blinked to clear her vision. There was something about a strong man being open about showing love and affection that stirred her emotions. It had been bad enough seeing Lizzie's beaming face when Hewitt had gathered her close and she'd kissed his cheek. Now seeing the depth of his bond with Quinn, her heart melted.

Ava crossed the lawn towards her. Hewitt's sister-in-law was tiny, too-thin tiny. But her blonde hair was thick and glossy and her skin possessed a healthy glow. The ring finger on her delicate left hand bore no wedding band.

'Thanks so much for having us to stay,' Ava said, her smile warm.

'It's my pleasure.' Fliss stepped forwards to hug her. She wasn't usually demonstrative with strangers but felt like she already knew Ava from their laptop chats.

'How was your trip?' Fliss asked as they turned to see Quinn sprint over to Ava's four-wheel drive to fetch a yellow and green toy tractor.

'Let's just say it will be nice to spend the next two days out of the car.'

Fliss nodded as Quinn bolted back towards his uncle. 'I can understand why your trip might've felt long.'

Lizzie came over to Ava and took hold of her mother's hand. The little girl stared at Fliss, expression cautious. From the amount of times they'd talked she was certain Lizzie wouldn't feel any shyness when they met face-to-face. But for all her confidence and bravado, Lizzie was still a young child who'd lost her father less than a year ago.

Fliss bent to talk to her. 'I've been looking forward to you staying and so have the puppies. They're sick of playing tug-o-war with me. Who would you like to meet first?'

A smile dawned in Lizzie's wide grey eyes. 'You're even prettier than on the computer, and much taller.' She put her small hand in Fliss's. 'Can I meet all of them?'

'You sure can.'

They'd taken two steps towards the garden shed when Quinn raced up to them. He thrust his tractor out for Fliss to see. The tractor was the same brand as the one pictured on his green and once white cap. She admired the toy's chipped green paintwork. 'I think your Uncle Hewitt had better book your tractor in for an oil change. It looks like it's ploughed lots of paddocks.'

Quinn's grin flashed before he ran away. Lizzie's hand tightened on hers.

'He likes you. He doesn't show anyone his tractor. Even Miss Annabelle at the Bush Mobile hasn't seen it.'

When they arrived at the garden shed, six puppies were jostling and yipping at the low wire panel Hewitt had constructed to keep them inside when the door was open. No sooner had Fliss lifted the panel than puppies rolled, slid and wriggled towards Lizzie. Fliss made sure the little girl didn't feel scared or overwhelmed. But Lizzie was fine. Giggling, she skipped over to the box of toys Fliss had left on the lawn. All six puppies followed and were soon chasing balls or chewing on the dog toys Lizzie dished out.

Fliss went to help Hewitt, Quinn and Ava unload the car. When all the bags were inside Hewitt and Quinn disappeared into the shed. Fliss gave Ava a tour of the renovated stables before offering her a cup of tea over in the main house.

Fliss made small talk while the kettle boiled but when they sat at the kitchen table, their china mugs in front of them, Ava's open expression turned serious.

'Fliss, I hope it's okay, but while we're alone I wanted to have a quick chat. We mightn't get another chance.'

'Absolutely. What's on your mind?'

'Firstly, I want to say thank you for having us this weekend and for giving Hewitt a place to stay. I was so worried about him but now it's almost like ... he's come back to us.'

Fliss nodded. Knowing how much Hewitt had been in pain made her throat ache.

'Secondly, I have something to tell him and I think it's best if he hears it while he's with you ... where he's got time and space to process things.'

'That makes sense.'

'It's not something bad. It's actually a happy thing, but it could be painful.'

Fliss stayed quiet, sensing Ava needed to say more.

'Brody came on a horse trek ride I was running and from that first moment he swept me off my feet. Before I knew it we were married and expecting twins. Life was complete. Then the cracks appeared.

I don't blame Brody. The twins weren't planned and fatherhood is demanding. But it soon became obvious Brody wasn't cut out to be a father.'

Ava stopped to trace a knot of wood in the table with her finger. 'It was Hewitt who'd stop to help when I was hanging out the washing. It was Hewitt who minded the twins so I could sleep. His parents were also great but the one person who wasn't was Brody. He was determined to keep his bachelor lifestyle.'

It didn't surprise Fliss that Hewitt had helped out, but what did shock her was Brody's immaturity and selfishness. She'd always assumed he shared his twin's kind and generous heart. 'I can see how this would have caused tension.'

Ava's laugh sounded hollow. 'You're right. There's only so many times a husband can come home drunk and wake two babies you've spent an hour getting to sleep. I hid from Hewitt, and his parents, how much trouble my marriage was in. I was the reason, not Hewitt, why Brody was bull riding.'

Fliss stilled, her mug of tea halfway to her lips. 'Hewitt's convinced he's the reason.'

'I know. I've told him he isn't, over and over. I've told him Brody made his own decisions and he wasn't riding for the prize money to buy Hewitt out. The truth is, and this is part of what I need to tell Hewitt, is that Brody was only riding bulls to prove a point. We'd had a huge fight and he rode to show me he could live his life any way he wanted. He didn't care if he had a family, he wanted to do the things he did before, even if they were high-risk.'

Fliss shook her head. 'Brody and Hewitt aren't similar at all. The little I know about Hewitt makes me believe that once he has a family, they will always come first.'

'They will. Hewitt has been more of a father to the twins than Brody ever was.'

'Did Hewitt know Brody wasn't the best father? He mentioned that Quinn used to follow Brody everywhere and work with him in the shed.'

'He did … for five minutes until Quinn touched something he shouldn't have. The only person Brody ever listened to was Hewitt. Hewitt would tell him to leave the rugby early to come home. Brody would look like he did, but really go to a mate's place.' Ava paused, her hands twisting together. 'I haven't been strong enough to make Hewitt realise once and for all that he wasn't at fault for Brody being back on a bull. I've been battling my own guilt. But I am now. You see … I've found someone else.'

'That's wonderful.'

'I just hope Hewitt doesn't think I'm betraying Brody by moving on. He knows who it is. It's our neighbour Dean who came to help with the crop when Hewitt had his motorbike accident.'

'Is this Dean your eastern neighbour?'

'Yes, the youngest brother.'

'Hewitt will be happy for the both of you.' Fliss reached over to squeeze Ava's hand. 'I'm sure.'

Hewitt, Quinn and Lizzie entered the kitchen. Fliss let go of Ava's hand but not before Hewitt's concerned gaze swept between the two of them.

Fliss gave the twins a sunny smile as she stood. 'Who wants to meet the green frog that lives in the laundry? We can wash our hands while we see him and then have a drink and an Anzac biscuit.'

In her peripheral vision, she saw Hewitt rub Ava's back before he sat beside her.

The afternoon passed in a flurry of activity. The twins rode Garnet and Flame and went in the ute with Hewitt to check the calves.

They then named the three red hens and black-and-gold rooster scratching around in the chook pen. While Ava rested, Quinn helped Hewitt add fallen branches to the garden rubbish he'd stockpiled beneath a tarpaulin to keep dry. Tonight they'd light the pile and enjoy a bonfire. Lizzie let the puppies sleep and came over to the main house to bake with Fliss.

After serious deliberation, Lizzie chose a vanilla fairy cupcake recipe from Fliss's mother's book. According to the handwritten notes, Fliss had enjoyed these cupcakes for her tenth birthday and the recipe had been passed on by Meredith.

Fliss watched Lizzie's cute face screw up in concentration as she stood on a stool and sifted flour into the mixing bowl. A longing to have her own little sweet Lizzie and energetic Quinn unfurled deep inside. A longing for children that she'd always repressed and had never had time to acknowledge before.

High-pitched boyish laughter sounded from outside. Through the kitchen window she saw Hewitt tickling Quinn on the lawn.

Lizzie rolled her eyes. 'They do that all the time.'

Fliss didn't reply. Laughter relaxed Hewitt's face and love for his nephew softened his mouth. The tug in her chest said it wasn't only the twins who'd activated her biological clock. Hewitt would make a loving and committed father.

When the shadows deepened and a chill stripped the warmth from the day, everyone sat around the table in the stables to enjoy the chicken Hewitt had roasted. Lizzie kept a watch for the first star through the kitchen window. When everyone's plates were empty and starlight glimmered, she wriggled in her chair. 'Uncle Hewy, is it dark enough for our bonfire yet?'

'It sure is.'

Fliss didn't know which child was the quickest out of their seats.

Around the wood pile Hewitt had set up hay bales that Fliss had covered with blankets. It wasn't until the twins were safely perched on a bale that Hewitt lit the fire. Flames flickered and sparks soared skywards as the bonfire took hold.

'Who's for dessert?' Fliss uncovered a tray of cones, marshmallows, bananas and chocolates she'd brought over from the main house.

The twins' excited chorus of 'I am!' made Fliss smile.

Lizzie filled her cone with a sensible amount of ingredients while Quinn stuffed his so full it took an extra piece of aluminium foil to secure it closed. Lizzie made a cone for Fliss and Ava while Quinn made one for his uncle. Hewitt carefully put the foil-covered cones into the coals to melt.

'And I thought maple syrup was sticky,' Ava said as she used a serviette to wipe away the melted chocolate from Quinn's chin.

Lizzie finished her dessert, not a smear of chocolate on her hands or mouth.

When the flames died down, and Quinn yawned from where he sat cuddled next to Hewitt, Ava got to her feet. 'Bed time.'

Despite their protests, the twins left their seats.

'See you in the morning,' she said to each sleepy five-year-old as they gave her a goodnight hug.

Hewitt went to help Ava tuck the twins in. Fliss busied herself with cleaning up and taking their dessert ingredients to the main house. She returned to keep an eye on the fire. When all the lights in the stables were switched off except for the one in the kitchen, she guessed Ava would be having her talk with Hewitt.

Grass rustled before Molly jumped up onto the hay bale. Fliss put an arm around the border collie and together they looked at the flames. Crickets chirped, frogs croaked and burning wood popped. Contentment filtered through her, silencing the whispers of her anxiety. She mightn't have the blood of her father's pioneering ancestors running through her, but she could still appreciate a campfire and the gentle touch of a balmy spring night. She could understand why her mother had said the bush was the best place to raise a family.

Footsteps sounded and Hewitt walked into the firelight. Shoulders rigid, he didn't speak as he circled the fire, tossing on the branches from the edge that had only burned part-way through. Molly yawned and jumped off the bale to head over to the shed where her babies slept. Fliss stayed quiet as Hewitt continued to stride around the bonfire. He tossed on a final log and after watching it for a moment, made his way over to her.

When he sat on the hay bale he didn't hide his grunt or the way he rubbed at his shoulder. Wrestling with Quinn had taken its toll on his shoulder.

Hewitt glanced at her, his eyes dark hollows in his carved features. 'Thanks for listening to Ava.'

'You're welcome.'

The silence stretched as Fliss gave Hewitt the space to talk. 'I'm so pleased for her and Dean and so ... angry at myself. How could I not have seen that Brody wasn't invested in his family?'

Fliss turned towards him. 'Because he didn't want you to see. Because you love those twins so much it never occurred to you that he didn't love them just as much.'

'How could he not?'

Fliss covered his hand with hers. For a moment he didn't respond and then he turned his hand over so their fingers laced. The simplicity of the gesture and its implicit message of thanks moved Fliss in a way words never could.

Hewitt stared into the fire. 'Dean's a good bloke and if things keep going the way they are, he'll be a wonderful father to Lizzie and Quinn.'

Fliss squeezed his hand. Desolation had thickened his words. 'Lizzie and Quinn love you. You will always be part of their lives no matter what the future holds. If Ava and Dean do get married then you'll have a chance to do what you wanted and make your own way.'

'Maybe. Mum and Dad have aged this past year and unless things change with Dad, I can't see myself living anywhere else. Someone needs to run Mayfield. If Ava and Dean do end up together then Dean running the farm might be an option, but that's not going to happen overnight.'

Hewitt stopped to press a kiss to the back of her hand. 'It's late and I'd better let you get to bed. I'll watch the fire. Quinn will be up before that new rooster of yours wakes us all at dawn.'

'I swear Popcorn has his times mixed up. He crowed well before dawn this morning.' Fliss worked hard to keep her voice even as Hewitt released her hand. The loss of his warmth was almost a physical wrench. She came to her feet. 'Night.'

Hewitt gazed at her but in the shadows she couldn't gauge his expression. 'Night, Fliss.'

Sleep was about as easy to come by as it had been letting go of Fliss's hand and watching her walk away. Hewitt sighed and flipped off the bedcovers. Even when the soothing sound of rain had fallen on the tin roof, he'd remained awake. He stood, raking both hands through his short hair.

If it wasn't enough Fliss slept across the hall, ever since his talk with Ava his emotions churned. Grief warred with anger. Loss merged with sadness. It broke his heart to think that Brody hadn't been committed to his family. Sure, he'd always liked to drink with his mates and this had continued after his marriage, but Hewitt had always assumed that Ava and the twins came first.

He reached for his jeans and slipped them on. Ava had confessed to keeping her misery private, instead trying to deal with Brody on her own. She hadn't wanted to cause a rift between him and their parents and especially between Brody and Hewitt. Not only were they brothers and friends, they were business partners. She'd hoped one day Brody would enjoy being a father. But that day had never come.

He could now understand Ava's insistence he wasn't to blame for Brody being back bull riding. But even though a layer of his guilt had been stripped away, he couldn't so easily absolve himself of the guilt for not being there when Brody needed him. His plans to leave had still set in motion a tragic chain of events.

He tugged on a black T-shirt, making sure he didn't aggravate his shoulder. Where had Quinn learned to rugby tackle so hard? He crossed the room, the polished floorboards cold beneath his bare feet. He'd sit on the veranda and see if solitude settled his thoughts.

As he walked along the darkened hallway, he noticed light peeping from under Fliss's office door. He paused, about to knock, when Molly's sharp bark cut through the night. Senses alert, he continued past Fliss's door. At the front door he pulled on his boots before heading to the veranda.

The rain had cleared. In the gloom, all he could see of the border collie were her white patches as she ran up the steps to him. He'd made the puppy panel low enough so she could jump out of the garden shed anytime she wanted to.

He touched her head. 'What's up, Miss Molly?'

He scanned the garden and stables before looking out over the front fence at the drive into Bundara. The screen door creaked and Fliss came to stand beside him. He shot her a quick sideways look, taking in her rugby top, grey pyjama shorts and alert gaze.

She stared out into the night. 'What is it?'

'A car, lights off, just sitting there on the road.'

'Where? I can't see it.'

'Before the dip.'

'What are they doing?'

'Checking us out.'

He reached for Fliss's hand and led her down the steps so she'd be less visible. He then waved his arm to activate the main house sensor lights. With Fliss following, and still holding his hand, he kept to the shadows. When they reached the stables, he again triggered the sensor lights before stepping back into the darkness. From beside him, Molly barked. He rubbed her ears to let her know everything was okay.

'What would they be after?' Fliss's voice was quiet but calm. 'Your quad bike?'

'Nothing tonight. This would just be a reconnaissance mission. They now know you have a dog and sensor lights. They will have noted the padlocked gates and no trespassing signs. There's also my ute, Ava's four-wheel drive and your car, so they know there's a few of us here.'

'Which hopefully will make Bundara too hard a target. I wish I could see the rego plate.'

Fliss still held his hand but the angle of her chin didn't bode well for any would-be thieves. Fliss would be no damsel in distress. She would have dealt with intoxicated and aggressive patients in her city emergency department.

'Have you had anyone stop and ask for directions or to see if you needed any odd jobs done?' he asked, making a calculated guess as to the make and model of the car.

'No. When I first moved in an old fellow came to see if he could have the grubs from the Kurrajong tree that had died along the fence line. He wanted to use them for fishing. I told him no as I was worried about insurance issues should he have an accident with his chainsaw. He came back a month later but since then I haven't had any unknown visitors.'

The slam of two car doors echoed through the thin night air. Hewitt eased his hand from Fliss's. Whoever was in the car would have seen them but this hadn't stopped them from leaving their vehicle. Molly growled low in her throat. He transferred his weight onto the balls of his feet.

Fliss slipped her hand around his forearm. 'Do I have to remind you about your broken shoulder?'

He didn't take his focus from the two blurred figures who'd moved to inspect a steel gate. A faint metal clink sounded. 'If they cut the padlock, remind me after I've talked to them.'

Fliss tightened her grip on his arm. 'There'll be no *talking* happening. You forget it wasn't only Denham's rodeo injuries I had to make sure he got help for.'

Hewitt didn't reply. No one was stealing anything from Bundara on his watch. The figures returned to their car. The engine rumbled into life before the sedan reversed, lights still off.

'Good riddance,' Fliss said, voice firm. 'If they come back you have my full permission to nip their ankles, Miss Molly.'

Hewitt looked at the border collie.

Fliss stiffened. 'Do you think they were after her and the puppies?'

'More likely they'd be after easier things to steal. Ice would be as much of a problem here as it is elsewhere. Last harvest the UHF radio was stolen from my header. It wasn't such a big deal, the radio isn't worth much, but the broken header window took three days to fix.'

'Harvest isn't a time when you want delays.'

'You can say that again. After he had a ute and tools stolen, Dean installed a camera that takes a picture whenever someone drives over his cattle grid.'

The sensor light clicked off and Hewitt lifted his arm to reactivate it. Now that the car had left, standing close to Fliss in the darkness only increased the risk of something happening between them. All he needed to do was dip his head and his mouth would cover hers. He stepped into the pool of bright light. Fliss took a last look at the darkened road before following. Her hand remained in his, the clasp of her slender fingers warm and strong.

He ran his thumb over her hand. 'Maybe Reggie should come to stay? Denham swears he's better than any watchdog.'

'Poor Reggie, he's much maligned. If you ever meet him you'll see he's a gentle giant.'

Hewitt lifted an eyebrow. He'd heard the story about Reggie ramming a car of trespassing teenagers. 'If I do meet him, I'm making sure he knows I'm at Claremont by invitation.'

Laughter kindled in Fliss's eyes. 'So you won't be feeding him any carrots?'

'Not if he thinks I shouldn't be in his paddock.'

Fliss took her hand from his to stifle a yawn. His fingers twitched at the sudden emptiness.

'I should have gone to sleep hours ago. I think I'm ready now. I'll shut down my computer and head to bed.'

They moved towards the house. At the veranda steps he stopped to pat Molly.

Fliss turned to face him. From where she stood on the second step their eyes were almost level. Beneath the sensor light she was all tousled hair, high cheekbones and large eyes.

She touched his jaw, her caress as light as the night breeze that swirled around them. 'I wouldn't have let you *talk* to those men alone.'

'I've no doubt you'd have had my back.'

He lost the battle to look away from the soft sweep of her bottom lip. Silence shrouded them. His heartbeat thundered in his chest. They'd both agreed there could be no second kiss.

Her hand slowly lowered. 'Night.'

'Night,' he managed, before she disappeared through the front door.

He scraped a hand over his face and waited until he could no longer hear the creak of the hallway floorboards before following her inside.

He could have a rodeo ground between them and it still wouldn't be enough to temper the awareness that he and Fliss were under the same roof. Fliss might now be able to sleep, but for him, sleep would be a long time coming.

As Hewitt had predicted, Popcorn the rooster crowed at dawn and all too soon two small bodies stormed his room. He tried to keep the noise and laughter down so as to not wake Fliss, but it wasn't long before she appeared at the bedroom doorway.

'I thought I heard the sound of little feet,' she said, voice sleepy.

'Sorry.'

She dragged her tousled hair off her face. 'I was awake anyway. It could have been worse, they could have been furry little feet.'

Lizzie giggled from where she sat cross-legged beside Hewitt. A large lump in her purple dressing gown wriggled before Poppy's tiny face appeared. Quinn reached behind him to produce the puppy named John Deere.

Fliss laughed softly. 'I might have known. I don't suppose anyone would like pancakes this early?'

Quinn and Lizzie scampered off the bed.

While Lizzie and Quinn took the puppies outside and helped Fliss cook pancakes, Hewitt took a shower. Ten minutes later, he entered the kitchen. His heart warmed. Fliss understood the twins so well. Lizzie had her own area of the bench, which was clean and neat. Quinn stood on a chair on the other side of Fliss, the bench beside him dusted with flour and smeared with batter. With Fliss's help, he slid a pancake that looked like the shape of Australia onto a plate.

Fliss glanced at him. 'Perfect timing. Quinn's cooked his first pancake. How was the shower?'

'Let's just say it's moved to the top of my to-do list.'

'That bad?'

'It would have been warmer swimming in the creek.'

Quinn's eyes lit up. Hewitt shook his head with a smile. 'Not so fast, Quinn. After all this rain the creek's running too fast to swim in. But there's a dam where we could catch yabbies.'

Ava joined them for breakfast. While Quinn's fingers and chin grew sticky with syrup, and Lizzie's face stayed clean, plans were made for a morning of yabbying. Despite the overnight rain shower, today promised to be clear and fine. When the final pancake had been eaten, Ava came to her feet to collect the empty plates.

Fliss stood. 'Please leave them. You're my guest.'

'Are you sure? I might have a quick shower before we leave.'

'Yes.' Fliss flicked Hewitt a teasing grin. 'I happen to know someone who's very good at washing up.'

Hewitt didn't miss the widening of Lizzie's eyes or her contented smile. She loved her fairy tales and anything with a happy ending. He had to be very careful her busy brain didn't have her believing that he and Fliss would end up together, let alone walking down the aisle.

When Ava returned, they piled into Hewitt's ute and her four-wheel drive. The convoy drove along the dry track on the higher side of the paddock to the dam. There was no missing the large body of water that reflected the sky and shimmered in the surrounding blanket of spring green.

Hewitt parked close to a flat area of the bank so the twins would have a safe area to throw in their yabby strings. Fliss laid out the picnic rug and unpacked the large basket she'd brought. Ava came to help and soon both women were laughing and chatting.

Quinn reeled in his first yabby. Hewitt looked away as Fliss came to watch. The black straps of her swimmers were visible beneath the collar of her pink shirt. He didn't need any reminders of how well she filled them out, or how she felt, wet and curvy, wrapped round him.

Quinn's yabby clung to the meat at the end of the string until, at the last minute, it let go. Quinn's frown would have stopped a road train.

Hewitt tousled his bright hair. 'You'll have better luck next time.'

His words proved true. It wasn't long before Quinn hauled another yabby to shore. Hewitt scooped it into the bucket. Lizzie caught a second yabby but then abandoned her string to sit on the picnic rug with Fliss and Ava.

Hewitt and Quinn took a break and everyone enjoyed a morning tea of lamingtons and fruit. Quinn didn't sit still for long and was soon running along the dam bank after a dragonfly. On his way back, he stopped to throw stones into the water. Spying a pile of larger rocks, he sped over, then slipped in the mud and fell. His instant cry was sharp and pained.

Hewitt reached him first and as Quinn lifted his head, blood dripped from his chin. Fliss knelt down beside them.

'You're okay, Quinn, just stay still.' She reached into her first-aid kit to unwrap a sterile white gauze pad. 'I'm going to hold this on your chin and then we'll sit you up.'

Fliss's voice was calm and reassuring but Hewitt didn't miss the unsteadiness of her fingers. She applied pressure to Quinn's chin and together they eased him into a sitting position. A single tear ran down his muddy cheek. Ava hugged him and kissed the top of his head. An uncertain Lizzie clung to her mother's arm.

Fliss met Hewitt's gaze. 'You'll need to go to … Woodlea.'

She hadn't said the word 'hospital' on purpose.

Fliss smiled across at Lizzie. 'Do you know where Quinn's tractor is? He was ploughing while he ate his banana. Maybe you could find it and wash it for him?'

Lizzie nodded and walked away, giving all the rocks a wide berth.

Hewitt helped Quinn to his feet. The white square patch of gauze was now red.

Fliss glanced at Ava who held Quinn's hand. 'Are you right to hold this on Quinn's chin for the drive in?'

She nodded.

Fliss showed Ava where to place her fingers. When Ava took over holding the gauze in place, Fliss pulled out her phone. She checked for signal before texting.

Hewitt carried Quinn over to Ava's four-wheel drive. While he settled him in his seat, Fliss read the reply text. 'Janet says Dr Sam's on duty. Quinn will be in safe hands.'

'Hear that?' Hewitt removed Quinn's cap and brushed his auburn hair off his too-pale face. 'You'll be feeling better soon.' He kissed Quinn's forehead. All the while Ava kept the pressure on his wound.

Lizzie came to the car door and passed Quinn his tractor. Hewitt's heart broke at the fear pinching her small face. He hugged her, whispering in her ear, 'We'll be back soon, sweetheart. Quinn will be all right.'

When he straightened, Fliss put her arm around Lizzie's shoulders. 'It looks like it's just us to finish our picnic. We get to drive Uncle Hewitt's ute home, play with the puppies and make something special for when Quinn gets back.'

Lizzie gave an uncertain nod, her bottom lip quivering.

Hewitt turned to Fliss. As strong and as calm as she sounded he didn't miss the way her shoulders were braced. Treating Quinn had unleashed all her fears and heightened her anxiety. Before he could think through what he was doing, he cupped the fine line of her jaw. Beneath his touch he could feel her tremble as reaction set in. Uncaring of his audience, he brushed his mouth over hers.

CHAPTER
14

'Some veranda furniture wouldn't go astray,' Hewitt said with a grin as Fliss passed him his morning coffee.

She nodded, thankful Hewitt had lightened the mood. They'd just farewelled Ava and the twins who'd stayed an extra night after Dr Sam had stitched Quinn's chin. Bundara already seemed too quiet.

She took her usual place on the top veranda step. Molly flopped down beside her. 'Are you complaining?'

'Not at all.' Hewitt patted the floorboards. 'These are as comfortable as the sofa I slept on last night.'

Hewitt had stayed in the stables to help Ava should Quinn have had a bad night.

'A sofa Lizzie and I covered with blankets and cushions to make sure your shoulder wouldn't be sore. It wasn't our fault you took them off and your feet hung over the edge.'

'A man does have some pride. I'm not sleeping with a fairy blanket or using a unicorn soft toy as a pillow no matter how much Lizzie pouts.'

'She does have that pout down to a fine art.' Fliss's tone sobered. 'Were you really uncomfortable?'

Hewitt took a sip of coffee, the tanned skin of his throat moving as he swallowed. 'No, I slept well and so did Quinn. It probably would have been better if he'd had a bad night as then he'd sleep on the way home. It's a long enough drive without him being in pain.'

Concern deepened Hewitt's tone as he stared in the direction Ava's four-wheel drive had taken.

'He'll be fine. They all will be. I'm not sure if it's a good sign or not, but I did see him poke Lizzie before they left.'

As she'd hoped, Hewitt's lips curved. 'Thanks again for all of your help.'

'It was a team effort.' Warmth crept into her face. 'Thanks too for … your support.'

His kiss had been designed to offer comfort. And it had. But it had left her wanting much more. One brush of his mouth on hers wasn't enough.

'No worries.' His gaze turned serious. 'Except I think my timing could have been better. Was it just me or did there seem to be a lot of wedding references from Lizzie this morning?'

'There was. She ran me through her favourite fairy tale couples and what she would wear if she was their flower girl.'

Hewitt closed his eyes. The grooves beside his mouth deepened.

She reached over to touch his denim-covered knee. 'Lizzie will understand. She just wants you to be happy. Besides, there still could be a wedding if everything works out for Ava and Dean.'

'I hope you're right. Lizzie's already experienced so much loss and uncertainty. As for a real wedding … Ava's going to talk to the twins about Dean when Quinn's feeling better. She's also going to chat to my parents. I offered to be there when she did, but she says she needs to do this on her own.'

'Which is great. Dean sounds like a nice guy and if everyone already knows him perhaps it won't come as such a shock.'

'I hope so.'

Fliss leaned back to dig in her jeans pocket for her phone as it buzzed. A picture of Ella holding a fluffy white puppy popped onto Fliss's screen.

'Hi, Ella. Any news?'

'Is Hewitt there?'

'Yes. Hang on, I'll put you on speaker.'

'Morning, Ella,' Hewitt said from where he sat on the other side of Molly.

'Morning. So … it's all been happening. A certain missing border collie was delivered to me this morning.'

'He was?' Fliss couldn't contain her joy or her relief. She shared a smile with Hewitt. 'Is Max okay?'

'Yes, he's thin and on edge but otherwise fine. That rego plate number you gave Daniel worked a treat. The ute was registered to a farm owner who didn't live far from the stock route you rode on. He was already under suspicion for being in possession of stolen property, so parked his ute there so the dogs wouldn't be seen. And get this. They were all stolen.'

'You're kidding.'

'No. Needless to say it's been a very busy morning.'

'So what happens to Max now?' Hewitt asked, stroking Molly's back.

'Thanks to the floods in France his owners are home from overseas early and are sending through the necessary paperwork. They'll drive up tomorrow to collect him.'

Fliss's stomach went into freefall. She hadn't ended up with an extra three weeks with Molly after all. 'Does that mean Molly and the puppies are going as well?'

'I'm sorry, Fliss, they would be. But the owners did ask if Max could stay with you tonight. They know once he's with Molly he'll feel safe. Apparently when the thieves swapped vehicles Max bit one of them, giving Molly an opportunity to escape.'

'Of course.' Fliss kept her words even to mask her sadness and deepening sense of loss. 'Do you want us to get him?'

'No, I'll bring him over after lunch. I have a foundered pony I need to see out your way.'

'Ella,' Hewitt spoke again, 'this guy who stole the dogs ... did he say where Molly escaped and if he'd been looking for her?'

'Yes, they lost her on Old Dairy Road which means Molly had a long way to travel to reach Bundara.' Ella paused. 'Daniel seems to think the guy knew you had her as he mentioned something about Molly having six puppies and how he could have made a fortune.'

Hewitt nodded. 'All he'd need to do was call the pound, or look on the local lost-and-found internet groups, and Molly and her details would have been easy to find.'

'That's right,' Ella said. 'I need to get back to work but I'll be there after lunch at one.'

'See you then.' Fliss ended the call.

Hewitt slid out his phone. 'Do you have Daniel's number?'

Fliss tapped her phone and held up her screen for Hewitt to see. She stayed quiet as Hewitt spoke to Daniel at the Woodlea police station. It soon became obvious that the white sedan that had paid Bundara a night-time visit had been the thieves assessing their chances of getting Molly and her puppies back.

Fliss only half listened as Hewitt chatted with Daniel about what would happen to the two men. She threaded her fingers through Molly's silken coat. What was she going to do without her? The border collie's bravery and sweetness had carved out a place in her heart. Molly nuzzled her hand.

Fliss hadn't realised Hewitt had ended the call until he leaned over to tuck the hair brushing her cheek behind her ear. 'I've no doubt Molly and Max are much loved. Their owners would have been worried about what had happened to them.'

'I know. This day had to come. I'm just wallowing.'

'There's nothing wrong with wallowing. Molly's a special dog.'

After Hewitt left to look at the hot water system, Fliss settled into her home office. She hadn't done much DNA work while Ava and the twins were visiting and she needed to see if she could find any birth, death or marriage certificates for Valda or Patrick Ryan.

The names hadn't been familiar when she'd checked with Cressy. But Meredith had thought she'd recognised the Ryan surname from when she'd known their mother in Sydney. Old electoral rolls had confirmed that a number of Ryan families had lived in the beachside area where their mother had grown up. Her father may very well have been a neighbour, school friend or family acquaintance.

Fliss re-read a paragraph on the internet page in front of her. When the content still didn't register, she shut her laptop. It was no use trying to distract herself. She couldn't forget that tomorrow Molly and her adorable puppies would be gone. She'd spend what little time they had left together outside playing and gardening.

Right on one o'clock, the Woodlea vet vehicle pulled up at the wrought-iron garden gate. Ella's time management was legendary.

Fliss was already seated on the veranda step with Molly. From over in the shed the puppies yipped. For the moment they'd stay behind the wire panel. Molly and Max needed space. Hewitt emerged from around the side of the house.

Fliss walked across the garden, Molly by her side. As soon as the border collie saw the dog the vet had on the lead, she whined and rushed forwards to jump the post-and-rail fence. Max swung around to meet her. The two dogs sniffed each other before licking each other's faces. Fliss had never seen Molly's tail wag so frantically.

Hewitt came to stand beside her.

'Now there's Lizzie's happy-ever-after.' Fliss wasn't surprised to find her words husky.

'It sure is.'

Ella led Max through the gate. Molly stayed close to him before running up to Fliss and Hewitt.

Fliss ruffled her thick neck. 'I know. Max's here. It's very exciting.'

Ella introduced Max to Hewitt and Fliss and the male border collie showed no fear or aggression.

Fliss rubbed behind his ears. 'You're a sweetheart, just like Molly.'

'He sure is,' Ella said as Max's tail wagged.

Ella unclipped his lead. Max bounded away, Molly following. Every so often Max stopped to sniff at a plant or a pot before lifting his leg. The whining and excited howls from the six fluffy faces pressing against the shed wire increased. Then his black nose touched those of his tiny offspring and peace fell over the garden. Molly sat close by, tail still wagging.

Ella checked her watch. 'As much as I'd like to stay and watch Max get to know his too-cute babies, I've a pony to see.' But instead of turning towards the gate, she glanced between Hewitt and Fliss. 'Neither of you have been to town lately, have you?'

Fliss shook her head.

'I thought so. Next time you go in, be warned, rodeo fever has nothing on this year's ball fever. The matchmaking has become worse than my year twelve formal.'

'That bad?'

'Believe me, it is.' Ella focused on Hewitt. 'Your name keeps cropping up, especially in connection to Bethany. Tanner's already sent me an SOS, otherwise I'd go with you. Taylor's bringing a mystery man so she isn't free to save you, which only leaves …'

Ella didn't complete her sentence, just raised a brow and stared at Fliss.

'Surely it hasn't come to that? We don't usually need partners for a charity ball.'

'Let's just say it's spring, the season of love, the yarn bombers have hung knitted red hearts all over town and Edna's in charge of the table seating.'

'Oh.'

'Yes, oh. On our table six spots have been taken, which leaves four. So either you and Hewitt go together or you'd better find partners before Edna assigns you ones. Otherwise we all know who'll be sitting next to Hewitt.'

Fliss frowned. 'But Edna knows it's unlikely Hewitt will even be here. Hewitt told her himself.'

'According to Mrs Knox, who was in the surgery today with her prize poodle, she heard from Harriet, who was talking to Christi, that Hewitt will still be in town. And we both know if Mrs Knox knows, Edna will know.'

Hewitt rubbed his chin. 'Christi was at the hospital when we took Quinn in. She chatted to him while we waited for Dr Sam.'

Fliss looked across at Hewitt. 'Even if you are here you don't have to go. I don't know if I'm going yet.'

'Yes you are,' Ella said, voice firm. 'You're going to have some fun.'

'Have you been talking to Cressy and Taylor? I'm starting to think there's a conspiracy going on.'

'No.' Ella slipped her arm through Fliss's as they walked towards the gate. 'But you should be talking to your sister. She'll tell you when it comes to getting the Knight girls out and about, I won't take no for an answer.'

Fliss groaned. Ella had made sure Cressy maintained a full social calendar in the years Denham had been riding on the American pro-rodeo circuit.

Ella looked sideways to where Hewitt walked beside her. 'We're all going to have a great night and raise lots of money for the hospital.'

Hewitt nodded. 'I'm in.'

Ella walked through the gate Hewitt held open for them. 'I knew I could count on you.' She slipped her arm from Fliss's. 'Taylor's going to do our hair, I have a whole wardrobe of dresses and I know you'd still have those heels you scared off that blind date of yours with.'

'Ella …'

The vet hugged her and whispered, 'You can do this.' She stepped away. 'Now I'd better go or I'll be late. I'll call you about the ball plans soon.'

Fliss waved Ella off and, as she turned, she realised Hewitt was watching her instead of the vehicle driving away.

The prospect of being in a loud and crowded cotton gin surrounded by tables of people made her palms clammy. But the idea of Bethany sitting close to Hewitt all night and flicking her long blonde hair made her blood fire.

Nevertheless, she wasn't falling into line so easily. She folded her arms. 'It's a new experience being railroaded.'

The corner of his mouth kicked into a half-smile. 'I gathered that.'

'I thought you really didn't want to go.'

'I wasn't sure if I would still be here.' His grin turned sheepish. 'If my shoulder had healed faster, I probably wouldn't be.'

Fliss bit the inside of her cheek at the thought of Hewitt not giving himself time to heal, but also at the thought of him leaving. The sadness she felt at Molly going tomorrow would be nothing compared to what she'd feel when Hewitt left.

Desolation stripped the warmth from the spring breeze. She rubbed at her arms. It was more important than ever that she keep things contained between them. Unlike in Lizzie's fairy tales, there couldn't be any happy ending, even if a ball was involved. Hewitt's family required all of him, both now and in the future. She'd never ask him to choose between them.

His eyes searched hers. 'I'm fine to partner Bethany if there's someone else you'd rather go with.'

Her chin lifted. 'No, we're foiling Edna's plans. You're stuck with me. Even if you were lying when you said you preferred brunettes.'

The sound of a car engine had Hewitt set his drill on the tack shed floor. He'd attach the other two metal saddle racks to the back wall later. It was time to say goodbye to the border collies he and Fliss had grown so fond of.

Max came to his feet from where he had been lying in the corner. The male border collie may have only arrived yesterday but he'd taken to being Hewitt's shadow. He'd even jumped in the back of the ute when Hewitt had gone to check the cattle.

Hewitt tickled behind the dog's ears. Maybe it wasn't just time for Fliss to get a dog. Maybe he should as well. He'd always enjoyed the company of the working dogs at Mayfield but he didn't have his own personal dog.

'Okay, Max. Showtime. We need to find Fliss and make sure she's okay.'

As comfortable and relaxed as Max had become, Fliss had only grown more subdued.

She too had heard the car. She walked down the veranda steps, her game face on. Instead of her usual farm jeans and cotton work shirt, she wore fitted jeans and a silky floral top with long loose sleeves. His jaw clenched as she gave him a strained smile. All he wanted to do was kiss away her sadness.

'Okay,' she said, shoulders squared. 'Let's do this.'

Together they walked to the garden gate, Max and Molly beside them. As a dual-cab ute pulled up, a roomy dog crate on the back, Hewitt touched the small of Fliss's back. She briefly rested her head on his right shoulder.

Even before the elderly couple left their vehicle, Molly and Max were at the gate, tails wagging and eyes bright. Hewitt sensed Fliss relax beside him. The bond between the border collies and their owners was unquestionable. The slight woman and the bow-legged man laughed as they greeted the dogs through the gate before moving inside to pat and hug them.

The man came over to Hewitt and Fliss. His handshake was firm and his palm callused from a life lived on the land.

'I'm Elliot, and this is Alison. We can't thank you enough for what you've done.'

Alison's brown eyes held tears as she shook their hands. 'We thought we'd never see Max and Molly again.'

'You're very welcome,' Fliss said, words warm. 'It's our pleasure. They're wonderful dogs.'

Elliot looked to where Molly now sat beside Fliss. Max had settled himself beside Hewitt's boots. 'They are. They're also the best workers.'

Fliss turned to lead the way over to the garden shed. 'I hope it's okay but we've named the puppies.'

Alison smiled. 'Thank you. This is Molly's third litter and I'm running out of names. My daughter's children are too little to help me think of some more.'

While Elliot and Alison played with the puppies, Fliss disappeared inside to make two coffees and a pot of tea. Hewitt went in search of another camp chair from the stables. Soon they were all seated around the recycled-door table. Hewitt made sure he sat beside Fliss. When his knee brushed hers in a silent message of support she gave him a quick, thankful glance.

Fliss offered everyone a banana muffin and talk soon revolved around what had happened to Max and Molly. The conversation then moved on to the couple's adventures on their overseas tour of Europe.

Fliss's laughter was genuine and her questions sincere but she failed to eat any of the muffins or sip at her tea.

When there was a lull in the conversation, Elliot cleared his throat. 'You have a great place here and are obviously a very nice couple to do what you've done for Max and Molly.'

Hewitt didn't answer, just took a swallow of coffee and watched Fliss from over the rim of his mug. The concept of them being a true couple shouldn't have filled him with such need or made his chest tighten.

'That's very kind.' Faint colour washed her cheeks. 'We're just friends. Hewitt's helping me fix up Bundara.'

Elliot looked around the manicured garden and across to the tidy sheds. 'Well, together you've done a great job.'

'Thanks.'

Alison spoke. 'There's something we'd like to discuss with you, Fliss. Please feel free to say no but, you see, we'd like to travel more and our son-in-law who runs our place already has his own working dogs. We'd also like Max and Molly to stay together. We were wondering if you'd be interested in having them ... permanently?'

Fliss didn't hesitate. Eyes shining, she leaned forwards. 'I'd love to. I'm honoured you feel I'd give them a good home. They're valuable working dogs so I must pay you for them.'

Alison touched Fliss's hand. 'You've already done more than enough. We're happy to give them to you and won't accept any payment.'

'Maybe I could make a donation to the working dog rescue group?'

'If you'd like to.'

Fliss nodded and looked across at Hewitt. He'd never seen her eyes such an intense amber. Happiness flushed her cheeks and tilted her lips.

Elliot bent to pick up Patch who'd waddled close to his boots. He settled the puppy into his lap. 'As for the puppies, we've already found homes for four of them. You're welcome to have the remaining two, or you might know of suitable owners?'

Fliss bent to pat Molly's head. 'We have a friend called Tanner who's looking for a working dog pup. We can vouch for him.'

Hewitt spoke quietly. 'I'd love one for my father. He's going through a rough patch and used to have border collies as a kid. One of the quieter pups, like Poppy, would make a perfect companion dog.'

Elliot extracted his fingers from Patch's mouth. 'I like the sound of that. What do you think, Alison?'

'I do too. Poppy's a gentle soul and would make a loyal and loving friend. Have a think about which puppy would suit Tanner best. We brought the paperwork to sign the dogs over just in case things worked out this way.'

'Thank you.' Fliss's smile was so beautiful it made Hewitt's heart ache.

She selected a muffin and while she ate, her hand disappeared under the table to feed Molly crumbs.

When everyone had finished their tea, Fliss offered Alison and Elliot lunch.

'Thanks,' Elliot said, coming to his feet. 'But we'd better complete this paperwork and get going. We've a long way to travel to our friends' place where we're staying the night. The longer we stay the harder it will be to say goodbye.'

The forms were completed and arrangements made for Tanner and Hewitt's father to compete their sections. It then came time for Elliot and Alison to say farewell to Molly and Max.

Hewitt caught the shimmer of tears in Fliss's eyes and moved to stand beside her.

Alison wiped the corners of her own eyes as she gave Molly a final pat.

'I'm so relieved Molly found her way to you,' the older woman said, voice choked as she embraced Fliss.

'So am I.'

After Alison had also hugged Hewitt, Elliot shook his hand. The older man looked between him and Fliss, his bushy grey brows lifting. 'Just friends, eh?'

Hewitt nodded.

'I once said the same thing.' He shot his wife an affectionate look before moving to Fliss and clasping her hand.

If she'd heard Elliott's comment, it didn't show in her open smile. 'Anytime you'd like to visit and see how Molly and Max are going, please feel welcome to call in.'

'Thank you. We will.'

When they could no longer see the dual cab in the distance, Fliss looked down at the sheaf of papers in her hand. The pink pages confirmed she was now Max and Molly's new owner.

'I can't believe it. I have not one but two incredible dogs.'

She hugged Molly and then Max and before Hewitt could read what she was going to do, she flung her arms around his neck and smacked a kiss on his cheek. 'Okay, you and me, shopping road trip, *now*.'

Hewitt kept his touch on her waist light and prayed she'd move away. Every second she remained pressed against him was another second for his self-control to slip. The warmth of her smooth skin beneath her silky shirt flowed into his palms. Her soft breaths feathered across his jaw.

Her arms suddenly lowered and she stepped away. 'Sorry, I'm not normally impulsive. You don't have to come to Woodlea if you don't want to.'

'You can be as … impulsive as you want.' The huskiness of his voice betrayed how close he was to forgetting why it was a bad idea for them to be more than friends. 'Maybe just give me more warning.'

'Is that a yes?'

Her voice was steady but a pulse beat at the base of her throat.

'Only if we take my ute.'

'Are you sure? Your ute will fit in more than my car.'

'I'm sure, and I'll drive.'

There was no other way he was going to keep his hands off her.

Fliss hadn't been joking about needing the ute to fit in all her shopping. After their first stop, dog kennels and beds filled the trayback.

Ella walked out of the Woodlea Veterinary Hospital and handed Hewitt two heavy bags. 'Fliss being a dog owner is definitely good for business.'

'Funnily enough, that's what the guy at Woodlea Rural said.'

'I'm sure he did. It's great to see her so happy and back to her old self. She's always been super organised and efficient.'

Hewitt nodded.

'So,' Ella said, her expression turning serious. 'Tell me, before Fliss finishes her shopping spree, is she still holding out on not going to the ball?'

Hewitt glanced at the red-knitted hearts wound around the nearby tree. 'No, she's going and with me.'

'Wonderful. That worked out well.'

Before Hewitt could answer, Fliss walked out of the vet hospital door carrying a third bag.

'Sorry,' she said as she joined them, 'I sent Lizzie a picture of the pink lead on my phone and she liked the sparkles so I got it as well.'

'Lizzie's not alone. That lead's our best seller.' Ella stepped onto the footpath. 'I'll get back to work and let you get going so you can meet Cressy and Denham at Claremont. Say hi to them for me.'

As they headed out of town, Fliss turned to look at the laden ute. 'Now all I need to do is sort out where the kennels should go.'

Their conversation revolved around the safe topic of the border collies until they reached Claremont. Hewitt drove along the poplar tree-lined drive to where the sprawling homestead, with its multiple red-brick chimneys, pushed against the sky. He kept to the left and parked outside the round yard beside Denham's Land Cruiser ute.

Denham whistled as he and Cressy walked out of the stables. 'Someone's been busy.'

'I claim full responsibility.' Fliss rapped the closest kennel with her knuckles. 'Needless to say I got every item on my list.'

Cressy opened the Land Cruiser ute door to reach for a box. 'I hope there's room in there for these books and the rest of Flame's gear.'

'There's plenty.' Hewitt lowered the tailgate. 'I should also be able to squeeze in some hay.'

'Perfect.' Cressy slid the box into the ute tray then turned to scan the nearby trees. 'Mr Magpie has been in fine form today protecting his chicks so unless we want to be swooped we'd better keep moving. Fliss, how about you and I see what you need for Flame while you boys get the hay?'

'Sure. We can take my ute.' Denham turned towards the Land Cruiser. 'There's a bucket with our combined body weight's worth of carrots to go to Reggie and it's not even his birthday.'

From the corner of his eye Hewitt thought he saw Fliss shoot a frown towards her sister.

Denham drove past the stables to the rodeo yards he'd built for his bucking bulls and where Tanner trained his horses. But before they reached the yards, Denham stopped as a mountain of a bull lumbered towards them.

'So that's the infamous Reggie.' Hewitt took in the power of the Brahman-cross bull's shoulders and his athletic gait. 'I'll say this ... he's no pussy cat.'

'His offspring are showing they'll have his conformation as well as that bad-ass attitude Cressy and Fliss swear he doesn't have.'

Hewitt shook his head as the mottled grey bull eyeballed him. 'Nope, no bad-ass attitude there. He's all peaches and cream.'

'The thing is, when he's around Cressy and Fliss, he really is as gentle as they believe. I've never seen anything like the bond he has with them.'

Denham's phone rang. 'Sorry,' he said as he glanced at the caller ID. 'I need to take this.'

'No problem.' Hewitt reached for the bucket beside his boots. 'Reggie and I will get to know each other.'

'I forget you like living dangerously,' Denham said as he lifted the phone to his ear.

'Let's just say that feeding Reggie will be nothing like living across the garden from Fliss and seeing her every day.'

Sympathy flashed across Denham's eyes before he answered his call.

If anyone understood his struggle to contain his emotions and keep his distance from Fliss, it was Denham. When the bull rider had returned to Woodlea and Cressy was back in his life, he'd fought a similar battle.

Hewitt's jaw locked as he headed for Reggie. But not because the bull bellowed as he pawed the ground. Unlike Denham and Cressy, for him and Fliss there could be no clear way forwards. His family needed him.

CHAPTER
15

Hewitt's early morning knock offered Fliss a welcome break. DNA was leading her around in frustrating circles. The cookbook clue had provided her only lead, and now she needed to find a way to confirm or eliminate the names she'd discovered. She still didn't want to disturb Lewis, but there had to be a way she could find out if Valda and Patrick Ryan were connected to her mother.

Fliss stood and rolled her shoulders. At least the hours she'd spent in front of the computer last night had clarified one thing: there was no Ryan surname in Cressy's family tree. Which meant that the Ryans she'd been matched to had to be through her father's side.

'Come in,' she called as she left her office. She may not have had to say goodbye to Max and Molly yesterday, but with every day that passed she remained conscious that Hewitt would soon leave. So until then, she'd make the most of his friendship and companionship, even if that wasn't all she suspected she wanted. It was all that she could have, and it had to be enough. She'd never come between him and the family he loved and was honour-bound to look out for.

Hewitt walked through the front door and her stomach did its usual flip-flop. Her steps slowed. Instead of being dressed in his usual western shirts, with stubble blurring his jaw, he was clean-shaven and wearing a pale blue shirt she'd never seen before. Nerves took flight in her midriff. He couldn't be leaving already?

'Morning.'

Seriousness edged his greeting.

'Morning.' If he was returning to his family, loss wasn't going to make her sound vulnerable or needy, no matter how much she'd miss the broad-shouldered man standing before her. 'You smell nice.'

Heat warmed her cheeks at her too-quick and inane comment.

'Thanks. I hope I always smell … nice.'

'You do.' She forced her words to slow. 'Are you off somewhere?'

'Yes. Ava called. Dad hasn't been well and she's struggling with Quinn. He's fallen off the swing and was lucky to not hit his chin.'

'I'm sorry to hear that. I also don't envy Ava trying to keep Quinn quiet.'

Mouth dry, she braced herself for what he was about to say.

'I'm heading home … for a day.'

She blinked. 'A day?'

'Yes. I was wondering if you'd like to come?'

Shock quickly dissolved into delight. 'Are you sure? Your family mightn't want a stranger visiting at a difficult time.'

Hewitt's eyes crinkled at the corners. 'You're not a stranger. I'm sure Lizzie wouldn't let me through the door if I didn't bring you. Quinn also asked if you were coming as he has another tractor to show you.'

'I'd love to come. I'll get changed.'

'No rush. I'll check the dogs and chooks have water and make a call. We've a stop to make on the way.'

Half an hour later, Fliss emerged from the homestead wearing wedges, black jeans and a simple, fitted black top. She said goodbye to Max, Molly and the pups and brushed off the resulting white dog hair as she walked through the garden to Hewitt's ute.

Hewitt slid into the driver's seat and she examined his profile as the engine roared into life. She hadn't yet heard if Hewitt had managed to feed Reggie a carrot. All she knew was that the carrot bucket was empty when he and Denham had returned with the hay.

She still couldn't believe Cressy had set up the Reggie test for Hewitt. A part of her didn't want to know whether he'd passed or not. The intensity of her reaction when she'd thought he was leaving this morning didn't bode well with how she'd cope when the bluestone stables were empty.

'So what is the stop we have to make?' she asked as they drove away from Bundara.

'I need to pick up a present for Lizzie. It's something that will appreciate all this forecasted rain.'

Fliss stared out the window at the knee-high grass rippling and swaying in the paddocks. She hoped there wasn't much more rain coming. The recent sunshine had lowered the creek and river levels but it wouldn't take much to raise the water table again. Cressy and the other State Emergency Service volunteers would be back on high flood alert.

'Knowing it's for Lizzie, it will have to be something cute and adorable. Can I have a clue?'

'It needs a name.'

'Does it waddle?'

'Yes, and I'm hoping it teaches the duck she already has how to be a duck again.'

Fliss smiled. 'And what did you get for Quinn?'

'A new tractor cap.'

'He'll love that.'

Fliss settled back and enjoyed the drive to Mayfield. The landscape stretched and flattened until the road before them ran ribbon-straight into the horizon. Long-legged emus strolled alongside the train tracks that ran parallel to the bitumen. Even out here where there wasn't always consistent rain, the crops grew thick and heavy. To their left, a crop-dusting plane swooped and soared as it top-dressed and delivered a burst of fertiliser.

On the outskirts of a small town adjacent to the main road, Hewitt stopped. The stand out the front of a house selling honey and fresh eggs was a giveaway as to what lay behind the neat front fence. But when Fliss left the ute she saw a shaggy black pony also inhabited the house yard.

When Lizzie's new Aylesbury duck, with its snow-white feathers and yellow beak, was safely stowed in its box, Hewitt continued west. Fliss must have dozed. When the ute's momentum slowed, and train tracks clicked beneath the tyres, she opened her eyes. They'd turned left to drive over the railway line and past a row of mailboxes that made it easier for mail to be delivered to the nearby farms.

Hewitt cast her a grin. 'We're almost there.'

Fliss returned his smile but inside she silently mourned. Hewitt's eagerness to see his family turned his eyes a light grey. The grooves beside his mouth had lessened. She didn't need any further proof how much it meant for him to be connected to the people he loved. People who relied on him.

This time it was a cattle grid that rattled beneath the ute's tyres. First a corrugated shearing shed and yards appeared, then an assortment of farm buildings. The main house stood beneath established trees that suggested the large house was far older than its modern brick exterior. To its right was a weatherboard cottage with a pretty garden filled with the soft colour of annuals. Beside the cottage sat a cubbyhouse shaded by a nearby plane tree.

'Hewitt, you have a lovely home.'

'Thank you.'

She glanced at him. Pain had rasped his words. She reached over to touch his clean-shaven cheek. 'I can understand why you needed to come to Bundara to heal. It must be hard having memories wherever you look.'

'It is. But it's not as hard today as it was on the day I left.'

'That's great to hear.'

Hewitt didn't reply. The front door of the cottage had burst open and two small figures raced along the path and out the garden gate.

Hewitt chuckled. 'Poor Ava. She really didn't stand a chance keeping Quinn quiet.'

Fliss let Hewitt exit the ute first. Quinn and Lizzie flung themselves at him. Just like on the day he'd greeted them with such love at Bundara, Fliss's emotions swelled. She blinked away the mist in her eyes before she left her seat. Lizzie and Quinn ran over, their little arms hugging her tight.

A woman with shoulder-length silver hair, wearing a blue fitted dress, walked over with Ava. Fliss could see where Hewitt had got his grey eyes and cheekbones. Even with age and grief etched into her face, his mother was a beautiful woman.

Ava hugged Fliss while Hewitt wrapped his arms around his mother. He then made the introductions. Fliss was surprised when Vernette, instead of speaking, stepped forwards to embrace her. It was only when she pulled away that the older woman spoke.

'Welcome to Mayfield, Fliss. I'm so thrilled you could make it.'

'Thank you.'

A quack from inside the box on the trayback stopped all further conversation. Lizzie's eyes widened and she stayed still as though not sure about what she'd heard. Quinn had no such doubts.

'Careful,' Ava said as Quinn used the ute tyre to clamber into the ute.

Quinn peered into the holes in the top of the cardboard box and then waved for his twin to join him. Hewitt helped by using his good arm to lift Lizzie. She peeked into the box.

Face beaming, she straightened to hug Hewitt. 'Thank you, Uncle Hewy. Jemima was so lonely.'

'I thought she might be.'

Lizzie again looked through the box holes. 'I wonder what we should call her?'

Hewitt moved to collect Quinn's tractor cap from inside the ute and settled it on his head. He then lifted the twins down. Ava took their hands and together they followed Hewitt as he carried the box over to where a duck sat with two fluffy silkie hens. The curtains in the nearby cottage moved before a white kitten jumped onto the window ledge to watch Jemima meet her new friend. As the two white ducks got to know each other, loud quacking sounded.

Vernette turned to Fliss. 'I'm sorry Wade hasn't come out to greet you. He cut his foot and it must have been deeper than we thought as it's taking a long time to heal.'

'I hope his foot feels better soon. I'm looking forward to meeting him.'

Vernette hesitated. 'Apart from Wade hobbling around, he isn't quite himself at the moment.'

'That's more than okay. I understand.'

Relief relaxed Vernette's smile. 'Thank you. From what Hewitt has told me I knew you would.'

Fliss glanced up as Lizzie waved to her from the front door of the main house.

Vernette laughed quietly. 'Lizzie has baked you vanilla fairy cupcakes and is desperate for you to try one.'

'I could easily fit one in before lunch.'

After two cupcakes Fliss found herself seated at a long dining table with Lizzie on one side and Quinn on the other. Hewitt, Ava and Vernette took their seats, leaving a single place empty at the head of the table.

Hewitt poured the adults a glass of wine. He looked across at his mother as he pushed back his chair. She gave a small shake of her head.

'Just give him five more minutes, dear. I told him lunch was ready. He's very slow at the moment with that bad foot of his.'

Hewitt nodded and remained seated.

Vernette passed Fliss a large bowl of pumpkin and feta salad. 'Let's start. Wade won't mind.'

Her light words were at odds with the tension that bracketed Hewitt's mouth.

Fliss took hold of the salad. 'Thank you. This looks delicious.'

Beside her, Quinn fidgeted. Every so often he glanced towards the closed door.

She turned to him with a smile. 'Salad?'

He stiffened before pulling a horrified face.

'The only green things he likes are lollies,' Lizzie said in a conspiratorial whisper.

Fliss winked at Quinn. 'Which leaves more for me.'

As she'd hoped, Vernette and Ava smiled. Quinn's grimace eased as she piled pumpkin salad onto her plate.

She passed the salad to Lizzie and selected a slice of creamy quiche. The aromas filling the dining room made her mouth water. Vernette loved to cook and Fliss could see why it had been important to Hewitt that he learn his mother's family recipes. She snuck a sideways glance at him. Even though he joked with Quinn while he helped him put a piece of quiche on his plate, the line of his shoulders remained rigid.

Cutlery clinked as everyone ate. The hum of conversation filled the dining room.

The door swung open and Wade slowly walked through. He didn't acknowledge anyone as he limped to his chair. His clothes hung loose on his angular frame and his weathered skin was ashen. Vernette reached for the jug of water and placed it next to his water glass. When he was seated, she introduced Fliss.

Wade gave her a curt nod, his pale blue eyes shrewd and assessing. Fliss had no doubt that though his physical strength had diminished, his force of character remained formidable. Wade's eyes softened as he looked at the twins before he spoke in a low tone to Vernette. His wife patted his hand and offered him the pumpkin salad. Cutlery again clinked and the chatter resumed.

Hewitt started a conversation about the winter oats crop and cattle prices. Wade contributed before his attention focused on Fliss. 'How are those border collie puppies?'

'As fluffy as they are mischievous.' Not knowing if Hewitt was saving the new puppy as a surprise, she didn't mention Wade now being Poppy's owner. 'They've chewed through two pairs of gumboots, ripped up three tea towels and buried my dustpan brush in the garden.'

Lizzie giggled.

Amusement sparked in Wade's eyes and then faded. 'They're good dogs those border collies.'

'They are.'

'So when do you think this hard-headed son of mine will be right to come home?'

Fliss didn't let Wade's abrupt tone fool her. She'd seen genuine concern when he'd glanced at Hewitt.

'Two to three weeks. I'll make sure the hospital does another scan so there's no doubt his shoulder fracture has fully healed.'

Vernette looked across at Hewitt. 'That sounds like a sensible idea, doesn't it, dear?'

From across the table Ava masked a smile as Hewitt sighed. His family knew full well he'd had no plans to check the progress of his injury. 'I guess so.'

Wade poured himself a second glass of water. Fliss's fork paused halfway to her mouth as a suspicion formed. There could be far more to why his foot hadn't healed than his wound being deep.

She needed to talk to Hewitt the first chance she could get.

After Hewitt helped clear lunch from the dining table and Fliss had followed the twins outside, he took the opportunity to see his father.

He walked into the living room that had become his father's haven. Here he could sit in his leather recliner and watch the news, read a book from the library along the back wall or use the computer Hewitt had set up on a side desk. The oversized window overlooked the shed and paddocks, enabling his father to see what was happening on the farm. Dean continued to help out and to manage Mayfield until Hewitt's return.

Hewitt didn't glance at the family photos covering the walls. He might be better able to cope with the memories woven into the fabric of his home but his conscience wouldn't allow him to look into the face of his twin. Brody's laughter would have echoed over the dining room table at lunch if Hewitt hadn't let him down.

He took a seat beside his father's recliner.

'Came to see Quinn, did you?' His father spoke without making eye contact. 'Those stitches haven't slowed him down.'

'I didn't think they would. I also came to see you.'

His father scowled. 'As you can see, I'm fine.'

'No, you're not.'

Hewitt readied himself for his father's irritation. Since losing Brody, his fuse had shortened. But instead of the expected gruff retort, his father studied him.

'You know Fliss will make sure that you have that x-ray.'

'I know.'

'And you'll do it.'

'Yes. Dr Fliss isn't to be messed with.'

A shadow of a smile shaped his father's lips. 'That's what I thought. Ava's like a daughter to us, but she was so young when she married Brody. He needed someone like Fliss to pull him into line.'

Hewitt stared at his father's rugged features. This was one of the few occasions when he'd mentioned Brody's name, and the first time in a long time he'd said a bad word about him.

Hewitt rubbed his chin. 'Was I the only one who didn't know he needed to be pulled into line?'

'Brody was very good at telling people what they wanted to hear. Your mother suspected he was shirking his family responsibilities but didn't know for sure. It's no secret Brody and I weren't getting along, but it wasn't the farm we were arguing over. I knew he was never at home. We also had a pretty heated blue about him bull riding again.'

Hewitt touched his father's arm. He'd had no idea their strong, unemotional father was racked with guilt. As much as he loved his twin, Brody's actions had caused so much pain and heartache.

'Dad, it's not your fault. Ava and I feel responsible for him being on that bull as well.' He clenched his jaw before glancing at the photo of Brody on the wall. 'But at the end of the day, the only person really responsible is Brody.'

His father grunted. 'Your mother and I didn't raise him to be selfish. But even as a kid he could be stubborn and not see sense. I'd like to think that one day he'd have grown up.'

'Has Ava ... spoken to you?'

'Yes.' His father's voice softened. 'I know she was worried about what we would think but we're very happy for her and Dean. The twins like him. He doesn't rush them and they enjoy his company.' His father paused and his stare hardened. 'As different as you are to Brody, you'll have no sense either if you don't start looking after yourself as well as you look after us.'

Hewitt shrugged. 'I'm fine. My shoulder's almost healed.'

'That's not what I'm talking about and you know it.' His father used the remote control to turn on the television. 'I'm sure you've better things to do than sit here with me. You have a guest to entertain. I'll see what the weather's doing and take my nap.'

Hewitt came to his feet. It wasn't belligerence roughening his father's words and shaking his hands but emotion. Hewitt clasped his thin shoulder. 'I'll come back later.'

Hewitt quit the room. He hadn't deliberately misunderstood what his father had said about looking after himself, he'd just been floored. Over the years his father hadn't ever meddled in any of his or Brody's relationships, even when they'd brought home girlfriends that were unsuitable. But he'd just made it clear that Hewitt needed someone in his life. As brief as the note of warmth had been when he'd mentioned Fliss's name, it was enough to tell him his father was impressed.

Shoulders rigid, he headed out to where Fliss was pushing Lizzie on a swing with Quinn playing in the sandpit next to them. He didn't need to be told that Fliss wasn't a woman to let get away. In a perfect world he'd hold on tight and never let go. But it was a far from perfect world and, even now Dean was on the scene, Hewitt's commitment to his family couldn't waver.

Fliss greeted him with a warm smile as Ava's voice sounded from over at the cottage.

'Coming, Mamma,' Lizzie called, using her feet to slow the swing. 'Mum wants us inside, Quinn.'

Her twin frowned but shook his tractor free of sand. He flashed Hewitt and Fliss a grin and raced off after his sister.

Fliss came to Hewitt's side before turning to wave at the twins who'd lifted the curtain in the cottage window to watch them. Snowball jumped onto the window ledge beside them. 'Is there somewhere ... quiet we can talk?'

'Yes, my place. Dad's having a rest and I suspect Mum is as well. I can pick up my suit for the ball while we're there.'

'Sounds great.'

They walked side by side towards his ute.

'Jemima and Puddles are already best friends,' Fliss said as the two white ducks swam by on the dam beside them.

'The dogs will be pleased.' Over near the stables the dog kennels stood empty. Dean would have the two liver-coloured farm kelpies out working stock. 'They can have their water bowls back. As big as Jemima is, she still manages to swim in them.'

After Fliss slid into the passenger seat, he started the engine. Once over the cattle grid, he turned left. Red dust rose in a vivid plume behind them. After the wet back roads around Bundara, it was a novelty to see dust again.

He hoped what Fliss needed to talk about wasn't Quinn's chin. Now he'd received stitches once, he wouldn't be so cooperative next time. 'Is Quinn's chin healing okay? It looks a little red.'

'It's fine. The stitches will be right to come out in another two days.'

'Those two days won't be able to pass quick enough for Ava.' He glanced at Fliss. Her expression remained preoccupied. 'Sorry if lunch wasn't very … relaxed.'

'You don't need to apologise. You never met my grandfather. He didn't suffer fools gladly and over the years we had some awkward and memorable meals when we had people over. I don't want to pry, but is it all right if I clarify a few things about your father?'

'Sure.'

'He's very thin now, but I'm guessing he was a bigger man once?'

'He's always been strong and solid but after we lost Brody the weight fell off him.'

'Has he had a medical recently?'

'I wish. You think I'm a bad patient; try getting my father to even walk past a hospital.'

'So he didn't see anyone about his foot?'

'No, he refused. But then again he refuses to go out at all so it mightn't just be the doctor he's avoiding.'

'He hasn't seen a grief counsellor?'

'Actually, he has. I made sure we all saw someone in the months … afterwards.'

'I'm glad you all had some professional support.'

Hewitt frowned as he drove up the driveway to a farmhouse with a neat lawn but no garden. 'Maybe I stopped taking him to see

Cheryl too soon. Knowing him, he wouldn't have talked as much as we all did.' He paused. 'Do you think Dad's depressed?'

'No ... but I think he could have type 2 diabetes.'

Hewitt parked out the front of the red-brick house and turned off the engine. 'Diabetes?'

'Yes. It all fits—the cut on his foot that won't heal and his excessive thirst, weight loss, tiredness, mood swings and irritability.'

Hewitt tunnelled a hand through his hair. 'So Dad's physically sick and how he's been this past year mightn't all be down to grieving for Brody?'

'Sorry, I believe so. He really does need to see a doctor and to have some blood tests done as soon as possible.'

Hewitt searched Fliss's face. Her solemn expression had cleared but her eyes remained serious. 'I take it this isn't exactly the best news?'

'Well, it depends on how you look at it. With a proper diet, exercise and medication he can feel better. This would have to have a positive impact on his mental health. But diabetes is a serious condition and one he'll have to manage for the rest of his life. The damage he may have done to his pancreas can't be reversed.'

'Anything that gets him back into the paddock has to be a positive thing, even if it means he needs to take his health more seriously. The life he leads now isn't a life at all.' Hewitt anchored his hands onto the steering wheel so he wouldn't be tempted to thank her with anything but words. 'Thank you. Dad could have gone on for months, even years, living with this, and no one would have known. I'll have a talk to him about seeing a doctor.'

As if sensing his self-control was unravelling faster than a ball of his mother's wool, Fliss pushed open her door. 'You're welcome.'

Careful to keep his attention away from her mouth, Hewitt led the way along the path towards the Federation-style farmhouse.

'I can talk to your dad if you like,' Fliss said as Hewitt unlocked the wooden front door. 'It might come better from me?'

'We'll see what mood he's in when he wakes up.'

Fliss stepped through the door he held open and walked along the hallway. She examined the two unfurnished front rooms. 'Now this is what I call minimalist decor.'

'That's one way of describing it.' He followed her into the kitchen. 'Another would be practical. I don't spend much time here.'

He looked around as though seeing the home he'd lived in since university through Fliss's eyes. The house was a reflection of his restlessness. There were no personal photographs or homely touches. The only sign that someone used the kitchen was the coffee machine and the single mug that sat beside it. When Ava and Brody were married he'd offered to swap the larger house for their cottage, but Ava had fallen pregnant and wanted to live close to Vernette and Wade.

Fliss stuck her head into the nearby room that served as his office. 'I can see you spend time in here—there's actually furniture. Can I take a closer look at the pictures on the corkboard? That sandstone house looks familiar.'

'Go ahead. I'll go find my dinner suit.'

He returned to find Fliss studying the properties he'd pinned to the board. Properties he'd seriously considered buying before Brody's death. Since then he'd been too focused on taking care of everyone to remove the pictures.

Fliss looked at him, expression thoughtful. 'These are all blue-chip properties and worth a small fortune. I recognise that sandstone house. It was on the market when I was looking.'

'I've worked hard, saved and been lucky with off-farm investments. Whichever property I bought would have been my home and … my future.'

Hewitt couldn't stop his words from deepening. He turned away to hide his torment. By following his dreams he'd only robbed Brody and his family of their own futures.

'Hewitt …' Fliss came to his side. 'You're not to blame for Brody being on the bull, remember?'

She didn't touch him, but the concern warming her voice comforted him as though she had.

'But I am to blame for him not making it.' He dragged a hand over his face. 'I should have been Seth's pickup partner when everything went to hell. I should have read the bull sooner and been in the arena quicker.'

Fliss laced her fingers with his. 'You could have been the pickup rider and you could have read the bull sooner and Brody still could have not made it. You can't be guilty of something that was beyond your control. Brody's death was a tragic accident. I'm sad to say in my line of work I know they can, and do, happen.'

Hewitt stared at her. The conviction in her words and the honesty in her eyes unlocked a possibility that before had been inaccessible. Was he not to blame for any part of Brody's death?

She spoke again, her gaze intense. 'That property you've always dreamed of, it could still be a reality. There will be a way to make looking after your family work alongside you living your own life. The best place to start will be with your father's health.' Fliss's grip on Hewitt's hand tightened. 'Let's go see him.'

The determination angling Fliss's chin hadn't lessened when they returned to Mayfield. They entered the kitchen where his mother was pouring tea into his father's favourite pottery mug.

'Hi, dear, your father's awake and wants a cuppa. Then we can sit and chat. I want to hear all about this ball. It's on this weekend, isn't it?'

While she spoke, she spooned his father's usual two teaspoons of sugar into his black tea. From the corner of his eye he caught Fliss's frown.

'Yes, it is,' he said, as Fliss approached the kitchen bench. Her eyes met his with an unspoken question. She wanted to be the one to talk to his father. He nodded. It didn't matter if his father was in a sociable mood or not, Fliss could more than deal with him.

'Vernette,' Fliss said. 'Is it okay if I take Wade his tea? We didn't get a chance to chat much at lunch.'

'That would be lovely. Thank you. Here ...' She placed two of Lizzie's vanilla cupcakes onto a white plate. 'He'll like these as well.'

When Fliss left, concern lined his mother's face. 'I hope your father's on his best behaviour. He can be a bear when he wakes up. He never used to be.'

'Fliss will be fine. She took Dad his tea because she needs to talk to him. Mum, Fliss thinks Dad might have diabetes.'

His mother moved to sit at the kitchen table.

Hewitt sat beside her and took her hand. 'Mum?'

'I'm fine, dear. I'm just ... relieved. I've known for a while something wasn't right.' She patted Hewitt's hand. 'This actually could explain a lot. Let's hope he's willing to see a doctor.'

'Fliss will make sure of it.'

Hewitt squeezed his mother's fingers before he went to make her a cup of tea. She hadn't taken more than three sips when Fliss returned.

Her smile at Vernette was serene. 'Wade said you'd have the number to call to make him a doctor's appointment?'

'I do.' His mother stood to clasp Fliss's hands. 'Thank you. You're a miracle worker.'

The joy faded from Fliss's smile as his mother moved to the top drawer where she kept her phone book. Fliss slid into the chair beside Hewitt.

'Everything okay?' he asked, voice low, feeling powerless against the guilt that refused to relinquish its hold on her. If he could he'd shoulder her burden at being unable to save a patient.

'Yes. Wade wants to see you.'

'Do I need to wear body armour?'

To his relief, her lips curved. 'No. I told him if anything happened to your shoulder he'd be the one sitting the two hours in the hospital fracture clinic while you're assessed and x-rayed.'

Hewitt returned her smile before heading for the living room. His father sat in his leather recliner staring out the window. Hewitt sat in his usual chair. Expression stony, his father turned to look at him.

'Fliss thinks I'm sick. What do you think?'

'I think she could be right.'

'I do too.' Hewitt wasn't sure what he was expecting but, just like in his mother's face, he glimpsed relief in his father's eyes. 'Do you know why I don't go to town?'

Hewitt shook his head.

'Because I can't last the trip without needing to find a bathroom. It's all this water I drink. Once I'm there I then need to go again. I just … don't want to be a burden. You all already have so much to deal with.'

Hewitt covered his father's hand with his. 'You'll never be a burden.'

His father swallowed. 'I sure feel like one. I just want to stop being so useless. I can't even walk outside with this foot.' His father stared out the window, his shoulders slumped. 'I just want to get back to the farm.'

'And you will.' Hewitt made no attempt to hide the emotion rasping his words. 'Let's get you checked out and go from there. Fliss will be with you every step of the way. It's how she is. She cares.'

His father didn't immediately answer as noise echoed from the kitchen. Lizzie and Quinn had come over to the main house. Fliss's laughter sounded, followed by a squeal from Lizzie.

His father spoke without looking at him. 'Remember what I said about looking after yourself.'

Hewitt stood and clasped his shoulder. 'I will.'

CHAPTER

16

'Earth to Fliss,' Taylor said, pausing as she coiled a section of Fliss's hair around a hair straightener.

'Sorry, I was off in la la land. What did I miss?'

Taylor grinned across at Cressy and Ella as they sat in the hair salon, their hair already in elaborate up-dos ready for the ball that evening. The girls were the last of Taylor's clients. 'Your sister saying I should be thankful you were quiet.'

Cressy lowered her magazine. 'Don't forget I have a lifetime's worth of proof that when you get your hair done you're usually more ... vocal.'

'I know I'm a control freak but I'm not that bad.'

Cressy kinked a brow.

'Okay, yes, I might have been a little worried that the Sydney hairdresser we went to as kids didn't know the difference between a trim and a crew cut, but you'll be happy to know I've mellowed in my old age.'

Ella nodded. 'I do believe you have. The old Fliss wouldn't ever have let Edna catch her wearing clothes covered in dog hair.'

It was true. The irony was that the more Fliss struggled to regain control the more she realised she didn't always need it. Even when covered in dog hair and when her lawn was strewn with stuffing from a cushion the puppies had torn, the sun still rose the next day.

Helping Hewitt through his grief had also helped her. She was beginning to understand it wouldn't have mattered what she'd done for Caitlyn, the young mother wouldn't have made it. Just like she'd explained to Hewitt, tragic things happened. Some things, like her feelings for him and her DNA, were simply beyond her control. She hadn't failed her patient, she'd done her best and it was time to try and take solace in the fact.

'I have.' She met Taylor's eyes in the mirror. 'I also have complete faith in Taylor so there's no need to say anything. As long as I don't leave here looking like a sexy fairy, I'll be happy.'

'If I do say so myself, that was some of my best work. Hewitt appreciated how gorgeous I made your hair look.'

Both Ella and Cressy lowered their magazines.

'What?' Cressy said, indignant. 'I never heard about this.'

'There's nothing to tell,' Fliss said. 'Hewitt didn't act any differently.'

And he hadn't on the day of the parade. She just hadn't mentioned the kiss that had exploded between them at the creek.

Taylor looked skywards. 'Please. The poor man couldn't look away. And you, Fliss, couldn't as well. But then again I couldn't either, along with the rest of the women. Hewitt and Tanner did make pretty impressive Highland warriors.'

'I love a man in a kilt,' Ella said, brown eyes dreamy.

Fliss tugged at the neck of the synthetic cape draped over her shoulders. She felt extra warm. She too was partial to men in kilts but only if they had an intense grey gaze and dark hair. 'There won't be any kilts tonight, just dinner suits. Men have it so easy not having to find something to wear.'

'They do,' Ella agreed. 'But you must admit it was fun trying on all those dresses.'

'It was.' Taylor arranged Fliss's hair into a messy bun. She stopped to glance at Cressy. 'One thing's for sure, you'll need a few lessons on your runway technique before you walk up the aisle.'

Cressy angled her chin. 'There was nothing wrong with my catwalk style. I happen to like wearing cowgirl boots with ball gowns.'

Fliss turned her head as much as she could with Taylor pinning her hair. 'Cressida Knight, don't even think about it. You're not wearing your dusty farm boots on your wedding day.'

Cressy's answering smile was all innocence.

Fliss looked at Ella. 'Ella …'

The vet winked at Fliss. 'It's okay. I'm with you. We've plenty of time to work out a compromise.'

Fliss made a mental note to search online for wedding cowgirl boots as soon as she could.

Taylor patted the last curl into place before showing Fliss the back of her elegant coiffure.

'Thank you. I love it.'

'You're very welcome.' Taylor reached for a can of hairspray. Fliss jumped from her seat as though she'd been bitten by a green ant.

Plans were made for Taylor to meet them at Ella's house after her mother, Sue, had straightened her hair for her. The boys were all meeting at Claremont, leaving their vehicles there, and using Meredith's four-wheel drive to travel to the ball. Whoever Taylor's mystery man was, he'd meet everyone at the venue. So far she'd given only one hint: it wasn't Rory.

The girls were getting dressed at Ella's and travelling the forty minutes to the converted cotton gin in her car. Designated drivers had already been decided and once the ball was over, Cressy and Fliss would ride back with the boys to Claremont. From there Fliss and Hewitt would head to Bundara.

Ella had stocked her fridge as a reward for surviving their marathon hairstyling session. Soon they had country music blaring and were sipping champagne and eating strawberries dipped in chocolate. The serious business of putting on makeup became a priority. Even tomboy Cressy spent time in front of the bathroom mirror.

Fliss applied her makeup in Ella's guestroom. Away from the others, her thoughts returned to Hewitt. He'd been the reason she'd been off with the fairies earlier. Since they'd returned from Mayfield three days ago, things had changed between them. It wasn't anything specific she could pinpoint. He still came by every morning to sit on the veranda and have a coffee with her. They continued their daily routine of riding around the cattle. She still went across to the stables to chat to his family over the internet. His father had seen the local GP and today had completed his blood tests.

She swept mascara through her lashes after realising she'd been staring at her reflection, her hand half raised, for several minutes. There was just a new intensity when Hewitt looked at her and a constant vigilance when they were in close contact. There'd been no more accidental touches when she handed him his coffee or when they'd help each other saddle the horses. It was as though a divide had opened up between them and Hewitt firmly remained on his side.

The doorbell rang. Ella's voice sounded as she invited Taylor inside and told her to make herself at home. Fliss finished her makeup and slipped on a classic black ball gown. She'd tried on a variety of Ella's and Taylor's dresses when they'd all come to Ella's for dinner the other night, but in the end she'd stuck with an old favourite. Her mother had helped her choose the strapless A-line gown for her university graduation ball. The style was simple and wouldn't make her stand out in the crowd. She added some crystal earrings and a bracelet and slipped on her blind-date-killer heels Cressy insisted she wear.

Her sister appeared at the doorway and Fliss stared. The no-frills cowgirl was unrecognisable. She was going to make the most breathtaking bride.

'Cressy, you look absolutely gorgeous.'

'Thank you.' Cressy swirled to show off the full deep-red organza skirt that fell below the fitted velvet bodice. 'I scrub up all right, if I do say so myself.'

'More than all right. You look so much like Mum in her younger photos.' Fliss touched the fine material of the skirt. 'You definitely didn't have this dress the other day.'

'No. When Denham and I went north I saw it in a bridal shop. I wanted to get ideas for wedding dresses but ended up trying this on as I loved it so much. But, you know me, I spend my life in jeans so decided not to buy it.'

'Let me guess … Denham bought it to surprise you.'

'Yes! I had no idea. It turned up yesterday.'

Fliss had no doubt that after Denham had seen Cressy in the dress he couldn't have left the gown in the store. It fitted her to perfection. The rich colour complemented the creamy hue of her skin and the glossy darkness of her hair. 'Denham's such a keeper.'

Cressy's expression radiated contentment. 'I know.' She held out a black clutch. The delicate crystals embedded in the clasp glittered. 'I bought this for you the other day when I made a flying visit to

Dubbo. I knew you'd wear your black dress and our grandmother's earrings. I thought it would match.'

'Thank you. You know me too well. It matches beautifully.' Fliss gave her sister a hug, careful not to crush Cressy's full skirt.

'I'm so glad you're coming with us.'

Fliss eased herself away. 'Me too.'

It wasn't only her control-freak side that had loosened up. Her anxiety at attending the crowded ball had subsided to a dull murmur. Lately she'd noticed that she had more days when her nerves didn't blindside her than days where she felt overwhelmed. She'd even been able to explain diabetes to Wade without faltering and had answered his questions with confidence.

Heels clicked on the wooden floorboards before Ella and Taylor entered. The smell of perfume filled the room.

Ella wore a fitted rose-gold dress that skimmed her curves and emphasised her long legs. Taylor also wore a slimline dress but in a powder blue that matched her eyes and highlighted the pale sheen of her blonde hair.

She lifted her phone. 'Come on, all you beautiful girls, gather round. I want to send Rory a photo.'

Everyone clustered close to the hairdresser.

'Smile.' Taylor's phone clicked.

Fliss scooped her phone from the bed. 'My turn. Best duck faces.'

It took two attempts to snap a photo between Cressy and Ella dissolving into laughter and Taylor doing dramatic dance poses.

Ella leaned over to check the time on Fliss's screen. 'How does leaving in ten minutes sound? Tanner texted and the boys have left but will save us a parking space.'

'Sounds great,' Fliss said. Taylor and Cressy nodded.

The women left to make final touches to their hair and makeup and Fliss was again alone. Laughter and chatter echoed through the house. All Fliss needed to do was transfer the contents of the plain black clutch she'd already filled to the one Cressy had given her.

Fliss opened the crystal-embedded clasp and her fingers stilled. Cressy had slipped a photograph inside. She slid out the picture. Knees unsteady, she sat on the edge of the bed.

The photo was of Hewitt feeding Reggie carrots. Not only did Hewitt look relaxed, Reggie's eyes had that glazed expression he wore when Fliss or Cressy scratched his forehead.

Hewitt hadn't only passed the Reggie test, he literally had Reggie eating out of the palm of his hand. She turned the picture over. Her sister had handwritten a single line.

Not just man enough for you, but a once in a lifetime man.

It wasn't just Cressy's words that caused Fliss's chest to tighten but the realisation that she'd always known Hewitt was a man like no other. From the day he'd arrived she'd been flung out of her comfort zone. Hewitt made her feel and want things she'd never thought she'd be capable of. Love. A family. The question was whether she should heed Cressy's message or keep playing it safe.

The line Hewitt had carefully drawn between them over the past few days would ensure their relationship didn't progress any further. It insulated them both from potential hurt and heartache. He'd been upfront in saying he hadn't come to Bundara to cause trouble. But she no longer wanted to colour between the lines. An unfamiliar recklessness flickered inside. She wanted to live in the moment and make the most of what life offered.

'Five minutes,' Ella called out.

Fliss came to her feet, knees now steady, and transferred the items between the two clutch bags. She slid the photo into the bag she'd emptied for safekeeping. She wasn't letting fear control her anymore. She'd start by bridging the divide Hewitt had built between them.

The trip to the cotton gin passed with much laughter and high spirits. Cressy had given Fliss an intent look when Fliss had placed the sparkly black clutch on her lap. Fliss had mouthed the words 'talk later'.

It didn't seem long before the rolling hills of Woodlea gave way to the flat contours of land being readied for cotton. Come autumn, the channel-irrigated rows of bare earth would be white and the adjacent roadsides would be dusted with cotton lint.

When they reached the cotton gin a parking attendant wearing a fluoro vest guided them into the sea of cars. Cressy called Denham and he gave them directions to where they were parked.

'The boys didn't get here much before us,' Fliss said, as Ella pulled up alongside Meredith's four-wheel drive. Tanner was shrugging on a dinner jacket and Denham was slinging a black bow tie around his neck. Intent on looking for Hewitt, Fliss almost missed the blond man who approached to shake hands with Denham.

She turned to Taylor. 'Rodger Galloway's your mystery man? Does Edna know?'

'Yes. She needs to move on.'

Cressy giggled. 'Go Taylor.'

Fliss smiled. 'I would have loved to have been a fly on the wall when Edna found out.'

'I believe,' Taylor said, with raised brows, 'she was speechless.'

'No way,' Ella said, opening her car door. 'Not possible.'

Taylor nodded. 'Rodger's girlfriend couldn't make it so Edna sat him next to Harriet Knox as her fiancé wasn't able to go either. So he was more than happy when I called.'

'I bet he was,' Fliss said as she caught sight of Hewitt. 'Edna and Mrs Knox have long been plotting a family merger.'

Fliss barely heard everyone's laughter as they manoeuvred themselves out of Ella's four-wheel drive in their dresses and heels. Fliss stayed in her seat and took a moment to breathe. Hewitt in casual clothes made her stomach flutter, but Hewitt in formal black and white made her breath stall. His grey eyes met hers through the window and she forced herself to smile. Hewitt wasn't the only one looking at her.

Cressy opened the car door. 'Everything okay, Fliss?'

'Yes.' She held up a pair of black heels she was thankful she'd taken off for the drive. 'I'm just strapping myself back in.'

Thankful for a distraction, she looked past Cressy at Rodger. She hadn't seen him since moving back home to Woodlea. Like Bethany, he was tall and resembled their reserved father. 'Hi, Rodger, great to see you. It's been a while.'

'It has. I'm looking forward to catching up over dinner.'

Fliss concentrated on securing her feet into her sky-high shoes. She left her seat, careful her heels didn't catch in the long skirt of her dress.

Cressy and Denham led the way to where guests were congregating at the cotton gin entrance. Fliss waited, heart racing, conscious that Hewitt hadn't moved. When it was just the two of them, he came to her side.

'You look ... stunning.'

In the waning light she wasn't sure but she thought a muscle worked in his jaw. He offered her his arm and she breathed in the cedar notes of his aftershave.

'Thanks. You don't look too bad yourself.' She slid her hand around the fine wool of his dinner jacket and gripped the hard strength of his muscles beneath. 'Don't tell Cressy, but I think I like her idea of wearing boots instead of heels. My power-dressing days are long gone.'

Hewitt laughed softly, the husky sound wrapping around her. She strengthened her hold on his arm. It wasn't anxiety rendering her light-headed, but anticipation. Tonight there were no more ground rules. Tonight there was no more need to play it safe.

Cressy turned to look back to where they were and smiled.

Thankful that Fliss was happy to walk and not talk, Hewitt kept his pace slow so she wouldn't struggle in her heels. He needed to collect himself and to reinstate his control.

Her swept-up hair exposed the elegant line of her neck and called for him to explore the smooth contours. Her perfume was a subtle floral scent that reminded him of the vases of summer flowers his mother displayed on the dining room table.

As for her mouth ... He risked a glance sideways. Whatever the not-quite-pink-but-not-quite-red colour was called, it highlighted the full sweep of her lips and reminded his testosterone it'd been far too long since he'd kissed her. He looked forward and forced himself to focus on where they walked.

Their trip to Mayfield had changed everything. Seeing Fliss with his family, and how patient she'd been with his father, only cemented how generous and compassionate she was. The fact she was whip-smart and knew her own mind only made him fall harder. His father had told him to look out for himself like he looked out for others, but the only way he could do that was if Fliss never left his side.

Tension dug across his shoulders. The reality was the person he had to look out for the most was Fliss. Tanner's big-brother talk had driven home how vulnerable she'd been after the loss of her patient. She'd also had to come to terms with knowing she wasn't connected by blood to the man she'd believed was her father. So over the past few days he'd made sure there had been no opportunity for things to develop further between them. He'd given his word he wasn't there to hurt her. He couldn't start something that would threaten the confidence she'd regained.

'The hospital fundraising committee has done such a wonderful job, haven't they?' Fliss's quiet words broke the silence between them. 'From the amount of people here they must have reached their target?'

'They have. Meredith took a call earlier and apparently the last-minute ticket sales exceeded the committee's expectations.'

'That's wonderful.'

Hewitt nodded as they joined the queue entering the ball. Fliss's hand stayed curled around his arm as the line moved. Every so often her body would brush against his and it took all of his strength to not put his hand around her waist and anchor her to his side. Ahead of them, the large cream steel shed that usually housed a working cotton gin had been transformed. A white marquee formed a stylish entrance in which fairy lights had been strung to form a graceful canopy. As dusk settled, the glow of the delicate lights intensified.

The white theme continued inside the main building. Rows of tables featured fragrant white candles surrounded by ivy wreaths. Each centrepiece rested on a round mirror that sat on a crisp white table runner. Thick white ribbons had been draped over the back of each chair.

Fliss stopped to touch an ivy centrepiece. 'No wonder the ivy covering Meredith's water tank looks like Taylor's taken to it with her hair clippers.'

From over to Hewitt's right, close to the makeshift dance floor, Cressy waved. The pathway between the tables narrowed and Fliss released his arm to weave her way over. Relief relaxed his jaw. As much as he missed her touch, he couldn't afford to be so physically close to her again. He couldn't trust that his control would hold.

They'd almost reached their seats when she came to an abrupt stop. His hands rested on her waist to prevent himself from running into her. His hard-won composure dissolved as she leaned back into his arms before moving away as the path in front of them cleared.

A figure dressed in fuchsia pink sailed towards him.

'Hewitt, how wonderful you're here.' Edna crushed him in a firm and cloying embrace. 'Don't you look dashing in your suit.'

Edna released him. She gave Fliss a thorough once-over before air-kissing her cheeks. 'So good of you to recycle a gown, Felicity. Now, Rodger has a steady girlfriend, even though he and Harriet would be so suited, so I've sat you on the opposite side of the table. I won't let you ruin his life again.'

'I wouldn't dream of sitting anywhere else.'

Fliss's dry tone appeared lost on Edna as she again zeroed in on Hewitt.

Behind Edna's back, Cressy winked as she rearranged the name cards on the table.

'Now, Hewitt,' Edna said, taking his arm, 'we must find Bethany. Even though you did go on the trail ride, I told her you mightn't be quite up to dancing. She's happy to keep you company. You had such a long chat when you first met.'

Edna glanced over Hewitt's shoulder. 'There she is. Even though Bethany's here with Drew Macgregor—I'm so thrilled he listened to reason and left the farm to come tonight—she of course would love to sit next to you during dinner.' Edna stiffened and her mouth fell open before she spoke through clenched teeth. 'That's *not* Drew Macgregor.'

Hewitt turned to see a dark-haired man accompanying Bethany. From the cut of his suit and his slick hairstyle he clearly wasn't a country boy. Behind the couple had to be Noel, Edna's husband. Bethany and Rodger shared the older man's square jawline and straight-edged nose.

'Excuse me.' Edna released his arm and bustled over to intercept her husband and daughter.

'Good on Bethany,' Fliss said quietly.

'Maybe.' Hewitt watched as the dark-haired man took a step back so Bethany bore the brunt of her mother's disapproval. 'As much as I hate to say this, Edna might be on the money about Bethany's city boy. She could do better.'

'I think you're right. If any man I dated used me as his first line of defence we wouldn't even make it to the table to sit down.'

'I'll remember that.'

Fliss smiled and he lost the fight to look away from her mouth. 'You don't have to. We don't need to go on any date. I already know I like what I see.'

The room closed in around him. Voices faded and lights dimmed. All he could focus on was the woman staring at him, her thick-lashed hazel eyes serious and her body angled towards his. With her heels, all it'd take was a dip of his head and her mouth would meet his. To think he'd once thought being out in public and being surrounded by people would guarantee nothing could happen between them. The kiss-me-now look she gave him would bring even the strongest man to his knees.

'Fliss …'

He hadn't realised he'd groaned her name until she blinked. Her chest rose and fell as she breathed deeply.

'Sorry.' She brushed the front of his jacket as if removing a piece of fluff. 'I forgot where we were. Edna's also right on another thing. You do look dashing in your dinner suit.'

She turned to find her seat. Hewitt followed and, avoiding both Denham's and Tanner's eyes, sat beside her. No one at the table would have missed what had just ignited between them. Cressy took the seat on his other side. Without saying a word, she passed him a beer.

To Hewitt's relief, conversation continued around him and he was soon discussing the forecasted rain and storms. Bethany came to the table alone and sat in the seat beside Taylor. The turbulence in her eyes said the cold weather front wasn't the only thing brewing trouble.

She reached for a bottle of red wine and poured a full glass. 'Men and mothers.'

Taylor chinked her wine glass with Bethany's. 'Here's to solidarity.'

Bethany's pretty face broke into a smile as she looked at her brother seated between Taylor and Fliss. 'Solidarity.'

Drinks flowed as they shared stories and laughter and soon the volunteer waitstaff delivered the first of the three courses. Once they'd finished their entrees of spiced lamb and pulled pork, a local dance troupe performed a sleek and glitzy dance routine. As the temperature within the cotton gin warmed up, Hewitt removed his jacket. Apart from small talk about the entree, Fliss spent her time reminiscing with Rodger, Taylor and Bethany. Hewitt didn't mind. The less interaction he had with Fliss the more their attraction would cool. There couldn't be any more intense and unguarded moments between them.

After the second course of pepper chicken and slow-cooked beef, Fliss excused herself and went to see a very pregnant Kellie who was sitting three tables over. Hewitt felt Cressy's attention on him as he watched Fliss move on to talk to Meredith and Phil. Tonight Fliss didn't wear her game face. Instead, quick with a natural smile, or a carefree laugh, she chatted with ease.

'Watch out world,' Cressy said, tone soft. 'The old Fliss is back.'

Before he could reply the party band burst into life. Music vibrated through the venue, bringing people to their feet. Tables emptied and the dance floor filled with people.

'Come on,' Cressy said above the noise of a saxophone, tugging his shirtsleeve. 'I'm sure Dr Fliss considers your shoulder healed enough to dance.'

Across the table Denham grinned in commiseration.

Cressy put her hands on her hips before marching around to drag him and Tanner to their feet. 'No smirking from you, Denham Rigby, or you, Tanner. One in, all in.'

Taylor came to her feet. 'Exactly. I've been waiting all night to dance and I'm not dancing on my own.' She flashed the boys a reassuring smile. 'Don't look so petrified. There can never be enough dad-dancing.'

Ella, Bethany and Rodger also stood. Bethany and Ella headed for the dance floor while Rodger made his way over to sit with his father.

'Safety in numbers,' Denham muttered to Hewitt as they headed after the girls.

The band's energy proved infectious. Denham's expression relaxed as he twirled a laughing Cressy before drawing her in for a kiss. The others danced as a group, with Taylor teaching them new dance moves. The whole time Hewitt kept track of where Fliss was. Her self-assurance may have appeared to have returned but he hadn't forgotten how adept she was at masking her fears.

The music tempo slowed and couples cuddled up on the dance floor. Ella fanned her hands in front of her face. 'I don't know about anyone else but I'm melting. I need a drink.'

Hewitt went to follow everyone to their table when he felt a hand on his back. He knew it was Fliss even before he turned. No other woman's touch fired his blood like hers did.

Her gaze held his in a silent question. He hesitated. Even with the time apart, he wasn't confident he could hold her close and not seek her mouth.

She linked her fingers with his. 'We're mature adults, remember?'

He couldn't reply, emotions pushed against his control, so he pulled her into his arms. He didn't imagine her sigh as she moulded herself against him. He held her tight. As one they moved to the music, but it was the connection between them that beat the loudest.

All too soon the song ended. Fliss didn't ease herself away. Instead she looked at him, her large amber eyes reflecting all the wants, needs and hopes that burned inside him. The moment had come to stop fighting what simmered between them. His hands tightened on her waist and he rested his forehead against hers. 'Not here.'

She tilted her head so her breath brushed his mouth. 'Where and when.'

He pulled back a little to look into her eyes. 'We need to talk first.'

'We do.' Her hand crept up to where he'd removed his bow tie and his shirt lay open. Her fingertips traced the indent of his collarbone. 'Tomorrow? When we can think clearly?'

He nodded. He could barely form a thought with Fliss touching him. If they tried to have a conversation later on tonight, talking would be the last thing on their minds.

She didn't move away. Her fingers stilled on the pulse in his neck. Whatever answers she read from the frenzied thud of his heart made her lips tilt.

'My place … early.'

'I'll be there, Dr Fliss.'

She slipped from his arms and disappeared into the crowd now jiving to an up-tempo number. Hewitt headed to his table. A beer already sat at his place.

Cressy pushed the glass towards him. 'I thought you might need one. It's okay, it's a light beer. I know you're driving.'

Hewitt took a long swallow. There was no point pretending Cressy hadn't seen what had happened on the dance floor. 'That sister of yours …'

'I know, words can't describe her sometimes. If it's any consolation, you're the only man who's ever handled her.' Cressy's eyes searched his. 'And you're the only man she's let get this close.'

Cressy didn't have to say the words that in all the time she'd known him, Fliss was the only woman he too had let get close. 'We're going to talk tomorrow.'

'Thank goodness, because if you don't do something about what's been going on since day one, these thunderstorms will have nothing on the electricity sparking between the two of you.'

Hewitt finished his beer while the girls went to dance. Tanner, Denham and Hewitt discussed the offset plough that had again broken before talk moved to the rodeo cattle and horses that would soon arrive at Claremont. Cressy returned to drag Denham back to the dance floor and every so often Ella and Taylor would sit out a song and rehydrate. Bethany had found a group of old Sydney school friends and now didn't seem to be missing her city man.

Taylor's ploy to take Rodger as her partner didn't appear to have worked. Edna's pride that her only son hadn't apparently been good enough for Fliss continued to colour her attitude towards both women. Edna's pursed lips whenever she glanced their way more than conveyed her disapproval about the altered seating arrangements.

Hewitt didn't see Fliss again until the last song was announced. She came to sit in the seat beside him. Before he could lower his arm from the back of the chair, she yawned and leaned against him. With everyone making the most of the final song, or finishing their drinks, no one appeared to notice them. He settled his arm around her and curved his hand over the warmth of her bare shoulder.

She lay her head in the hollow of his neck. 'I'm in trouble if I ever have to work another night shift. I'm out of practice even staying up late.'

His lips touched the silky darkness of her hair. 'You can sleep on the way home.'

Once the music finished, dinner jackets and discarded bow ties were collected and weary guests returned to the car park. Headlights lit up the night as a convoy of vehicles left the cotton gin. Hewitt drove Meredith's car with Fliss, Tanner, Denham and Cressy on board. Behind him Ella followed with Taylor. The vet would drive straight to Woodlea.

At Claremont, where Denham and Cressy were staying the night, Tanner repeated his offer for Fliss and Hewitt to also stay.

Fliss sent him a quick look before replying, 'Thanks but we'll head home. We've a busy morning planned.'

Hewitt helped a sleepy Fliss into his ute. After brushing her mouth over his, she snuggled into the seat and was soon asleep. The first of the lightning split through the night-blotted sky as he drove over Bundara's cattle grid.

CHAPTER
17

The crack of thunder almost directly overhead resounded like a stock whip.

Fliss sat up in bed and rubbed her tight temple. No luminous light glowed from her bedside clock. There had to be a blackout. The ache behind her eyes told her it must have only been a few hours ago that she'd crawled into bed after Hewitt drove them home from the ball. She'd taken a quick shower and vaguely remembered the splatter of raindrops as she'd fallen asleep.

Rain suddenly assaulted the tin roof. The force was almost deafening. Not bothering to throw her rugby top on over her black pyjama shorts and tank top she felt her way down the pitch-dark hallway into the kitchen. The vibrations of the storm rippled through the floorboards. The puppies would have to be scared even though they'd be safe and snug in the garden shed with Molly. Max had taken up residence in his kennel on the side veranda and, unless the rain turned horizontal, he'd remain dry.

She opened the first kitchen cupboard and took out a torch. At least Hewitt had fixed the loose guttering and secured the tin roof of the water tank. With this wind and wild rain she could only hope other parts of the old homestead stayed intact. She turned on the torch and shone the beam through the kitchen window.

There was no night sky, no garden view, just a wall of water. Clunking sounded as marble-sized balls of hail bounced off the glass. Quashing her unease, she headed for the laundry door to check the side veranda. Nearby trees provided shelter from the worst of the storm. Rain doused her, coating her arms and legs as she stepped onto the cold and wet floorboards. She peered into the kennel illuminated by a flare of weak lightning.

'How are you doing, Max?'

The border collie stretched and left his kennel to lick her hand. 'Look at you. You're not worried at all. You've seen this all before.'

Fliss bent to feel the blanket that hung over the lip of the kennel. It was damp. She turned the kennel around, making sure she angled it so Max would have room to get inside. He did so as soon as she stepped away.

A distorted light came from the direction of the shed. Hewitt would be checking on Molly and the puppies. A jagged lightning bolt hung suspended in the sky before a crack sounded. Fliss shivered. That was far too close.

She headed inside and along the hallway to the front door. Hewitt would come to check on her. Tonight there'd been a mutual acceptance, a recognition that they needed to stop resisting what was between them. And the knowledge brought with it both relief and peace.

The simple action of Hewitt holding her, of his lips touching her hair, didn't just affect her physically but also emotionally. Hewitt made her feel safe, adored, understood. The part of her that she'd always held back was no longer content to remain in hiding. She wanted to invest all of herself. She wanted the whole deal: a home, kids ... love.

Thunder clapped and she jumped. But that was a conversation for the morning. She had to be certain Hewitt shared her feelings and that he had worked through his grief and was ready for a relationship beyond friendship. There wasn't yet a clear way forward for either of them. She needed to decide whether or not to return to medicine, and if she didn't, what she'd do. Her savings wouldn't last forever. As for Hewitt, he had his family duty to honour as well as his dreams to run his own place.

She opened the front screen door which the wind tried to wrestle from her hands. Light bobbed before Hewitt jogged out of the rain and up the veranda steps. He wore a long oilskin coat and a broad-brimmed hat, and his jeans were dark where the rain had soaked the denim. He didn't try to speak. His gaze skimmed her face to check she was okay before he flicked off his torch. He set it beside the door and removed his hat to shake the water from the felt. Fliss moved aside to give him room to enter the house.

He stepped inside, the wind slamming the door behind him. It was impossible to speak over the noise so she shone the torchlight towards the hall rack where he could hang his hat and coat. But before Hewitt could shrug off the oilskin, lightning flashed with a simultaneous boom that reverberated like a gunshot. Fliss dropped the torch and grabbed the front of Hewitt's coat. She breathed in the smell of rain and the earthy scent of the wax-covered cotton. His arm came around her waist to steady her.

'It sounds worse than it is,' he said against her ear. 'The storm will pass soon.'

All she'd wanted was something to hold on to until her flight response settled. But when her knuckles felt the hot press of slick

skin and she realised Hewitt wasn't wearing a shirt, all she wanted
was him. She released his coat and ran her hands over the wet
ridges below. She couldn't hear the intake of his breath, only feel
the accelerated rise and fall of his chest. She hadn't even pushed the
oilskin to the point of his shoulders when his mouth claimed hers.

Just like in the creek, Hewitt's kiss took her to a place where only
heat and urgency existed. Never again would she think the whole
physical chemistry thing was overrated. Wherever Hewitt kissed,
nerve-endings flared into life and wherever he touched, her senses
burned. But it wasn't enough. She needed more. She'd waited a
lifetime to find a man like him.

She pressed kisses along the strong column of his throat as she
slid the oilskin coat free. It fell to the floor. As if in the distance,
thunder rumbled, but as his mouth returned to hers, she forgot
everything but the sensation of being pulled hard against him. He
wanted her as much as she wanted him. His hands found the skin
of her lower back and she shuddered as he traced the sensitive line
of her spine.

Breathing ragged, she entwined her fingers with his to lead him
along the hallway. The time for talking had passed. At the bedroom
door he framed her face with his hands and kissed her. His kiss was
so gentle and so tender it brought tears to her eyes. She knew what
he asked. She took hold of his right hand and raised his palm to her
lips. She had no fears or concerns about what was about to happen.
She'd never been so sure of anything in her life. She needed the
touch of the man before her as much as she needed her next breath.

She smiled, even though he wouldn't be able to see her expression,
before kissing him. She had his belt buckle undone even before
they made it to her bed. No words were needed to communicate,
no light needed to see. Their bodies had a language all of their own.
It wouldn't have mattered if the storm had blown the roof off from

over her head, all she could focus on was Hewitt and the way only he could make her feel.

Fliss awoke to the demure patter of rain and the warm weight of Hewitt's arm holding her close. The alarm clock blinked and light crept beneath the blind.

She hadn't thought she'd done anything to indicate she was awake except open her eyes, but Hewitt had known. His hand brushed the hair off her face as he kissed the top of her head. She eased away so she could examine his expression. His eyes were a clear grey and the lines beside his mouth were relaxed. He looked … happy.

She still had to ask. 'No regrets?'

His chuckle emerged husky and deep. 'Only that we can't spend the day in bed.'

She brought her mouth close to his to whisper, 'We can't?'

His hand caressed her jaw before his fingers slid into her hair. 'No. Hear that?'

'No.' All she could hear was the pounding of her heart. Waking up beside Hewitt made her happy, too. Then she heard a puppy howling. 'Someone's in trouble.'

Hewitt stole a quick kiss before leaving the bed to pull on his clothes. 'I'll go to the rescue.'

'I'll put the kettle on.'

Fliss enjoyed the view as Hewitt left dressed in nothing but his jeans. She slipped on her clothes that were strewn across her room. Once in the kitchen she answered Cressy's text asking if they were all right after the storm and busied herself making French toast.

Beyond the kitchen window leaves sparkled in the early morning sunshine and the trunks of trees glistened. But not all of the garden had appreciated the heavy rain and wind. Leaves and twigs littered the lawn and over near where they'd had the bonfire a larger branch had fallen.

Hewitt emerged from the stables wearing a grey T-shirt with his jeans. While he inspected the yard, the six puppies followed him. He disappeared from sight but soon the front door opened and closed. Fliss flipped the first piece of French toast as he entered the kitchen.

'That smells good.' He wrapped his arms around her waist and nuzzled her neck.

She smiled as his stubble scraped her skin and goose bumps rippled over her arms. 'That feels good.'

Hewitt stepped back. 'That's as good as it gets until we have our talk.'

Fliss spun around. 'Isn't it a little late for that?'

Hewitt moved to get two white plates from the hutch. 'I told Cressy we were going to so we will.' He looked to where Fliss's top lowered at the front. 'Because otherwise talking will be the last thing on our to-do list.'

After they'd eaten their French toast and Fliss lay curled up on his lap on the lounge, they made talking a priority.

Fliss went first. 'I know you've always said you don't want to hurt me but there's never going to be a right time between us. There's just now.'

Hewitt's fingers traced patterns on her thigh. 'True, but there can still be a wrong time. Is this … the right time?'

'It is for me. How about you?'

'I still miss Brody but I'm ready to live my life again.'

She touched her lips to his. 'And that's what it is, Hewitt, your life. I said earlier there will be a way to manage looking after your family and doing what you've dreamed of.'

When he stayed silent, she smoothed the stubbled line of his jaw. 'It's a little like my DNA search: the answer is in there somewhere, we just have to find it.' She slipped her arms around his neck. 'So until we do, how about we live in the moment? No pressure and no promises. When your shoulder's healed and you're right to return to Mayfield we can make decisions then about how we move forward.'

His eyes glinted as his mouth lowered to hers. 'You have yourself a deal.'

For the next three days life settled into a comfortable rhythm. Hewitt moved into the main house and they spent as much time together as possible. Fliss didn't know that such contentment was possible. She was such a slow learner. Having Hewitt by her side made her feel like she could do anything and that anything was possible. His laughter, companionship and the nights spent in his arms brought a joy and stability she hadn't realised her life lacked.

The storms delivered the promised rain and more. Huge mushrooms sprouted in the back lawn and moss grew on the bricks around the overflow of the rainwater tank. Catchments were again saturated and the run-off caused creeks and rivers to rise. The white wooden bridge was close to going under as water surged impatiently below. They'd made a slippery trip to Woodlea to stock up on food in case the roads closed. On the way they'd passed a bogged tractor and ute at a front farm gate. On their return trip the vehicles hadn't moved. It could be weeks before the farmer would be able to get them out.

Her DNA research continued and the Ryan list had been whittled down to five names. She'd found an online photo of a man with the Ryan surname who was still living in the beachside suburb where her mother had grown up. It might be wistful thinking, but there was something about the shape of his face that seemed familiar. He also was tall with tanned skin.

Hewitt's father's type 2 diabetes diagnosis had been confirmed and he'd surprised them all with his readiness to do what needed to be done. He was determined to get well so he could venture into the paddocks. She answered his text letting her know what day his meeting was with the dietitian and put her phone beside her computer. She'd run some more DNA segment comparisons before Hewitt returned from cleaning the quad bike after checking the calves. He'd sent the twins a photo and Quinn had been very impressed with how muddy Hewitt had made both himself and the four wheeler.

She'd just opened a file when her mobile rang. Cressy was calling from her landline.

'Hi, sis,' Fliss said.

'Afternoon. You sound cheerful.'

'You sound tired.'

'I am. We had two State Emergency Service call-outs last night. One because someone thought it was a sensible idea to drive through floodwater. The other one was to help move livestock.'

'This rain has to stop sometime, right?'

'Even if it does, it's too late for the rodeo and campdraft. The committee's cancelled this year's event.'

'That's a shame. Now Denham's not riding bulls, I was looking forward to sitting back, relaxing and enjoying the events.'

Cressy chuckled. 'No, you weren't. I bet life's very dull now he doesn't have any injuries for you to boss him around about.'

Fliss should have known better than to stay silent while she thought about how life definitely wasn't dull with Hewitt no longer sleeping in the stables.

Cressy's sharp intake of breath was audible. 'Felicity Anne Knight, are you holding out on me?'

'No, not on purpose. I have left you messages.'

'Actually, you have. And I've tried to call. You're forgiven. So I take it your talk with Hewitt went ... well.'

'Yes. We're just taking things slow and will see where things go.'

'I'm so pleased. Denham would be too. We knew you'd be good together.' Cressy's voice turned teasing. 'See, Reggie knows what he's doing. Hewitt and Denham are the only ones to have passed the carrot test.'

Fliss laughed. 'I still can't believe you set Hewitt up. Thanks for the photo. It helped put everything into perspective.'

'I hoped it would.' Cressy paused. 'Fliss ... I'd better go. Denham's just texted. There's been a two-vehicle crash on Tathra Road and it's closed. I'll get ready in case there's an SES page.'

'Okay. Talk soon. Be safe.'

Fliss ended the call and frowned at her phone. She hadn't been mistaken. She'd felt a rush of adrenaline at the mention of the accident. But could she trust this as a sign that medicine still called her? She didn't have faith her fears wouldn't undermine her confidence if she returned to the career she'd loved.

Deep in thought, she resumed her DNA segment matching. When her mobile rang, she didn't look at the caller ID, assuming it was Cressy ringing about something she'd forgotten to mention.

But it was Kellie's breathless voice on the other end. 'Hi, Fliss.'

Fliss's brain switched into action. 'Hi, Kellie. Everything okay?'

'I'm not sure. Jase's out helping move stock to higher ground at Drew Macgregor's. The creek cut the road so it will take him a while to get back. It's two weeks too soon for the baby but I don't feel ... right. I've a few niggles. I don't think they're contractions, just Braxton Hicks. My back's not sore.'

'Have your waters broken?'

'No. I would call the hospital but there's been that crash. I don't want to drag an ambulance out here if it's nothing. With all the water around others might need help. I'm probably just overthinking things but … after last time … I'm worried.'

'Sit tight. Hewitt and I'll come and stay with you until Jason's home. We can then take you to town if you need to go. Where's Zoe?'

'Are you sure? She's gone to Alice's for the day. I'll see if she can sleep over. Alice is always asking her to even though Zoe says no because she thinks she'll get scared.'

'I'm sure. I don't want you driving. I'll call the hospital so they're ready, just in case.'

'Fliss … thank you.'

Silence filled the stables' kitchen and the laptop screen went black as Hewitt ended the call to Lizzie and Quinn. He was stretching to ease the stiffness in his shoulder when urgent knocks hammered on his front door. He came to his feet. He hadn't seen Fliss come over from the main house.

Movements hurried, he tugged on his boots as he opened the wooden door. Another snake could be in the garden.

But when the door swung open, Fliss stood with her arms full of bags. She'd changed from her farm clothes into a neat blue shirt and jeans and pulled her hair into a practical ponytail. Her words were calm and measured but her eyes shone with an anxious intensity.

'Kellie called. Jason's out and she's worried her baby might be coming early.'

'Right. I'll get my keys.' He glanced at Fliss's overnight bag. With the floodwaters rising she wasn't taking any chances. 'And some clothes.'

'Thanks.' As if sensing his next question, she continued. 'The dogs have been fed and are in the shed so will be right for tonight.'

She'd turned to head to his ute even before he'd nodded.

They hadn't made it to the white wooden bridge before the brooding sky ripped open.

'Can there be any more rain?' Fliss frowned at the frantic pace of the windscreen wipers.

'It's just a localised storm. See, over there, there's blue sky.'

She looked to their right where the sun shone, but the tension lining her brow didn't ease. He was sure she was mentally willing him to drive faster. Lips pressed together, she checked her phone for a third time.

'Fliss ... relax. We've plenty of phone signal and we'll soon be there. If Kellie's in labour, we'll take her to the hospital.'

Fliss blew out a breath. 'You're right. I'm not going to have to deliver a baby on my own and without the proper equipment. It's just ... if anything happened to either Kellie or the baby ...'

Hewitt reached for her hand and linked her tense fingers with his.

'You brought your first-aid kit which is a mini-hospital in itself. And I'm guessing you would've been trained to deliver a baby?'

'I have. I've had a hospital rotation in obstetrics.'

He squeezed her hand. Her voice sounded stronger, more sure. 'See ... whatever happens, you'll be more than able to handle it.'

She nodded and settled herself deeper into her seat.

He slowed as a sudden onslaught of rain hampered his visibility. The ute swayed as the wind gusted, whipping leaves onto the windscreen.

'I'm glad you're driving,' Fliss said, above the noise of raindrops pelting glass and metal.

Through the heavy veil of rain, hazard lights flashed to their left where a small car had pulled over on the side of the road to wait out the storm.

'We're almost through the worst of it. I'd be surprised if it's even raining at Bundara or at Kellie's.'

The rain eased and the white lines on the black bitumen became easier to see. The number of passing trucks kicking up water confirmed that flooding had already closed some local roads. The traffic would become more congested over the upcoming days as creeks and rivers peaked. The council would have some impressive potholes to fill once the floodwaters receded.

Fliss leaned forwards to peer through the windscreen. 'Kellie's is the next turn, then left at the cream mailbox.' Fliss slipped her fingers from his so she could type a message. 'I'll let her know we're almost there.'

Fliss's phone whooshed almost straight away. As she read the message, her shoulders squared.

'Kellie's waters have broken.'

Fliss texted again before holding her mobile to her ear. Using a professional tone, she organised for the ambulance to head to Kellie's farm. She then left a voice message for Jason. As she lowered her phone, her teeth caught on her bottom lip.

'You can do this,' Hewitt said softly.

'Yes.' She leaned over to press a quick kiss to his mouth. 'I can.'

The cream mailbox loomed and they swapped bitumen for red dirt. Mud pelted the underside of the ute as Hewitt raced towards the green tin-roofed farmhouse. Gum trees sheltered the brick home and a cluster of sheds and silos. The white tape of electric fences fluttered. From inside a small paddock, a round grey pony lifted his head as they approached.

Hewitt sped over the cattle grid and pulled up as close as he could to the front door. Two kelpies barked from over where they were tied up to their kennels near a small shed.

'I'll do whatever you need me to,' he said as Fliss unclipped her belt to reach for the bag at her feet.

'Thanks.' She touched his cheek. 'See you in there.'

Then she was out of her seat, running across the yard and up the house steps. Hewitt moved the ute closer to the garage where it wouldn't be in the way of the ambulance and carried their bags inside.

Voices sounded from a room to the left that he assumed was the master bedroom. Feeling useless, he flicked on the kettle. An empty hot water bottle sat on the bench and might be needed. He then filled the sink with water and cleared away the lunch dishes.

Fliss appeared, a handful of folded towels in her arms. Her hands were steady and her expression composed. He could imagine her doing the rounds of an emergency ward, a stethoscope around her neck. It was only the strain lines around her eyes that hinted at the nerves churning beneath her composure.

'This baby's going to beat both the ambulance and Jason. Everything looks in order and Kellie's going well but it could get a little noisy as this baby's in a hurry.' Before Fliss disappeared along the hallway, she turned. 'Kellie said there's farm magazines in Jason's office if you need a distraction and beer in the fridge if he needs one when he arrives.'

'I'm fine. Don't forget I'm here for anything you need.'

The sweet smile she flashed over her shoulder stayed with him as he finished cleaning the kitchen. At a loss, he inspected the fridge. There was no way he'd sit around reading magazines. Over the upcoming days Kellie and her family would need some pre-prepared meals and snacks. Zoe liked chocolate brownies as much as her tubby pony liked apples. She hopefully would also be partial to lasagne like Lizzie and Quinn were. Hewitt collected what ingredients he needed from the pantry along with a tin of hot chocolate. At the very least, Fliss would need a sugar rush after delivering Kellie's baby.

By the time the lasagne and chocolate brownies were in the oven, the sounds from the bedroom indicated Kellie had reached an intense stage of labour. Knowing Fliss would call if she needed him, he took to pacing the kitchen. Ava once said labour was the worst pain she'd ever experienced. She'd also said holding her babies made everything worthwhile and she'd do it again in a heartbeat.

But hearing what Kellie was going through, he couldn't imagine how any woman would be willing to experience childbirth. He scrubbed his hand over his face. Give him the stress of a rodeo wreck anytime. He needed a beer as much as Jason soon would.

CHAPTER
18

Fliss lifted her chin and banished the last of her self-doubt. She wasn't going to risk Kellie or her baby's life by faltering. She was ready. Hewitt was right. She could handle whatever happened in the next ten minutes.

She rubbed Kellie's back while Kellie knelt on a pillow and leaned against the seat of a wooden chair. 'Your body's done this all before.'

'Tell me about it.' She gave Fliss a brief, pained smile. 'I can't believe I thought it was a good idea to go through this … again.'

All conversation stopped as another intense contraction gripped Kellie. Fliss encouraged her to focus on keeping her breathing rhythmic and steady. She'd already helped Kellie into a hot shower to ease her discomfort, but the frequency of contractions meant she was nearing the end of the transition phase. It would soon be time to push.

'It won't be long now.'

Kellie didn't reply as another contraction stole her breath and twisted her expression. Fine beads of sweat filmed her brow. Fliss did a quick check to confirm the baby's head had crowned.

'You're doing so well, Kell. Just catch your breath and next contraction, push.'

Kellie did as Fliss instructed and the baby's head appeared. Fliss made sure the umbilical cord wasn't wrapped around the tiny neck. 'Almost there. All we need now is one ...'

Fliss hadn't finished before the warm weight of a baby boy filled her gloved hands. She made an Apgar score assessment. The blue tinge to his hands and feet appeared normal, his breathing regular and as he opened his mouth the strength of his cry let everyone know he was fine.

'Oh, Kell ... it's a boy and he's just beautiful.'

Kellie turned, cheeks wet. Fliss placed the newborn against his mother's bare skin. Making sure they were both warmed by a soft towel, she helped Kellie into bed before performing a second Apgar assessment on the baby. From outside, the farm dogs barked in welcome. The ambulance had arrived.

Fliss tucked a blanket over Kellie and together they stared at the tiny face nestled against her shoulder.

'Fliss ... I have no words ... thank you just doesn't seem enough.'

'You don't need to say anything. Seeing you with your baby is thanks enough.' She cleared her throat. 'Shall I take a photo for Jason?'

'Yes, please.'

Fliss snapped a picture of an exhausted but radiant Kellie as footsteps sounded in the hallway.

As Fliss turned to greet the paramedics, Kellie grabbed her hand. 'To use Zoe's words ... you *are* the best doctor ever.'

For the first time since she'd arrived back in the bush, Fliss didn't flinch at being referred to as a doctor. She squeezed Kellie's hand and went to update the two tall paramedics. She was once again Dr Fliss.

'You look happy,' Hewitt said the following morning as Fliss stood at the doorway of Kellie's kitchen and studied the tidy room.

After Kellie and her new baby had left with the paramedics, and the dogs and horses had been fed, Hewitt had spent the evening helping Fliss make the house sparkle. To everyone's surprise Zoe had agreed to have a sleepover at Alice's and had stayed the entire night. Jason had remained in Woodlea to be close to Kellie and his son.

All the beds in the farmhouse now sported clean sheets, the washing had been folded, the freezer filled with meals and the lawn mowed. When Kellie and baby Garth came home from hospital, there wouldn't be anything left to do except enjoy being together as a family.

'I am.' Inside there was no trace of nerves, just a sense of confidence. She centred the vase of spring flowers she'd placed on the table. 'How could I not be? Yesterday I delivered the most beautiful baby boy.'

Hewitt came to her side and pressed a kiss to her temple. 'Yes, you did. You more than handled Garth's early arrival.' His tone deepened. 'Just like I knew you would.'

His unconditional faith moved her just as much as his heartfelt words.

She turned to put her arms around his waist and hug him. 'Thank you for all your help getting the house ready. Your hospital corners make mine look second-rate. I'll tie up the dogs and then we're right to head to town to see how we can help out with the floods.'

They had only just driven past the cream mailbox when her phone whooshed. She read the text aloud as Hewitt turned onto the bitumen.

'Cressy says the bridge is only just hanging in there and to be safe she's taken the dogs to Glenmore. She made sure the horses have hay and are on high ground and that the self-feeder for the chooks is full.'

'Juno will be in hyper-dog heaven with all those puppies to run riot with.'

'She would be. I'm so lucky to have Cressy. I don't know what I'd do without her.'

'I've heard her say the exact same thing about you.'

Fliss's mind whirled as she created a new to-do list. 'It's time I got back to planning her the best wedding possible.'

'Don't let Lizzie hear you say that. She's still obsessed with weddings.'

'I hate to break this to you but I don't think Lizzie will ever lose her love for all things that sparkle. Just like Quinn will never stop liking noisy farm machinery.'

'So another generation of conformists?'

'Yes, but there's nothing wrong with being a conformist.' She leaned over to run her fingers through Hewitt's hair. 'As long as a certain uncle wears a motorbike helmet to model good behaviour so a certain nephew … and his uncle … never end up in my emergency department.'

'Message received loud and clear, Dr Fliss.'

Her phone vibrated, a can of hairspray appearing as the caller's photo. She shook her head. Taylor must have had fun with her mobile when she wasn't looking.

She held her phone against her ear. 'Nice profile picture.'

The hairdresser laughed. 'I thought so too. I couldn't resist when you left your phone on Ella's kitchen bench while you were getting ready for the ball.'

'And you just happened to have a can of hairspray nearby?'

'Of course. You never know when one will come in handy ... like on a trail ride.'

Fliss groaned.

'Come on, admit it.' Laughter threaded Taylor's words. 'It's all thanks to my hairspray that you and Hewitt have been missing-in-action since the ball.'

'No, we haven't, not really.' Cheeks warm, she glanced at Hewitt who gave her a crooked grin. 'It's been wet.'

'True. I guess you have been to town. Just a heads-up, next time you kiss Hewitt in the walkway off Main Street and think no one's looking, think again.'

'Oh no ... not Edna.'

'No, relax, just me. I was having lunch and saw you walk past so followed to say hi. Fliss ...' Taylor's tone turned serious. 'I'm really happy for you both.'

'Thanks. So am I.'

'Now, are you sitting down?'

'Yes.'

'Edna just said a nice thing about you.'

'She has? Wait, I have to pick myself up off the floor.'

'She really did. We were preparing food in the hall for the SES volunteers and she was telling Mrs Knox how proud she was of you for delivering Kellie's baby. And then ... she smiled at me.'

'We are talking about Edna Galloway, whose memory is more extensive than an internet search engine.'

'The one and the same. But all jokes aside, Kellie's baby safely arriving has given everyone a lift. It just doesn't seem as though this rain will end and people are getting tired.'

'They must be. Hewitt and I are almost in town. What needs to be done?'

'There hasn't been any water in any houses yet, but backyards, sheds and garages have been flooded. There was a call-out earlier for people to help fill sandbags at the SES headquarters.'

'Great. We'll be there soon.'

After Fliss had spent the morning filling hessian bags with sand from the mountain in front of her, she could understand why volunteers were feeling fatigued. Even with the bags only being filled two thirds full, and not needing to be tied, her back ached and her palms were raw beneath her gloves.

She swiped a hand across her forehead. She'd rolled up her sleeves on her thin purple shirt and still felt warm. To everyone's relief the rain had held off but the humidity was cloying and the low clouds ominous. Forecasts predicted another storm for tomorrow.

Hewitt appeared at her side and passed her an open water bottle. 'I can take over if you like?'

She took a sip of water. Quinn wasn't the only Sinclair who liked to play with sand.

'I'm sorry you can't get your hands dirty. As well as your shoulder feels, these bags weigh a tonne. Wasn't there a forklift you were having fun with?'

Hewitt had been in demand once it was known he held a forklift licence from his university days of working in a stockfeed store.

He looked at the pile of sand and sighed. 'Yes.'

Even though other volunteers shovelled beside her, Fliss stood on tiptoe to kiss him. From the sideways glances when they'd arrived, Fliss guessed her and Hewitt being together was the town's worst kept secret. For once, the attention didn't make her feel uneasy or self-conscious.

Hewitt settled her cap on her head after it had tilted when she'd kissed him and left with a smile. Fliss filled another sandbag and dragged it over to the wooden pallet Hewitt would later lift and load onto a truck.

'Need a partner in crime?' Ella said, as she opened a new hessian bag for Fliss to shovel sand into.

'Yes, please. You look like you've been busy?'

Tiredness dulled the usual glow of Ella's brown eyes.

'Yes. There's already been livestock losses. I've just checked over a dog that was trapped with its owner when their car was swept off a causeway. The SES had to use the bucket of an excavator to lift the woman and kelpie to safety.'

'The water must have been running fast. I'm glad they're okay. When did you last sleep?'

'I had a few hours last night.' Ella reached for Fliss's shovel as she finished filling the sandbag. 'I hear you had a busy afternoon yesterday. I'm so pleased you were there. I can't imagine what Kellie would have gone through giving birth alone, especially if things had gone wrong.'

Fliss held open Ella's bag for her to fill. 'I'm so grateful Hewitt got me there in time. In the end I didn't really do anything. Kellie did all the work.'

Ella stopped digging to return Hewitt's wave from where he sat on the orange forklift. The vet glanced at Fliss before she continued shovelling.

'You're not going to let him go, are you?'

Fliss heard the pain in Ella's voice. Whatever had happened overseas still left deep emotional scars. Ella wasn't even close to wanting a new relationship.

'No, I won't. I promise. I'm not sure exactly what shape our lives will take when Hewitt leaves, but I do know that without him my life wouldn't be the same.'

Ella gave her a quick hug. 'It shouldn't be any other way. Anyone could see the two of you were meant for each other.'

They filled three more bags before the volunteers around them put their shovels down, many rubbing at their lower backs. Fliss swapped smiles with people she knew and didn't know. The solidarity of the bush in times of crisis made her glad she lived where she did. It didn't matter if her mother, and likely her biological father, had been raised in the city, the outback was where she belonged. It'd taken a heartbreaking loss and much soul-searching but she now had no doubts about where her future lay. Just like Cressy, it was in the rolling hills and the close-knit rural community of where they'd grown up.

Janet approached with a group of ladies carrying baskets of food and drinks. Fliss removed her gloves. When the flood crisis eased she'd visit Dr Sam and discuss what she needed to do to make working in Woodlea a reality. The town would then have one less rural doctor to find.

She glanced at Hewitt as he used the forklift to lift a pallet of sandbags. It wasn't the right time now, his family needed him, but she'd heard the farm next to hers might come up for sale. The next generation had all made lives elsewhere. The property had twice as much land as Bundara and contained valuable river flats and irrigation pivots. There'd been pictures of similar river flats in Hewitt's home office.

She accepted a cream-topped scone from Freya, the new teacher in the one-teacher school west of town at Reedy Creek. Zoe already spoke highly of Miss George. With her glossy auburn hair, quiet eyes and pretty smile Fliss could see why she'd won over her tiny students as well as the youngest Ridley boy.

She left Ella talking to Freya to go over to where Hewitt and Tanner were standing beside the forklift. Whatever they were talking about appeared serious. Tanner clasped Hewitt's shoulder before he stepped forwards to hug her.

'So, Dr Fliss, how does it feel to be the local hero?'

'I'm no such thing. Kellie did all the work and is the one everyone should be proud of.' She looked around. 'Besides, everyone here helping out with the floods is a local hero.'

'I agree. But you are still a hero among heroes. Babies scare me more than that bull of your sister's.'

'Not you too. I thought you'd be fine with Reggie? Look at the horse you ride. Arrow isn't exactly bomb proof.'

'Arrow's a lamb compared to Reggie. I offered him carrots and he refused to eat them.' Tanner shot Hewitt an aggrieved look. 'He gave me this glare as if to say I shouldn't even think about trying to befriend him and stalked off.'

Fliss pressed a hand to her stomach to stop her laughter from taxing muscles she'd overused while digging. 'Here I am thinking you're a tough guy. Ask Hewitt, Reggie's harmless and as for babies, you just haven't met the right person yet.'

Tanner shuddered. 'Babies and Reggie, that's the stuff nightmares are made of.'

Fliss was still laughing when Edna called her name. 'Felicity.'

Tanner lowered his voice. 'Actually, I'd include Edna on that list. The word around town is Bethany's now officially single as she's given her city boyfriend the boot.'

Fliss didn't have a chance to reply before Edna's strong perfume engulfed her and she was crushed against her ample chest. 'Felicity, or should I say *Doctor* Felicity. Well done on delivering Kellie's baby.'

Fliss pulled away before she was smothered. 'Thank you. I was at the right place at the right time.'

'You've always been so humble.'

Fliss blinked.

Edna continued on, without drawing breath. 'But so misguided. You'd have made Rodger the perfect wife.'

Hewitt and Tanner worked hard to keep a straight face.

'Edna,' she said firmly. 'You know I wouldn't have. I'm too bossy.'

Edna patted Fliss's cheek. 'Exactly.' She frowned at Hewitt. 'You have a special one here so make sure you take care of her. Did I tell you I happen to know Mrs Quigley who knows your mother?'

'No, you haven't, but it's no surprise you know Mrs Quigley.' Tone wry, Hewitt slipped an arm around Fliss. 'Just like you, she knows everyone.'

'Of course she does. We're both such social butterflies. Now …' Edna's expression assumed her commander-in-chief focus. 'I have horses that need to be moved. They are at Old Clarry's. He's had a fall and is up on the hill with Dr Sam. They are his daughter's horses, the one that left town with the miner. I'm not sure how many there are, but they need to go into the paddocks behind the house.'

'Hewitt and I'll go.' Fliss didn't need to glance at him to know he'd be thinking the same thing.

'Thank you. I'll cross the horses off my list.' Edna's crisp voice softened. 'The back road to Bundara is open but if it closes and you can't get to Cressy's, Bethany's at home and our spare beds are made up.'

'Thanks.'

Edna's gaze sharpened. 'Of course, Rodger's room's out of bounds.'

Fliss sighed. Her reprieve from feeling the brunt of Edna's wounded pride had ended. 'Of course.'

Edna turned to Tanner, a gleam in her eyes. 'Now, Tanner.' Edna took his arm, giving him no choice but to walk with her. 'I saw you having several dances with Bethany at the ball.'

Hewitt shook his head. 'Our local queen bee, Mrs Quigley, has nothing on your Edna Galloway.'

'Tell me about it. I must say she's full of surprises. I had no idea she cared.'

'By threatening me with gossip to make sure I don't do the wrong thing by you?'

Fliss laughed. 'No, by offering us a bed to sleep in.' She looked across to where Edna kept a firm grip on Tanner's arm. 'Do you think we need to rescue him?'

'No, Taylor's arrived and by the looks of it she's braving Edna to run a rescue mission.'

As they watched, whatever Taylor said to Edna made her press her hand to her chest with false modesty. Tanner slipped his arm free and, after a thumbs up to Taylor, strode away before Edna could latch onto him again.

Lightning flashed on the storm-dark horizon before distant thunder grumbled. Hewitt flicked on his headlights. It was early afternoon but the poor light made it feel much later.

Fliss stifled a yawn. 'I don't know why I'm so tired.'

'It's not every day you shovel a pallet load of sand.'

Fliss flexed her fingers. 'My hands are telling me that's very true.' She gazed out the window, expression pensive. 'I hope there are enough sandbags. There's so much water.'

Puddles pooled across the road and along the roadsides. The soil was at saturation point. Water covered low-lying land and, in the creeks they passed, swollen streams rushed to go someplace new. Crops were waterlogged, pastures flattened, fences under threat and stock displaced. Hewitt slowed as they came to the Bell River whose power had once carved out the fertile valley. The bridge arched over the surging mass of water and a heavy round bale of hay bobbed as it was swept along.

Hewitt let the conversation lapse so Fliss could relax. She rested her head against the headrest and closed her eyes. His gaze lingered on the beauty of her profile.

Warmth flowed through him. Words couldn't describe how the past few days had been being with her. It was time to admit the dream that had always gone hand in hand with buying his land had a face and a name. *Fliss*. Right from the start she'd affected him like no other woman ever had. She filled the vast loneliness behind his restlessness. She centred him, grounded him, and made him feel deep emotions of happiness, joy, contentment. He could spend a lifetime loving her and it wouldn't ever be enough.

He stared at the low-lying cloud cover beyond the windscreen. But the admission that what he felt for Fliss was love didn't usher in any sense of release or freedom. Instead, emptiness chilled him. Once he received the all-clear on his broken shoulder his time at Bundara would end. He'd be lying if he said he shared Fliss's faith there could be a way forward. On the rodeo circuit he'd seen firsthand how distance could corrode even the strongest relationships. Just like the rail tracks running west to Mayfield, their lives could prove impossible to merge.

She'd turned her run-down farm into a home not only for herself but for Max, Molly and Flame. It had been to Cressy and the Woodlea community that Fliss had run in her time of uncertainty and need. He could no more ask her to leave than he could abandon his family. Even with the improvement in his father's health, and Dean being with Ava, it could be years before Hewitt would be free to lead his own life.

Fliss shifted in her seat. Her eyes opened as they passed an ornate farm entrance with a fancy scrolled steel gate.

He relaxed his tense grip on the steering wheel. Fliss couldn't know of his fears or his doubts. 'Let me guess ... Edna's place?'

'Yes. After Mrs Knox updated her front gate Edna decided her entrance also needed a makeover. Old Clarry's will be the next farm over the hill and after the cattle yards.'

When they turned past the battered old mailbox, water already covered the dirt road. On the high ground on the other side of the gully stood a farmhouse. Black cows, with a white band around their middle, occupied the house yard and had made themselves at home on the veranda.

Fliss smiled. 'That's Old Clarry for you. He lives alone and his Belted Galloways are like his family. I can't see any horses, though.'

Hewitt drove through the water, maintaining a steady pace as spray funnelled over the ute. The wipers worked hard to clear the windscreen.

He glanced to his right. 'There's two on that strip of land near the fence. I can see why Clarry was worried. They're already hoof-deep in water.'

'From their size they're thoroughbreds. Imagine if Minty was here—the water would be over his little fetlocks.'

When Hewitt stopped at the front gate, Fliss reached behind her seat for her glossy black gumboots. 'I thought these might come in handy.'

Organised Fliss was always thinking ahead. No wonder she and Lizzie got on so well.

Fliss opened and closed the gate. Hewitt parked near the machinery shed on a patch of gravel. His getting bogged days were over.

He left the ute to scan the farm yard. The five cattle occupied the large house yard, leaving two small paddocks behind the house. Each had a tin lean-to so whichever paddock they put the horses in they would have shelter. Behind a shed door he found a tack room.

He grabbed two full-sized halters and lead ropes and returned to see that Fliss had opened the gate into the closest spare paddock. All they had to do was catch the horses, lead them past the ute, sheds and house and their job would be done.

But as they walked through the mud to the swollen creek, Hewitt's unease grew. The two bay thoroughbreds jostled against each other on the wet strip of land, the whites of their eyes showing. One of the horses neighed, a shrill, piercing sound.

'Fliss, be careful. This isn't going to be easy.'

'It's okay.' She slid her hand into the pocket of her lightweight navy jacket. 'I brought some bribery. I kept an apple from our afternoon break.'

'They don't look like they've been handled in a while. The gear in the tack room was dusty.' He glanced at Fliss, already knowing her answer. 'How about you stay here at the gate? I'll get the one with the star on his forehead. The mare looks like she'll follow.'

'I don't think so.' She shot him a firm look. 'I didn't bring my gumboots for nothing.'

The mare took a step towards them as though seeking their help. The longer they delayed the more anxious and unpredictable the horses would be.

'Okay. But if things get hairy look after yourself. I'll be fine.'

Fliss didn't answer, just started walking.

Together they waded through the water until they reached the horses. Hewitt talked to the spooked gelding to gain his trust, remaining acutely aware of where Fliss was. One kick from a terrified horse and Fliss could end up in the hospital with Old Clarry.

The thoroughbred gelding shook beneath Hewitt's touch but allowed him to slide on the halter and slip the noseband into place. The mare flicked her tail but stood still so Fliss could also put her halter on. She sniffed at the apple Fliss offered but didn't take a bite.

'Ready?' he asked, voice low.

'Ready.'

The gelding proved reluctant to walk into the fast-flowing water but with gentle encouragement he followed Hewitt. Water splashed as Fliss and the mare left the higher ground. Hewitt looked over his shoulder. Fliss had let a safe space open up between them. She worked hard to keep the mare walking at a sensible pace as the bay surged ahead, her snorts nervous and loud.

When the gelding's hooves cleared the water and he saw the open gate ahead, his ears pricked forwards. Fliss and the mare left the floodwater and walked up alongside them. Both horses now appeared calmer and glad to be on firm ground.

Fliss sent him a smile.

An agitated neigh trumpeted from behind them. Jaw tight, Hewitt spun around. A third horse left the trees to gallop towards them. He held on to the gelding's halter as the thoroughbred threw his head up, ears flattened.

Fliss's mare's nostrils flared as she pranced and side-stepped. Fliss rubbed her neck and led her towards the gate to make room for the additional horse.

The chestnut ploughed through the floodwater. This horse was trouble. Large and big-framed, there was a reason why he'd been by himself and why the mare had partially healed marks on her legs.

Hewitt looked for Fliss. 'Watch this one with your mare. He's bad news.'

'I will.' Fliss kept the flighty mare walking.

Hewitt led the gelding forwards. They needed to get the horses through the gate where there'd be more room. The front farm gate was closed, so the third horse would be safe running loose. There'd been a bag of lucerne chaff in the tack room and experience told Hewitt that's what they needed to catch the rogue chestnut.

Hoofbeats thundered as the horse left the water.

'Easy there.' Hewitt soothed the gelding as he shied at a falling leaf.

The chestnut came in from the right, bucking and kicking. Ears pinned back, he crowded the gelding who lashed out an unshod hind hoof. A thud sounded. The herd bully didn't slow. Focused on the mare in front of him, his head snaked forwards.

Hewitt yelled. 'Fliss—'

The chestnut's overgrown teeth fastened on the mare's rump. She squealed and lunged sideways, knocking Fliss over.

Hooves flashed, colour blurred, and the two horses were gone.

Fliss lay on the ground.

Hewitt didn't know he'd again called her name until the echo penetrated the fog of his horror. This time he wasn't in a rodeo arena. This time there was no devil of a bull. But this time it was the woman he loved who lay broken on the ground.

Not taking his eyes off her, Hewitt unclipped the lead from the gelding's halter. The horse galloped to the left of Fliss and over to where the chestnut chased the mare.

Hewitt covered the ground in three strides and sank to his knees. Against the darkness of the mud, Fliss's skin appeared white and her lips colourless. Blood pooled at her temple and trailed a vivid red path across her cheek. He bent to check she was breathing.

Nothing.

Fear strangled his own breaths.

Then her lashes fluttered.

'Hewitt?'

'I'm here.' His voice was nothing more than a hoarse rasp. 'Lie still.'

'I'm fine, just … winded.' She touched a hand to her head then reached for his arm. 'I need … to sit up.'

He eased her into a sitting position and she pulled her knees to her chest. He tugged off his collared woollen jumper and wrapped it around her shoulders. Blood dripped from her jaw.

He pressed a kiss to her forehead. 'Are you right while I get that fancy first-aid kit of yours?'

The corners of her mouth briefly tilted.

Once he'd pressed a wad of cotton dressing against her temple, the blood flow slowed, then stopped. Colour returned to her lips and cheeks. He made another trip to his ute for her makeup bag.

She used a small mirror to examine her wound. 'I don't need a steri-strip or any stitches.' Her eyes met his. 'And I definitely don't need to go to the emergency department.'

Hewitt didn't answer. The cold fear inside him hadn't yet thawed.

'I'm okay, Hewitt, really.' She touched his cheek. 'It looks far worse than it is. Scalp wounds can bleed a lot, even if they are only minor.'

He caught her fingers and kissed the inside of her wrist. It continued to be a struggle to speak.

She looked around. 'You were right. This wasn't easy. Where are the horses?'

He cleared his throat. 'The two we rescued are where they're supposed to be. The chestnut's tormenting the cows.'

Fliss frowned as she slowly turned to look to where the chestnut was cantering alongside the house yard fence. 'We can't let him get to the mare again.'

'We won't. After I'm sure you're okay, I'll put him in his own paddock.'

'I'm fine. Please do it now. He's such a brute. Tomorrow I'm calling Old Clarry, as well as Denham and Tanner. They have one mean horse to sort out.'

Hewitt smoothed hair from off her cheek. Mud and blood smeared her chin and she trembled as shock kicked in.

'Sit tight. I'll deal with the chestnut and then, I'm not taking no for an answer, we'll head to Edna's so you can have a hot shower and get cleaned up.'

When the last of the orange sunset streaked across the sky, Hewitt tucked a blanket around Fliss as she lay asleep in Edna's frilly guest bedroom. Clean and warm, she'd struggled to stay awake when Bethany had served pumpkin soup for an early dinner. Fliss was adamant she hadn't knocked her head, so she didn't have concussion, but did concede she was tired and sore. The rain had started again and after she'd smothered another yawn Fliss had given in to Bethany's insistence they stay the night. Relieved, Hewitt had collected Fliss's duffle bag from the ute.

Now Fliss was safe and they were alone, Hewitt allowed his control to slip. He touched his mouth to hers and she smiled in her sleep. But her response brought no joy or comfort. The terror that had been unleashed by seeing her lying on the ground writhed and thrashed until it consumed him. He couldn't think. He couldn't rationalise. All he could do was feel.

And the emotions weren't ones he'd ever wanted to experience again. Anguish. Despair. Torment. Losing Brody had carved off a piece of his heart, but if anything happened to Fliss he'd never be whole again.

He gave in to his flight response and came to his feet. He needed air. He needed to breathe. He thought he'd moved on enough in his grief to be ready to start the life he'd always wanted with the only woman he'd ever truly love. But the brutal truth was he hadn't.

Fliss's accident had taken him back to a place he'd never wanted to revisit. The metallic scent of blood, the frenzied racing of his heart, his absolute powerlessness had all triggered a desperate, deep-seated fear. A fear that dragged him under and suffocated him.

There was a reason why his duffle bag was still in his ute. Every moment he stayed with Fliss only increased the hurt he'd promised he'd never cause her. Until he faced his demons and could fully invest in the relationship she deserved, he had no place being by her side. Lizzie wasn't going to have the wedding and happy-ever-after she believed in. With his heart breaking and soul numb, he bent to give Fliss a final kiss.

He would head to Bundara to pack and collect Garnet. There'd be no sleep for him tonight. When the sun rose, he'd return here for when Fliss woke up to say goodbye.

CHAPTER
19

Something wasn't right.

Fliss opened her heavy eyes and through the haze of sleep realised she was in an unfamiliar, darkened room and that Hewitt wasn't beside her. Then she registered the ring and too-bright flashes of her phone on the bedside table.

It took two attempts but her fingers connected with her mobile. She held the phone to her ear but didn't speak.

Cressy's worried voice sounded. 'Fliss?'

'I'm here.'

'How are you feeling?'

She dragged the hair off her face and winced. 'Never better.'

Her light reply failed to erase the concern in Cressy's voice. 'Are you still at Bethany's?'

'Yes. What time is it?'

'It's eight o'clock at night. Hewitt's not with you?'

'He's out talking to Bethany.'

'Are you sure?'

'Yes, why?'

'I called him to see how you were, as I tried you earlier. He didn't talk long but … Fliss, I know when someone's talking hands-free on their phone in their car.'

Fliss pushed off the bedcovers, ignoring the protest of stiff and bruised muscles. 'When was this?'

'About ten minutes ago. Did he say he was going anywhere?'

'No. If anything, he was determined we'd stay. He said I needed to rest.'

She came to her feet. The plush carpet cushioned her bare feet as she went to the window to pull back the heavy curtains. The pale wash of moonlight showed the ripple of raindrops on puddles and an empty space where Hewitt's ute had been.

Mouth dry, she swallowed. 'You're right. His ute's gone.'

'Fliss, as much as I don't want to say this, I don't think Hewitt's left for a simple reason. I know him well enough to sense when he's shutting down. His voice was grave, tight, like when he arrived.'

'He was quiet when we got here but otherwise seemed fine.' She rubbed her forehead, trying to sift through their dinner conversation. 'Where would he be going? Why didn't he tell me he'd be leaving?'

'I don't know. What exactly happened at Old Clarry's?'

'Nothing … except, like I messaged you, I got winded by one of the horses.'

'So you got hit?'

'Yes, I was knocked over but I wasn't lying there for lo—' Fliss grabbed her jeans that lay over the back of a winged chair. 'I have to go after him. I would have been sprawled on the ground, just like Brody would have been.'

'That's what's upset him. He'll need to be with the twins; they're the ones who got him through after Brody died.'

Fliss pulled on a white shirt over her pyjama tank top. 'That's what I think as well. But he'd never leave without Garnet so he'd be going to Bundara before the bridge closes.'

'Fliss … would you listen if I said to call him and not go after him until the morning? It's raining and the roads are going to be bad.'

She slung her handbag over her shoulder. 'I'll be fine. Bethany will have a four-wheel drive I can borrow. I need to banish my fears and learn to drive in the mud.'

Despite the strength of her words, Fliss drew a steadying breath as she left the bitumen and sent Edna and Noel's farm Hilux onto the red dirt road that would take her home. She could do this. She had to. She'd driven with Hewitt enough times to notice how he handled the slippery road conditions. She kept to a careful speed. When the ute slid, she kept her front wheels pointed in the direction of the slide and eased herself back onto the muddy road. When she needed to slow she didn't slam on the brakes.

Her headlights shone on the mass of water lapping at the bottom of the white bridge. She was taking a risk heading home. The river peak would soon be passing through and the road would be closed. She could only hope Cressy had caught Hewitt on the way to Bundara, not on his way out. Otherwise she'd have a long drive west to Mayfield.

The old wooden planks on the bridge rattled and her knuckles whitened on the steering wheel. But it wasn't driving on the rickety bridge that caused her concern, but what lay ahead.

Professionally she could understand how Hewitt seeing her on the ground had reawakened the memories that haunted him. Walking into the Woodlea hospital had taken her back to the moment she'd lost Caitlyn. But personally she couldn't understand why Hewitt would run and close himself off again. She'd thought they had a connection that was stronger than the fears they faced.

She'd tried to call twice but his phone had gone to voicemail. What if he wouldn't talk to her? What if she couldn't convince him to stay? She squared her shoulders. The only thing she was sure of was that she loved him and she needed to let him know how much he meant to her. She had to hope it would be enough.

She drove past her milk-can mailbox and negotiated the dip in the road filled with fast-flowing water. When she saw the black gleam of Hewitt's ute parked outside the stables she released the breath she'd been holding. But her relief was short-lived. The empty horse float was attached and the quad bike loaded. Hewitt might still be there, but he wasn't planning to stay.

At the soft patch in the curve of the road beside the garden gate, she kept the ute's momentum going until she pulled up beside Hewitt's ute.

She left the driver's seat and the glare of the sensor light revealed the layers of mud covering Edna and Noel's silver farm ute. If it'd been any other time she'd have acknowledged she'd just passed some sort of rite of passage. But tonight it was all about holding on to the man she wasn't going to let go. No matter how strong and stubborn he might be.

Hewitt stood in the doorway of the stables, dressed in a black T-shirt and jeans. Just like on the day he'd arrived, his easy, casual stance didn't tell the whole story. Beneath the bright glow of the outside light his face was all harsh angles and shadowed hollows. But it was his eyes that caused her steps to falter. Hooded and dark, they spoke of untold suffering.

His intense stillness broke her heart. His emotions were locked down so tight she wasn't sure she had the power to release them. She didn't say a word, just closed the distance between them and walked into his arms. He slid a hand into the hair at her nape and wrapped his arm around her waist. He smelt of fresh soap and the cedar tang of aftershave. Scents that had come to signify home and belonging.

Hewitt didn't speak, just held her as though he'd never let her go. Fliss wasn't fooled. His words would convey a message far different to his touch.

His hoarse voice sounded in her ear. 'Fliss ... I have to go.'

She pulled away a little to see his face. His expression remained tight, guarded.

'You can't just ... leave.'

As hard as she tried she couldn't stop pain from choking her words.

A muscle worked in his jaw. 'I wasn't. I was planning to see you in the morning ... to say goodbye. But with the bridge going under, I was going to take Garnet home and come back to see you.'

His deep, anguished tone gave her hope his emotions were battling the iron grip he kept on them.

'Were you planning to sleep anytime in the next twenty-four hours?'

'No.'

'Do I need to give you a lecture on the dangers of sleep deprivation?'

An almost smile shaped his lips. 'That won't be necessary, Dr Fliss.'

'Which just leaves us to talk about us.'

'It does.' Strain carved grooves beside his mouth.

His arms dropped from around her and he stepped away from the doorway. She entered the stables to sit on the sofa. His full duffle bag sat on the bottom step of the wooden staircase that led to the bedroom.

He sat on the sofa, careful to keep his distance, and faced her. She stretched out her hand to curl her little finger around his. To her relief, he didn't shift his hand away.

Voice low, he spoke first. 'I'm sorry. The last thing I've ever wanted to do was hurt you.'

'I know.'

'Seeing you on the ground … if I lost you like I did Brody … it would break me … I'd be no good for anything or anyone.'

She nodded, unable to speak. Hewitt wasn't afraid of anything and yet his feelings for her had brought him to his knees.

'If I go now it will save you hurt in the long run. I thought now was an okay time for me. I was wrong.'

'I'll wait.'

He slipped his hand free and folded his arms. 'I can't ask you to do that. It's asking too much.'

'No, it isn't. And I'm waiting, even if you ask me not to.'

She kept her voice calm, even though her instincts told her she was losing him. His eyes were bleak, empty, and his shoulders rigid. He'd gone into lockdown mode.

'Fliss … I don't know if I can ever move past this … fear.' He slid to the edge of the sofa, readying himself to stand. 'There can be no way forward for us.'

She searched for the right words to reach him. The fight for their future wasn't ending here. Once he came to his feet there'd be no way she could stop him walking out the door.

'Hewitt … when there's a wreck in the rodeo arena, which way do you ride? To the wreck or in the opposite direction?'

'Is this a trick question?'

She gave a small smile. 'Only if you want it to be.'

'Always to the wreck.'

'No matter what might happen?'

He slowly nodded as a spark of understanding flared in his eyes.

Hope fluttered inside. She placed her palm on his cheek, uncaring he'd feel how much she was shaking. She had to keep him with her. 'I love you.'

The warmth of his hand that covered hers gave her the courage to continue.

'I can't let you leave. It would break me. I've spent my life going out with people who I knew were wrong for me because I didn't want to risk my heart. But with you … I have to take the risk because you're the only man I'll ever want. I know seeing me on the ground today was tough, but you don't need to ride in the opposite direction. We can face your fears together. You don't have to shoulder this alo—'

Hewitt's kiss silenced her. His hands tangled in her hair. His heat burned against her skin. His mouth told her without words he'd spend a lifetime riding towards whatever came their way. She accepted everything his touch offered and gave as much in return.

When they broke apart, light had eclipsed the darkness in his eyes. She'd never seen his irises such a smoky grey or his smile so tender.

'From that first day, I knew … you're the only one for me. You're right. I can't let fear hold me back. You have no idea how much I love you, Dr Fliss. Especially when you have an answer for everything.'

The raw, intense emotion in his voice touched her even more than his husky words. As strong as he was, Hewitt was capable of feeling deeply. He was a man to spend forever with.

She held his gaze, knowing tears would be shining in her eyes. The battle for the man she'd loved had been won.

She slipped her hands beneath the soft cotton of his black T-shirt. 'No, I don't know how much you love me. You're just going to have to show me … over and over again.'

Thanks to Hewitt having already packed his bags, the permanent move into the main house took less than ten minutes. Thanks to the bridge going under they had three uninterrupted days for Hewitt to show her how much he loved her.

When the floodwaters receded, they still had a week until his shoulder scan appointment. Once Hewitt had the all-clear, he'd return to Mayfield. They would live between his house and Bundara until he was no longer needed to run the family farm fulltime. Fliss had mentioned the adjoining property coming up for sale and Hewitt had paid their elderly neighbour a visit. When Hewitt hadn't returned after three hours she knew they'd bonded over their appreciation for yellow and green farm machinery.

Having Hewitt in her life filled a void Fliss had refused to acknowledge in her quest to be a doctor. All her yearnings for a home and a family were no longer hidden in the shadows. It was as though he'd completed a part of her that had been missing.

She sighed as she fed another Ryan family tree she couldn't be connected to through the paper shredder. If only the DNA part of her that remained missing could be found.

'Another strikeout?' Hewitt entered her office carrying the box containing her mother's old novels that Cressy had given her on the day he'd passed the Reggie test.

'Yes, but that's okay, I have two Ryan names left on my list. I have to be getting close. Who knows, by this afternoon I might have found a link and we'll be making a mad dash to Sydney.'

She walked over to where Hewitt sat the box on the floor. He drew her close and rested his head on hers as they looked at the new bookshelf he'd made out of another old door. Sections had been removed and small shelves built to hold books and other items. Hewitt's man-cave now had almost as many power tools as Denham's shed.

'It looks so good. Cressy's going to want one of these too.' She paused as rain sounded on the roof. 'No way. I only just hung out the towels.'

'I thought you were being optimistic doing a load of washing.' He snuck a kiss. 'I'll get them off the line before they get wet and hang at the perfect puppy-grabbing height.'

After Hewitt left she opened the box. Her DNA could wait for a little while. A special bookshelf called for special things and these were her mother's favourite books. She and Denham's mother, Audrey, had been avid readers, with Audrey even having had a personal library over at Claremont. Fliss arranged a selection of novels on the bottom two shelves. The old fabric covers in hues of blues, greens and reds suited the distressed white finish of the wood.

In the middle of the box she found a dark gold-embossed copy of *Pride and Prejudice*. She smiled and flipped through the book. Her mother had given her and Cressy their own special copies. On rainy days like today the television series of the book had been their go-to entertainment. When Cressy had been young she'd taken to calling it the Mr Darcy show.

Fliss went to put the book on the third shelf when she saw a small gap in the pages. Her mother often pressed flowers and there could be an old violet she'd missed. But when Fliss opened the book, a photograph fell out. She made no move to pick it up.

The picture was of a man standing beside a rock pool looking out to sea. It was only a profile shot, but it was enough. Her heart beat too loudly in her ears. Her breaths emerged too short and too shallow. The last two Ryan names would have also been strikeouts. For her biological father's surname wasn't Ryan ... it was Barclay.

She slowly sank to sit on the floor. The man in the photograph was Lewis.

Hewitt looked across to where Fliss sat still and silent in the passenger seat of his ute.

'It was like Christmas had come when I took the dogs to Cressy's. Even Tippy was glad to see the puppies.'

Fliss cast him a subdued smile. 'Hopefully we won't be in Sydney long and they can all be home soon.'

'Cressy said there's no rush. You might find you want to stay more than two nights.'

'Maybe.'

Ever since Hewitt had returned to the office and seen Fliss sitting on the floor staring at a photo, she'd been hard to read. One minute she was relieved at knowing who she was and the next she was angry.

'How could Lewis be my father? Why didn't they tell me?'

Hewitt took hold of her hand. 'I'm sorry I don't have the answers, but Lewis will. Meredith didn't know?'

'No, she's just as shocked as I am. She still doesn't know how Mum even knew him. Cressy has no idea how this could have happened. She's always liked him, so she's actually really pleased.'

'If Cressy's met him, did your father meet him too?'

Fliss pursed her lips as she thought. 'No. The only time he would have was at my university graduation. But Jean wasn't well so Lewis came and went quickly. But I've mentioned him countless times over the years and never once did Mum or Dad react in a strange way.'

The strain in her voice was reflected in the furrows in her forehead. Hewitt ran his thumb across the back of her hand. 'Did you end up calling Lewis to let him know we were coming?'

'No. I was going to, but then if he doesn't know, it will also be a huge shock to him. He's just lost Jean.' Fliss's grip tightened on Hewitt's hand. 'So many secrets. I wonder if she knew? Jean always said I was the daughter she and Lewis couldn't have.'

'We'll find out the truth soon enough.' Hewitt reached behind his seat for the blanket he'd thrown in the ute along with their bags.

'We've still got a long way to drive, so why don't you sleep? I have a feeling it'll be a late night once we get there.'

'Thanks for coming with me.'

He kissed her hand. There wasn't anywhere he'd ever want to be but by her side. With Fliss with him, fear no longer wielded any power. He'd never run in the wrong direction again. Whatever life threw at them, they'd face it head-on and together.

'Anytime.'

Soon her breaths were soft and her lashes lay dark against her skin. When she stirred, he tucked the blanket around her.

The rain followed them as they headed east and only eased as they climbed the escarpment. Once past the Blue Mountains the traffic slowed as they hit peak hour. The urban landscape beyond the ute already made him yearn for the open space of the bush. A horn squealed as an impatient driver registered their annoyance at the car ahead of them.

Fliss woke and busied herself with finding last-minute accommodation close to Lewis's home. Hewitt made sure she had something to eat, even though she picked at her hamburger they'd bought from a trendy roadside steakhouse. As streetlights cast a sombre glow and house lights spilled from between half-drawn curtains, they pulled up outside Lewis's home.

Hewitt brushed hair from off her cheek. 'Good luck. I hope you find the answers you're after. I'll wait here until you're done.'

'Come with me. Please. I want … I need you there.'

The sudden vulnerability in her eyes had him lean in close to kiss away her fears.

The question of whether Lewis knew he was Fliss's father was answered the moment he opened the door. A sharp, intelligent stare raked over Hewitt with an intensity and protectiveness that left Hewitt in no doubt he wasn't the only one who loved Fliss.

Lewis stepped forwards to hug her. 'This is a surprise.'

Fliss didn't return his hug. 'Is it?'

Expression thoughtful, Lewis studied Fliss's face. Even in the poor light Hewitt could see subtle hints they were father and daughter. As much as Fliss resembled her mother, Hewitt could see Fliss's skin had her father's golden tone. She also shared his height along with his long, slender hands. As their eyes met and neither looked away, he guessed they shared the same tenacity.

'No, it's not. I knew … hoped … this day would someday come.'

He moved away to allow Fliss to walk past. Lewis looked at Hewitt, eyes narrowed.

'Your name had better be Hewitt, or you'll have to wait outside.'

Hewitt held out his hand. He already liked Fliss's straight-talking father. 'Yes, it's Hewitt.'

'Just as well.' Lewis shook his hand before stepping aside. 'Come in. I already know you don't like vectors, vodka shots or bubbly blonde interns.'

At the end of the hallway Hewitt could see Fliss pacing in the living room. He sat on the brown leather lounge and she came to sit beside him. Her thigh pressed against his as if needing the reassurance of physical contact. He rested his arm across the back of the lounge behind her. Her quick, soft glance gave him all the thanks he needed.

Lewis sat in a wing-backed chair opposite them and crossed his legs. He almost appeared at ease, as though a huge burden had been shifted from him.

The older man opened the conversation. 'I'll answer any question you have with nothing but honesty. Where do you want to start?'

Fliss stared at him for a moment. 'You knew my mother?'

'I did. I also loved her.'

Fliss's back straightened. 'But Jean was your wife. I know how much she loved you.'

Sadness clouded Lewis's eyes. 'I loved her, but in a different way to how I loved your mother … and never stopped loving her.'

'Did Jean know?' Anger clipped Fliss's words.

'Yes. Maybe it's best if I start at the beginning.' Lewis stood and moved to a dark mahogany sideboard and slid open the top drawer. He took out a framed photo and handed it to Fliss.

The picture had been taken near the same rock pool and on the same day as the one Fliss had found. Except in this one, a woman who resembled Fliss had her arms wrapped around Lewis as they smiled at each other.

'Jean took that at the beach near your mother's house. We were all friends.'

Fliss stared at the photo and her shoulders relaxed. 'Mum looks so happy, so young. She loved you. I can see it in her eyes.' Fliss looked back at Lewis and when she spoke her voice had lost its hard edge. 'What happened? What went wrong?'

Lewis sighed. 'Life. You know I met Meredith when she was staying with Audrey's family because I used to mow their lawns to pay my way through university?'

'I do.'

'Well, I did odd gardening jobs for several families. Even though I had a scholarship for Sydney University, it wasn't enough. My mother was a single mother and I had two younger brothers to support.'

'And your father?'

Lewis's mouth thinned. 'Let's just say he drank too much and left my mother for a girl half his age. From the day he walked out we never saw him again.'

'I'm so sorry.'

Lewis nodded. 'I worked for Jean's parents as well as your mother's as they were neighbours. It had been a hot summer and on my first day at your mother's house she brought me a cool drink. When I ripped my shirt, she offered to patch it.' Lewis paused. 'She was like you, Fliss. She cared so deeply about people.'

Fliss reached for Hewitt's hand.

'But her parents were overprotective and they had money. Their daughter having a relationship with the gardener wasn't exactly what they'd hoped for her. So we kept our meetings on the beach secret. Jean always knew as she helped us arrange times to be together. But somehow your grandparents found out and they whisked your mother away to Europe for a two-month grand tour.'

Lewis rubbed his temple, a gesture Hewitt had seen Fliss make. 'What happened next was my fault. I missed your mother so much I would go to the beach where we'd meet. Jean started to come and see me. I didn't think anything of it. Jean knew I loved your mother but ... one wet afternoon when we were walking back she slipped on the steps near the lifesaving club house. I helped her up and she ... kissed me. I didn't kiss her back and very gently told her I couldn't be anything but a friend. Upset, she ran up the steps and out into the car park ...'

Lewis stopped. His lips compressed together.

Fliss's hold tightened on Hewitt's hand. 'And she was hit by a car.'

'She was.' Lewis briefly closed his eyes. 'I felt so much guilt, so much remorse. Jean suffered a brain injury that affected her vision and speech and meant she'd need lifelong support. It soon became obvious her family wouldn't be there for her. They were happy to pay for whatever help she needed, otherwise they were preoccupied with their own lives. I sat by her bed for days and when she could understand what I was saying I promised I would always be there for her.'

Silence cloaked the room before Fliss asked, 'What happened when Mum returned?'

'She'd known Jean loved me and felt immense guilt for not warning me. That night was our last night together. She knew her parents would never approve of us marrying. She also knew I'd honour my promise to Jean on top of providing for my mother and studying. I think she believed she would only make everything worse if she stayed with me. She went on a trip with her parents out west to visit family friends. Within three weeks she was engaged to their son and within six weeks they'd eloped.'

'Then I arrived.'

A light returned to Lewis's weary gaze. 'Yes, you did. You were the most beautiful baby.'

'Mum told you?'

'Yes. She told everyone who needed to know. Otherwise it wasn't common knowledge.'

Fliss blinked. 'Everyone?'

'Yes. Your father, his parents, her parents, Jean and myself.'

'And they were all okay ... about me?'

'Yes and no. Your mother's parents never accepted you, even when you grew older. But your father's parents already loved your mother like a daughter and they loved you just as much.'

'And Dad?'

'Let's just say he had his own reasons for not wanting to cause trouble. His parents had the grandchild they'd wanted and a daughter-in-law they adored and this allowed him to fly under the radar and live a life they wouldn't approve of. In his own way, I believe he loved you as if you were his.'

Fliss looked at the photo resting on her lap. 'Did you ever see Mum again?'

'I did. At first she sent letters and photographs. Then when you came to boarding school she'd visit Sydney and we'd catch up for a coffee or go for a walk along the beach. But we were never ... together again, if that was what you were asking?'

'It was.'

'Your mother did care about your father and tried to make it work, and I would never have dishonoured the promises I made to Jean. She wasn't a jealous person and when you came into our lives you became very special to her.'

'She was special to me too.' Fliss touched the corner of her eye. 'If everyone knew, why didn't you tell me?'

'It was your mother's decision. Your happiness and wellbeing meant everything to her. We'd planned for me to bump into you at uni and to go from there. But, it was almost as though life was trying to make amends when Meredith asked me to look out for the daughter of her dear friend. Then your mother went to Tasmania ...'

Lewis's hoarse words revealed how much he still mourned the loss of Fliss's mother. He cleared his throat before he spoke again. 'To be honest ... with Jean and your mother no longer here, I've been wrestling with whether to tell you or not.'

Fliss smiled her beautiful smile at the man who'd always been like a father to her. 'Thanks to DNA and to Mum keeping a very well-hidden picture of you, I worked it all out and ... here I am.'

Fliss passed Hewitt the framed photo before standing to cross the living room. Lewis came to his feet and they exchanged a long and tight embrace.

When Fliss pulled away, the tears in her eyes made Hewitt's chest ache. The woman he loved, and who had filled his world with colour and light, now had all the pieces of her life returned to her.

EPILOGUE

'You know we really do need to use the veranda furniture,' Hewitt said, voice husky as she leaned back against him.

Fliss snuggled into his arms. Having Hewitt hold her while they sat on the top veranda step was as much of a morning ritual as it was drinking her tea with Molly and Max sprawled beside them. Except today the border collies had had their coats brushed and were tied up near their kennels. They'd be let off later when everyone arrived.

Fliss glanced at the white wicker furniture they'd bought together. A vase of the last of her pale pink iceberg roses sat on the glass-topped table. Summer still staked its claim during the day, but once the sun descended, autumn's chill made it known winter was not far away.

'Why use a chair when the floorboards are as comfortable as a sofa?' she said with a grin.

Hewitt laughed and Fliss loved the way the deep sound made her stomach flutter. He continued to move her like no man ever had.

The deep connection and happiness she'd always yearned for, and seen Cressy and Denham share, was hers.

They now lived at Bundara fulltime and Hewitt had recently exchanged contracts on the property next door. Bundara had become a sizable holding and Hewitt had the property he'd always dreamed of. Bundara's bluestone homestead would remain their home and Hewitt would rent out the new farmhouse.

Wade had his diabetes under control and was out in the paddocks again where he'd always wanted to be. Poppy was his constant companion and when she wasn't in the ute she was lying by the sandpit watching Quinn or going for walks on her pink sparkly lead with Lizzie. Ava and Dean had announced their engagement and plans were underway for Dean to leave the family partnership with his brothers to run Mayfield with Wade. Vernette's knitting and craft had taken over the house. When Fliss had been looking for a blanket in the linen cupboard she'd discovered a shelf of embroidered woollen baby blankets and handmade quilts.

From over at his kennel, Max barked.

Fliss turned to look at Hewitt. 'Who do you think will arrive first?'

'It won't be Ava. They'd all still be half an hour away. It would be Ella. She's always on time.' Hewitt's arms tightened around Fliss as he lowered his head. 'Which means I'd better do this before we have a garden full of guests.'

Hewitt's kiss left her wishing they had more time before everyone arrived for the belated housewarming.

As predicted, it was Ella's car that appeared first. She parked near the stables and gave them a wave as she opened the garden gate. Dressed in a fitted white dress and heels, the sunlight showcased her blonde beauty.

Fliss sighed. 'I worry about her. She could have anyone she wanted but she still doesn't seem interested in dating. Which is more than fine, but sometimes she looks so lonely.'

'She'll get her happy-ever-after, you'll see.' Hewitt stood and pulled Fliss to her feet. 'We did.'

She pressed a last kiss to his mouth and smoothed down the skirt of her black-and-white dress. Tanner's blue ute navigated its way through the dip in the road. His silver bull bar glinted in the sun.

'Let's hope Tanner does too. Kellie's bringing baby Garth, who's just the cutest, happiest little fellow, and yet Tanner avoids him like he's contagious.'

Hewitt chuckled as they walked down the veranda steps. 'The tougher they are, the harder they fall. Tanner will meet his match one day and then all he'll be thinking about is babies.'

'I hope so.'

Soon the carefully tended garden filled with guests. When she wasn't being Dr Fliss in town or at the hospital she spent as much time as she could gardening. She could understand why her mother had been such an avid gardener; it made her feel closer to Lewis.

Fliss smiled across at the man who she was open about introducing as her father. He returned her smile from where he stood under the cedar tree talking to Phil and Meredith. Lewis was a frequent visitor to Bundara and would now stay a week to help Hewitt put in the winter oats crop. Despite being an academic and medical professional, her father too proved to be a conformist. He shared Hewitt's masculine interest in farm machinery.

Laughter sounded as Zoe and Lizzie ran past trailing a row of bubbles. Taylor had finished French braiding their hair. Quinn ran behind carrying his tractor. He'd made sure he stayed well away from the hairspray-wielding hairdresser.

Seeing that a water jug needed refilling, Fliss headed inside. Heels sounded behind her and she turned to see Edna enter the kitchen.

'Well, this all looks very nice, Felicity. You wouldn't recognise the house.'

'Thank you.' Fliss filled the jug with ice from the refrigerator dispenser. 'There's still some work to be done but it's slowly taking shape.'

Edna moved to a shelf where Fliss had sat a cluster of family photos. Edna picked up a silver frame and spoke without looking at Fliss. 'Your mother's secret was safe with me. She'd be so pleased Lewis is here today.'

Ice cubes scattered across the floor as Fliss turned and the jug moved away from the dispenser.

'She told you?'

'No. She didn't have to.' An unfamiliar softness tempered Edna's sharp stare. 'Do you know how I knew you'd recycled the gown you wore to the ball?'

Fliss shook her head.

'It's because your mother showed me your graduation photos. I saw the dress but I also saw … this.'

Edna passed Fliss the photo frame she held in which Fliss was wearing a black academic gown and trencher. Lewis had his arm around her shoulders as they smiled at each other.

'This is how a proud father looks at the daughter he loves.'

'Edna …' Fliss was lost for words. The one person she wouldn't have trusted with the truth had known the answer all along. Edna, Woodlea's most prolific gossip, had honoured her mother's secret.

Fliss set the jug on the bench and hugged the woman before her. 'Thank you.'

Edna returned her embrace before stepping away. 'Don't thank me.' Her tone was crisp once more. Edna picked up the water jug.

'I did it for your mother. She was a dear and caring friend. You're still not off the hook for breaking my poor Rodger's heart.'

Just before Edna sailed out from the kitchen, she gave Fliss a smile.

Fliss returned the frame to the shelf before collecting another bowl of freshly popped popcorn. She'd seen Quinn eating handfuls and, when Lizzie wasn't looking, stick some in her hair.

Fliss paused on the top veranda step and looked over the people she loved. She'd come here adrift and anxious and had found herself, her place in life and a strong man to love. To her right, Cressy waved her hand as she spoke to Denham. Light flashed from her ring finger. Today the no-frills cowgirl wore a pretty denim dress. Fliss had found a perfect pair of white cowgirl boots and had made sure Cressy and Denham's wedding plans were on track. She was going to give her sister the best wedding possible.

Fliss sought Hewitt's eyes as he looked over to her from where he stood beside his father. Her heart swelled. It was all hush hush for now, as they didn't want to spoil Cressy and Denham's big day, but when spring turned Hewitt's canola crops yellow and brought the white butterflies to her garden, the historic Woodlea church bells would again ring out in celebration of a wedding.

ACKNOWLEDGEMENTS

I'm so grateful to have again spent time in Woodlea, my small town of windmills, and owe many people my heartfelt thanks. Thank you to HarperCollins and the Harlequin Mira imprint team. *The Red Dirt Road* has taken many forms and Rachael Donovan and Julia Knapman have again worked their magic. As always thanks to my writing buddies, Allison Butler, Rachael Johns and Mel Teshco for all their support. Thanks to my dear friend Anne Vail for her medical expertise and insights. Any mistakes are my own. Thanks to my children—Angus, for the firsthand experience of broken bones and for proving that pancakes can be made in the shape of Australia; Callum, for not having any emergency department visits and for his enthusiasm towards his blue AU falcon ute; Adeline, for her love of animals and the knowledge that ducks can swim in a dog's water bowl; and Bryana, who temporarily swapped red dirt roads for historic cobbled streets. Special thanks to Luke, my brains trust, my hero and the reason why I can write. Last but not least, thanks to everyone who has turned a page of my books, left a review or asked for more stories. I appreciate each and every one of you. Without such loyal readers an author is only ever writing into the wilderness.

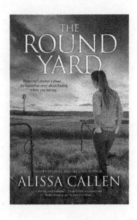

Turn over for a sneak peek.

THE
ROUND
YARD

by

ALISSA CALLEN

Available February 2019

CHAPTER
1

Neve Fitzpatrick walked out the front door and into a scene of mass garden destruction. Dismay anchored her boots onto the dusty veranda floorboards. No wonder the two willie wagtails perched on the nearby wooden fence had been scolding.

The three-year-old girl she carried on her hip stopped wriggling. The five-year-old sister standing close beside her stilled. They all stared at what had been ordered rows of vegetables filling the raised beds in the right corner of the garden. Now, carrots and strawberry plants littered the red dirt path and the rows of staked tomatoes slumped as though they suffered from heatstroke. The scent of crushed rosemary tinged the breeze.

'Uh-oh.' Maya slipped her small, sticky hand into Neve's. Her chatterbox voice lacked its usual volume.

'Uh-oh,' Kait repeated in her high-pitched tone, shaking her head so her red curls glinted.

'Uh-oh, all right.'

'We need Mr McGregor who chased Peter Rabbit,' Maya said with a frown.

'Or a better fence.' Neve sighed. 'We have a bigger problem than rabbits. Make that two big problems.'

Loud crunching sounded. The grey-and-white donkey feasting on a carrot turned to look at them with large amber eyes. The taffy pony beside her snatched at a head of lettuce before peering at them through his long blond forelock.

Neve shook her head. To think she'd been worried about locusts, when the threat had been far closer to home. She'd watered and nurtured the rows of vegetables through the summer heat and now, just when the cooler autumn weather had arrived, she'd have to start over again.

'Don't give me that innocent look, Sebastian,' she said to the pony as a lettuce leaf hung from his mouth. 'I know it was you who busted you and Delilah out.'

The pony took a second bite of lettuce.

'Bassie's going to get a tummy ache.' Worry pinched Maya's heart-shaped face and her hold on Neve's hand tightened.

A brain tumour had robbed the sweet sisters of their mother last spring. On the days they spent with Neve, while their father worked in Woodlea as a livestock agent, she made sure she provided stability and fun. She pressed her lips closed against the emptiness that didn't seem to fill despite the calendar pages she turned. She knew firsthand how losing a mother could strip the warmth from the sunshine and dull even the brightest of blue skies.

Neve released Maya's hand to place an arm around her delicate shoulders. 'He'll be fine and if he's not we'll call Ella.'

The concern straining Maya's expression eased. Both girls knew and liked the local vet, as she'd looked after their kelpie when he'd fallen off the farm ute. Ella was also the reason why Neve had a shaggy donkey and a sassy pony in the paddock of her rented farmhouse. Both animals had been neglected and in need of a loving home.

As a child Neve had been horse mad and she hadn't outgrown the dream to one day have a horse of her own. She just wished Ella had sent out a how-to manual along with the bales of hay. Growing up in the city hadn't exactly equipped her with the skills to outsmart her two escapees.

Kait wriggled on her hip and Neve bent to set her on the veranda beside Maya. With their burnished curls, big brown eyes and pale, round cheeks, the sisters were a mirror image of each other. When she took them to town they'd often been mistaken by tourists for her daughters, except her auburn hair was a lighter, more strawberry blonde and her eyes were green.

Footsteps sounded in the hallway behind them before the screen door opened.

'Sorry, the hospital calle—' Fliss stopped, her mouth rounding. 'Not again.'

Neve moved to take hold of the tray of iced cupcakes that tilted in the local doctor's hands.

'Yes. Again.' She set the tray on the nearby outdoor table. They'd have afternoon tea before she attempted mission impossible to return the donkey and pony to their paddock. 'This time they didn't just eat the hedge. I was sure the extra row of electrical tape would work.'

'I was too.' Fliss ran a hand through her glossy, dark hair. 'It's time your free-spirited duo met their match. If Denham and Tanner can sort out that chestnut bully of Old Clarry's, they can handle a big-eared donkey and pretty-boy pony.'

'Thanks, but Denham's busy with his wedding and I've not met Tanner.' She poured water into a plastic cup. 'I'll work it out.'

It didn't feel right relying on others. Usually, she was the one offering to problem-solve and to help. Life had taught her to be self-sufficient. After her father had died when he'd fallen from a ladder, it had only ever been her mother and her, and for a too-brief while, her grandmother.

Fliss helped Kait into a chair before passing her a cupcake on a blue plate. 'Tanner's home from droving and Denham would welcome any distraction from working out table-seating arrangements.'

'I couldn't ask Denham. It isn't just the wedding keeping Cressy and him busy, they're also getting ready to go away for their honeymoon.'

'Which leaves Tanner. He'd be able to keep Bassie and Dell in their paddock and work with them to make them easier to handle.' Fliss smiled at Maya and Kait. 'Bassie's also supposed to be broken in. You'd like to ride him, wouldn't you?'

Both bright heads bobbed.

Neve didn't realise she was chewing her bottom lip until Fliss glanced at her. She turned away to sit beside Maya. 'I'm sure Tanner knows what he's doing. But it's fine. Really.'

To her relief, Fliss also sat and the conversation lapsed. Wings *whoosh*ed as a flock of cockatoos landed in the old gum tree that threw shade across the trampoline. Dell and Bassie weren't the only ones who'd been eyeing off the ripening strawberries.

Silence settled over the veranda as everyone enjoyed the cupcakes iced in white and sprinkled in edible pink glitter. The girls liked baking and Neve made sure they cooked recipes that reminded them of their mother. A mouthful of cake lodged in her throat. One day she'd cook her own mother's favourite vanilla cake recipe.

Avoiding Fliss's gaze, she stifled a cough and reached for her water. Her new neighbour was far too perceptive and had already done enough to help her keep busy. Three months ago, she'd organised for Neve to look after the girls five days a week until Graham found a more permanent arrangement in the spring and before Maya started school.

Kait giggled as Dell plucked a fresh carrot from the garden bed and Bassie tried to steal it from her.

Fliss laughed softly. 'I know those two are incorrigible, but they really are cute.'

Neve joined in with the laughter. 'I'll remind myself of how adorable they are when it takes me at least an hour to get them into their paddock.'

'I can help.' Fliss selected another cupcake. 'I'm not on night duty, so I'm not in a rush to get home.'

Fliss and pickup rider Hewitt lived at nearby Bundara, and the house Neve rented was on their second farm. It was no coincidence she'd chosen the small town of Woodlea to move to. Bundara had been her mother's family home and she lay buried alongside her parents in the historic local cemetery.

Thanks to kind and generous Fliss, Neve had since been a frequent visitor to the bluestone homestead she'd visited as a child. Sometimes the memory of her mother's laughter would echo as she walked through the high-ceilinged rooms. The summer scent of white gardenias took her back to eating Anzac biscuits on the cool veranda with her grandmother.

Neve took hold of the empty water jug. 'Which means you can spend a quiet night in with Hewitt.'

'Wouldn't that be wonderful. He's been working late on the new adventure playground so I've barely seen him.' Fliss's hazel eyes searched her face. 'Are you sure?'

She nodded, ignoring the way Bassie threw her a sly sideways look. There'd be a battle of wills as soon as her boots hit the lawn.

Fliss dug in her jeans pocket for her phone. Neve stood and headed inside before Fliss could again mention Tanner and offer to text him. If she was honest there was more to her refusal to enlist his help than her ingrained independence. If Denham wasn't so busy she'd possibly ask him, but Tanner was a definite no.

Tanner was Woodlea's man of mystery. His name was usually mentioned in wistful tones or with a dreamy expression if it was a young cowgirl speaking. When he wasn't away droving, it sounded as though the horse trainer only hung out with a few select mates and rarely attended social events. From the variation in the stories murmured about him, it was obvious the majority of the district hadn't personally met him.

She'd only seen him once, but it was enough. Edna Galloway was justified in having the broad-shouldered cowboy at the top of her future-husband list for her daughter. Even from across Main Street, his easy grin as he'd greeted Denham had caused Neve to forget what she'd been heading to the grocery shop for.

It wasn't only Dell and Bassie she was ill-equipped to handle. Good-looking, single men also ticked such a box. It wasn't so much the combination of his dark-blond hair and tanned, sculptured features that triggered her need for self-preservation, but how he carried himself. Confident and in control, he wore his self-assurance as well as he did his faded denim jeans.

Water jug full, she turned to retrace her steps. Sure she'd had boyfriends, but between university and her mother's multiple sclerosis, and then starting up her Sydney occupational therapy practice, relationships had been put into the too-hard box. Being an introvert hadn't helped either when she'd sold her business to become her mother's full-time carer. She hadn't wanted to waste a moment of their final two years together by going out on yet another awkward date.

Her shoulders squared. She had enough to deal with without feeling tongue-tied around an eligible bachelor who'd think her useless for not coping with her new charges.

Before she reached the front door, Fliss entered holding Maya and Kait's hands. Pink shimmered on the girls' cheeks and chins. Fliss held up the sisters' hands; they too were covered in glitter. 'Turns out Bassie and Dell like being fed cupcakes as much as they like carrots.'

'Why doesn't that surprise me?' Neve said with a laugh as Fliss disappeared into the main bathroom with the two grinning little redheads.

Neve went to clear off the outside table and to check she didn't have a donkey and a pony making themselves at home on her front veranda. When she returned, a clean Maya and Kait played in the toy corner, while Fliss stood at the sink.

The tall brunette turned with a grin. 'I know ... I'm not supposed to do the washing up.'

Neve opened a drawer to take out a folded tea towel. 'I didn't say a word.'

Fliss's laughter filled the small kitchen and the lonely crevices of Neve's heart. The farmhouse hadn't felt like a home until she'd started babysitting the girls, and Fliss, her sister Cressy, and Ella had befriended her. Now the house was busy, noisy and a riot of colour. Just how she liked things. Light caught in the pink specks scattered across the kitchen bench. And today it sparkled.

She smiled and took hold of a plate to dry. Fliss glanced at her. 'All this glitter reminds me of the hoof polish the ponies wore in the trail-ride parade. I'm sure the girls would love some for Bassie and Dell.'

'I'm sure they would too.'

'I'll ask Kellie where she got her pink polish from when we see her at the small-hall festival. You're still right to go?'

'I won't have the girls and Ella's determined I come along.'

'Trust me, if Ella's set on you going, you'll have no hope of backing out. She's dragged Cressy and me halfway around the countryside to make sure we had some fun.' Fliss placed a bowl in the dish rack. 'I can't wait to see the Reedy Creek Hall decorations. It always looks so different to when it's used as an emergency control centre. Touch wood, there're no more floods and that Drew Macgregor's header is the only thing to go up in flames.'

Neve nodded. She was still to meet many of the locals, but she'd heard about the flooding spring rains as well as the Christmas harvest fire.

Gravel crunched and a diesel car engine chugged. She glanced at the clock. Graham was here early to pick up the girls. Usually, she'd give them dinner and a bath before he took them home.

She didn't need to call out to Maya and Kait. Toy horses in their hands, they raced out the door and down the veranda steps to hug the man walking along the garden path. Bassie and Dell stood in the shade of the garden shed and barely flicked an ear as Graham passed by. If only they'd stay so placid. Who knew such short, stubby legs could move so fast.

Graham picked up Kait, and then, holding Maya's hand, joined Neve and Fliss on the veranda. He assessed the destroyed vegetable garden beds. 'Someone's been busy?'

Neve grimaced. 'Yes, but don't worry, the girls and I will still make the carrot cake we promised you. You're here early.'

'I thought I'd take the afternoon … off.'

As he looked down at his daughters, Neve swapped a concerned look with Fliss. The anguish of losing his wife was imprinted on Graham's weary face. Fresh silver glistened in the cropped brown hair at his temples.

He dipped his head at Fliss. 'That Hewitt of yours has been hammering up a storm in the adventure playground.'

'He says another two weeks, and a final working bee, and it'll be done.'

Maya's smile beamed as she tugged at her father's hand. 'Neve's taking us. We're going to be the first ones to play on it.'

'That sounds like fun.' Graham's voice deepened and he paused to clear his throat before glancing at Neve. 'Thank you for all that you do for the girls. I don't know how we'd cope without you.'

She didn't immediately answer. She was the one who didn't know what she'd do without Maya and Kait. Their tight cuddles and cute chatter never failed to keep her loneliness at bay. The brutal ten months after her mother's funeral and before they'd come into her life had proved she wasn't used to being on her own or not having anyone to care for.

Even with packing up and selling her Sydney family home, she'd felt purposeless. She'd never made a decision that only involved herself. She'd never had spare time that required filling. Since she'd been at high school, she'd done the washing, cooking or shopping whenever her mother's joints had ached or she'd been unable to stand due to her poor balance.

Fliss slipped an arm around her shoulders. 'It was Woodlea's lucky day when Neve called to rent this place.' She paused to glance at the nearby pony and donkey. 'Especially for those two.'

Fliss's amusement dispersed the heavy emotion. Neve went inside to collect the girls' backpacks. Through the screen door she heard their excited voices filling their father in on what they'd done today. The knowledge that she'd kept them busy and made their day happy eased the ache in her throat.

After she and Fliss had waved Maya and Kait goodbye, Fliss turned to hug her. 'Thanks for afternoon tea. See you and Ella on Saturday night and … good luck with the destructive duo.'

'Thanks.' She crossed her fingers and held them behind her back. 'I'll have them out of the garden in no time.'

Even an hour had been an optimistic estimate of how long it would take to get Dell and Bassie back into their paddock. The usual bribery of hay failed to work, so Neve used their need to evade her to eventually direct them through the gate.

If either animal had been wearing a headcollar she would at least have been able to catch them. But the day after they arrived both headcollars had been removed. She hadn't been close enough since then to put them on again. She still didn't know who the clever culprit was who'd taken them off.

Once Dell and Bassie were where they belonged, Neve made sure the electric fence was intact and the red light of the charger blinked. As purple shadows dappled the lawn and the first blush of sunset brushed the sky, she went inside.

A coffee in one hand and her phone in the other, she settled onto the end of the living-room sofa. From such a position she had an uninhibited view of the electric fence through the large front window. She'd kept watch before, and if she had any hope of outwitting the terrible twosome, she needed to stay one step ahead. The only way to do this would be to discover how they escaped.

She was swapping texts with Ella about what to wear to the upcoming festival when Dell and Bassie approached the two strands of electrical tape that formed the gateway. The plastic-handled metal hooks that slipped into the loops on the corner post didn't carry any charge. Bassie and Dell appeared to sniff at the hooks. Dell then pulled the bottom hook free even before Neve realised one strand of white tape sagged onto the ground. If she wasn't so dumfounded, she'd have been impressed.

She sprang off the lounge and used her phone to film Dell ducking under the remaining wire and Bassie pawing the ground before he followed. The donkey and pony touched noses then ambled towards the pots of sunflowers growing alongside the garden shed.

Neve headed outside. Logic told her that Houdini Dell had more than one escape method as this was the first time the tape at the gateway had been removed. She had more hope of plugging holes in a bucket than of keeping Dell and Bassie where they were supposed to be.

Another hour and a half later, and with only the pale wash of moonlight to see by, Dell and Bassie were in their paddock. Neve double-checked the knots on the baling twine she'd used to secure the gate hooks.

'Sleep tight,' she said, rolling her shoulders to ease her weary muscles. Dell lifted a heavy eyelid to give her a placid look. Bassie ignored her. 'I know I will.'

But as Neve lay in bed, a loud bray from outside her bedroom window startled her. She groaned, rubbed at her forehead and reached for her phone on the bedside table. It didn't matter how awkward or out of her depth she'd feel around Tanner, it would soon become a safety issue if the girls were in the garden with Dell and Bassie. She also couldn't impose on an already flat-out Denham. Stomach swirling, she texted Fliss for Tanner's number before her self-preservation had a meltdown.

Tanner Callahan parked in the shade of an established cedar tree. He made no move to turn off the ignition of his blue ute. The V8 engine rumbled, masking the thundering of his heart. He stared at the woman and two young children waiting for him beyond the garden gate on the neat green lawn. Sunlight glanced off their auburn hair.

He could ride an unbroken brumby and offer carrots to a grumpy mountain of a rodeo bull, but he was in no hurry to leave his ute. Only two things unnerved him: anyone under four feet in height and small-town matchmaking. Not that the woman before him would threaten his bachelor status; she was already spoken for. He'd passed a man in a white four-wheel drive not far from the front cattle grid. When Fliss had given him directions she'd said no one else lived along this road.

He turned the ute key and the sudden silence magnified the pounding in his ears. In this woman's case, what dried his mouth was what she represented. The way she held one child and had her arm around the other conveyed her deep love and warmth. All the homely scene needed was a white picket fence and he'd be looking at the embodiment of a perfect family. He reached for his battered felt hat on the passenger seat and jammed it on, making sure the brim was low enough to hide his expression.

He may have found Meredith, his birth mother, and he may have worked through the childhood self-doubts associated with having been adopted, but his fears refused to fade. Abandonment continued to coil inside, striking out at any tentative sense of stability. Common sense argued that a woman to love, a home and children would fill the chasm within him. Yet, his self-control insisted that giving in to such yearnings would only make him a fool. He couldn't again risk having his trust, let alone his heart, broken.

LET'S TALK ABOUT BOOKS!

JOIN THE CONVERSATION

HARLEQUIN
AUSTRALIA

@HARLEQUINAUS

@HARLEQUINAUS